A Quarter
for a Kiss

MINDY
STARNS
CLARK

HARVEST HOUSE PUBLISHERS

EUGENE, OREGON

Cover by Terry Dugan Design, Minneapolis, Minnesota

Cover photo © Alain Brin/Blue Glass Photography

Lyrics from "A Quarter for a Kiss," words and music by David Starns, © Copyright 2003 by David Starns, are used herein with all rights reserved and by permission.

A QUARTER FOR A KISS

Copyright © 2004 by Mindy Starns Clark
Published by Harvest House Publishers
Eugene, Oregon 97402
www.harvesthousepublishers.com

Library of Congress Cataloging-in-Publication Data
Clark, Mindy Starns.
  A quarter for a kiss / Mindy Starns Clark.
     p. cm.—(Million dollar mysteries ; bk. 4)
  ISBN 0-7369-1293-2 (pbk.)
  1. Nonprofit organizations—Fiction. 2. Saint John (V.I.)—Fiction. 3. Widows—Fiction. I. Title.
  PS3603.L366Q37 2004
  813'.54—dc22   2003020826

Printed in the United States of America

04 05 06 07 08 09 10 11 / BC-CF / 10 9 8 7 6 5 4 3 2

For my mother,
Jacquelyn Dickerson Starns.
You are my rock,
my friend,
and my inspiration.
I love you!

Acknowledgments

Thank you so much:

John Clark, J.D., C.P.A., for everything. Your generosity of time, resources, and love never ceases to amaze me.

Kim Moore, for being the best (and the sweetest) editor on the planet.

David Starns, my wonderful brother, for penning the song "A Quarter for a Kiss" and then bringing it to life in the studio. You are the single most amazing musician I have ever known.

Steve Laube and Frank Weimann, for your representation. What a pair!

Daniel Scannell, for outstanding research assistance.

Kay Justus, for brainstorming, researching, and providing invaluable contacts.

Jackie Starns and Shari Weber, for reading and proofing.

Shana Smith, for "coining" the right phrase to give the book its title.

Ken Weber, for creating and maintaining my website.

Janet White, for gracious hospitality.

The brilliant minds at Chi Libris, MMA, Dorothy L, and Sisters in Crime, for tremendous advice and support.

And a big thanks to those who have answered questions and expanded the base of my knowledge in the course of writing this book: Daniel Bailey, Tim Barker, Bob and Sue Butler, Alice Clark, Emily and Lauren Clark, Jeff Cohen, Kathy Coon, Jonathan King, Craig Kozan, R. Troyan Krause, Warren Levicoff, Jack Liddy, Dave Redinger, Douglas T. Reindl, Robert M. Starns, M.D., Corinne Weaber, and the helpful staff of Northeast Scuba Supply of Trooper, PA.

*There is nothing concealed that will not be disclosed,
or hidden that will not be made known.*

MATTHEW 10:26

One

"Come on, Callie," Tom urged. "You can do it. You know how."

Ignoring the burning in my calves, I kept my gaze on Tom, who had reached the top of the wall almost effortlessly and now waited there for me to join him.

"There's a grip at two o'clock, up from your right hand about six inches," he guided, speaking in the low, soothing tones I teasingly called his "rock climbing" voice. Glad for that voice now, I released my handhold and reached upward, my fingers easily finding and grasping the tiny ledge. "Now your foot," he said. "Slow and easy. You're almost there."

As I went I concentrated on all I had learned about rock climbing in the last few weeks. It was Tom's passion, and we had spent a number of hours practicing on a real rock face while he taught me the basic tricks and techniques. Now we were in an indoor gym, on a simulated rock wall, climbing much higher than we had ever gone in our practice runs. And though I was wearing a safety harness that was roped to the ceiling, that didn't make it any easier or any less scary—particularly where the wall actually bent outward, pitching me at a difficult angle.

"You are one step away, Cal," he said, excitement evident in his voice. "Most of the people won't make it half this far."

With a final burst of daring, I slid my toes against the next hold and straightened my knees, rising high enough to touch the ceiling at the top of the wall.

"You did it!" Tom cried, and only then did I allow myself to smile and then to laugh.

"I *did* do it!" I echoed, slapping a high five with Tom and feeling the rush of pleasure and relief he said he experienced every time he finished a challenging climb. Of course, to him "challenging" meant the Red Rocks of Nevada or Half Dome in Yosemite. For me, a big wall in a rock-climbing gym was a pretty good start.

We repelled down together, my legs still feeling shaky once I was on solid ground.

"That was great," the teenage worker said as he helped unhook me from the harness. "And to think you were worried. Are you sure you haven't done this before?"

"Not that high and not indoors," I said.

"Well, you're a natural."

"I had a good teacher," I replied, glancing at Tom, who was busy removing his own harness. He and I had spent the last three weeks together vacationing in the North Carolina mountains. During that time, we had enjoyed teaching each other our favorite sports of climbing and canoeing—though I liked to tease him that my hobby was the superior one, because one false move with a canoe paddle wouldn't exactly plunge a person hundreds of feet to their death. Tom had replied that if one were canoeing above Niagara Falls, that wouldn't exactly be true, now would it?

As the teenager moved on to help the next set of climbers, Tom gave me an encouraging smile.

"Hey, what did you say this is called?" I asked him, pointing at my visibly wobbling knees. "Sewing legs?"

"Sewing-machine legs," Tom replied. "A common climbing malady. Come on. You need to rest for a bit."

He bought us two bottles of water from the snack bar, and then we found a quiet corner and sat on a bench there, leaning back against the wall. I felt thoroughly spent, as if I had pushed every single muscle in my body to its very limit.

I sipped on my water, feeling my pulse slowly return to normal, looking around at the activity that surrounded us. Across the giant room, a new group of climbers was being instructed by a guide while about ten more people waited in line for their turn. In the front window was a giant banner that said "Climb for KFK," and beside the cash register was a table where pledges and donations were being accepted for "Kamps for Kids," a charity that provided summer camp scholarships to impoverished children. Instead of a walkathon, they were calling this event a "climbathon." I liked the idea as well as the whole atmosphere of the place, from the easy joviality of the people waiting in line to the upbeat encouragement of the instructors who were manning the ropes and providing assistance as needed.

"So what's up, Callie?" Tom asked. "You haven't been yourself all morning."

I shrugged.

"Sorry," I said. "This is my work mode, I guess. You have to remember, we're not just here to have fun. We're on the job, so to speak."

Tom nodded knowingly and then leaned closer and lowered his voice.

"So how does this happen, exactly?" he asked. "Do you just walk up to the people and say, 'Hi, here's a big whopping check'?"

I smiled.

"Oh, sure, that's usually how it goes. I call that my Big Whopping Check speech."

"Don't be hard on me," he said, grinning. "I've never done this before."

I leaned toward him, speaking softly.

"Well, first of all, you have to wait for the proper moment," I said. "Like just before you're about to leave."

"Okay."

"Second," I continued, "you have to have the full attention of the correct person. You don't want to give that whopping check to just anybody."

"Get the big wig. Got it."

"Finally, the act of presentation takes a little bit of flair. It's a huge moment for them. You want to help them enjoy it."

"I think I understand."

"You also want to bring them back down to earth a little. I actually do have a short speech I give every time I hand over a grant. I remind the recipient where the money's coming from and what it's for. That seems to go over well."

I felt funny explaining how I did my job to Tom, because he wasn't just my boyfriend, he was also technically my boss. Though he lived and worked on the other side of the country, far from our actual office, Tom was the kind and generous philanthropist behind the J.O.S.H.U.A. Foundation. I worked for the foundation as the director of research, and basically my job was to investigate non-profits Tom was interested in and analyze their suitability for grants. If they checked out okay, I then had the pleasure of awarding them grant money. That's what we were doing here today. For the first time ever, Tom was joining me as I gave a little bit of his money away.

"Hey, Tom! Tom Bennett!" a man cried, interrupting my thoughts.

The fellow bounded toward us, grinning widely. He was tall and wiry, with deep laugh lines in a tanned face, and when he reached us, we stood and the two men shook hands warmly. "You said you might come, but I didn't believe you."

"I'm glad I was able to work it out," Tom replied, smiling.

He introduced his friend as Mitch Heckman, owner of the gym and co-organizer of the event. I told Mitch how impressed I was with the gym and with the climbathon concept.

"Most of the credit goes to my wife," Mitch said, shaking my hand. "I'm just glad we could use the gym to help out a good cause."

"Have you raised much?" Tom asked.

"Our goal for today was twenty-five thousand dollars," Mitch said. "You can see how we're doing on that poster over there."

He pointed to a drawing of a mountain with a zero at the bottom, amounts written up the side, and $25,000 at the top. Sadly, it had only been colored in about half of the way up—and the event would be over in another hour or two.

"Of course, we had a pretty big learning curve in putting the whole thing together," Mitch said. "I'm sure we can make up the difference with some bake sales or car washes or something. We'll get there eventually. *Mai pen rai*, huh?"

"Yeah, *mai pen rai*."

They chatted for a few minutes more, and then Mitch was called up to the front. After he was gone, Tom explained to me their acquaintance, that they had met a few months ago while mountain climbing—specifically, while scaling the limestone cliffs off of Rai Ley Beach in the Krabi Province of Thailand. Tom had been working hard in Singapore and had taken a weekend off to visit the nearby mountain-climbers' mecca, where he met Mitch atop one of the peaks after a particularly challenging climb. As the two men rested, they talked, and it turned out that they were both avid climbers and eager to explore an unfrequented jungle crag nearby. Together they had hired a guide and ended up having an incredible day of climbing. Though the two men hadn't seen each other since, they had been in touch off and on ever since via e-mail.

"What were you saying to each other just now? My pen…"

"*Mai pen rai*," Tom replied. "That's Thai for 'no problem' or 'never mind.' The guides say it to encourage you while you're climbing, kind of like 'you can do it.' 'Don't worry.' *Mai pen rai*."

"Does Mitch know about the foundation?"

"Nope. He thinks I'm just another rock jock."

"He's in for a nice surprise, then," I said. "This is fun, giving a grant to someone who never even applied for one."

This wasn't our usual mode for doing business, that was for sure. But this particular charity was so new—and the amount we were donating so relatively small—that the investigation hadn't been all that complicated. Since KFK had never applied for a grant from us, I hadn't really had the authority to go in and do an extensive investigation. But they did belong to several good nonprofit watchdog groups, so I had felt confident doing the research from our vacation home in North Carolina, mostly over the internet and on the phone with the foundation's accounting whiz, Harriet, the day before.

"Anyway, now you'll finally have the pleasure of making a donation live and in person," I added. "Something I've only been bugging you to do for two years."

"Almost three years now," he corrected. "And, yes, I'm hoping this might shut you up for good."

"Oh, you want me to shut up, do you?" I asked. "What about—"

He silenced me with a finger against my lips, which he allowed to linger there.

"No," he whispered, gazing a moment at my mouth. "Don't ever stop talking to me. I want to listen to you forever."

We looked into each other's eyes as everything else in the room blurred into the background. My legs shivered again, but not from climbing this time.

"We need to get going," Tom said gruffly, standing and then helping me to my feet. I squeezed his hand, and then we separated into the men's and women's locker areas to get cleaned up.

After a shower I dressed quickly in a pair of black slacks and a soft blue knit shirt. I towel-dried my short hair, combed it out, and took a moment to put on some lipstick and a touch of mascara.

As I looked in the mirror, ready to leave, I was suddenly overwhelmed with sadness. In a few short hours Tom and I would go our separate ways, boarding two different flights to head toward our homes on opposite coasts—him to California and me to Maryland. For three glorious weeks we had done nothing more than shut out the rest of the world and spend time together, but we couldn't hide out and play forever. Our work and other responsibilities awaited us, and as one week had turned into two and then to three, we had already stretched the length of our available time to the very max. Soon our idyllic vacation together would officially be over, and Tom and I would be back to our long-distance romance as usual.

Slinging my bag onto my shoulder, I decided to take this day moment-by-moment. Despite the difficulty of parting, we still had a job to do. We still had a grant to give out.

I emerged from the locker room to find Tom also showered and dressed, standing nearby and squinting toward the front of the room. He had in his hand a check from the J.O.S.H.U.A. Foundation, dated today and made out to the charity, though the amount had been left blank.

"Callie, can you read that figure?" he asked. "I need the exact amount they've raised so far."

I walked a little closer and then came back to report that they were up to $11,043. Quick with numbers, Tom didn't even hesitate before he filled out the check for $13,957.

"That will bring them to the full twenty-five thousand," I said after doing the math in my head, not surprised one bit by his generosity.

"Making sure they meet their goal is the least we can do, don't you think?"

He tried to put the check in my hand, but I pushed it back.

"No, you don't," I said. "Enjoy the moment."

Carrying our bags, Tom and I walked to the front of the gym, where his friend Mitch was chatting with a woman that I assumed was his wife. We were introduced, and I liked her firm handshake and the way she looked me directly in the eye. She thanked us for coming and then moved on to speak with someone else.

"We're going to head out," Tom said to Mitch, "but I wanted to give you a check first. I talked my company into making a small grant."

Of course, the way Tom had said it, you'd never know that it was *his* company, nor *his* money—nor that he was using "small" as a relative term. Mitch took the folded check without looking at it.

"Listen, buddy, every bit helps. Thank you so much, and thanks for coming."

The two men shook hands, and then Mitch shook my hand as well. We said goodbye, and Tom and I departed, walking silently through the packed parking lot toward our rental car.

"You were right, Callie," he said nonchalantly, pressing a button on the key chain to unlock the car. "Giving away the money in person really is kind of fun."

I was about to reply when we heard Mitch calling Tom's name. We turned to see the man running toward us, breathless, his eyes filled with disbelief.

"I don't understand," he gasped, holding up the check. "This is so much. Is it some kind of joke?"

"No joke, Mitch," Tom said. "We're affiliated with the J.O.S.H.U.A. Foundation. That's a grant."

"A grant?"

"Yeah, we give them out all the time. Callie, what is it you like to say when you give grants to people?"

I smiled.

"Basically," I said, going into my spiel, "we want you to know that the best way you can say thanks is to take that money and use it to further your mission. The foundation believes strongly in what you're trying to accomplish, and we just wanted to have some small part in furthering your efforts."

To my surprise, Mitch's eyes filled with tears.

"Your generosity leaves me speechless," he said finally. "Won't you come back inside? Let me tell my wife. She'll be so excited. Maybe we can get a picture for the newsletter or the website or something."

I looked at Tom, but he seemed decidedly uncomfortable.

"Mitch," I said, "we really prefer to do this in a discreet manner. Just tell Jill that the J.O.S.H.U.A. Foundation gives the money with love and with God's blessings. We'd rather not receive any individual recognition."

Bewildered, he looked back down at the check.

"And you promise this isn't a joke?" he tried one more time.

"No joke," Tom laughed. "I give you my word, buddy. It's for real."

With a final sincere thanks, Mitch turned and headed back to the building. We stood there and watched until he went inside and the door closed behind him.

On impulse, I turned and threw my arms around Tom's neck. Startled, after a moment he hugged me back.

"You are such a good man," I whispered, feeling absolutely, utterly, and completely in love.

He laughed, pulling me in tightly for an embrace.

"Wow," he replied. "This giving-away-money thing gets better all the time."

Knowing the clock was ticking closer toward our flight times, we managed to pull apart and get into the car. He started it up and pulled out of the parking lot, driving toward the airport.

We were quiet as we went, both lost in our own thoughts. As we wove our way through traffic, I considered our relationship and the long and winding path my life had taken since my husband's death. This coming summer would mark four years since Bryan was killed, and in one way it seemed like yesterday, and in another it seemed like decades ago. My husband had been my first true love, the sweetheart I had met at 16 and married at 25. We'd had four wonderful years together as husband and wife, but that had all come crashing to an end that fateful day when we went water-skiing and Bryan was hit by a speedboat. The boat's driver went to prison for manslaughter, but I also went into a sort of prison myself—a self-imposed prison of mourning, of loneliness.

Only in the last six months had I allowed myself to consider the possibility that there might be life for me beyond my husband's death. Tom and I had developed a good, strong friendship through our many work-related conversations over the phone, and then, slowly, that friendship had started taking on other dimensions. We finally met in person last fall, when Tom received word that I had been hurt in an investigation and raced halfway around the world to be by my side and make certain I was all right. We had spent a mere 12 hours together—just long enough to begin falling in love—and then we were forced to endure a four-month separation while he went back to Singapore on important business and I healed from my injuries and continued my work with his foundation in the U.S.

Then three weeks ago, in the very heart of spring, we had been joyously reunited. Showing up in a hot air balloon, Tom had swept me away to a gorgeous vacation spot in the North Carolina mountains, where we planned to stay a week or so and give ourselves the opportunity to see if our relationship really could work face-to-face. What we had found was that we were so compatible, so comfortable, and so suddenly and deeply in love that it was nearly impossible to end our vacation and return to our regular lives.

Now, however, our time together had come to an end.

"There's the car rental return," Tom said suddenly, pulling me from my thoughts. He followed the signs and turned into the lot, but instead of heading straight to the busy rental return area, he veered over to an empty parking spot nestled behind a big truck. He put the car in park but left the motor running.

"Maybe we should say our goodbyes here," he told me, "instead of out in the middle of the busy airport."

I nodded, surprised when my eyes suddenly filled with tears. I didn't want to say goodbye at all! He took my hand, stroking the back of it with his fingers.

"Callie, have I told you that the past three weeks have been the happiest three weeks of my life?" he asked.

In the quiet warmth of the car, I held onto his hand and searched his handsome face, finding only love reflected there.

"It has been incredible," I replied, knowing there were many, many moments we had shared that I would relive in my mind in the coming days. "I don't know if I have the strength to say goodbye to you or not."

Tom reached up and smoothed a loose lock of hair behind my ear. Such tenderness was in his gaze that I thought it might break my heart.

"Callie, I have something for you," he whispered. He started to reach into his pocket, and I swallowed hard, wondering what it could be.

Then his cell phone rang.

By the time he got the phone out from his gym bag, the call had been disconnected. Tom was pressing buttons, trying to see who had called, when my phone started ringing from my purse. I dug it out, surprised to see that the number on my screen matched the number that had just called his.

"Hello?" I asked somewhat hesitantly.

"Callie?" a woman's voice cried from very far away. "Is that you?"

"This is Callie," I answered. "Who is this?"

"This is Stella," the voice said. "Stella Gold."

I put my hand over the phone and mouthed to Tom, *It's Eli's wife.*

Eli Gold was my mentor, a friend of Tom's, and the person responsible for bringing the two of us together.

"Stella?" I asked, trying to picture a woman I didn't know very well at the other end of the line. I had met her the day she married my dear friend Eli, but she and I had not really spoken since, except for those times when I called their house and she had been the one to answer the phone. "What's up?"

"Oh, Callie, I'm so glad I finally reached you. I need you. I need your help. I need Tom Bennett, also, if you know how to reach him."

"What is it?" I asked, my heart surging.

"It's Eli," she sobbed. "He's in the hospital."

"In the hospital?"

"Callie, he's been shot."

Two

Eli had asked for both of us to come. So while Tom dealt with returning the rental car, I went straight to the airline ticketing counter and made the necessary changes to our flights. Because Stella and Eli lived in Cocoa Beach, Florida, we would fly into Orlando and then rent another car and drive east to the coast. According to Stella, Eli was in the hospital in Cape Canaveral and about to go to the operating room.

The best I could do was a connection through Atlanta that would get us to Orlando around midnight. We probably had another hour's drive from there to the hospital, so once everything had been arranged, I called Stella back and told her to expect us between 1:00 and 2:00 A.M. It was going to be a long night.

Tom and I met back at security, and then we filed through and found our gate. Mostly, I was operating on autopilot, somewhat in shock. The flight to Atlanta seemed to take forever, and the connection from there on to Orlando felt like an eternity. Despite the comforts of first class, my mind was filled with so many emotions I had to remind myself several times to breathe.

Tom and I had barely said two words to each other on the first flight, though once the second plane took off out of Atlanta, he reached for my hand and asked me if I was okay, if I wanted to talk.

"No, and no," I said softly, giving his hand a quick squeeze before pulling mine away. How could I begin to explain all of the confusion that was swirling in my brain?

Eli had been shot, caught in the chest by a sniper's bullet, and now he lay in the hospital teetering between life and death. I leaned away from Tom and rested my head against the seat, my heart pounding as strongly as it had since we first received Stella's phone call. I was relieved that Tom didn't press me to talk but simply took out his laptop and turned his attention elsewhere.

Don't die, Eli! my mind shouted. I knew I should be praying, but I was paralyzed with shock and fear, too numb to do anything but hold in my sobs and keep from screaming.

Eli was like a father to me, and the thought of him dying was difficult enough. But for him to have been senselessly shot in some random act of violence was so horrifying that it defied explanation. I closed my eyes, unable to stop the image of him walking down the street toward Stella and then suddenly falling down, his chest struck with the bullet that nicked his right lung and tore through his liver. She'd said the sound was far away, like an echo without an origination, and when Eli first fell to the ground she had merely thought he'd tripped. But then she ran to him and saw blood on his shirt and knew that something was terribly wrong.

According to Stella, she had been so consumed with getting help for her bleeding husband that it hadn't even occurred to her until later that she might've been in danger too. But the sniper had not shot at anyone else.

Now she was at the hospital, waiting as Eli went through surgery. The last thing Eli had said to her before he lost consciousness was that he needed to talk to Tom right away and that he needed me as well. Stella wasn't sure what that meant, but Eli had been so adamant that she had attempted to reach the two of us before she called anyone else, even her own children. As we flew through the nighttime sky, we were left to wonder why Eli had asked for us—and if the violence perpetrated against him had been random or deliberate.

I opened my eyes and glanced at Tom's computer screen. He was composing an e-mail to his office staff, telling them he wouldn't be flying home tonight as planned. Not wanting to be nosy, I caught the words "unexpected emergency" and "will be in touch" before turning my head away. I realized I didn't know much about Tom's relationship with Eli or how or when they first met. I knew only that they were friends and that they shared a great mutual respect for each other. Eli was the original connection between me and Tom, the person who first recognized the fact that a man who wanted to give away some of his millions could do worse than employ a woman who held a private investigator's license and a law degree with a specialty in the nonprofit sector. Eli had coordinated the entire employment process, putting Tom in touch with me so that he could offer me the job of director of research for the new J.O.S.H.U.A. Foundation and then convincing me to take the job Tom was offering.

I owed Eli everything, not only for introducing me to Tom and for my wonderful job, but also for the years he spent training me to be a detective and for his continued guidance and friendship now that he was retired and married and living in Cocoa Beach. It made me physically sick to think of the sniper in Florida who had positioned himself in some secluded spot so that he could shoot our beloved Eli.

"Callie, you're trembling," Tom said, his arm pressed against mine.

I shook my head in denial, but he closed his laptop, put it away, and turned toward me.

"You might not want to talk," he said in a soft voice, "but you can't stop me from praying."

Gathering my hands in his, he bowed his head and whispered a long, soothing prayer, asking for protection and peace and healing. About halfway through, I began to calm down, and by the end I knew that whatever happened, the Lord had His hand on Eli—and on us as well.

"Please don't shut me out," he said, handing me a clean hand-kerchief from his pocket. "Talk to me, Callie."

"It's just hard," I admitted. "I'm scared. I don't want someone else I love to die."

"He'll be out of surgery by the time we get there," he said. "You'll be able to talk to him yourself and see that he's going to be okay."

"I hope so, Tom." Tears threatened to fill my eyes again, but I blinked them away and sat up straight when I saw the flight attendant approaching.

She asked if we would like anything to drink and we both asked for coffee, knowing we would probably be up the rest of the night. I thought about what this sudden trip did to my own schedule, and I used the seatback phone to call my friend and coworker Harriet, to let her know I wasn't heading home after all. After that I dialed Lindsey, the girl who cared for my dog whenever I was out of town. This was the third extension in three weeks with her, and I was grateful she was being flexible again, as usual. I thought of my little Maltese, Sal, and felt a twinge of guilt. One of these days I was going to come home and Sal wasn't even going to remember me.

The rest of the flight was uneventful. Looking around, I realized that the first-class cabin was empty except for one woman who sat in the front row. I could see only the side of her carefully coifed hair and her left hand, which sat on the arm rest, a diamond ring the size of a small country on her fourth finger. I glanced down at my own hand, at my wedding ring, the simple gold band Bryan had slipped onto my finger the day we were married. I had promised to love him until death, and then I had been forced to fulfill that promise far too quickly.

Eli had never made any promises to me like that, except that he would always be there for me. Now it was my turn to be there for him. I could only hope that whatever he needed me to do, I was up to the challenge. Certainly, I was willing to move heaven and earth to keep him safe and make him whole again.

We arrived at the Orlando airport right on schedule, and then we claimed our bags and found our rental car. Tom drove as I navigated, the Florida roads dark and flat and straight all the way to Cape Canaveral. When we reached the hospital parking lot, I thanked

Tom for being such a calm and reassuring presence in this difficult time.

"I know how much you love Eli," he said simply, choosing a parking spot. "I'm just glad I was here to help."

"What about you?" I asked as we got out of the car and walked quickly toward the building. "You care about him too."

Tom held the door for me and we went inside. At the information desk, we were directed to intensive care.

"I respect Eli and I like him very much," Tom said. "But he and I don't have the history you two share."

I thought about that history as we took the elevator up to the fifth floor. Eli had simply been a friend of my father's when he gave me a summer job the year I was 16. Little did I know, that summer job would help determine the course of my life, and Eli would eventually become one of my very best friends. I worked for him for nine years, until the day I graduated from law school.

We reached intensive care and asked at the desk if we could see him. We were told he was still in surgery, but the nurse pointed us toward the waiting room and said his wife would be in there.

At first I didn't recognize Stella. She was the only person in the room, a tiny blonde woman asleep in a chair in a corner, wearing a costume made entirely of faux fur. From her toes to her neck, she was fuzzy and brown, with a lighter brown furry circle at her tummy. I tried to reconcile that with the woman I had seen on her wedding day, wearing an expensive rose-colored silk suit.

"Stella?"

She sat up and then jumped up, racing over to grip me in a fierce, furry hug.

"Callie, Tom, I'm so glad you came!"

Then she burst into tears. I put my arm around her and guided her back to the chairs, where we sat.

"How is he?" I asked.

"They were able to repair the damage to his lung, but he's lost a lot of blood. Right now he's still unconscious and hooked up to a bunch of machines."

"Are you here by yourself?" Tom asked.

"Yes. My sons said they'd come tomorrow. I can't reach my daughter—she's been traveling."

Tom and I glanced at each other, and I wondered if he knew Stella's three children. I had had the pleasure, if you could call it that, of meeting them at the wedding. All three seemed petty and spoiled and suspicious of the man who had stolen their mother's heart. Stella was quite wealthy, and I think they saw Eli not as a companion for their mom in her later years but as a threat to the nest egg that she was supposed to leave to them someday.

"It was all so fast," she said tearfully. "Today—well, yesterday, I guess—was hug day at the home, and I—"

"Hug day?" I interrupted.

She gestured toward the seat across from us, and I turned to see a large teddy bear head sitting there, a furry match for the costume Stella was wearing.

"Every Friday afternoon I go to the local nursing home dressed as a teddy bear and give out hugs," she explained. "It's my ministry."

"Your ministry?" Tom asked, and Stella looked at him defensively.

"Everybody needs hugs," she said, "but when you're old and alone, no one ever touches you. So I go in there dressed like a teddy bear, and I hug all of the old folks. For some of them, that's the only hug they'll get all week."

Tom reached out and patted Stella's furry hand.

"I'm sorry," he said. "I think that sounds wonderful."

"Anyway," she continued, "Eli always picks me up at five-forty so we can make it to the Speedy Sailor for the Friday Night Special. You can get crab cakes and a bowl of oyster stew for a dollar ninety-nine if you're in your seat by six o'clock."

"Wow," I said, stifling a smile. Despite her healthy bank account, Stella was known for her eccentric money-saving habits.

"Yes, but this time we weren't going to make it, and I was mad at Eli for making us late. I came out of the nursing home at five fifty-five, and he was just walking up the street toward me from where he had parked the car about half a block away. Then, all of a sudden, he just fell down onto the ground. I was getting ready to fuss at him for being late, and the next thing I knew he had collapsed."

She went on to repeat the description she had given me earlier of the fall and then the distant gunshot and then the blood.

"Thank goodness we weren't alone. I started screaming and people came running. Pretty soon an ambulance and the police were there too."

"Were any other shots fired?" Tom asked.

"No, and the cops didn't catch anybody. They weren't even sure what direction the shot had come from. It's a busy area, with a lot of buildings. I'm sure it could've been done from any number of places."

"Do the police think it was just a random shooting?" I asked, leaning forward.

"The cops are presuming it was random," Stella said. "But I know better."

"What do you mean?" Tom asked.

"As soon as Eli got shot, he told me, 'Nadine said he was coming. You have to call Tom Bennett. Show him my notes.'"

I looked at Tom, who seemed genuinely confused.

"Call me about what?" he asked. "What notes?"

"I don't know. He just kept saying, 'Promise me you'll call Tom. Nadine was right.'"

"Nadine who?" I asked.

"I don't know," Stella replied. "We don't know anyone named Nadine."

"Tom?" I pressed. "Do you know someone named Nadine?"

He shook his head no.

"He wanted you here too, Callie," Stella said. "He was kind of talking out of his head, but he said only you would know where the notes are."

I sat up straight, completely stumped. How would I know where his notes were? What notes? While we often spoke on the phone, Eli had never mentioned anything that even remotely gave me an idea about what was going on with him.

"Stella, why would I know where he kept something like that? He's never said anything to me about any notes."

She shook her head, the expression on her face one of desperation.

"Eli's been up to something," she said. "Some kind of investigation. For a while now."

"Was he working for someone?"

"Not that I know of. It started a few months ago, down at our vacation house in the Virgin Islands. One day he said something about 'running a license plate.' Next thing I knew, he was going out on surveillance and talking about security systems and rounding up all kinds of odd little tools."

"Tools?"

"Like, detective things. I don't know. I wish I had paid more attention, asked more questions. He'd been so bored since he retired, but once this case got rolling, it's like the old spark was back. I was just glad to see him so alive and active. I let him do his thing and I did mine." Her eyes filled with tears. "Oh, why didn't I see what he was getting himself into? I should've been more involved."

I pictured Eli at the height of his game, back when he and I worked together in his detective agency. Between cases, he always seemed sort of lost and depressed, but once we were on the trail of someone or something, it was as though every part of him came alive. I tried explaining that to Stella, tried to make her understand that he had always been that way, that none of this was her fault.

"But this time," she cried, "whatever he was doing, he ended up getting shot! What if he dies, Callie? What if they come back again and try to kill him? You have to help us!"

She grabbed the box of tissues on the side table, pulled out a handful, and then bent forward and sobbed into them. Tom looked at me intently over the top of her head.

"First things first," he said softly. "I'll make some calls and get some round-the-clock security in here. Don't you worry, Stella. No one's going to get near Eli now."

He patted her on the arm, stood, and walked away, heading for the bank of pay phones by the elevator.

"It's okay, Stella," I assured her, slipping my arm around her shoulders. "Whatever Eli was doing, whatever got him into this mess, I promise you this: Tom and I will figure out what is going on."

Three

By 3:00 A.M. Stella was finally allowed to see Eli. They let her stay for exactly five minutes, and when she came back out, she was as white as a sheet. Apparently, her beloved husband was still unconscious, covered with tubes and wires and breathing through a respirator, his tenuous heartbeat flashing on a screen behind the bed.

"They said the next twenty-four hours are the most critical," Stella told us. "They don't know if he'll make it to the morning."

Once again, the thought of losing Eli made my stomach suddenly whoosh out from under me, like a giant drop on a roller coaster. Eli was always so full of life! *How could he possibly die?*

At 3:30 A.M. the private security Tom had hired showed up, a big, muscular man with a crew cut, wearing a suit and tie. He went with Tom to speak to the hospital staff and iron out the details of Eli's protection, and while they were gone I had Stella give me of a list of things she wanted from home. She wasn't going to leave the hospital anytime soon, and I thought she at least might like a change of clothes.

It was nearly 4:00 A.M. by the time Tom and I drove out of there and headed toward Stella and Eli's condominium. I was very torn, because a part of me wanted to be with Eli as well, but another part of me was anxious to get to the house to see if I could figure out where Eli might have stashed the "notes" he had spoken of. If he were still in danger, the best way we could protect him was not by sitting around in the waiting room and staring at each other but by unearthing whatever had gotten him shot in the first place.

The complex where Eli and Stella lived was an expansive community of pastel-hued buildings that lined both sides of a series of tidy, winding roads. The buildings looked so much alike—and there were so many of them—that if it hadn't been for the giant street signs that marked every corner, we never would have found our way to their home. It was at the very end of the farthest street, in what had to be the priciest section of the entire community because of its proximity to the water. Careful to park in a "visitor" spot and not one of the assigned spaces, we got out of the car and headed up the walk. Theirs was an end unit, and by the light of the nearly full moon I could easily see around the side of the building to the wide sandy beach that lay beyond. Everything was so quiet and still I could even hear the gentle lapping of the waves in the distance.

Stella had given Tom a key, but when he tried to put it into the lock, the door simply swung open.

"What the…" Tom said as he reached inside and flipped on the light.

We gasped.

The living room had been completely destroyed, the couch torn to shreds, the drawers dumped onto the floor. Shards of glass littered the carpet along with dirt from a number of upended potted plants.

Tom moved forward as if to check out the rest of the house, but I grabbed his arm and held him back.

"No," I whispered. "Someone could still be in there."

I was thinking we could call the police from the car. We were just backing out of there when we heard the word "Freeze!"

Looking up, we saw a woman across the room, standing in the shadows, holding up what looked like a gun. Instinctively, Tom moved in front of me, his arms held out by his sides.

"What are you doing here? Who are you?" the woman demanded.

I squinted, looking closer, and realized the "gun" she held was simply a small black blow-dryer. I stepped forward, pushing Tom's arm down and out of my way.

"We're friends of Eli Gold," I said calmly. "Who are you?"

She hesitated, the blow-dryer visibly trembling in her hands.

"I-I'm Jodi," she said. "Stella's daughter."

Stella's daughter? From what Stella had told us at the hospital, Jodi was on an extended trip and couldn't be reached.

"We won't hurt you, Jodi," Tom said. "You can put down the gun."

"It's not a gun," I said dryly. "It's a blow-dryer."

At that the girl lowered her arms and stepped forward into the light.

"I remember you from the wedding," she said, looking at me.

"Is there anyone else here?"

"No," she said, and I could tell she was near tears. "Where is my mother? What's happening?"

"Have you called the police?" I asked, ignoring her questions for the moment.

"No, I just came in and saw all of this…" Her voice trailed off.

"I'll do it," Tom said.

He pulled out his cell phone, dialed information, and headed outside. As he asked for the number of the local police, I convinced Jodi to walk outside also, away from the crime scene, and wait on the sidewalk with Tom. Then I went back in by myself and walked carefully through the entire condo to view the damage that had been done. It was awful. Every single room had been destroyed. Obviously, someone had been here looking for something. If Eli had hidden his notes in this place, they were no doubt gone by now, whether that's what the person was looking for or not.

I felt certain this confirmed that Eli truly was in danger, and that it had not been a random shooting. My guess was that he was on someone's trail, and they had taken a drastic and potentially deadly step to stop him.

By the time I went back outside, Tom was off the phone, Jodi was pacing back and forth on the grass, and the security guard for the complex was just striding up the walk. He was a short, chubby man in a navy blue uniform, and though he carried no gun he did wear a badge pinned to his crisp shirt.

He seemed quite upset, and I realized he was afraid this incident might cost him his position. He kept wringing his hands and saying, "I told management this job is too big for one person!" Tom tried to calm him down by reassuring him that if someone wanted to break in somewhere badly enough, there wouldn't be enough security in the world to stop them.

The police showed up about ten minutes later, and though they weren't using their sirens, the flashing lights and the sounds of their voices roused some of the neighbors. A large crowd gathered on the front lawn, mostly made up of senior citizens in pajamas and slippers.

As they learned of Eli's shooting and the break-in, they seemed to grow quite upset. I was glad to hear a small cluster of women decide to go to the hospital later in the morning to sit with Stella.

As for me, I tried to get as close to the action inside as I could, finally convincing the police officer manning the door that I was both a private investigator and a friend of the Golds, and that I needed to know what had happened for the sake of my own investigation into the matter. He didn't ask for my PI license, which was fortunate since I didn't have one for Florida. Chances are, one of the other states I was registered in had reciprocity, but I hadn't had the time to find out. The officer *did* ask if I had a permit to carry a weapon, and I told him that I did not, that I was primarily a business investigator and that I never carried a gun.

In any event he finally let me come inside and observe the goings-on there. The police seemed to be processing the break-in very slowly, which I supposed was good, considering the sniper shooting earlier in the evening. Though the detective handling the attempted murder didn't actually come to the scene of the break-in, he did communicate by telephone. I was glad to see they were taking fingerprints of the whole place, and though Tom and I hadn't touched anything inside, Jodi had, so the cops rolled a set of prints for her merely as an elimination.

The sun was coming up by the time the police decided they were finished at the scene. They gave us the telephone number of a service that specialized in crime scene cleanup and suggested we call later in the morning. They also requested that Stella come home as soon as possible to look through everything and file a report on whatever might be missing.

Tom agreed to stay at the condo while Jodi and I drove to the hospital to get Stella. I wasn't too worried about leaving him there in any danger because, now that it was daylight, half the neighborhood was clustered on the lawn. Any criminal who might choose to return to the scene of the crime would have to make their way through a squadron of agitated senior citizens to get there.

I hadn't talked much to Jodi at the scene, but once we were alone in the car, she peppered me with questions about all that had happened. I tried to answer her as thoroughly as I could. She said she didn't know Eli all that well, but he seemed a nice enough guy and it was a shame he'd been shot.

"Now I wish I'd taken the time to get to know him better," she lamented. "I wasn't very nice to him at the wedding."

"How long has it been since you were home?" I asked.

"Last fall," she said. "I went to France to do some graduate work. Then I kind of got sidetracked."

"Sidetracked?"

"There was this guy. He wanted to tour Europe, wanted me to go with him…you know how it is."

"I see," I said, not really knowing how it was at all.

From what I recalled of Jodi, she was a sweet person but rather immature for her age. She was somewhere in her mid-twenties, the kind of woman who looked quite striking when she was all done up with fancy hair and makeup—and quite plain when she wasn't. I met her at her loveliest, at Eli and Stella's wedding several years before, and when I saw her the next morning in her housecoat and glasses, with no makeup and her hair askew, I barely recognized her.

She more closely resembled that person now, wearing dirty jeans and a faded button-down shirt, her hair pulled back into a messy ponytail. She seemed tired, and as she described the hours and connections it had taken her to fly back home to the States, I understood why.

"I had been thinking about coming home for a while," she said, "and yesterday there was a flight available, so I took it. I didn't think I'd miss Franco at all, but I do."

She wiped at her face, and I realized she was crying.

"Franco?" I asked gently.

"My boyfriend. Ex-boyfriend. We broke up yesterday."

"Oh. I'm sorry."

"He just wanted me for my money." She shifted in her seat, leaning her head against the glass of the passenger window and closing her eyes. "I just had my twenty-fifth birthday, and that means now I can have access to the trust fund my daddy left me. I've been thinking a lot about the money and what I'm going to do with it. When I told Franco that I've decided to give it all away to charity, he went nuts. He was like, 'I've waited all this time for you to get your inheritance, and now you tell me you're just getting rid of it? You're just giving it all away? I've been wasting my time.'"

"Wow."

"I'm such a sucker when it comes to men. I have always made bad choices."

We reached the entrance to the hospital, and I slowed to turn in.

"I thought I was getting older and wiser," she added, "but once all this happened with Franco, I realized I'm still making the wrong choices. I decided I needed to come home, get back into therapy, and maybe let Mom take care of me for a while."

We were silent as I parked the car, but before we got out, I turned to look her in the eye.

"You understand that that's no longer an option," I said. "At least not right now."

"What do you mean?"

"Your mother's husband has been shot. Her home has been destroyed. If anyone needs to be taken care of, Jodi, it's her."

She looked back at me, rather startled, and then she finally nodded.

"Of course," she said softly. "Of course."

As we walked into the hospital together, I warned Jodi that her mother would be wearing a fur costume thanks to hug day at the nursing home.

"That sounds just like her," Jodi said, rolling her eyes. "She once picked me up from school in a full beekeeper's uniform. I nearly died of humiliation."

"A beekeeper's uniform?"

"She had been helping a friend with the bees in his orchard, and she didn't take time to change clothes."

"That's funny."

"The problem with my mother," Jodi continued as we rode up in the elevator, "is that she lives in her own little world most of the time. She just doesn't realize how nutty her actions look to other people."

I thought about the way Eli and Stella first met. Stella's two sons had wanted to have Stella declared mentally incompetent, so they hired Eli to investigate their mother and provide proof. And though Eli had followed Stella around and snapped photos of her doing things like break-dancing in the park and spontaneously picking up trash along the highway, he also found himself falling head over heels in love with her. In the end, he gave the sons back their money and told them their mother wasn't incompetent, just eccentric. Afterward, Eli began courting Stella, and a year later the lifelong bachelor married the eccentric widow. As far as I knew, things had been wonderful between them since.

We found Stella in the intensive care waiting room, right where I had left her, though now she was speaking with two police officers. I was afraid that, after the shooting, learning of the break-in might just send her over the top, but she seemed perfectly calm.

"I'm so sorry, Stella," I said, giving her a hug after the cops were gone. "It looks like they got into everything."

"Don't worry about it," she replied. "Compared to what's happened with Eli, it's nothing. It's less than nothing."

She saw Jodi hanging back behind me and gasped.

"My baby!" Stella cried, reaching for her daughter and pulling her into a tight embrace.

I stepped away from them for a few minutes while they shared tears and words of love. I could hear things like "missed you so bad" and "gone too long," and I was glad to see that the two of them seemed to be very close despite the daughter's eight-month absence. Stella would need Jodi now more than ever.

Finally, I suggested that perhaps I could stay at the hospital while Jodi drove her mother home to change clothes and to assess the damage to her home. They agreed, and Stella cleared me with the security guy before walking with me to the nurses' station.

"Yes?" the nurse asked, looking up at us.

"Kathy, I'm going to run home for a bit. This is Callie Webber. She'll be here if Eli wakes up."

"I'm sorry," the nurse said. "Only immediate family can go in."

"My dear," Stella said defiantly, standing up straight. "Callie *is* immediate family."

"Oh, I'm sorry," the nurse amended, checking her watch. "I didn't realize. That will be fine. Next visit is from six to six-oh-five."

I walked Stella and Jodi to the elevator, thanking Stella for her little fib.

"That was no fib," she replied softly, tapping her chest. "In Eli's heart, Callie, you are his family."

Four

Eli didn't look like himself. The five minutes I was allowed next to his bed were half wasted on simply gazing at all they had done to him, trying to find the man I knew under the equipment.

His skin was pale, his bald head splotchy in the fluorescent light. I finally found his hand among the tubes and squeezed it, though of course he didn't squeeze back. Then I knelt there on the floor next to the bed, still holding his hand, and prayed that God would please, just please spare this one soul from heaven a while longer.

"I need him more than You do, Father," I whispered. "Please don't take him away now."

The nurse made me leave at 6:05 on the dot, and as we walked out, I asked her when she thought he might regain consciousness.

"Oh, honey," she said, one hand on my arm. "Let's just get him through the next twenty-four hours. Then we'll worry about that."

Her words were sobering. As I sat in the waiting room staring into space, I thought about the life of Eli Gold. He had grown up in New Jersey, the only son of doting parents. His father was an attorney, though Eli passed on college in favor of joining the Navy. Military testing landed him in the Navy's radio training program, where he worked in signals intelligence.

Parts of Eli's life story were a bit fuzzy to me now, but I knew he had left the Navy at the end of his two years and then lived for a time in the Florida Keys. Eventually, he had settled in Virginia, gone to the police academy, and become a cop. He and my dad were partners for ten years, until Eli grew tired of the bureaucracy and decided to quit the force and open his own detective agency.

The Gold Agency was a mere five years old when Eli heard I was looking for a part-time job. He offered me a position after school and on weekends, typing and filing for him. I was 16 at the time, too young to legally work in a detective agency in the state of Virginia, so he employed me under the facetious title of "personal social secretary."

Luckily for me, Eli had several very fascinating, very complicated cases going on that summer, and my duties began to expand as I helped him handle all of the paperwork that went with them.

I recalled the time he puzzled over a cheating spouse case. The wife was absolutely certain her husband was fooling around with someone. Eli had followed the husband for several weeks with no results before turning to the man's paper trail, desperate to find some kind of proof that the guy was cheating. Unfortunately, everything seemed squeaky clean—that is, until the day I noticed a big discrepancy between his household financial records and his tax return. A number of his credit card bills showed a $50 charge to a place called "Helping Hands." And though in his household records he had earmarked those charges as chartable deductions, he hadn't taken the deduction from the corresponding tax return, even though he had itemized every other item in that category.

I pointed that out to Eli, who followed up on the lead and found out that the husband was driving once a month to Tennessee, where he would spend the afternoon at the Helping Hands Massage Parlor in the company of a certain red-haired "masseuse" named Brandy Flambeaux. The man had falsified his records to hide his indiscretion from his wife, but he hadn't dared to commit fraud on his tax return.

"You have the gift!" Eli proclaimed to me a few days later as we celebrated his hefty paycheck over Chinese takeout.

After that, he began to involve me more in his cases, and it really did seem as if I had a knack for detecting. It wasn't long before Eli was using me as his sounding board, asking me to play devil's advocate as he worked out different facets of his cases aloud. The fact that the work I did for him was mostly confidential taught me to keep my mouth shut and my eyes open. For the next few years, Eli seized every opportunity to give me on-the-job training on all he knew about detecting.

By the time I turned 18, the Gold Agency was thriving. Eli hired a real secretary and officially made me his assistant. I worked with him all through college, and though I knew he hoped I would stay with him once I graduated, I decided to go to law school instead. I loved detecting, but I was also fascinated with the law, and I wanted a career that didn't include hanging upside down from a fire escape to get good photographs of errant spouses. Eli's graduation gift for me was one-third ownership in the agency, but I tearfully turned it down and told him to give me a "retirement" watch instead.

Of course, life never quite goes as we plan. My career in law went well for the first several years but then ended once my husband was killed. After Bryan's death, I resigned from my job and basically from life, moving to Maryland's Eastern Shore and entering a self-imposed exile from the world. It took the gentle, constant prodding of Eli to finally get me out of the house and back into the workforce again—this time in a job that combined my detecting abilities with my legal skills. I loved working as the director of research for Tom and the J.O.S.H.U.A Foundation, and I had Eli to thank for talking me into taking a second chance on life. Though Eli had no business connection with Tom or the foundation, he was the mutual friend who put us together. Now, I realized, not only did I have Eli to thank for telling me about an amazing job opportunity that was a perfect match for my skills and experience, I also had him to thank for bringing me to the man who showed me I could love again.

I glanced at the clock and wondered how much longer I would be here before Jodi came to relieve me. I didn't mind sitting and waiting for the next hour's visit, but I thought my energies might be better spent back at the house, trying to find the notes Eli had said only I would be able to locate—*if* the person or people who trashed the house hadn't found them already.

Why would I know where Eli kept his notes?

I tried to think of all of our recent conversations, if he had told me anything during one of our phone calls that might have tipped me off. Sadly, I had to admit that just about the only time I talked to Eli anymore was when I needed his help on a complicated case. Why didn't I ever call to ask about him and how he was doing? Why didn't I ever call just to say hello?

Taking a deep breath, I decided to put off the guilt trip until later. For now, I had to figure this out.

Notes. Where had Eli stashed his notes? And why did he think I would know where that place would be?

There were really only two possibilities: Either he had told me recently and I just wasn't paying attention, or he was using a hiding place he had used in the past that only I would know about and would be able to figure out. Since I couldn't recall any conversation between the two of us about notes or a case within the last few years, I decided to concentrate on the latter.

Think, Callie.

Remembering back to the days when we had worked together, I closed my eyes and tried to picture Eli with his notes. He always kept a running file of every case, and that file was usually on his person when the case was active. When he left the office, he carried the file in an old brown satchel.

When he wasn't working a case, perhaps taking a weekend off, he would leave the file at the office. Depending on the security level of the case involved, that meant either putting the file in his top desk drawer or locking it away in the office safe.

But Eli had no office now, so there would be no desk nor any office safe. I decided to ask Stella if perhaps they had a home safe that Eli might have used, or if he still kept that old brown satchel around.

I dug through my bag for a phone card and my address book and then went to the pay phones next to the elevator and dialed Stella's home phone number. Tom answered and we spoke for a moment, each of us making sure the other was okay. Then he handed the phone to Stella, who sounded distracted. I got right to the point and asked her my questions, but unfortunately she said they had no safe, no real desk other than a small rolltop where they kept stamps and envelopes, and no satchel. I said I'd like to examine the desk, if she didn't mind, and she told me that was no problem, that Jodi should be showing up any moment to relieve me here at the hospital.

I hung up the phone and returned to my seat, desperately trying to think of other possibilities.

Over the years, I recalled, there had been a few cases where security had been especially high. At those times, Eli had stored his notes in a safety deposit box at a local bank. But that was too inconvenient for ongoing cases. That was usually for situations when he had wrapped up his notes and then simply needed to store them for a time; for example, while waiting for a case to go to trial. I wondered if perhaps that might be the situation here, though I doubted he was waiting for any kind of trial since surely he would have told Stella that.

So what did that leave? At the very least, I should call Stella back and ask her if they kept a safety deposit box at the bank. I was about to return to the pay phone to call her again when Jodi came strolling up the hall.

"Hey, Callie," she said, looking even more tired than before. "How's he doing?"

"About the same. How are things going there?"

"Not good. Most of the geezers on the lawn have gone back home, but my mom's kind of in a frenzy. Nothing's been taken that she can tell. Now she's even more determined for you to find those notes. She doesn't understand what's going on or why someone would trash the joint if they weren't out to steal something."

I glanced at my watch, surprised that it was nearly time for the next hourly visit with Eli. I told Jodi I wanted to see him one more time, and then I would return to the condo. Nodding, she settled down in the waiting room, stretched out across a row of seats, and promptly fell asleep. Grateful that at least someone would be here to continue the vigil, I walked to the nurses' desk to see if they would let me in to see him one more time.

Five

My second time at Eli's bedside was somewhat easier than the first. The tubes and wires and machines weren't quite as shocking to me, though it was still difficult to hold his hand and not feel him holding mine back. This time I leaned close to his ear and told him, firmly but nicely, that I needed for him to snap out of it.

"Come on, Eli," I said, squeezing his limp hand. "It's time to tell everybody what the heck is going on."

A few minutes later, in the car on the way to Stella's, I thought about the final words Eli had said on the street after he was shot and before he lost consciousness. According to Stella, he rambled on about Tom and me and someone named Nadine. Certainly, Eli and I had never discussed anyone by that name. I knew I would remember if we had.

Back at the condo, Stella had changed into her version of "regular" clothes—a bright floral shirt and lime green slacks. The fact that nothing had been stolen from her home seemed to have rattled her completely, especially since she had several valuable pieces of jewelry that could have easily been removed from the jewelry box atop the dresser but hadn't been. As Tom walked through the house with the insurance adjuster, Stella grabbed my arm and held on tightly, jabbering almost nonstop in a nervous patter.

"Why does someone break into a home if not to steal?" she kept asking, almost pleading with me for an answer. Unfortunately, at this point, I didn't really know. I would have thought it was simple, random vandalism if not for the fact that Eli had also been shot.

"We need to focus here, Stella," I said, leading her to the couch and sitting down beside her. "If Eli thinks I can find his notes, then that has to be my number one priority."

"I know, I know."

"I'm thinking he may have stored them in a safety deposit box. That's one of the things he used to do with sensitive material, and something he would've expected me to remember. As far as you know, does he have one?"

"We share a box," she said, "but there's not much in there. A few documents, some jewelry. That's about it."

"When was the last time you looked in it?"

She thought about that.

"A few weeks ago," she answered finally. "A CD matured, and I needed the certificate."

"Where do you keep the key?"

"I think it's still in my purse."

"Does Eli have his own key?"

"No," she replied. "Why would he need one? We share."

I shrugged, thinking it was possible that Eli had put his notes in the box for safekeeping without Stella's knowledge.

"Do you think you could run by the bank when it opens and take another look?" I asked. "See if there's anything in the box you don't recognize?"

"I guess I could," she said, on the verge of tears, "but I need to get back to the hospital. What if Eli wakes up and I'm not there?"

Tom had overheard this last exchange and stuck his head around the corner to speak to us.

"Stella, as soon as we're finished here, I'll drive you over to the bank and then straight from there to the hospital. We'll get you back there as quickly as we can."

I glanced at my watch, surprised to see that it was after 8:00.

"Okay," she sniffled, seeming somewhat comforted. "I think on Saturdays it's open from nine to noon."

"In the meantime," I said, "have you eaten anything today? Maybe we should fix you some breakfast."

"I suppose a bowl of cereal might make me feel better."

There was a knock on the door, and I opened it, expecting to see the cleaning service. Instead, it was a man in his mid-forties, dressed casually in shorts and a T-shirt. Stella seemed happy to see him, so I left the two of them to talk while I went into the kitchen in search of cereal. Most of it had been poured out onto the kitchen floor by the vandals, but I found a few inches left in the bottom of a box of Raisin Bran. Careful not to cut myself on the broken glass on the counter, I found two intact bowls and spoons, washed them thoroughly, and cleared a space for us at the table.

Stella joined me there a few minutes later and sat down to eat. Between bites she told me about the man who had been at the door, the son of a neighbor. He had just heard about the vandalism and had come to offer us the use of his father's condo until the mess here had been cleaned up.

"Norman fell and broke his hip last week, so his place will be empty for a while," Stella said. "Jim told me where he hides the spare key and said for us to feel free to use his dad's home as much as we need to."

"That was nice of him," I said, pouring some cereal for myself. It wasn't what I usually chose for breakfast, but at this point I was so hungry I was happy for anything. The night without sleep followed by a morning without food was combining to give me a killer headache.

"His unit is in the next building over," Stella continued, gesturing to her left. "Number seventy-six. It's a three-bedroom, so there should be room for all of us, if need be."

"Good."

I chewed absently, listening as she described the location of the flowerpot under which we could find the spare key. It struck me that I hadn't even asked how the vandals had broken in here last night, and I wondered if Stella kept out a spare key as well. I asked her.

"My kids each have a key to the condo," she said. "But, no, I've never put one outside like some folks do. Never saw the need."

"What about the people who broke in and did all of this? How did they get in?"

Tom and the insurance adjuster entered the room at that moment.

"They busted through the back bedroom window," the insurance adjuster said, his voice nasal and high. "According to the police, they used towels to muffle the sound and protect themselves from any shards of glass. The report said there were a few fibers along the sill, so at least they left some evidence."

"Towels," I repeated. "That means they came prepared."

"Oh, yes," the man said. "From what I've seen, this person—or people—weren't here merely to vandalize. Seems to me they were professionals searching for something specific. They certainly knew every conceivable place to look. The damage here is quite extensive."

He joined us at the table and finished filling out the paperwork on his clipboard, assuring Stella that she would get a check to cover the damage within ten days.

"Do you need an emergency check now," he asked, "to cover the cleanup and get you a place to stay in the meantime?"

"Oh, no," she said vaguely, waving away the thought. Obviously, the man wasn't aware that Stella was wealthy and could afford to do whatever she needed to get through this crisis. Like many older folks, she lived on a shoestring, but I knew for a fact her bank accounts and other assets were quite hefty.

As they reviewed the papers and she signed on the dotted lines, I thought about the break-in and felt a surge of dismay. Had Eli been outmaneuvered by professionals? Was I chasing after something that had already been found and removed from the premises?

Suddenly, the dismay gave way to a glimmer of hope. Eli Gold was no amateur either. If he had hidden something important, I doubted anyone would be able to find it easily, even if they were pros.

I think Eli realized that himself and that's why his words to Stella were for *me* to find the notes. He knew they were hidden too well for anyone else to discover them. Wherever he had put them for safe-keeping, they certainly weren't going to turn up just by random searching.

Once the adjuster left, Tom and Stella prepared to head to the bank. I thought about going with them but decided my time would be better spent here taking one last look around. One of us needed to stay behind anyway, to let in the cleaning people when they came.

"Stella, may I ask you a question?" I said as she was stepping out the door. "Do you mind if I poke around your home myself? Is there any area you wouldn't want me digging through?"

Stella looked back at me, her expression baffled.

"Eli and I are two old folks who play canasta and have a fond-ness for mocha chocolate chip ice cream. What do you think you might find, Callie? Our secret collection of nuclear weapons?"

"I just want to respect your privacy."

"Everything I own has been dumped out onto the floor!" she cried. "I don't have any privacy left. Help yourself."

Six

I went to work the moment the door shut behind them. There was a big difference between poking around when a homeowner was there and digging through things when they were not—especially digging with permission.

This time I didn't just look for physical evidence of Eli's notes. I also skimmed documents and letters, rooted around the files that had been dumped all over the floor next to their small filing cabinet, and generally stuck my nose deeply into all sorts of places that it didn't belong. In the process, I decided that Stella was involved in an incredibly high number of activities—from bunco to bingo to volunteering to civic work to church activities and on and on and on. No wonder she hadn't paid much attention to what Eli had been doing; she was too busy!

I also read enough of her kids' letters to decide that the sons were a pair of greedy little jerks. That had always been my impression, but some of the communications they had sent to their mother served to confirm that fact.

Sadly, my biggest revelation upon digging through Eli's private possessions came from seeing the reminders of his advanced age: a tube of denture cream, a bottle of Metamucil, a prescription for anti-inflammatories. Somehow, I had managed to ignore the fact that my friend Eli wasn't exactly a spring chicken anymore. He was getting older—maybe so old that he might not pull through this whole thing after all.

That sobering thought was on my mind when I found a small box of mementos that had been dumped out on the side of the bed, obviously taken from the bedside table. On the floor were a few of Eli's most precious keepsakes: the good citizenship medal he received at his eighth-grade graduation; dog tags from his time in the Navy; a photo of him and me together, snapped at my wedding. I held the picture in my hands, remembering that my dad had taken the shot, posing us in front of the table in such a way that made it look like wedding cake was sprouting from the top of Eli's head. I had tossed the photo aside but Eli had asked if he could have it. I had no idea he had held onto it all these years.

Under a few other photos of people I didn't know, I found the small black cap that had been Eli's boyhood yarmulke. Holding the small satin cap in my fingers, I said another prayer for this gentle Jewish Christian who had been such an important figure in my life.

Please, God, heal him. Heal him now.

Wiping tears from my eyes, I put the mementos together in the cigar box they had come from and slid it into the empty bedside drawer. I was at a loss for what to do next, so I bent down and picked up a few other items, putting them back in the drawer where I assumed they belonged. It wasn't until I came to Eli's old prayer shawl that I felt a small tingle at the back of my neck.

The prayer shawl.

The yarmulke.

Both symbols of his faith.

I stood up, memories rushing back to me in a flash.

The mezuzah!

The mezuzah held the key!

There had been two cases years ago where the safety and security of Eli's files had been paramount. In one situation, Eli had been called to testify against the leader of a major crime network; in the other, he had gathered evidence against an important politician. Both times he had needed to store his files in an absolutely impenetrable location, safe from the long arms of those he was going up against.

Eli had used a safety deposit box, as he did for other important cases, except each of those two times he had rented a new box in a different town where no one knew him. Then he had taken steps to make sure that no one would be able to locate the box and get it open unless they knew three separate things: where the key was hidden, the name of the bank, and the number of the box. He had provided me with enough information so that I could figure those things out for myself if worse came to worse and something bad happened to him. But I had never needed to take those steps.

Chances are, it was time for me to take those steps now.

I ran through the condo, grabbing a screwdriver from the spot in the laundry room where a small toolbox had been dumped out on the floor. Then I dragged a chair to the front door, opened it wide, and set the chair on the threshold.

The phone rang just as I was climbing up on the chair, and so I paused to answer it. Tom was calling to tell me that he and Stella were finished at the bank and were on the way to the hospital. They had looked into the safety deposit box and it was empty except for the items Stella had already described to me.

"That's what I expected to hear," I said, and I'm sure Tom was a bit confused by the excitement in my voice.

"Are you okay?" he asked.

"Just another idea I had. I'll call you back if it pans out."

I hung up before he could reply.

Back on the chair, I inhaled deeply at the sight of what I had been hoping to see: Mounted on the right doorpost and set at an angle was Eli's old mezuzah. I used the screwdriver to remove it, and as I worked I tried to remember what Eli had told me about this traditional Jewish fixture.

According to him, a mezuzah was simply a small case inside of which rested a tiny scroll containing several special passages of

Scripture from the Old Testament. Many Jews had mezuzahs mounted on their doorframes as a constant reminder of God's presence and a response to the directive in Deuteronomy 6:9 to put God's commandments on the doorframes of their houses.

Before Eli became a Christian, he followed the Jewish tradition of paying respect to the mezuzah each time he went in or out of his home. After he gave his life to Christ, he left the mezuzah in place but no longer followed the rabbinical directives that accompanied it.

One time he needed to leave a message for me outside of the office, and I facetiously suggested that he write it on a little piece of paper and stick it in the mezuzah. He told me that he felt that would be disrespectful, but that I might be onto something nevertheless. When it came time for him to hide the key to his safety deposit box, he removed the little mezuzah, hollowed out a flat space for the key behind it, and then remounted it. He didn't think God would have a problem with that; he also liked the idea of hiding something in plain sight, something I would be able to get to easily if the need arose.

My hope was that he had taken the same actions here in Florida, and seeing the mezuzah on his doorframe was a good indication that he had. As soon as the little box was loose I would know for sure.

I managed to poke the screwdriver behind the box, pressed it like a lever, and watched one side of the box swing loose. I gasped, my heartbeat pulsing in my throat. There, hidden behind the mezuzah, was a small, flat key. I pushed aside the mezuzah, pried it loose from the wood, and turned it over in my hand.

"Excuse me, is this the Gold residence?"

I nearly tossed everything in the air at the sound of the person who had snuck up behind me. Spinning precariously on the chair, I spied two women standing on the sidewalk, their arms loaded with cleaning supplies.

"Sorry," one of them said, "we didn't mean to frighten you."

"That's okay," I replied, smoothly pocketing the key, "I'm just a little jumpy."

"No wonder, judging by the condition of the house," the other woman said, leaning to one side to look into the condo behind me. "We're here to clean up the mess. You called this morning?"

I climbed down from the chair and smoothed out my clothes.

"Yes. Thanks for coming."

"No blood, right?" one of them asked. "We didn't bring the right stuff for that."

"Just…vandalism," I replied, turning so that they could come inside.

They seemed quite blasé about the mess, and I supposed that came with the territory. If their job was to clean up crime scenes, then they probably saw much worse things than this every day.

They decided to start at the back of the house and work their way forward. That was fine with me, and as soon as they got started, I went to the kitchen, pulled the key from my pocket, and studied it.

It looked a lot like the key to my own safety deposit box, same size, same basic shape. Slipping it back into my pocket, I closed my eyes and tried to remember the other two steps I needed to take that would lead me to the correct box at the correct bank.

A bookcase. It had something to do with a bookcase—but it had been so many years since Eli told me about these things, I didn't fully remember.

I walked into the empty living room and crunched my way across the mess to where all of their books lay strewn in a heap at the foot of a big bookcase. *Second shelf, far right,* I could almost hear Eli telling me, and in a flash the entire memory came flooding back: Inside a book, he found the page number that corresponded with his box number and he had drawn a circle around it with a pen. Then he had placed it on the shelf, second one from the top, at the far right.

Unfortunately, his books were no longer on the shelves, so I didn't know which book he had put the clue in! I would have to go through each and every one just to find the page I wanted. With a small sigh I cleared a small space on the floor, sat down, and began. I figured I would flip quickly through each of the books and see if anything jumped out at me. If that didn't work, I would go back through them more thoroughly a second time.

It took a while, but after thumbing through 15 books, it dawned on me to check the fattest books next, back to front, because the odds were that the box number was high. I struck gold with a heavy tome titled *The Riverside Shakespeare:* On page 1569, at the bottom right corner, the page number was circled in black ink. By coincidence, I noticed, the last line on the page was from *The Winter's Tale,* and the quote seemed ironic, considering the situation: *Would they else be content to die?*

Now that I had the correct book, I was to look for two more notations that would tell me the correct bank, and these were harder to remember. Something about a square and a triangle and "x marks the spot."

I held the book to me and closed my eyes, praying that God would bring the memories I needed back to me. It had been so very long since Eli had told me all of this; what had given him the right to believe I would still remember after all this time?

Frustrated, I started on page 1 of the nearly 2000-page-long book and flipped through, page after page, until I found what I was looking for. On page 17, a small triangle had been lightly drawn around the number, and then, on page 43, the same thing had been done with a square. I knew I was supposed to use these numbers to find the page and listing of the correct bank in the phone book.

I had seen a telephone directory in the kitchen, so I stood and made my way back to there, first checking out the seventeenth listing on page 43 and then the forty-third listing on page 17. One was a personal residence and one was a dog groomer. Neither was a bank.

Back to square one. I put the phone book down on the counter and tried, again, to clear my mind. *What now, Lord?* I prayed silently.

X marks the spot, I could almost hear Eli say in reply.

X marks the spot—of course! I wasn't supposed to use the local phone book, because the box hadn't been rented locally. Heart pounding, I ran to the guest bedroom, where I remembered seeing five or six other phone directories for the state of Florida.

They were still in a heap on the floor, and it didn't take long to look inside each directory's back cover until I came to the one with a big "X" marked across it in black ink. The directory was for the Orlando area.

Hands trembling, I sat on the edge of the bed and turned to page 43, the seventeenth listing.

Boss Lumber.

I tried again, page 17, the forty-third listing.

American Fidelity Bank.

Bingo.

Seven

"Hey, Harriet," I said into my cell phone as Tom steered us toward the interstate. "It's Callie. I need some banking info."

"Sure," Harriet replied. God bless her, she always knew when my tone meant "right away, no time to chat." At the moment, though I was sure she was dying to ask me questions, she held her tongue. "What can I tell you?"

"Can I get into a safety deposit box without showing ID?"

Because Harriet had worked for a bank before becoming office manager of the J.O.S.H.U.A. Foundation, she was always my go-to gal for banking procedures.

"Depends," she replied. "Do they know you there?"

"No. I'm trying to get into Eli's box. But I feel sure they don't know him, either."

"Hmm…" she said, and I could picture her chewing her pencil—or twirling it into her deep red hair. "There's a chance they won't ask, but if they're doing their job right, they will. Everybody's more careful these days, you know. If I had to lay odds, I'd say there's about a ninety percent chance you're gonna have to show your driver's license to get into that box. And the name on the license has to match the name on the box or you're out of luck."

"I was afraid of that," I said.

"Even if they don't ask for ID," she said, "you'll have to sign the signature card, and it has to look just like the sig they already have on file."

"Oh, that's right," I said, wishing I could be the one to do this instead of Tom. Eli and I had learned to write each other's signatures years ago, a skill that had come in handy considering the flow of papers that came through our office. Of course, I couldn't exactly march into the bank now and claim to be "Eli Gold"—even if I could make the signatures match.

"I mean, you can give it a shot," Harriet said. "Ask for the box by number, and if they say 'we need to see some ID,' tell them you don't have any with you but you'll go get it and come back. Then hightail it out of there fast. Banks don't look kindly on fraud. If they figure out you're trying to get into a box that's not your own, they just might call the police."

"All right, Harriet," I replied, looking out at the flat Florida landscape. I could hardly believe only three days ago I had been relaxing deep in the Smoky Mountains. "Thanks for the advice."

"You okay, hon?"

"Yeah. I'll call you when I have some time to talk."

"I'll be holdin' my breath 'til then, you know."

I disconnected the call and told Tom all that Harriet had said. The drive took nearly an hour, and we tossed out different options all the way there. Tom had some banking connections, of course, so there was always a chance he could pull some strings. But despite the influential names in his Palm Pilot, he was doubtful any of them could give him access into another person's safety deposit box—at least not without causing a big stir.

I knew we could always go the police route and do this legally, but that would take too long—not to mention that then the police would confiscate the contents of the box and I would never get to see them at all.

In the end we both decided that the quickest, easiest way to get into Eli's safety deposit box was to take that ten percent chance the bank wouldn't ask for ID. If our plan didn't work, we would follow Harriet's directive to "hightail" it out of there.

Then we would decide on a Plan B.

Once we reached downtown Orlando, the bank was easy to find. We parked on the street at a meter and then spent some time in the car with paper and pen as I tried to teach Tom how to write Eli's signature. When he had the hang of it, we got out of the car and crossed the street to the bank.

"It's showtime," he whispered as he held the door open for me.

We walked across the lobby together, our footsteps clicking on the shiny marble floor. Shoulders high, Tom approached a bank representative confidently and announced that he would like to have box 1569 please. Then he glanced at his watch, insinuating he was in a hurry.

"Of course," the woman replied, and she walked immediately to a filing cabinet. As she turned to go, I noticed the red blush along her hairline, a common response to Tom and his handsome presence.

I looked around the bank as we waited for her to pull the file, noting the beautiful ornate moldings that lined the ceiling. This was an older building, filled with elaborate architectural details, dignified whispers, and the distinctive smell of money.

"I just need for you to sign your name right here on this line," she said softly, returning to place a card on the counter in front of him. Smoothly, he pulled a pen from his pocket. I was about to distract the woman by commenting on the lovely building when she spoke again.

"And, of course, I'll need to see some ID, Mr. Gold."

Tom hesitated and I stepped forward, my pulse surging.

"Oh, we were afraid of that," I said. "He lost his wallet last night at the restaurant. Isn't the signature enough?"

I could feel Tom's foot pressing against mine, and I knew I wasn't following our plan. But we were so close to getting to that box! I simply couldn't help myself.

"It's for your own protection," the woman explained. "I'm sure you understand."

"Of course we do," Tom said, taking my arm. "We'll just run over to the restaurant and see if they found the wallet yet. If so, we'll come right back."

I was about to try another plea when the woman picked up the card and tapped it on the table.

"Sorry about that," she said, a flicker of suspicion crossing her features. "But that's our policy, you know."

"Wait!" I cried, gesturing toward the card though I could feel Tom's fingers pinching into my arm. "I still have *my* wallet."

The woman and Tom both looked blankly at me. Then she gazed down at the card, turning it over to see what I had just glimpsed.

"Are you Mrs. Webber?" she asked.

"Yes, I am," I replied, grinning foolishly as I reached into my purse for my driver's license. *Good ol' Eli,* I thought. He had put my name on his box as a backup, forging my signature just like the old days!

I signed on the back of the card next to my name. Within ten minutes, Tom and I were back at the car, a manila envelope weighing heavily in my hands.

"That envelope better be worth what we just risked to get it," he said.

"It will be," I replied, running my fingers across the front. "If I know Eli, it will be."

Eight

We found a little restaurant on the way out of town and asked for a table off to ourselves. With a knowing smile, the hostess led us to a booth near the window, but there were still people within earshot. Tom gestured toward an empty dining room at the back, slipped the woman a twenty, and asked if we might sit there instead.

"Honey, for twenty bucks," she said, pocketing the cash, "you can come home with me and sit at my kitchen table!"

As soon as we were seated in the back room and had placed our orders, I pulled out the envelope and opened the clasp. Inside I found two items: Eli's old address book, falling to pieces but held together with several rubber bands, and a thick file with Eli's familiar handwriting scribbled across the front. I carefully removed the file and set it down in front of me.

"Aw, shoot," the waitress interrupted, bringing in two glasses of water. "You wanted privacy for a business meeting. I thought y'all was sweet on each other and just wanted a little solitude, if you know what I mean."

She must have picked up on our mood because she left the room without much more chatter. Once she was gone, Tom moved over to sit next to me so we could go through the file together.

The word Eli had written across the front of the file was "Nadine." My heart pounded. All of my hunches in finding and securing this file were about to pay off.

We opened it up to find Eli's typed notes, the first entry dated December 28 of last year.

"He started this file four months ago," Tom said, pointing to the date.

Though Eli used a shorthand way of writing, his notes were always thorough, containing impressions and observations that lesser detectives might have missed entirely. As he had taught me years ago, you never know what's going to be important in a case. Better to write it all down as it happens so that you can refer back to it later if need be.

Now, Tom and I both read the entry silently to ourselves.

12/28 6 P.M.—Ferry St. Thomas to St. John on way to house. White female passenger on ferry looks familiar. Attractive brunette, age approx. late fifties. Expensive watch, well-cut clothes. Carries two shopping bags—one orange with big white sunflower, the other brown with big cursive signature logo. Based on time of day, I assume she's been shopping in St. Thomas and is now headed back to St. John for the night. I puzzle over it the whole way; getting off the ferry, I realize what it is: She reminds me of Nadine Peters! Face is different, though.

Think nothing more of it, must deal with my own luggage. Leaving the dock with porter, observe woman again, from behind; she is reaching up to unzip sunroof from car. Her movements raise the hem of her skirt, exposing ugly scar on thigh just above her knee. Coincidence? It has been many, many years. And Nadine is dead. I saw her die. Shot her myself. Still, that scar. Those movements. Something about that face...

I make note: Plate JAB 6944, Suzuki Vitara, gray.

She drives away immediately; impossible to tail without being obvious or explaining to Stella. Distract Stella with the bags and then ask two cabdrivers; neither claims to know her. Vendor at dockside stand thinks woman is a local but that she doesn't get out much or mingle in the community.

That was the full entry for that date. Tom and I looked at each other, and he didn't even have to ask the question for me to answer it.

"No," I said, shaking my head, "I never heard of Nadine Peters. Have you?"

"No," he echoed.

"I don't get this about the ferry, though. Why is he on a ferry?"

"There's no airport in St. John. To get there, you have to fly into St. Thomas. The islands are fairly close to each other. I think the ferries run all day long, and you can get from one to the other by boat in less than an hour."

"So that's what he was doing when he first saw her. Eli and Stella had flown to St. Thomas and they were taking the ferry over to St. John, where Stella has a house."

"Yes. And while they were on that ferry, he thought he recognized someone from his past. Someone of significance."

"But then he says, 'Nadine is dead. I saw her die. Shot her myself.' Now he thinks he sees her alive. He must've been stunned!"

Tom reread the notes.

"Has Eli shot many people in his lifetime?" he asked.

"I don't know," I replied. "He's been a detective and a cop, and he was in the military. I suppose in all of that, there might have been at least a few times he had to shoot at someone."

We moved on to the next entry, both fascinated by the detailed notes.

12/29—Can't get woman out of my mind. One screaming question: Could it be Nadine????? There is simply no way. Nadine is dead!!!

12/31—7 P.M.—Bring bottle of good champagne to A. to toast the New Year; convince him to run plates; leave with name and

address info from lic. plate. Plate JAB 6944, Suzuki Vitara, is regis-
tered to Earl Streep, Turtle Point, East End. Husband?

1/10 noon—Can't stop obsessing, have to investigate just to
rule this out. Locate Turtle Point out on the East End of St. John.
Driveway to house is long, winding road up mountain with no way
to approach without being seen. Posted as "Private Drive, No Tres-
passing." Let it go, just coincidence.

"Hmm," I said. "Looks like he tried to let it go, for a while at least.
The next entry is about six weeks later."

"February 28," Tom said. "That was just two months ago."

"I know. I guess he couldn't let it rest forever."

We continued to read.

2/28—BIG SURPRISE! Go to St. Thomas to get bracelet for
Stella for birthday. Spot same woman shopping in town. I purchase
camera with zoom and tail on foot. Two hours of shopping, visit to
private home 3344 Ketch Alley for approx. 45 minutes. Ferry back
to St. John. Take chance of getting on ferry, afraid she will spot me.
She sits front, right, so I go back left and get some photos. Not
spotted. Stella picks me up. Drop photos for development. Decide I
will set up surveillance near bottom of driveway to her house.
Across the street is a small beach.

3/1 10 A.M.—First day of surveillance. Warm and sunny. Beach
umbrella, ice chest, chair—I'm set. Camera at the ready, car
parked not ten feet away. Let's have some action.

6 P.M.—Time to pack it in. No one in or out all day. Local on
beach says "big estate" at the top of that driveway. No comment
from him on frequency of activity (or lack thereof) in and out of
driveway.

8 P.M.—Back in Stella's car for night surveill., park several
blocks away. No easy night cover here, small restaurant but it's
closed tonight, no other activity.

9 P.M.—Police car passes twice, acting suspicious, so I hang it up
for the night. Will try again tomorrow.

"He sounds very determined," Tom said, turning the page.

"That's Eli," I replied. "Like a bulldog when he gets started on something. You have no idea."

Before we could go on, the waitress showed up with our food. She set it down in front of us, asked if we needed anything else, and then left us to our papers. Tom reached for his hamburger and took a bite. I was too excited to eat, but I stabbed at my chef salad anyway, spearing a chunk of ham and a little lettuce before sliding the plate away and returning my attentions to the papers.

3/2 9 A.M.—Back on the beach.

1:30 P.M.—At last, some activity!!! Delivery car from Island Foods, bringing groceries.

1:45 P.M.—Delivery car exits. Decide to follow and perhaps engage in conversation. Long trip back to town; two more deliveries are made on the way. Finally, over mountain and into Cruz Bay, pull into Island Foods lot; make note of delivery man.

Pick up a few things in the store. Delivery man is stocking shelves, his name tag says Gerald. I complain about how much I hate shopping, wonder aloud if the store has delivery. He says with a fee. Where is my house? I say East End, he says $50 del. fee plus tip. (Wish I could shrink myself down into a box of macaroni and have myself delivered there.)

3/3—All day surveillance. No activity.

3/4—All day surv. No activity. Pick up photos—some good shots. This woman just has to be Nadine. I bring the best pics to Z. at the deli in Coral Bay since he knows almost everyone on the entire island. Does he recognize her? He says, yes, that's Dianne Streep. She lives out on the East End. Keeps to herself. Married? Yes, her husband is Earl. Know anything about them? Just that they don't really mingle with the community. Been living out on Turtle Point for a long time. Big estate. Nice little beach around back.

3/5—Need new approach. Call P. in Seattle for satellite photos of the area. He e-mails them; I download and study. Big estate. Tennis court. Pool. Walls. No other houses in vicinity. No vantage point for better look. Too old to climb mountain on foot! Would probably be caught anyway. Am ready to give up search. Call A. and get *reference for local PI out of St. Thomas. For $200 they'll do some research into the estate's security. Costs are mounting, but I give the go-ahead. They will have report by the end of the week. Get tips from them on purchase location for certain items. Do some shopping and then organize h.c. with new tools.*

In the meantime, call around to see if T. is still in the area, still has that sailboat.

"What's with the initials?" Tom asked. "Who is 'P'? Who is 'T'?"

"Eli always did that to protect his sources—though we'll probably be able to figure out who's who since we have his address book."

"Oh yeah," he said, glancing toward the envelope.

"I have a feeling 'P. in Seattle' is probably Paul Tyson," I said, "a guy I use sometimes too. A real computer genius. Not always operating on the right side of the law, you understand."

"Nothing illegal about getting satellite photos. You can get them off the internet."

"Maybe. But if I know Paul, his photos were downloaded straight from the CIA's satellites or something. He's a real hacker, and he has a way of going places most people don't see."

"You sure keep some interesting company, Callie."

"I learned at the hand of the master," I replied, gesturing toward Eli's notes.

"What's 'h.c.'?"

"Haven't a clue," I said, rereading the sentence: "'Do some shopping and then organize h.c. with new tools.' Some kind of storage area? Maybe a special carrying case? Those would be my best guesses."

We continued.

3/6 8:30 A.M.—Out on T.'s sailboat with telescope in hand. Have a good glimpse of the main gate, though house is obscured by trees. No activity.

We sail around back side. I'm pleased to see a private road from estate down to small beach. Activity on beach, though not her. Three dogs and a native. Anchor boat and swim over. Though the beach is public, there are "No Trespassing" signs about every 10 feet along brush line. I try to look nonthreatening, say I'm a little seasick & need to stretch my legs. He is responsive but not overly friendly.

Conversation tough, don't want to be overeager. Says he works for the Streeps and points up the hill. Brings dogs down twice a day for run on beach. Apparently the dogs are Mrs. Streep's pride and joy. I say it's a swanky place, curious what they do for a living. He says Mr. Streep is retired, Mrs. Streep is an art dealer. She works from home as a consultant. I don't let anything show on my face, but I can't believe it. Nadine Peters minored in art history in college! If she's living here in a new life, art consultant is perfect fit.

Time's up. He yells for Bob, Eve, and Alice. I'm expecting three people to appear, but it turns out he's calling for the dogs. We shake hands; he is William.

"Dianne Streep," I said. "An art dealer."
Tom didn't reply. We kept reading.

3/7—Report from Windward Investigations. Security on estate is extreme!!! Protective barriers include:

1. Three watchdogs

2. One night security guard

3. Alarm system on doors and windows

4. Biometric entry system on all doors

5. Internal and external motion sensors

6. Internal thermal sensors

7. Internal and external cameras

8. Acoustic/electromagnetic shielding for secure room

9. Backup generator for electronic security devices

10. Closed computer network

Protective measures are far above and beyond the norm. This more than anything convinces me that Dianne Streep and Nadine Peters are one and the same. Bigger question: Is the art dealer thing really her job now or is it a cover? Is she still an active agent?????

3/8—Windward calls to tell me that subject has gained knowledge of their security inquiry. Not good. Surveillance will have to wait for now. Must convince Stella we've got to go back to States a week early. Risk factor high. Need to approach from different direction.

3/9—Home in Florida; book morning flight to Baltimore without Stella.

3/10—Flight to Baltimore. Meet with R., now docent at the museum. Confirms Nadine's death as eyewitness. Says imagination plays tricks, forget it.

3/11—Under Freedom of Information Act read all declassified info on Nadine. Learn nothing new. Sold secrets to Russians during CMC, worked as mathematician for NSA.

"What does that mean?" I asked. "What's 'CMC'? What's 'NSA'?"

Tom didn't reply, but I could feel his arm muscles stiffening as he sat there next to me.

"Tom?" I asked.

He simply shook his head and pointed at the next paragraph of the report.

"Looks like Eli and this woman were a couple," he said.

File contains full reports of her relationship with me! Including photos of us together at cabin. Partial report of discovery of her betrayal; my interrogation; her escape and subsequent death at cabin. File closed with "Deceased." Autopsy report included. Photo of body.

Compare to current photos I took. Bring photos back to R. He says he will look into it and get back to me. Could take weeks—he says to be patient.

3/12—Return to Florida and wait. Put file into highest security storage until I hear back from R.

CODE YELLOW.

"That's it," I said. "That's his last entry. The twelfth of last month."

Tom and I looked at each other and then back down at the stacks of photos, reports, and documents.

"What's code yellow?" Tom asked.

"Like a traffic light," I replied. "It means 'slow down and wait.'" Tom nodded.

"I guess while he waited, somebody decided to shoot him."

Nine

~

"We have to go back to square one," Tom said as we pulled onto the interstate. "Recap the whole thing again."

We had finished our lunch while looking through the stack of photographs, reports, and computer printouts that had been included with the file. As always, Eli's records had been thorough. This case was too complicated to take it all in at once.

"Okay," I said, holding the case notes in front of me and turning in my seat a bit to get comfortable. We had an hour's drive back to Stella's place. Though I would have preferred to spend the time sleeping, I knew Tom was as exhausted as I was, and I needed to stay alert in order to keep him from falling asleep at the wheel. Before I went over everything, I reached out and took his hand.

"Are you all right?" I asked. "At some point we both need to lie down and take a nap."

"Maybe when we get back to Stella's," he said. "Right now, my mind is racing too much to sleep anyway."

"Good. Then you drive while I go it through again."

"Go for it."

"The short version is that Eli saw a woman from his past he thought he recognized, a woman he had had a relationship with and then apparently shot and killed. He investigated to find out if it was really her, and then he ended up getting shot by a sniper."

"Take me through the long version," Tom said grimly.

I paged through everything and then began.

"A few months ago, right after Christmas, Eli and Stella went down to their vacation house in the Virgin Islands to stay for a while. They flew into St. Thomas first and then they took a ferry from St. Thomas over to St. John, which is where their house is. While they were on the ferry, Eli thought he recognized one of the passengers, an older woman who reminded him of someone named Nadine Peters. He kept looking at her, trying to decide if it was her when he saw a nasty scar on her leg—a scar in the very spot where apparently he shot this woman Nadine years before. That more or less confirmed it for him."

"Except that Nadine was supposed to be dead."

"Exactly."

I dug through the papers until I came to the computer printout from the St. John police, showing the name and address registered to the woman's license plate number.

"Anyway," I said, "Eli stewed on it for a few days before finally taking the plate number from the woman's car down to someone named 'A.' The plate checked out for an address on the East End of the island under a completely different name. Eli went over there and looked for her house, but all he found was just a long driveway up a mountain with a 'No Trespassing' sign. He decided it was too much trouble, just coincidence. He let it go."

"For a while."

"For about six weeks. Then at the end of February he accidentally spotted her again, this time while shopping in St. Thomas. Unable to resist the opportunity, he quickly bought a camera and then tailed her while she was shopping. She stopped at someone's house for a while, and he wrote down the address. He got photos of everything."

I flipped through the pile until I came to the pictures, all of which had been blown up to 8 x 10 size. I studied the ones that showed the woman's face, though most were in profile. She wasn't unattractive, but there wasn't anything conspicuous about her either.

"That's a nose job, for sure," Tom said, glancing at the pictures in my hands. "Face lift too. Maybe the chin."

"How do you know?"

"I live in Southern California. You get to know the look."

I rolled my eyes and continued.

"After that second sighting, Eli decided to set up a surveillance on her house—well, on her driveway at least. He used the beach across the street from there as a cover, and he sat and waited for some action for…" I counted the dates in his notes. "Well, for a day and a half, until she received a delivery of groceries. Eli tried to make some headway with the delivery guy, but it was a wash."

"Gerald at Island Foods, right?"

"Very good," I said. "After that, Eli continued the surveillance for two more days, all to no avail. Then he decided to take a different approach."

"The satellite photos."

"Yes," I replied, pulling the computer-printed pictures from the pile. They were very interesting to look at, a vivid bird's-eye view of the woman's estate. There were about five photos, all very similar, all showing a gorgeous mountaintop home and the different facilities surrounding it. She really had the whole hill to herself, a wonderful fortress for someone who didn't want to be observed by anyone in any way.

"I'd like to live like that," Tom said. "High up on a hill, away from the world."

"You would?"

"If you were there with me."

I looked down, knowing I felt the same. Not that it would be the wisest course of action, but there was something about being in love with this man that made me want to steal away with him and shut out everything but each other.

"That's when he hired the local private investigator too, right?" Tom asked, snapping me from my thoughts.

"Yeah. Windward Investigations," I said, pulling their report from the file. "He paid this local guy two hundred dollars to research the security level of the estate. Big surprise when it turned out that the place was locked down tighter than Fort Knox."

"In the meantime Eli stashed away some spy tools and hired a sailboat."

"Yes, somebody he calls 'T' took Eli out on a sailboat with a telescope. He got a better look at the place, and then he spent a little while on her private beach, talking with a man named William who apparently worked for her."

"He tried to question the guy about Nadine."

"Except her name now is Dianne."

I pointed down at Eli's notes.

"What does this mean, 'Is she still an active agent?'"

"I don't know," Tom said, but I could see something shift in his expression, as though something just closed off. I wanted to ask him what he was thinking, but he interrupted my train of thought.

"You understand the significance of the woman's name, don't you?" he asked.

"Dianne?"

"Dianne. Nadine. Peters. Streep. She's playing word games. Scramble the letters for Nadine and you get Dianne. Scramble Peters and you come up with Streep."

I stared at the names on the page in front of me, mixing up the letters with my eyes. He was right.

"Leave it to you to notice something like that," I said.

"I'm good at word puzzles," he replied. That was the understatement of the year. With all of the board games we had played in North Carolina, I learned not to go up against him in anything that required using letters or numbers to win.

"So then he and Stella returned to Florida, and the next day he flew to Baltimore," Tom said, interrupting my thoughts again.

"Where he met with a docent at a museum," I continued. "A docent he calls 'R.' Apparently R. tried to tell Eli that Nadine was definitely dead, and that this new sighting was all in his imagination. Eli used the Freedom of Information Act to pull some old reports on Nadine anyway."

"Reports that showed she sold secrets to the Russians during the Cold War. She must've been an NSA agent."

From the file I pulled out a stack of papers that was about an inch high, old documents from the early '60s detailing this woman's activities as a double agent and, sure enough, she worked for the NSA. I knew that when we had time, we could probably glean a lot more data simply by reading each and every page—though many of the pages were black with ink from a Magic Marker. Even with the Freedom of Information Act, certain types of information could be legally withheld.

"According to Eli, he already knew she was a spy. Here's where I get confused." I held up Eli's notes and read them out loud. "'Sold secrets to Russians during CMC, worked as mathematician for NSA.' What's CMC? What's NSA?"

Tom hesitated.

"I would think NSA is the National Security Agency," he said finally, his voice sounding tight.

"Of course," I said. "What's the old joke about the NSA? They're so secretive, 'NSA' stands for 'No Such Agency'?"

I tried to think of what I knew about the National Security Agency. I thought it was located outside of Baltimore, around Ft. Meade. I had seen signs for it when I traveled the Baltimore/Washington Expressway, and signs for the new Cryptological Museum located next door.

"What does the NSA do?" I asked. "Aren't they intelligence, kind of like the CIA?"

"More like code breaking. Code making. Transfer of information."

"Hey, maybe that's the museum where R. is a docent—that new museum of cryptology."

"If Eli was dealing with the NSA, that would be the likely one," Tom said.

I looked at him and noticed a strange expression in his eyes.

"What's wrong?" I asked.

He shook his head dismissively.

"Nothing," he replied. "I'm just tired."

Certainly, we were both tired at this point. But there *was* something odd in Tom's eyes. I took a deep breath and decided to pursue it later.

"So Eli pulled some files on Nadine," Tom said, continuing on with our recap, "that confirmed she used to work for the NSA but that she sold secrets to the Russians. The files also confirmed that she was dead."

I dug through the stack for the gruesome pictures at the bottom, the autopsy photos of Nadine Peters. She sure looked dead to me, though, certainly, the photos could have been staged. From the looks of it, she had about five bullet wounds—four in her back and one in her leg. The one in the thigh must have been the shot that Eli had made.

Under those were some photos of an old, dilapidated cabin in the woods.

"This must be where they went to have their affair," I said. "He says here, 'Full reports of her relationship with me! Including photos of us together at cabin.'"

I studied the pictures more closely and realized that one of them showed a very young Eli embracing a partially disrobed Nadine, seen through one of the windows of the cabin.

"So, basically, what we're thinking," Tom said, "is that years ago Eli fell in love with a woman who turned out to be a spy for the Russians? That he was there when she was killed? That now in his golden years he realized she isn't dead after all?"

"Yes," I said, turning that over in my mind.

We drove along quietly for a moment, each of us lost in thought. Eli had dated a few women over the years, but as far as I knew he had never been in love, not until he met Stella. Now, I realized, that might not be the full story. Perhaps Eli had been in love once before, years ago, with a woman he ended up shooting. Perhaps Nadine thought turnabout was fair play and now she had come to Florida and shot him. I suggested the idea to Tom.

"Doesn't work," he said.

"Why not?"

Tom accelerated to pass a slow-moving truck.

"Because when Eli was shot, he told Stella 'Nadine said he was coming.' That leads me to believe that Nadine had recently made contact with Eli in some way, and that she had warned him of something—or someone, rather."

"*He's* coming? But who's 'he'?"

"I don't know. But why would Nadine warn Eli of something and then turn around and shoot him herself?"

He shook his head without speaking. I knew there was much going on here he wasn't saying. Suddenly, the biggest question on my mind—after who shot Eli, of course—was why Tom was involved here at all. I mean, I understood why Eli had asked for *me* to come. As his former partner, I knew him and his ways well enough to figure out the location of this sensitive file. But what about Tom? Eli's words to Stella were to *show Tom the notes.*

What did Tom bring to this situation that I didn't understand? Why would Eli want Tom to see these notes?

I looked at him, at his broad shoulders, at his serious face. There was so much about Tom I didn't know, so much he kept from me. As I thought about all of the questions that remained unanswered between us, a wave of exhaustion swept over me. Would I ever know all of this man's secrets?

I closed my eyes and leaned back against the headrest, thinking about our brief history together. So many things about Tom had always been an enigma to me, but he had laid out the privacy ground rules in the beginning of our relationship, and that was how it had remained. Though I had come to know him on a number of levels, there were still important facts about his life he simply would not share.

Once, several years ago, when he had first hired me at the foundation, I had become so curious about my new boss that I had attempted, discreetly, to use my investigative skills to investigate *him*. I'm not sure what kind of security systems he had in place, but as soon as I started putting out some feelers, he found out about it.

Angrily, he told me that I could investigate him or I could work for him, but that I could not do both.

I agreed that I wouldn't investigate him, but only because of our mutual connection with Eli. Eli had said that Tom was a good (but very private) man, and I would have to leave it at that.

Many things had changed since then. Yet now here we were, back to that same old line drawn in the sand.

"There are things about this case you're not telling me, aren't there?" I asked in the quiet of the car.

"Yes," he answered softly, letting out a long, slow breath. "For one thing, I understand now why Eli wanted me here."

"Can you tell me about it?"

"No," he said. "I'm sorry, but I can't."

I looked out at the blue, blue sky, at the flat ground, at the scrubby brush and palm trees.

Somehow, despite the man sitting beside me, I felt very much alone.

Ten

It was almost 4:00 P.M. by the time we were back in Cocoa Beach. There were so many directions we could go with what we had learned, so many avenues to pursue, but I was starting to feel nauseous from lack of sleep. Tom wasn't looking much better; dark circles were visible under his eyes.

We went to the condo and found the women still cleaning it. They had made a lot of headway, but with one room left to do, they would be around for a while longer. I called the hospital to learn that Eli's condition was still listed as critical. Tom suggested that he and I get some rooms at a local hotel to catch a quick nap, but I reminded him of the friendly offer from the neighbor to use the empty condo as needed. Too tired to resist, Tom followed along behind me as I dug around for the spare key and let us into the place.

It was a mirror image of Stella's home, though it smelled musty and stale, as if it had been closed up for a while. We opened some of the windows and the light sea breeze swept through almost immediately. Tom and I sank onto the couch, where the air flowed best.

We were silent as we rested there together, Tom lightly tracing a pattern across the back of my hand with his fingers. I closed my eyes and exhaled slowly as his hand moved up to caress and knead the knots at the back of my neck.

"Mmmm…" I sighed, relaxing into the steady, pulsing movements of his hands.

Soon, shivers of desire began to whisper through me. My breath caught, and in an instant I knew we were entering dangerous territory. How wonderful it would be, I knew, to close out the rest of the world for a while and simply make love to each other.

But we couldn't. As Christians, Tom and I were both committed to celibacy outside of marriage. And though it hadn't been easy, we had managed to get through the past few weeks without ending up in bed together. I wasn't about to use the excuse of our current troubles to compromise now.

In North Carolina, it had helped that I had stayed out in the guest house, Tom slept in the main house, and Wilbert and Ida Jean Miller—an older couple who served as the caretakers of the property—resided between us in a small cottage. In the past three weeks, we had turned the two of them into sort of ad hoc chaperones, inviting them over to the main house for board games on the evenings whenever we found ourselves feeling especially tempted. In the last three weeks, the four of us had played many games of Scrabble, Monopoly, Clue, Trouble, Life, and Yahtzee.

Fortunately, during the daytime hours, Tom and I seemed to have developed a sort of tag team approach to chastity—just when he was feeling weakest, I would be strong, and vice versa. Once hands or thoughts began to wander, that's when we knew it was time to go out and do something constructive to clear our minds and occupy our bodies. It was no wonder I had learned to mountain climb in a mere three weeks' time! Tom was getting to be a pretty good canoer too.

"It's tag team time," I whispered now, leaning back into the caresses of his hands.

"I know," he moaned, shifting forward to wrap his arms around me, his breath sweet and warm against the back of my neck.

I realized I would have to be the strong one this time, and so finally, reluctantly, I pulled away.

"You rest here," I whispered. "I'll find somewhere down the hall."

He let me go with a deep groan.

"And what's to stop me from following you there?"

I stood and smoothed my hair and then gave him a smile.

"You know the answer to that question as well as I do," I said.

Leaving him on the couch, I found one of the back bedrooms and opened a window. What we had to remember, what we had to keep telling ourselves, was that even though we were alone together, we were never completely alone. Our Savior was always watching, and He's the one to whom we were both accountable.

A fresh ocean breeze swept into the room, and I lay down across the bed, exhausted. Despite all that had just happened, I felt myself slipping into sleep almost immediately. I closed my eyes, inhaling the smell of the sea.

Slowly, I became aware of a hand on my arm, gently shaking me. The light in the room was soft and shadowed, and it took a few seconds to remember where I was. Tom was there, sitting on the side of the bed, saying my name.

"What time is it?" I asked, sitting up.

"Almost seven," he replied.

We had slept much longer than either of us had intended. He stood as I slid my legs to the edge of the bed, trying to clear my foggy brain.

"I'm really sorry about earlier," he said. "I wasn't thinking straight."

"It's okay," I replied, smiling up at him. "We've had a tough day."

I went to the bathroom and splashed some water on my face. What I really needed was a nice, long shower. I looked at my reflection in the mirror. A very pale, very tired Callie looked back at me. Using the few items I carried in my purse, I tried to freshen up, smoothing my hair and putting on a bit of mascara and a dab of lipstick. I took a deep breath and let it out, wondering when I could get an entire night's sleep.

When I returned to the living room, Tom was standing at the door, jiggling his keys. He seemed to have pulled himself together also, managing to finger-comb his dark hair into place.

"Let's go back over to Stella's," he said, looking somber, "and see what's up there."

He had closed and locked all of the windows, so I locked the door, stashed the key under the flowerpot, and followed him down the sidewalk to Stella's unit.

It was empty, but the cleaners had left a bill for their services on the kitchen counter. "Sid's Glass" had also shown up and replaced the broken window, as their bill sat on the table next to that of the cleaners.

"Poor Stella," I said, putting down the note. "Imagine having to deal with this while your husband clings to life in the hospital."

"You should probably get down there," Tom said. "I'm sure she's wondering what's going on with us."

"I don't think we should tell her much about what we've learned," I said, thinking of the more intimate details of this case. "Not yet, anyway."

"Whatever you think's best."

"I also don't know how much we should tell the police, either," I said. "Some of the things Eli did in his investigation aren't exactly—"

"For now, we don't tell the police a thing," Tom interrupted. "Let them work the case from their own angles."

He was acting odd, almost antsy, still jingling his keys. I wanted to talk, but something in his face was closed off to me. Instead, I reached for his hand.

He squeezed mine in return but then let it go and gestured toward the door.

"Come on," he said. "I'll drop you at the hospital so you can sit for a while with Stella."

"Then where are you going?" I asked.

He looked away.

"I have to make a phone call," he said finally.

"A phone call?" I asked. "Why don't you make it here before we go?"

He shook his head, not meeting my eyes.

"I need to make a call on a secure line."

I studied his face for a moment, trying to understand what he was telling me. Secure, as in private?

Or digitally secure, as in scrambled?

"And where will you go to make this phone call?" I asked slowly. "Is this regarding Eli's situation or something of your own?"

He looked at me for a long moment.

"Both," he replied finally. "I have to make a digitally scrambled call, Callie, which means going somewhere that has that type of telephone equipment."

"Like where?"

"Like a local FBI office, maybe, or a military base. Something like that."

"You should try the Kennedy Space Center," I said. "It's not far from here. I bet they could help you."

"Good idea. Either way, this is not a call I can make on just any telephone. And I'm sorry, but you can't come with me."

There it was. Laid out for me, plain and simple. Except I didn't understand it one bit.

From the set of his chin, I could tell the conversation was over for now. Without responding, I picked up my purse and walked past him to the car.

We didn't speak on the drive. When we pulled under the front awning of the hospital, I reached for the file, but Tom put his hand on it.

"I'll keep it for now," he said.

We sat there with the engine idling. I removed my hand and placed it on my lap.

"How long will you be gone?" I asked evenly.

"I'm not sure," he replied. "As long as it takes. But I'll pick you up when I'm finished."

I nodded, a part of me wanting to reach out and grab his shirt by the collar and shake the truth out of him. Instead I opened the door and got out.

"Take as long as you want," I said, shutting the door a little harder than I probably needed to. Then I turned and walked into the hospital as quickly as my legs would carry me—uncertain if my overriding emotion was one of anger, hurt, or fear.

Eleven

~

Once inside the hospital, I walked across the lobby, around a corner, and then doubled back and hid behind a large plant. I watched Tom's rental pull out of the hospital parking lot onto the road. I quickly ran back outside, thinking that if there were a cab anywhere in the vicinity, I would jump in and say "Follow that car!"

Unfortunately, no cabs were to be seen. I stood there a moment on the pavement and watched Tom's car disappear around a corner. Suddenly I decided I was now ready to cross that line in the sand.

What was it he had said to me that time he caught me digging around? *You can investigate me or you can work for me, but you cannot do both.* I wondered what he would say if I investigated him now.

Half of me knew that would be wrong. Tom was a good man, and if there were secrets in his life, they were necessary secrets. The other half of me burned to know what it was that connected Tom with this case, and I didn't care what it would take to get some answers. I didn't have much time, and I didn't have many resources, but I thought if I could spend at least one hour searching for the connection, and if I could find something, it would shed a whole new light on what was going on. I told myself that if something about Tom had an impact on this case with Eli, then I had the right to know what that was.

The woman at the hospital information desk said that the nearest public library was three or four miles away. She offered to call a cab for me, and I waited for it under the portico out front.

By the time I got to the library, it was 30 minutes to closing time. At least it was a nice facility, very clean, with ample space for bookshelves and groupings of chairs. Fortunately, I didn't need a library card to use the computers. I chose the one in a back corner where I could use it without anyone seeing what I was doing, and then I got down to business.

I worked quickly, hoping to get as much information as I could in the time I had. I knew that any number of my actions could somehow trip Tom's security and alert him to what I was doing. At this point I didn't care. I told myself that my main concern here was Eli. I would do anything to figure out exactly what was going on.

I started with a simple search for the name "Tom Bennett": Basically, I signed onto a search engine, typed Tom's name in the "Search" box, and then clicked on the button that said "Go." Instantly, the screen listed hundreds of websites, pictures, articles, and more that included the name Tom Bennett.

Unfortunately, it wasn't that uncommon of a name, and that single input netted me pages and pages of hits that seemed to have nothing to do with the Tom Bennett I was interested in. I swiftly skimmed through listings about artists and lawyers and even a commissioner—all named Tom Bennett. All not him. I tried again with "Thomas Bennett," but it simply returned more of the same.

Sitting back in my chair, I decided to type "Tom Bennett" along with certain keywords to pull up only articles that featured his name *plus* the additional word or words. I tried "Tom Bennett + Eli Gold." "Tom Bennett + NSA." "Tom Bennett + spy." "Tom Bennett + Russia." All of my entries netted a lot of sites to wade through but no true hits.

It wasn't until I tried "Tom Bennett + computer" that I got something that caught my eye.

It was from an old archived magazine article about a famous cryptographer who created an unbreakable e-mail computer encryption program. With the article was a photo of a group of people, and the caption on the photo said "Water walkers—the best and the brightest." It went on to list the names of the people in the photo, including Tom Bennett. I would've thought it was another useless site except that there, in the picture, was a younger Tom—*my* Tom—looking back at me.

"Water walkers?" I whispered. I had never heard that term.

Suddenly, the loudspeaker announced that the library would be closing in ten minutes. I had spent 20 minutes finding something, and now they were telling me to wrap it up!

I skimmed the article, and what I read made my heart pound.

Apparently, "water walker" was a cryptology term for a person who seemed to know exactly what direction to take when breaking a secret code. Like walking on water, they seemed to perform miracles in code-breaking, almost effortlessly.

Was Tom really a water walker, a breaker of secret codes?

I sat back in my chair and thought for a moment. I didn't know all that much about cryptology. I knew it was a science that dated back thousands of years but one that had changed drastically with the advent of computers. I knew that the World War II allied code breakers were credited with shortening the war when they finally broke the great German code, Enigma. I knew that even in times of peace the government had legions of code breakers working around the clock to decipher messages from across the globe. But that was about all I knew.

Time was running short, too short to sit and simply think, so with one eye on the clock, I clicked on the links that were attached to the article. I finally hit pay dirt on the third one.

It was an article from a 1996 issue of *Time* magazine, a list of the 25 most influential people on the internet. "Most of these people you've never heard of..." the article began, "but rest assured they are the key movers and shakers of the internet revolution." The introductory paragraphs were followed by a photo and a short profile of each person. There, at number 19, was Tom Bennett. Beside his name was the heading "Crypto Genius."

"The library will be closing in five minutes," the voice on the loudspeaker said. Looking up, I saw a library employee headed my way, trying to catch my eye. My time was up.

I clicked "Print" and hoped this computer allowed printing. Sure enough, there was a small printer next to the machine, and after a moment it sprang to life.

"I'm sorry, you'll have to get off the computer now," the woman said to me sweetly. "We'll reopen again at nine o'clock Monday morning."

"How do I pay for this?" I asked, pointing to the printer.

"Ten cents a page. You can pay at the desk," she said before walking away.

When the printing was finished, I removed my pages, clicked off the website, and went to the front counter to fork over 60 cents. From the corner of my eye, I watched the employee return to the computers and shut them down. Then I folded the pages I had printed into thirds and walked out into the street.

It was growing dark, too dark to stand there and read the entire article, though I desperately wanted to. I called the cab company on my cell phone, and while I waited for them to pick me up, I read as much as I could. My heart quickened as I reached the part about Tom:

19. Tom Bennett, Crypto Genius

> Looking more like a movie star than a techno-nerd, Tom Bennett has emerged as one of a handful of bright young cryptologists to set the world of internet privacy on its ear. Bennett's e-mail encryption program allows users to encode computer messages for complete e-mail security. Though Bennett is a hero of privacy advocates and civil rights leaders worldwide, he is also the target of an ongoing FBI criminal investigation regarding the violation of U.S. export restrictions.

Criminal investigation? The FBI?

Hands shaking, I folded the paper, tucked it into my purse, and climbed into the cab that had pulled up in front of me.

"Cape Canaveral Hospital, please," I said, my head spinning.

Was this Tom's big secret? That he'd been convicted by the FBI and sent to prison? All sorts of wild scenarios played out in my head. He often alluded to the work he did "for the government." Maybe he'd been convicted and had negotiated a trade: code breaking for the FBI in exchange for his freedom?

I refused to believe it! Tom, my Tom, my sweet and generous Tom, would not have broken the law, would not have kept from me a secret of this magnitude. As we sped toward the hospital in the darkness, I decided I would give him the benefit of the doubt. I'd show him the article and let him tell me what had really happened.

By the time we reached the hospital, I was convinced it was all a terrible mistake. Whatever connection Eli shared with Tom, it could be explained. Whatever FBI matter this article alluded to had certainly come to naught.

The cab pulled under the portico, and I paid and got out, nearly walking into Jodi and Stella in the lobby.

Stella looked terrible. She was leaning heavily onto Jodi, who wasn't looking much better herself.

"Hi," I said, trying not to look flustered. "Looks like I caught you on your way out."

"Our pastor came and prayed with us," Stella replied. "The deacons are going to take turns staying through the night. They're insisting we go home and go to bed. I don't think I've stayed up for this many hours straight since Jodi was a baby."

I felt a surge of guilt that this afternoon, while Stella was keeping the vigil at her husband's bedside, Tom and I were napping at the neighbor's. Still, he and I were pretty much running on empty as well. It had been a long day, long night, and another long day.

"How is Eli?"

"Exactly the same," said Jodi. "He's still unconscious, still listed as critical."

"Do you have any news for me?" Stella asked, leaning toward me. I saw desperation in her eyes, and I wished I could answer her in the affirmative.

"I'm sorry, Stella," I said. "We've been investigating all day, but so far we don't have any solid theories." She looked so devastated, I added, "Though we do have some leads."

"The police are being idiots about the whole thing," she said. "They've been questioning Jodi, questioning my sons—"

"Are your sons in town?"

"No. They can't get here until tomorrow."

"Oh."

"The police refuse to look at the obvious, which is that Eli was working on a case and it got him shot."

"That's why Tom and I are here," I said softly. "To take that theory and run with it."

The three of us talked for a moment longer, but they were looking so tired I suggested they go on home. Stella insisted that we come and stay there too, and though she was mostly being considerate, I think a part of her was frightened as well and she wanted safety in numbers. After her husband's shooting and the subsequent looting, I didn't blame her. I said we would pick up something to eat on the way and meet them back at the condo where we would, indeed, stay the night.

Fortunately, Tom showed up to get me not long after they left.

"How's Eli?" he asked as soon as I got into the car.

"About the same," I replied.

Except for a quick stop at a Wendy's, the rest of the ride was silent.

As we steered across town and then through the maze of the condominium complex, I wondered what he was thinking. Had his secure phone call netted him any sort of information? Was he ready to sit and tell me everything he had learned? As exhausted as I was, I didn't think I would sleep until I knew where he had gone and what he had found out.

Whether I was willing to tell him the same about myself, I just wasn't sure.

Twelve

Dinner was a somber affair, with Tom, Stella, and me eating at the table and Jodi nearby at the counter, alternating bites of her food with returning the numerous phone messages that had been left on Stella's voice mail. Certainly, Stella and Eli were popular, as there must have been at least 20 calls from friends who had heard the news and wondered how he was and if there was anything they could do. Many offered cakes or casseroles, which made me smile. That was the Southern way, I knew: When tragedy strikes and all else fails, *bring food*.

Jodi handled the calls with surprising aplomb, thanking each person for their concern, updating them on Eli's condition, coordinating meals so there would be something here to eat all week, and conveying her mother's request for prayers. For their closer friends, Jodi also organized times that each of them could come and sit at the hospital, either with Stella or in her place. By the time all of the calls had been returned, I was exhausted just listening to them.

"That was impressive," I said when she rejoined us at the table. "You sure know how to get all your ducks in a row."

"Oh, you have no idea," Stella said, beaming at her daughter with the first smile I'd seen on her face all evening. "We call Jodi the Great Coordinator. She was born to administrate."

"A weird sort of skill, I'm sure," Jodi added modestly.

"Don't be shy," Stella said. "Jodi was student body secretary in college, not to mention president of her sorority."

Stella went on to talk about her daughter's numerous accomplishments, which served to embarrass Jodi and enlighten me. I had to admit, until then I had been thinking of her as a bit of a lightweight.

I was most interested in the work Jodi had done between college and grad school, supervising several large fundraisers on behalf of some local nonprofits—a golf event, a formal ball, and a few auctions. According to Stella, each event had gone flawlessly and had brought in record-breaking donations. As she talked I was reminded again of Jodi's desire to give away her trust fund to charity, and I made a mental note to talk to her about it sometime when we were alone. I thought it was a wonderful idea, of course, but I felt I could give her some guidance for choosing the appropriate charity.

"We were so disappointed when Jodi traipsed off to Europe to study fashion design," Stella said, rolling her eyes. "Forget all that! If ever there was a born MBA, this is the girl."

Jodi shrugged, looking down at her plate.

"I didn't get very far with it anyway," she said. "So it doesn't matter now."

Sensing a minefield between mother and daughter, I feigned a yawn and steered the conversation toward sleeping arrangements. This was only a two-bedroom condo, so I suggested that either Tom or I sleep over at the neighbor's place.

"That sounds good," Tom said, jumping into the conversation for the first time since dinner began. "I'll stay there."

I didn't blame him, as I'm sure he wasn't all that comfortable sharing a bathroom with three women, two of whom he hardly knew. Stella offered me the guest room, but I insisted on taking the couch. I had a feeling Jodi might be here a while, and she might as well get settled into the spare room from the beginning.

"I *told* Eli we needed a three- or four-bedroom unit for when company comes," Stella said, looking as if she might tear up. "But there wasn't much available at the time, and we had to choose between the extra bedrooms or the ocean view. We took the view."

I realized I hadn't even peeked out of the window. I had heard the waves and felt the ocean breezes, but I hadn't had the time to step out on the deck and take a look. As a real water person, that was quite unusual for me.

A little while later, after Jodi and Stella had turned in for the night, I asked Tom if we could go for a walk on the beach.

I took a deep breath as we stepped out through the sliding glass door. Even in the dark, I could smell the water and hear the waves. Tom pulled the door shut behind us, and we crossed the deck and let ourselves out through the gate to the beach. We kicked off our shoes and left them there as we stepped out onto the sand.

Oh, it was wonderful!

The warm air was so inviting, the wide sand so smooth and cool under my toes. I walked toward the water, looking up at the moon that was nearly full.

The light illuminated the small white tops of the gentle waves, looking like tufts of frosting on the black water. To my surprise, after a moment Tom took my hand in his. I had felt far from him for the last few hours. In contrast, this simple gesture spoke volumes. We strolled for a bit along the firmer sand of the shoreline, the warm waves teasing at our feet.

"I know why you brought me out here and I'll tell you what I can," he said finally, out of the blue. I kept my mouth shut, willing him to talk. "First of all, you need to know why I'm here, why Eli told Stella to send for me."

As that was the question of the hour, I was eager to hear his answer.

"It's because of my contacts," he continued, "and not any previous involvement with this case or any of these people. Until we read the file, I didn't know a thing about what was going on, and I couldn't understand why Eli wanted my help. Once we read it, I understood.

Eli knows I can get answers where others can't. He knows I have some knowledge and some connections that could be of use."

I thought about this afternoon, when we were going over the papers in Eli's file. Tom had stiffened up at about the time the notes mentioned the NSA.

Was that where his connections were?

"What about your phone call today?" I asked. "Were your connections able to tell you what's going on here?"

"No," he said. "After all the trouble of finding a secure line and tracking down the people I needed, I don't have anything new to add. I'm stumped."

Suddenly, it felt as though I could take this conversation further in the direction it needed to go if I were completely honest in return. I let go of his hand as we continued walking.

"I have to tell you something," I said.

"Sure."

"This evening, while you were making your phone call, I didn't go into the hospital. I went to the library and did some internet research."

"You did? Why didn't you tell me?"

"Because I was researching you."

That seemed to leave him speechless for a moment. I looked out at the dark horizon, at the endless series of waves that washed the shore.

"Years ago," I continued, "you told me I could work for you or I could investigate you, but I couldn't do both."

"I remember that conversation."

"I have honored your request for three years, Tom. Today, after you dumped me off to go make your secret phone call, I decided the time had come to do some digging. I didn't access any secret files. I didn't talk to anyone or ask any questions. I only did some simple internet searches using your name, and I only turned up information that is fully in the public domain."

"And what did you learn?"

"For one, that you're a cryptologist."

"What else?"

"That you were investigated by the FBI."

"What else?"

"That's about it. My time was up."

He nodded and looked away, his chin set. I decided not to speak again but simply let that sit between us until he had formed a response. When he did reply, he didn't sound angry, much to my relief. If anything, he just sounded tired.

"I wasn't convicted, if that's your question," he said finally. "It's a long and complicated story, but in the end I was exonerated."

"Good," I whispered, knowing that was the answer I had fully expected to hear.

"One of my partners, however, wasn't so innocent," Tom continued. "He's still in prison, though the charges ended up going way beyond a simple violation of export restrictions. Again, it's a long story."

"Is it a story you can tell me?" I asked. Though we had wandered far off track from Eli and his situation, I knew all of this had to be resolved before we could proceed with our investigation. I needed to know what Eli knew, both to help with this investigation and also to give me peace of mind.

"No. I'm sorry, but I can't go into it."

I nodded and looked back out at the water. I supposed that would have to do. For now.

"Now that you know, I might as well tell you that today at the restaurant, when we were reading Eli's notes, one thing jumped out at me. Nadine may have been a mathematician back in the sixties, but I'd be willing to bet that she was a cryptologist too."

"How do you know that?"

"Her dogs."

I pressed my toes into the warm sand.

"Her *dogs?*"

"Alice, Bob, and Eve. I knew right away. Those are cryptology terms. I don't need to bore you with details, but whenever someone discusses encryption, they usually put it in terms of Alice, Bob, and Eve. For example, 'If Alice wants to send Bob a secure message, but Eve wants to intercept it and read what it says…' It's a simple method for making complicated terms more clear. If you ever hear someone refer to Alice, Bob, and Eve, they are talking about cryptology, encryption, security, or something similar. It was actually pretty nervy of Nadine to give those names to her dogs. It's something I would never do. She might as well hang up a sign."

"A sign few people would 'get.'"

"True. Maybe she just thinks it's an inside joke."

We strolled further. An odd peace descended on my heart despite our current circumstance.

"For what it's worth," he said softly, "a big part of me feels really bad that my own girlfriend has to do clandestine internet searches to find out the facts of my life. I never minded the secrecy my work entails until I met you, Callie. But the closer you and I become, the more these things become a burden to me."

"But why *does* everything have to be such a big secret, Tom? You know that you can trust me implicitly."

He answered my question with a question.

"You tell me, Callie: Why do you think I keep so many secrets?"

My mind raced for answers.

"I don't know," I whispered.

"There are some places a person can work," he said, "and they aren't even allowed to say they work there."

"But you work for yourself."

"I have a computer company, yes. But there are people there who handle the day-to-day operations. Most of my time is spent as a contractor to the U.S. government."

I thought about that. I knew he did some consulting work for Uncle Sam, but I didn't know the nature of it, nor the extent. Certainly, he had some very high-reaching connections within the government, not the least of which was his buddy the attorney general. Now that I understood Tom's background, that he dealt with codes, I had to wonder if perhaps he was a code maker or a code breaker for U.S. intelligence. My heart surged at the thought.

"I read once," I said carefully, "that people who work for the NSA can't even say they work for the NSA. When pressed, all they'll admit to is that they work for the Department of Defense."

"That's true."

"So who do you work for, Tom?" I asked, my heart pounding. He took my hand again and held it.

"Ah, Callie," he replied, exhaling softly and looking out at the horizon. "I guess you could say I work for the Department of Defense."

Thirteen

I didn't think I'd get any sleep, but I did. I dreamed I was surfing, with great waves that carried me high above dark water, past dangerous rocks and jetties, all the way to the shore. When I awoke, the sun was streaming in my face and the clock said 8:15. I hoped that was the correct time. If it was, then I had just slept for almost nine much-needed hours.

"Callie?" Jodi whispered, tiptoeing into the room and carrying a bottle of water. She was dressed in shorts and a T-shirt.

"Hey," I said, trying to sit up. "What's going on?"

"Mom's still asleep," she replied softly. "I just called the hospital and Eli still hasn't regained consciousness. They're now officially calling it a coma."

I ran a hand through my hair, closing my eyes. A coma.

God, please don't let him die.

"Have you heard from Tom?" I asked.

"No. I figured if he hasn't surfaced in another hour, we should knock on his door. For now, I was about to go for a run. I was hoping you'd join me."

"Oh, sure," I said, swinging my legs off the couch. "I'd love to. What about church?"

"I don't think Mom's going to go. But you can, if you want. It starts at eleven."

"Good," I said, standing. "Time enough for a run first."

I wasn't a big fan of jogging, but suddenly the thought of speeding along the shoreline in the morning sunshine seemed like a very good idea. It had been a stressful couple of days, and I could use the release.

Jodi said she'd wait for me on the deck, so I dug through my bags to find shorts and a T-shirt of my own and then headed to the bathroom. As I dressed and quickly brushed my hair and my teeth, I thought about Tom and our conversation of last night.

With his admission that he worked for the DOD—and his insinuation that he worked for the NSA specifically—Tom and I had formed a sort of truce. At least now I could understand why he wasn't free to share certain things with me. Considering the current crisis, I thought it best to leave the bigger questions for later and concentrate all of our energies here. I really felt that between Tom's contacts and my investigative know-how, we just might be able to figure out what had really happened, who shot Eli, and why.

Our first order of business was to read the entire inch-thick file Eli had accumulated on Nadine—not the notes and things we had already gone over in detail, but the old documents about Nadine Peters he had collected under the Freedom of Information Act. As Tom said, we needed to understand what had happened in the past in order to set things straight in the present. For now, I was going to clear my head and start my day with some exercise. I felt myself slipping into a dark mood, but I couldn't let my feelings overwhelm me. Eli needed me to be clear and proactive for his sake.

I found Jodi on the deck doing some stretches. I followed suit, feeling the strong pull down the backs of my calves as I did.

"Tom and I went rock climbing Friday morning," I said. "It really did a number on my leg muscles."

She hopped down onto the sand and began to jog in place.

"Rock climbing, huh?" she asked. "Is that how Tom stays so buff?"

I looked at her, surprised to see her grinning.

"Don't worry," she said. "I know he's taken. I just think he's pretty hot…for an old guy."

I bent forward, put my hands on the ground, and straightened my knees.

"Old guy? He's the same age I am!"

"Yeah, I know," she said, grinning. "To me, everybody over thirty is old."

She turned and took off jogging across the sand. I finished my stretch and then followed suit, laughing.

"Thanks a lot," I called after her, struggling in the loose sand. "You'll be there in a few years yourself, you know."

I caught up with her on the firmer sand, at the edge of the water. We settled into an easy pace, matching stride for stride.

"On the drive home from the hospital last night," Jodi said, "Mom was talking about you guys. She said it looked like you had finally become a couple. She said Eli would be thrilled to know."

"Eli has always pushed for me and Tom to get together," I said fondly. "So, yes, he will be thrilled." *If he makes it,* I wanted to add but didn't.

"Is that weird, like, dating your boss?"

I ran for a minute, enjoying the beautiful morning while framing my reply. The temperature was perfect, and the beach just went on and on. Gorgeous.

"Not really," I said finally. "Technically, I suppose, Tom is my boss, but it's not like we work together in an office or anything. I don't think of him that way."

"So what do you do? What's your job?"

"I'm an investigator for the J.O.S.H.U.A. Foundation. My job is to check out charities that apply for grants and see if they qualify."

"Oh cool," she said, sounding as if she meant it. "So when Mom said you could help me make some decisions about donating my trust fund, she wasn't kidding."

"No, she wasn't kidding."

"How do you investigate a charity?" she asked.

"It's pretty straightforward, really," I replied. "I have a list of criteria to go by, and the charity has to measure up or they don't get the money."

"Like what?"

"Well, most importantly, do they fulfill their mission? Are they financially sound? Do they have annual audits? Things like that. I don't mean to make it sound simpler than it is. Sometimes it gets really complicated. But for those places that come out squeaky clean in the end, I have the pleasure of handing them a big, fat check."

"That's super."

"It is very rewarding."

We ran on silently for a moment.

"And what about Tom?" Jodi asked. "Is he really as rich as Mom says?"

It was my turn to laugh.

"Yes, Jodi," I said. "He really is."

"That can be a mixed blessing," she replied thoughtfully. "Take it from one who knows."

"I can imagine," I said.

"I cashed out my trust fund yesterday. Now I've got three hundred thousand dollars in bearer bonds to give to the charity of my choice."

"Wow. Why bearer bonds?"

She shrugged.

"I knew I had to get the money out of the bank," she said. "Otherwise, my brothers would try to boss me around about it. But if the money's not in there, they can't do that. For all they know, I've already started wasting it away on beautiful clothes and exotic travel. To them, that's probably a more logical choice than using it for the good of some nonprofit!"

"How sad."

We continued running, chatting whenever something came up, falling silent when we were lost in thought. Now that she was over her jet lag and the initial shock of the breakup with her boyfriend,

Jodi had really rallied, and I found her to be both engaging and witty. The time passed quickly, and we eventually ran about two miles before agreeing we ought to turn around. The sun grew warmer as we headed back, and by the time we reached the condo, it was positively blazing. Jodi and I slowed to a walk once Stella's place was in sight, trying to cool down from the run.

"I have to take Mom back down to the hospital once she gets up," she said. "But maybe later we could talk some more about all of this nonprofit stuff. If I'm giving away my money, I want to make good choices."

I had been curious about her financial situation and the upcoming trust fund issue, but I hadn't wanted to pry. Now, however, seemed an appropriate time to ask for more details.

"So tell me again," I said, "you have a trust fund that your father set up for you…"

"Well, I've been receiving an annuity since I was eighteen. It gives me about three thousand a month after taxes. I'll continue to live off that. This other thing that just came due is a lump sum deferred inheritance trust."

"I see."

"The bottom line is, I don't really need it. Franco thought I was crazy, but I don't see why having more money or more stuff is going to make me happy. Look at my brothers! They're loaded and they're miserable. I'd rather keep my three thou a month to live on and see that the rest gets put to good use with a nonprofit."

"Where are you thinking of donating it?"

"I've narrowed it down to a couple of choices."

"Well, good. I'll be happy to give you some guidance."

Up ahead, I noticed someone in the water at the edge of the beach, and as we drew closer I realized that it was Tom, just going in for a swim.

"Hey!" I called, and as he looked our way, he greeted us with a smile and a wave. Judging by his warm expression, he also seemed to feel as if last night's discussion had cleared the air between us.

"Look at you two!" he said. "I had a feeling you were out running. I knew I couldn't catch up, so I thought I'd swim instead."

"You want to go to church?" I asked, glancing at my watch. "It starts at eleven."

"Sure. That'll give me time for a few laps first."

He waded out of the water to give me a peck on the cheek, but I was so sweaty I held up a hand and stepped back.

"Don't come too close," I laughed. "We just ran about four miles in this heat."

He looked at Jodi and winked.

"Guess you need to cool off then," he said.

Then he came nearer, picked me up, and carried me kicking and screaming into the water.

Fourteen

We followed Stella's directions to her church and made it to the service just as it was starting. Tom and I were both a bit over-dressed, which came as a bit of a surprise considering that we were at least 20 years younger than most of the people in the congregation. Feeling very conspicuous as a brunette in a suit amid a whole lot of gray heads wearing golf shirts, I led the way to a spot about halfway up and joined in the singing of the opening hymn.

The service was fairly traditional, and we were particularly blessed by the soloist, a young redhead with a big voice that filled the room. She sang one of my favorite hymns, and when she came to the chorus I closed my eyes and simply let myself feel the very heart of the music through her amazing range. *How great Thou art, indeed,* I thought.

During the announcements, a special prayer request was made for Eli Gold, who was said to be "in a coma at the hospital," with no mention of the shooting, the sniper, or the vandalism. I supposed the pastor didn't want to upset his more delicate parishioners.

Through no fault of the choir, I found my mind wandering during the anthem. Tom and I had both felt it prudent to keep Eli's notes with us at all times, and I just couldn't concentrate knowing that right now the whole file was stuffed in my largest bag, which was on the pew next to me. I wanted to be in a worshipful mood, I really did, but I kept going over the case in my mind, working through it bit by bit. I knew if we couldn't find more answers by pouring through Eli's files, our next step would probably be to get on a plane and go down to St. John and investigate Nadine firsthand.

I asked the Lord to help me focus, and I was blessed in turn by a wonderful sermon. The pastor spoke of trust and faith, reminding us that even in the midst of an evil and sometimes-frightening world, God is still firmly in control. I realized that all of my prayers of late had been merely prayers of petition—give me this, help me with that. I resolved to spend some time on my knees tonight before going to bed, remembering to praise God for His sovereign magnificence.

Once the service was over, we made a beeline for the door, knowing we didn't have time to get caught up in any long conversations. We passed the red-headed soloist in the parking lot, and I did stop to take a moment to thank her for the beautiful song.

"Kierstin, right?" I said, recalling her name from the bulletin. "That was amazing."

"Thanks," she said, smiling shyly, and I realized she wasn't more than 17 or 18 years old.

"That's a lot of voice for one so young," I said to Tom as we drove away. "I'd give anything to be able to sing like that."

"I used to be a singer," he said. "Had a garage band and everything."

"Are you any good?" I asked, laughing.

"I'll put it this way," he replied. "There's a reason we never got out of the garage."

We found Stella in the intensive care waiting room, as expected. Tom offered to run down to the cafeteria to get her a sandwich, which she gratefully accepted. Apparently she had had a steady stream of visitors all morning, but none of them had come bearing food.

I was allowed to go in with her for her next visit, and together we spent those precious five minutes talking to Eli and encouraging him to wake up.

Jodi was there in the waiting room when we came back out, so Tom and I left Stella in her capable hands and headed back to the condo to proceed with the case.

By the time Tom and I arrived at the house again, I was eager to get down to work. As soon as the next-door neighbor saw us pull up, she came running over with several food items that well-wishers had brought. Tom handled her with warmth and charm while I disappeared into the bathroom to change into something a bit more comfortable. I slipped on jeans and a knit shirt and then hung my suit carefully on a hanger.

Once the neighbor was gone, I came back out to the living room and tried calling my parents in Virginia. My dad needed to know that Eli had been shot, and I thought I ought to be the one to tell him.

I reached my brother, Michael, instead, who had just stopped by our parents' house to drop off some tools he had borrowed.

"They're not here," he said. "I think there was a dinner on the grounds after church today or something. I went to the early service, so I didn't pay much attention."

I glanced at my watch, calculating when they might be getting home.

"You wanna leave a message for 'em?" he asked. "I can stick it on the fridge."

"Sure," I replied, wondering what kind of message to leave. They didn't need to find out the bad news from a Post-it Note. "Just put 'Call Callie ASAP.' Let me give you the number."

I glanced up to see Tom gesturing to me. He was going into the kitchen to get himself some food, and he wondered if I wanted anything. I shook my head.

"Where are you calling from?" Michael asked, not recognizing the area code.

"Cocoa Beach, Florida. I'm at Stella Gold's house."

"Oh, cool. How are they?"

"Not well. Eli is...Eli's in the hospital."

"Gosh, is he okay?"

"No, he's in a coma right now. He was shot by a sniper."

"You gotta be kidding. What's going on? There's not some new nutcase on the loose down there, is there, some random-shooting wacko?"

"No, this seems to have been something altogether different. Eli was working a case, and I'm pretty sure it was related to that."

Michael was a cop, and as he asked me questions about the shooting, I could hear his voice slipping into "detective" mode. All business now, he wanted to know the who, what, when, why, where, and how of what had happened. I told him what I could but said that he needed to keep everything to himself for now. He promised not to tell a soul.

"So what's being done for Eli's safety in the meantime?" he asked.

"Tom hired a security service. They're keeping a guard on duty around the clock."

"Good. Tom who?"

"Tom Bennett," I said, looking up to see him just coming back into the room, carrying a plate piled high with food. "My boss."

Tom looked up at that comment and raised one eyebrow.

"Your boss?" Michael said. "Oh, that's right. He knows Eli too."

"Yeah. He does."

I wanted to elaborate, to say something that would indicate Tom had become more than merely my boss. My family knew I had been thinking about dating again, but I wanted to ease them into this boyfriend thing as gently as I could. Michael wanted me to move on with my life, but he also had loved Bryan like a brother, and I knew it wouldn't be easy for him to see me with someone else.

"Tom's great," I said. "I think you'd really like him."

"Hey, he pays you to go around and give his money away. Sounds like a pretty cool guy to me."

"That he is, Michael," I said, smiling up at the man I loved. "A cool guy for sure."

Fifteen

After finishing the call with my brother, Tom and I settled at the dining room table to work.

"So what's the game plan here?" he asked.

Because his government contacts had not been of any help to us after all, I realized this case would have to be solved the old-fashioned way, with some serious sleuthing. We would begin by reading the photocopies of the old documents Eli had collected from the National Archives. There might be information in and among the blackened-out pages that could help us learn more about Nadine Peters and what she had been involved with back in the '60s.

"Let's just read and take notes for now," I said, opening the database on my computer screen for the input of facts.

We divided the papers in half and got started. My intention was simply to read each page as we got to it, but it was too confusing. Soon, it became obvious that we needed some sort of system. After a bit of discussion, we decided to try and put the different reports and memos and letters and things into chronological order. Better to start at the beginning, if possible, and work our way up through time. As Tom sorted the papers into piles, I served myself from the delicious food in the kitchen, ate quickly, and then put my empty dishes in the sink.

Back in the dining room, we scooted our chairs side by side and read each page together. I thought it might be hard to concentrate with Tom sitting and reading with me, but I was soon lost in the story that unfolded in the papers in front of us.

The documents started with Eli's military career, which began in the late '50s. He joined the Navy right out of high school, and according to his training placement papers, because he was already an accomplished ham radio operator, the Navy sent him to school for signals intelligence—SIGINT for short. He eventually was promoted to seaman first class and assigned to the *USS Oxford*, a communications ship that hovered off the coast of Cuba, intercepting radio signals.

Judging by several memos with his name on them, Eli seemed to be one of the people monitoring the cargo manifests of Soviet ships sailing into Havana. Eventually, of course, the United States confirmed that those Soviet ships were bringing in more than small shipments of palm oil or farm equipment: They were bringing arms and ammunition, light aircraft, military vehicles, and equipment for military installations. The buildup of arms and equipment so close to the United States eventually came to a head in 1962 with the Cuban Missile Crisis. I didn't know much about that period in American history, but I found it fascinating to learn that Eli was one of the unsung heroes of the U.S. military at that time.

"CMC," Tom said, nodding his head.

"What?" I asked, watching as he grabbed Eli's case notes and began flipping through them.

"'Sold secrets to Russians during CMC, worked as mathematician for NSA,'" he said, reading from Eli's notes. "I thought so. CMC is the Cuban Missile Crisis. Nadine sold secrets to the Russians during the Cuban Missile Crisis, while working as a mathematician for the National Security Agency."

"Of course," I said. "Wow. What a traitor. How do you think Eli got mixed up with her?"

"I don't know," he said. "Let's keep reading."

It didn't take long to see what had happened. Apparently, when the crisis was over, Eli was debriefed in Key West, where Nadine was stationed. Her name was even on the list of people who signed off on his debriefing sessions.

"Eli and Nadine must've hit it off and started a relationship," I said.

"Yeah," Tom replied. "Too bad it had to end with him shooting her."

We kept paging through the documents, and it looked to me as if Eli had stayed on in Key West and done some SIGINT work for the NSA after his discharge from the Navy, though whether as an employee of the NSA or as a consultant, it wasn't clear.

"He never told me," I whispered, looking at a memo with Eli's name on it. Though some of the lines had been blacked out by a censor's permanent marker, Eli was definitely working for the NSA in January of 1962.

"I knew," Tom replied softly. "I knew he worked there."

I glanced at him and then back at the papers.

"But this was back in the early sixties," I said. "You weren't even born yet."

"No, I mean Eli told me. He told me when we first met that he had done contract work in the past for the NSA."

I took a deep breath and let it out slowly, surprised to find myself feeling hurt. In a way, I was closer to Eli than anyone on this planet—with the exception of Stella and maybe my father. Had he really kept a secret of this magnitude from me all the years we had known each other while volunteering the information to Tom the first time they ever met? Surely there was more to the story than that.

"Why did he tell you, Tom?" I asked. "How did you and Eli meet in the first place?"

There was a long silence before he finally spoke.

"There was an…intersection of interests," he replied evasively.

I glared at him, so he tried again.

"Eli was working a case as a private investigator," he said. "His investigation led him to me because of the person he was investigating. There were connections there."

"Connections?"

"Eli came to me and said that he was a former NSA agent and that he knew the rules about secrecy, but he needed my help in understanding this particular situation with this particular person. I did as much for him as I could. We became friends after that."

"When was this?" I asked, running through Eli's old cases in my mind. Even when I was completely distracted with college and working for Eli only a few hours per week, I always kept up with his cases. I knew for a fact none of them had ever involved the NSA.

"Several years ago," Tom said. "It was after you had left the agency."

We continued through the pile, frustrated that most of the interoffice documents were full of secure information that had been blacked out by a marker. But we could read enough to understand that Eli and Nadine worked together for nearly a year. I expressed the assumption that they had fallen in love during that time, a guess that was confirmed by an internal affairs report regarding the "emotional and sexual ties" between Nadine Peters and Eli Gold. Eli and Nadine began spending weekends together in the privacy of an old fishing cabin on one of the smaller keys. I looked again at the fuzzy photos of the dilapidated shack that were with the file, particularly the one that showed the two of them through the window.

I sat back, wondering what that must be like, to learn that your employer had been photographing your extracurricular activities with the woman you loved. With a shudder, I wondered if Tom were ever followed and photographed as well.

"What gave the NSA the right to do this?" I asked softly, studying the picture.

"This, apparently," Tom said, lifting the next batch of papers from the pile. It was a dossier on the illegal activities of one Nadine Peters, paid informant for the KGB.

He read through the dossier, describing a woman of humble beginnings who had been irresistibly wooed into selling U.S. secrets to Russian operatives. Her duplicity started with $1000, which Nadine was given in exchange for some key settings to a cipher machine. The KGB had then used that information to decode certain U.S. military communications.

From there, Nadine and one of her coworkers developed an ongoing relationship with a KGB operative, a man who coordinated "dead drops" for the exchange of money for information.

"What's a dead drop?" I asked.

"Making an exchange without ever actually having any contact. For instance, they put the money in a bag and leave it beside a trash can. You pick it up there and then drop your papers near a predetermined park bench."

"I see."

"It says they would occasionally meet in person. Whenever one of them wanted to call a meeting, they would put an innocuous-seeming ad in the Sunday *Washington Post* classifieds that would specify the date, time, and location."

"Doesn't sound very secretive to me. Anybody could read that."

"It was all done in code," Tom said. "See here? We have some examples."

I looked at photocopies of newspaper classified ads. One said "Midnight blue couch for sale. Call 721-0800. Ask for Piper Firve." Another read "Midnight lace satin gown. Call 903-2300. Ask for Lomus Baer."

"These look like normal ads," I said. "I don't see what's so secret about them, except maybe those names are a little weird. And they both start with 'midnight.'"

Tom took the paper from my hand and looked at it for a moment. Then he held it out to me and traced his finger along it.

"If I had to guess," he said, "I'd be willing to bet this is a request for a meeting on July 21 at eight o'clock in the morning at Pier Five, wherever that is. This one is for September third at eleven P.M. at some place called Lou's Bar."

I looked at the ads again.

"How did you get all of that?"

"I'd be willing to bet there's no 721 exchange for the DC area, especially not back then. The 721 is the date, the 0800 is the time. Pier Five comes from removing every third letter of the person's name. Same with the other one. Lomus Baer becomes Lou's Bar. It's an extremely simplistic code, but I guess it served their purposes."

I stared at it for a moment, finally nodding.

"Which is why you're a cryptologist and I'm just an investigator," I said.

He smiled.

"Look at this," I said, moving on to the next set of papers. It was a heavily censored report on the interrogation of Eli Gold, dated December 1962. I read what I could, trying to understand what I was seeing. The best I could tell, the NSA had finally made their move by bringing in Eli and questioning him exhaustively to see what he knew about Nadine's ongoing espionage. From the looks of the report, Eli was found to be innocent of any knowledge and absolved of any complicity in the matter. I could only imagine how heartbroken he must've been, however, to learn that the woman he loved was a traitor to him and to the country.

That was it for the official documents, except for the autopsy report on Nadine and a December 1962 police report about the facts of her death. That hadn't been censored at all, and I could only assume Eli hadn't obtained that particular report from the NSA but from an old police file.

"What's it say?" Tom asked, handing it to me and rubbing his eyes. After scanning all of these old documents, my eyes were feeling tired and sore as well.

"Looks like Nadine was caught trying to flee the area about an hour after Eli's interrogation ended. She was shot down by five armed gunmen."

"Wow."

I read further and then looked up at Tom.

"Here's a list of the gunmen," I said. "One of them was Eli Gold."

"The shot in the thigh, I'd bet," he said. "No wonder he recognized the scar."

I put down the paper and closed my eyes. I could understand Eli feeling betrayed and angry and upset with Nadine. What I couldn't comprehend was how he could have shot her. Betrayal was one thing. Shooting the woman you loved in cold blood was quite another.

"She was 'killed' in December 1962," Tom said softly. "What do you know of Eli's life since then?"

I shook my head and opened my eyes.

"I know he moved to Virginia at some point and enrolled in the police academy. He and my dad graduated together, somewhere around sixty-three or sixty-four. Eli stayed with the force until he quit to become a private detective in seventy-five."

"I wonder if your father knows any of Eli's secrets."

As if on cue, the phone started ringing.

"Maybe that's him calling back," I said. "We can ask."

Sure enough, the voice at the other end of the line was my father's. Once I explained what had happened and where I was, he was understandably angry with me.

"Come on, Callie," he said. "You shoulda called me the minute you heard. Eli was my partner for almost ten years! Doesn't that count for something?"

"I'm sorry, Dad," I said. "At first, I was just concerned about getting here. Then I hit the ground running. I haven't stopped."

"Well, just remember you're not the only detective in the family. Do the police there even know Eli is a former cop? I guarantee you, this situation would get a lot more attention if they did."

"I don't know if Stella told them or not. I'll be sure to mention it to them either way."

"What have they been doing? Are they keeping you apprised of their investigation?"

"No," I said, looking out at the beautiful beach and the blue sky beyond. "I'm working the case from a different angle, Dad. There's a history here the police don't know anything about. It's hard to explain."

"Try me," he said, and I knew from his tone of voice there was no use arguing. I moved from the table over to the couch and sat down, crossing my legs under me.

"Eli used to work for the NSA," I said bluntly. "Did you know that?"

"The NSA?"

"The National Security Agency."

He was quiet for a moment, and then he let out a low whistle.

"No, I did not," he said. "In the beginning, there was a rumor around the force that he was some kind of former agent—people said CIA or FBI. I asked him straight out and he said no. Never crossed my mind to ask if he worked for the NSA. How do you know?"

"He had a case file going. I've got old interoffice documents with his name on them right here."

I tried my best to explain that apparently Eli had become involved with a female coworker while at the NSA, but that it was discovered that the woman was selling secrets to the Russians. She was shot and killed by a group of agents, including Eli.

"But that would've been years ago," he said. "Why is it relevant now?"

"Because though the woman was shot and killed in 1962," I replied, "a couple of months ago, Eli saw her."

"He *saw* her?"

"Alive and well down in the Virgin Islands. He thought it was her, so he started investigating. I guess he just wanted to know how she could still be alive when he knew for a fact she was dead."

"And what did he find out?"

"He worked the case for a few months," I said. "Long enough to confirm that it was her and to raise suspicions that she was still involved in some kind of spy work. A few weeks ago, Eli brought all of the evidence to one of his buddies at the NSA, and while he was waiting to hear back from him, he was shot."

"Do you think she did it? She shot him?"

"It's a possibility, but I doubt it. She came here to see him before he was shot, to warn him that someone was coming. We just don't know who the someone was."

"The NSA? Maybe he was targeted by the NSA."

I glanced toward the kitchen, where Tom had gone to pour himself a glass of water. I hadn't mentioned it to him, but the possibility had also crossed my mind.

"I don't think they do that sort of thing," I said. "But it's possible, I suppose."

"Who else could it be? The Russians?"

"In this day and age? The Cold War's over, Dad."

"Maybe somebody had a vendetta," he said. "Those Russians, they've got long memories, you know."

In my lifetime I had seen the Berlin Wall topple and the Russian's Soviet empire splinter to pieces. The Russia I knew was a different animal from that of my father's generation.

"So what's your next step?" he asked.

"Darned if I know," I replied. "I'm tempted to go down to St. John and knock on the woman's door."

"Don't do that, Callie. Promise me you won't do that."

I smiled at his tone, knowing we could talk like fellow detectives for a little while, but in the end he was primarily my father.

"Okay, Dad," I said. "I might go down there, but I promise I won't confront the woman directly."

"I just don't know what I think about all of this. If Eli's poking around ended up getting him shot, it seems like you're putting yourself in the very same danger by following up on things."

"I'm very discreet, Dad," I said, trying to sound reassuring while all the while I knew what he was saying was true. How did I know that Tom and I wouldn't be next in the crosshairs of a sniper's gun?

"Anyway, in the meantime I think I'll make a few calls myself," he said. "Talk to the officer in charge. Make sure this is getting top priority."

"Just don't share any details of what I've told you, okay? The last thing I need is to have this file confiscated by the local police force."

"Don't worry. I'll keep my mouth shut. I just want to know what they've accomplished from their angle."

He promised to get back in touch with me once he knew something. I hung up the phone just as Tom was coming back into the room.

"Well?" he asked.

"Well," I replied, exhaling slowly. "it looks like it might be time for you and me to take a little trip."

Sixteen

That night we prepared to go to the Virgin Islands to pick up the investigation right where Eli had left off. Tom insisted on putting everything on his credit card, but he asked if I would please make the arrangements since he needed to spend the next few hours tying up some loose ends with his office. He went back to the neighbor's apartment to do his work in the quiet there. I stayed at Stella's, plugged the phone cord into my computer, and went online to find a flight.

I had reserved our seats and was looking for hotel accomodations when Jodi came home, seeming exhausted. She grabbed a cold soda from the fridge before joining me at the dining table, sitting crossways on the seat so that her feet dangled off the side.

"What a day," she said, taking a sip from the can. "Milton's in town."

"Milton?"

"My oldest brother. Ugh! To him, I might as well be twelve years old. Did you ever know someone who doesn't even really look at you? Like they look right through you? That's Milton. I'm just a blip on his screen. I'm just white noise in the background."

I smiled at her description. From what I recalled of Eli's wedding, Milton didn't seem to notice much besides himself. I felt a surge of gratefulness for my own brother, who was a real sweetheart and one of my best friends.

"How's Eli?" I asked, and Jodi gave a report of the events of the afternoon. His lung had collapsed and they had to do some sort of procedure to get him breathing again. She said Stella had rallied fairly well. Once Milton showed up and sort of commandeered the waiting room, Jodi had felt a little superfluous.

"Maybe I should go back to Europe," she said, playing with the metal tab on the top of her soda can. "At least Franco was fun when he wasn't being a greedy idiot."

I started to reply, but she held up one hand.

"Kidding," she said. "Sort of."

"Speaking of going somewhere, Tom and I are going down to St. John," I said. "We leave in the morning."

Her eyes opened wide.

"You're going off on vacation *now?*"

"It's not a vacation. We're investigating Eli's shooting. The investigation has led us down there."

She spun her legs around and sat up.

"Oh, let me go with you!" she said. "I haven't been down to the house in almost a year."

"I don't think—"

"Come on!" she urged. "I can help. I can follow people. I can collect evidence. I watch enough detective shows to know how it's done."

"What about your mother?"

"She doesn't need me now that Milton's here. C'mon. Please?"

My first reaction was to object, but as I thought about it, I realized it might not hurt to have a third person along. I had absolutely no contacts down there, and Jodi was familiar with the island. On the other hand, Stella would have my head if I let anything happen to her daughter.

"The house is gorgeous," Jodi said. "I don't know if Mom showed you the pictures, but you'll love it. We've got two cars there too. Oh, and maybe some of the girls are in town. This is perfect! One of the charities I'm considering is located down there, so I can even investigate it. You can help me."

"The girls?"

"Friends of mine. Like me, their parents have houses there. We used to coordinate so we'd all be down at the same time. Gosh, I haven't talked to any of them in ages, except Sandy and I e-mail a lot. She's the one who works with the charity."

Suddenly, it felt as if Jodi's accompanying us was a done deal.

"If you go," I said, "you absolutely cannot tell a soul why we're there or what we're doing. This isn't a group activity, Jodi, it's an investigation. For me and Tom."

"Can't I help?"

"You can show us around and get us oriented," I said. "Beyond that, I doubt it. Though if I have any spare time, I'll be happy to give you some guidance with the nonprofit there."

She thought about that for a few moments.

"Okay," she said finally. "I can do that. We'll fly down tomorrow, I'll give you the whole island tour, and then I'll stay out of your way. But I'll be there if you need me."

"And you won't tell your friends what's going on?"

She held up three fingers, like the Girl Scout pledge.

"On my honor, I will keep my mouth shut," she said. "Now what time's our flight?"

"Eight o'clock in the morning. That means we need to leave for the airport at five."

"I'll be ready."

I guess it would be three to the islands, then. I hoped Tom wouldn't mind that I had told Jodi yes without consulting him first.

Because we wouldn't be needing a hotel, I clicked the reservation form off my screen and went back into flights, adding a reservation for Jodi. I reserved a car because Tom and I would be more comfortable driving a rental. If something came up where we needed another car, then we might borrow one of Stella's.

Jodi happily went off down the hall to do laundry, and I used the time to go through my e-mail. I had a note from Lindsey, asking me if she could register Sal for the Osprey Cove Mayday Parade. There was a pet costume contest and she wanted to dress Sal as William Shakespup. (Lindsey was dating a guy who was active in community theatre, and everything she did lately seemed to relate somehow to the stage.) I wrote back and said it was okay with me, as long as the costume wasn't personally humiliating for Sal and I didn't have to have any part of it—including leading my dog around on a leash while she sported a pleated ruff and a doublet.

I took some time to send a long note to Harriet, telling her about my vacation in North Carolina. She and I still hadn't had a chance to chat, and I felt guilty about that. Maybe one day soon I would give her a call. In the meantime, I needed to go through all of my stuff, get organized, and figure out what I would be bringing with me.

Stella checked in with us around seven, sounding tired but hopeful. Eli had had an EEG, and it showed definite brainwave activity.

"The coma is because his body is still in shock," she said. "But the doctor said his vital signs are better. He's starting to feel confident that Eli might pull through after all."

"Oh, Stella, thank the Lord."

"Thank the Lord indeed."

I told her Tom and I were still working on the investigation, but that it had become necessary for us to go down to the Virgin Islands. Our flight to St. Thomas was in the morning.

"I *told* you that's when Eli started acting funny," she said. "When we went to St. John."

I was afraid she was going to ask me about the particulars of the investigation, but instead she simply started talking about the house down there, where she kept the key, how to turn the hot water on, and all of that. Finally, I told her that Jodi was "thinking" about coming with us.

"Oh, that would be good," Stella said, surprising me with her reaction. "She'll be a big help to you."

Before we hung up, I told her that I needed to ask her one more question, and that she could think about it and call me back if she needed to.

"Eli had some…equipment," I said. "I think you called them his 'little tools.' I need to know where he might have kept them."

If he had things like tape recorders and binoculars and stuff, and if we could get our hands on them, it would save us a lot of time, money, and trouble.

"Oh, sure," she said, not even hesitating. "They're in the hidden compartment."

"The hidden compartment?"

I thought of Eli's notes, where he said he organized the "h.c." with his new tools. It didn't get much more straightforward than that.

Stella described the hidden compartment in her house in St. John. It was at the back of the pantry in the kitchen, a false wall that slid open when you twisted the cup hook that was mounted next to it.

"I think it was originally built for drying spices," she said. "I never needed it. When Eli asked me if he could use it, I said sure. I didn't care."

"And you're positive he left all of that stuff down there?"

"Oh, yeah. He said it was the best hiding place he'd ever had."

"Wonderful. Thank you, Stella. That'll be a big help."

I was all packed by nine and feeling tired enough to go on to bed. I brought some supper over to Tom at the neighbor's apartment, where he was still on the computer trying to take care of business before we left the country.

"Are you sure you can do this?" I asked as I handed him his plate. "You can miss even more time from the office?"

He shrugged as he smiled up at me.

"It's my company," he said. "What am I going to do? Fire myself?"

Seventeen

Tom had more work to do on his laptop in the morning, so on the plane he switched seats with Jodi, and she and I sat together all the way to Miami. The arrangement worked out well because she had an opportunity to pick my brain about how to choose a good charity. She had made up a list of the three places where she was considering donating her money, and at first she was wondering if I would do the investigations for her. With my time at a minimum and my attentions focused elsewhere, however, I was able to convince her that she could do the investigations herself and merely use me as a reference.

I wrote down the list of criteria I always used for evaluating nonprofits and then explained the first two steps—"a good charity serves a worthwhile cause" and "a good charity adequately fulfills its mission statement, showing fruits for its labors"—in detail.

"But how do I know if they're doing all of that?" she asked.

"First, get a copy of their mission statement," I said. "Then take a look at what they do. Talk to people. Read the literature. Visit their facilities. You can get a good idea of how a place is run by connecting with volunteers, employees, and the population they serve.

You know, you have an extra consideration here I don't usually have to worry about."

"What's that?"

"The number one rule when donating to a charity."

She perked up, giving me her full attention.

"Jodi, it has to be a cause that's important to *you*. You personally. It's your money. Most good fundraising consultants know that when all is said and done, the person who *gave* the money should be just as happy and excited about their donation as the people at the place who *got* the money. It's all about supporting a cause you feel is important. Which one of these three causes lights the biggest fire inside of you?"

She took a sip of her juice.

"This one," she said, pointing to the third entry on the list, something called SPICE. "I mean, the other two are great causes. My dad died of cancer, you know, so that's why I was thinking of that one. And I have a friend who was helped a lot by this other one— it's a halfway house for substance abusers. But this third listing is the one that interests me the most personally."

"SPICE? What is that?"

"It's a group of people working to preserve the rich history of the entire Caribbean. SPICE stands for the Society for the Preservation of Indigenous Ethnicities. Their primary goal is to collect, compile, and present a true picture of the Caribbean and its people up until the time that Christopher Columbus first came there. My friend Sandy is overseeing a dig in St. John, studying the ancient Taino culture. Eventually, the Columbus Foundation hopes to raise enough money to build a giant museum of the Caribbean, either in St. Thomas or San Juan."

I sat back in my seat, fingering the list in front of me.

"Now that's an interesting choice for you," I said. "What is it about the project you find so exciting?"

She thought about it.

"Probably that no one has ever done this, at least not on a grand scale. There are entire cultures, entire ethnic groups, that have disappeared from the world's radar because nothing was done to preserve or promote their heritage. The Tainos are extinct, for example, but by understanding their culture, their traditions—even their diet—we can learn so much about the islands, the history, and the heritage of the people who live there now."

"I didn't realize you were such a history buff," I said.

She shrugged.

"I'm not. I just…as a kid, you know, going down to St. John was the highlight of my year. And it wasn't just the scenery or the swimming that I loved. It was the people, the music. The food. The smells. The stories. I had a babysitter there who loved to tell me the ancient legends and fables of the island. In almost every story, there was such sadness, such loss. It was almost as though I could see their heritage disappearing before my eyes. SPICE is going to keep that from happening. They will preserve the past."

I smiled, pleased with the excitement that clearly shone in Jodi's eyes as she talked about the charity.

"What?" she asked, noticing my smile.

"You should see yourself," I said. "We in the business of nonprofits call this the 'fever.' You've got the fever for this particular charity, Jodi. I think you should investigate it, and if it checks out, make your donation to them."

"I think you're right," she replied happily. "Thank you, Callie."

"You're welcome. Now let's talk about how you can get started."

Because Jodi already had a friend on the inside, I suggested she exploit that resource fully.

"The single best way to find out if a nonprofit really has their act together is to talk one-on-one with the folks who work there. If they feel they can be honest with you, they will tell you things you might not find out any other way. Concentrate on spending, salaries, administration, planning—things like that. You want to know if this is a good group, if they are doing what they claim to be doing in a responsible, cost-efficient manner."

I wasn't sure if Jodi would understand the nonprofit mindset, so I tried to explain how there were industry standards for things like salaries and benefits—and how they rarely matched the rates paid in the for-profit sector.

"Working for a nonprofit can sometimes require a lot of sacrifice, monetarily speaking," I said. "But what you lack in income you usually get back in job satisfaction. Imagine working where you *know* you're making a difference in the world. For most people who do it, it's well worth it."

I was just writing down the website where she could look up appropriate salary ranges for this type of charity when the captain announced our descent into Miami.

"Thanks, Callie," Jodi said, checking her seat belt. "You've given me a lot to think about."

"You're welcome, Jodi."

Because I was sitting on the aisle, I couldn't see out of the window all that well, but the glimpses I caught of the turquoise blue water nearly took my breath away. Glancing at Tom, I saw him put away his laptop and then flash me a smile. My heart did a little flip-flop in return.

We changed planes in Miami, and Tom and I sat together for the flight from there to St. Thomas. I was glued to the window this time, astounded at the beauty of the Caribbean as we flew overhead. There were a lot of islands down there, more than I would have thought, and they were all like tiny green emeralds sparkling from the sea.

Once we had landed in St. Thomas, we claimed our bags and then listened as Jodi explained our choices for getting to the island of St. John.

"We can pay fifty bucks apiece and catch a luxury boat right here," she said, "or we can take a taxi to the harbor in town and catch the regular ferry for three dollars. Either way, the boat ride takes about forty-five minutes."

I thought Tom was going to opt for the luxury boat, but he surprised me by suggesting the ferry instead.

"Let's do it just like Stella and Eli did," he said. "We need to get a feel for that ferry."

I agreed. The three of us easily found a taxi outside, a battered old van with a friendly driver and reggae music playing on the radio. We had to wait until most of the seats in the van were full before we could leave, but that didn't take too long. The airport was a busy place, filled with incoming passengers.

"Welcome to St. Thomas!" the driver said as he climbed in behind the wheel and started up. "Have you folks ever been to our island before?"

"Never!" the woman behind me exclaimed.

Her whole group was very chatty, saving us from having to make conversation. My eyes were focused out of the window, taking in the surroundings and trying to get used to a new perspective from driving on the left side of the road.

The roads were surprisingly good, though my heart was in my throat a few times with the speed at which our driver took some of the hairpin curves. As we went I was amazed at how developed the island was, with houses and shops and schools and churches on every side. I had expected it to be a bit more deserted, but the lush vegetation seemed to be dotted with structures and people from one end to the other.

As we came over the hill above Charlotte Amalie, I actually gasped, it was so beautiful. There below us was the quaint capital of St. Thomas, situated along a wide, curved harbor. Two magnificent cruise ships rested just offshore, their white hulls a marked contrast to the rich turquoise of the water. Other islands rose in the distance, hills of forest green among the blue.

"Wow," I whispered, and Tom took my hand in his.

"Really something, huh?" he said. "I had forgotten."

The ride down through town was chaotic, with honking horns and friendly shouts and a thousand different smells. We passed bars and restaurants overflowing with tourists, underdressed teenagers clutching handfuls of shopping bags, and island natives serenely ignoring it all.

By the time we arrived at the ferry, I was feeling a bit overwhelmed.

"After all of this," Jodi said as Tom paid the taxi driver, "you'll welcome the peace and quiet of St. John."

Certainly the ferry was peaceful. We had a choice of sitting inside in the shade or on the top deck out in the sun. We chose the shade because it was after 1:00 P.M. and the day had become rather hot. Also, in Eli's notes, he referred to sitting in the back, to the left, so that's where we went too. The ferry was big enough and crowded enough to understand why Nadine hadn't spotted him sitting there and watching her. He would have been easy to miss.

As the ferry neared St. John, I went outside to stand at the railing, soaking up the sun and the amazing view. We were headed into another, smaller harbor, on an island that seemed completely different from the one we had just left. The downtown area was much smaller, for one thing. There also seemed to be a lot less congestion of people and traffic. We glided past a number of anchored sailboats, and I couldn't helping thinking that the beautiful scene in front of me—the blue water, the white sand, the coral-colored roofs on the tan buildings—looked just like something out of a watercolor.

The large ferry glided smoothly up to the cement dock, and as the workers began to land it, I went back inside to find Tom and Jodi. We grabbed our bags and stood in line to file off the ship. Then the three of us followed the cement walkway toward a semicircular drive filled with parked taxicabs.

A man was waiting for us next to a car with a big sign that said "C and C Rentals."

"C and C?" I asked.

"Bennett?" he replied.

We nodded and he sprang to life, first taking our luggage and then helping Jodi and me into the tiny back seat. Much to my surprise, once we were seated, he piled the suitcases in on top of us.

"I'm sorry dis is all we had," he said in a lilting island accent, gesturing for Tom to take the passenger seat. "When you rent at the last minute, you have to take what you can get."

Without waiting for a reply, we were off. Our driver zipped through the adorable town of Cruz Bay, up one street and down another until he made a sharp right turn and pulled to a stop in front of a tiny shack.

"Come on in here to do de paperwork, and den she's all yours," he said.

Smiling, Tom did as the man said while Jodi and I extricated ourselves from the pile of suitcases and reorganized things. The first order of business was unzipping the convertible top from the small Jeep and then piling our bags on one side of the backseat. I sat in the space that was left, insisting that Jodi take the front passenger seat so she could navigate.

"This is nuts," she said. "Maybe we should run by the house and unload our bags first."

"Good idea," I said, a suitcase handle digging into my thigh.

Tom came out of the little building, tucking his credit card into his wallet. He climbed behind the wheel, adjusted the rearview mirror, and then turned to give me a smile.

"You trust me to drive on the left side of the road?" he asked.

"I trust you to do anything," I replied, smiling back at him.

He seemed to get the hang of it quickly enough. As Jodi directed him out of town, I took in the sights, thinking that this island was even more beautiful than St. Thomas. It seemed a little wealthier, for one thing, which meant cleaner streets and nicer homes. And it wasn't nearly so crowded. As we drove, Jodi explained that most of this island was protected by the U.S. National Parks system. In some places, the boundaries of the park even extended out into the water, and one beach featured the park system's only underwater snorkeling trail.

Fortunately, Stella's home wasn't very far away. We were less than a mile from the downtown area when Jodi directed Tom to take a right on a steep and winding one-lane road. We passed several driveways shooting off of that, each one steeper than the one before. Finally, Jodi pointed to the one that was ours, and my heart leapt into my throat as Tom made the turn that dropped us a good twenty feet sharply downward. At the bottom of the drop, the driveway widened, and Tom pulled to one side, leaving room for Jodi to get her mother's car out of the garage.

Because of all the greenery, we couldn't tell much about the house from there, but Jodi dug the keys from her purse and led us up the walkway to the door. Once inside, my breath caught. The opposite wall was a floor-to-ceiling bank of windows looking out over the beauty of the island.

Though it had been modernized, the place was obviously quite old, a treasure from St. John's historic past. It was oddly laid out, almost as if the builders had added one big room at a time, with each sort of flowing into the next. There were a total of five bedrooms, three bathrooms, a really nice kitchen, an expansive family room, and an incredible hot tub on a deck that spanned the length of the entire house. I was in awe.

"This is really something," Tom said, looking out at the view. "How long has your mom had this place?"

"It was a wedding present," Jodi replied. "To my mom from my dad."

We carried in our suitcases and set them in the entranceway. Jodi opened a few windows to let in some fresh air, and then she gave us each a set of keys for the house.

"Callie, if you need a second car while you're here," she said, leading us to the garage, "you can take the Explorer. I like the Side-kick."

She showed me where the keys hung on the wall, and then she opened the garage.

"So what's the agenda?" she asked, all business, as we piled into the SUV.

"Just get us oriented," Tom said.

He and I looked at each other, and I thought of how far we had come just to get a glimpse of Nadine's driveway.

"We're particularly interested in the East End of the island," I added. "So we can get a good look, just drive us around."

Jodi surprised me by laughing.

"Well, there really is no 'around' on St. John. It's more like up and down and twist and turn. I hope you're not prone to car sickness!"

"Not usually," I said.

"Then hold on to your hat," she replied, "and I'll introduce you to paradise."

Eighteen

Our island tour took about two hours. Jodi began back in Cruz Bay, where we had gotten off the ferry and rented the car. She drove around the streets of the town to show us the Island Foods grocery store, the National Park Visitor's Center, and a big shopping area known as Mongoose Junction. From Cruz Bay, she said, there were two ways to get to Coral Bay, which was St. John's smaller town at the other end of the island.

"We'll take Northshore Road going," she said, "and Centerline Road coming back."

What proceeded was one of the most incredibly beautiful drives of my life. The Northshore Road hugged the coastline, and around every curve was another sweeping vista, another pristine white beach. I saw road signs for beaches, bays, hiking trails, camp grounds—even ruins—and as we went I decided that Tom and I would absolutely have to come back here as tourists. At one point the road took us uphill, away from the coast, where it joined with Centerline Road.

"So when you're coming from the opposite direction," Jodi said as she pointed out the landmark ice cream stand that sat at one side of the intersection, "you can fork either right or left. Either way will get you back to Cruz Bay."

Centerline Road carried us to the top of the mountain, where a heart-stopping curve revealed an astounding view: the rest of the island, the Caribbean sea, and other islands in the distance. From there the road plummeted downward and around toward the smaller, scruffier town of Coral Bay.

"The road splits here too," Jodi said once we reached sea level, veering to the left. "This takes you down to East End. There's not much out here but hiking trails and houses. When we come back out, I'll go the other way and show you Coral Bay and Salt Pond and all of that."

I watched for Nadine's address, which came up quickly. Just as Eli's notes described, it was a simple driveway with a "No Trespassing" sign, across the street and down just a bit from a public beach.

Jodi kept going, telling us some of the history of the island as we went. She listed the different Indian tribes that had lived here—including the Arawaks, the Caribs, and the Tainos. Then she described several centuries of slave labor for the sugarcane industry, including a slave revolt in the 1700s that ended with a mass suicide of over 300 slaves jumping from the cliffs rather than being brought back into captivity and torture.

"There's a lot of ruins around," she said, "like old windmills and sugarcane plantations. You can tour some of them. There's some petroglyphs, too, you can hike to. You know, cave drawings. They're cool."

Eventually, she turned around in a steep driveway to head back the way we had come. We passed Nadine's peninsula once again as we went.

"Nowadays, about two-thirds of the island is owned by the U.S. National Park Service," Jodi said, reaching the fork in the road and turning left. "That's why it's not as crowded. It's mostly national park."

We drove slowly through the tiny town of Coral Bay, stopping to let three little goats cross the road. Jodi said goats, chickens, and even donkeys freely roamed the island.

There were a few shops and restaurants and bars sprinkled along the way, but otherwise there didn't seem to be much going on at all.

"Didn't Rockefeller donate a bunch of land here?" Tom asked.

"Yes," Jodi replied. "Back in the fifties. He bought up a lot of it and then gave it over to be permanently preserved as a national park."

Beyond the town of Coral Bay, the island seemed to grow more arid. We drove for half a mile or so, and the farther we went, the more it felt as though we were driving into a desert.

"This road ends a few miles ahead. Do you want me to take it all the way?"

"I think we've seen enough," Tom replied. "You can head back now."

Jodi turned around again in someone's driveway, narrowly missing a giant cactus at the corner.

"Well, that's it, then," she said. "That's the island."

"It's beautiful," I told her.

The drive back to the house seemed a lot quicker, probably because we took a more direct route, following Centerline Road, which literally hugged the centerline of the island's mountains. Jodi talked almost nonstop as we went, but I tuned her out and focused on the amazing scenery surrounding us. We were almost back at Stella's place when I realized I was humming "How Great Thou Art" under my breath.

Back at the house, Jodi made a few phone calls while Tom and I "got settled." Really, we were just killing time until she left, as we were both eager to get to Eli's hidden compartment and see what tools we had to work with.

Luckily, Jodi was able to locate her friend Sandy, and they made plans to meet up with each other right away. Before Jodi left, she gave me her cell phone number, assuring us that our phones should work fine throughout the island, thanks to two new cellular towers that had recently been built.

"Oh, I'll pick up some groceries for us while I'm in town," she added.

"Great."

"If you need me, you call," she said. "Otherwise, I'm going to stay out of your way. Okay?"

"Thanks, Jodi," I said. "For everything."

"No problem!" she cried. Then she hugged me, grabbed the keys to the Sidekick, and headed out the door.

"She sort of grows on you, doesn't she?" Tom asked after she was gone.

"Very much so," I replied, crossing the room to stand in front of him.

"Hey, you sort of grow on me too," he whispered, closing his eyes and leaning down for a kiss.

A few moments later I suggested we focus back on our investigation and get a look at Eli's stash of "spy tools." We found the pantry, and as it turned out, the shelves were actually built into the door. Opening that door exposed the back wall, and when I twisted the large cuphook, it sounded as though I had undone some sort of latch. I had expected the door to magically slide open after that. Instead, it just sat there, so I reached out and pushed it. It rolled away into the wall easily enough, revealing Eli's hidden stash inside.

We gasped.

When Stella had called it a spice cabinet, I was picturing something small, but this thing was floor to ceiling, with about eight shelves, each one a good ten inches deep. Much to our shock, the cabinet was almost completely filled with...well, with spy tools. There was nothing else to call them.

"This is incredible," Tom whispered, stepping closer.

"Eli was always big on the tools of the trade," I said. "The more high tech his subject, the more high tech his arsenal. Man, he went all out for this one."

"Where did he *get* all of this stuff?"

"Didn't the file say something about getting tips from the local PI about where to purchase 'certain items'?"

"Yeah, but come on! Some of these things..."

He reached out, picked up a box, and opened it to reveal two rows of tiny black disks—12 in all.

"What's this?" he asked.

I took the box from him and studied the contents, my heart suddenly in my throat. They were bugs. Eli knew better. Any PI caught with a bug in his possession faced the automatic loss of his investigative license.

"Ah, Tom," I said softly, "Eli was treading some dangerous ground here. These are so illegal. I can't believe he was willing to risk everything for the sake of this one investigation."

I put the box back and reached for a small pile of similar disks with wires.

"More bugs," I said, shaking my head.

"They're all so tiny."

"They probably come with some kind of transmitter. Yeah, here."

I grabbed a square, camouflaged container about the size of a small toaster.

"You plant the bugs throughout the house, and then you put this somewhere within range, maybe fifty feet away. The signals are sent from the bugs to the transmitter, and then from there out to a listening station."

I bent down to point at the biggest box, at the bottom, which had a reel-to-reel tape recorder and headphones and looked like a suitcase.

"I don't understand," he said. "Why a transmitter? I thought they made bugs nowadays that can transmit for several miles all by themselves."

"They do," I said. "But here's the thing. You want the signals to be strong enough to transmit, but weak enough that they won't be detected by antibugging devices. This kind of bug is much less likely to be discovered. Very clever, considering the level of security on Nadine's house. I bet she has built-in sweepers."

Tom knelt down next to me to inspect the listening station more closely.

"Callie, if this stuff is so illegal, how come you know so much about it?"

I shrugged.

"When I was first starting out with Eli, he taught me everything he knew about electronic surveillance. But laws have changed since then. The world has changed. No PI in his right mind would touch this stuff nowadays."

"Wow."

"The only way I would ever use bugs would be if I were working in cooperation with the police and I had a Title Three warrant in my hand."

"Really."

We went through the rest of the closet, noting that most of the tools were for watching and listening: binoculars, cameras, bugs of all kind. Eli had a telescoping directional microphone, pinpoint cameras, and several different sets of disguises. On a low shelf was a dog bone, and when I inspected it more closely, I realized that it contained a small bugging device as well.

"Here's a clever one," I said, handing the bone to Tom. "You let the dog plant this bug for you by throwing it in the yard and hoping he'll carry it into the house."

"Incredible."

I played with the listening station a bit, checking the wires, fooling with the dials.

"I bet Eli was hoping to get a better feel for what was going on inside that house before he made any sort of overt move."

"But near the end of his notes, didn't he say something like 'the surveillance tools will have to wait for now'?"

"Yeah. 'Risk factor high.' They must've figured out he was onto them."

Tom stood up and stepped away from the closet, brushing the dust from his knees.

"So what's the plan, Callie?" he asked. "Any ideas?"

"Yeah," I replied. "Let's leave this stuff alone for now."

"And?"

"And...maybe we should pay a visit to Windward Investigations. See if they can give us a better idea of what they know about the situation."

Nineteen

We pulled out Eli's file and carried it to the kitchen table. I also had his address book, which was falling apart at the seams.

I turned to the last page of Eli's notes and reread the entry:

> *Windward calls to tell me subject has gained knowledge of their security inquiry. Not good. Surveillance tools will have to wait for now. Must convince Stella we've got to go back to States a week early. Risk factor high. Need to approach from different direction.*

That certainly sounded to me as though Eli felt he might be in danger.

I pulled out the initial security report and looked at the header information. Windward Investigations was located on Redhook Road in St. Thomas, and the report had been provided by a man named Chris Fisher. I didn't want to cross back to the other island unless we had to, so I hoped we might be able to do this by phone. It was late in the day on a Monday, but as I dialed, I prayed that someone would still be in the office.

A tough-sounding woman answered, and when I asked for Chris Fisher, she said, "Speaking."

"Oh, good," I replied, trying not to sound surprised that Chris was a woman. I told her my name was Callie Webber and I was a friend of Eli Gold's. I said I was following up on an investigation he had been working on regarding a house on Turtle Point, and I was hoping she could help me to understand some of the notes in a report she had done for him.

Not surprisingly, the woman wasn't exactly cooperative. She let me go through my whole spiel, and then she said curtly, "Sorry, can't help you."

"I'll gladly pay you for your time," I replied quickly. "I just need to ask you some questions about the report you did for him."

"I'm not sure I remember the case in question."

"You're one who put together this report," I said. "You signed off on it, anyway."

Knowing her reluctance might simply be a matter of needing to verify my identity, I gave her my license number and explained that Eli and I had worked together for a number of years. I said she could contact his wife in Cocoa Beach, if she wanted a reference.

"Nope," she said simply. "That case is closed."

"Maybe I'm not making myself clear," I said, glancing at Tom. "Eli Gold has been shot. I'm here trying to follow things up on his behalf."

At least that seemed to give her pause.

"Sorry," she said finally, sounding almost as if she meant it.

Then she hung up.

I sat with my cell phone in my hand for a minute, wondering why the conversation had gone so wrong. Fellow investigators were usually quite helpful and certainly more than willing to spend time—especially paid time—doing something as simple as going over notes.

"What now?" Tom asked.

"I don't know," I said, flipping through Eli's file.

I looked at the notation for December 31:

> 12/31 7 P.M.—*Bring bottle of good champagne to A. to toast the New Year; convince him to run plates; leave with name and address info from lic. plate.*

"Let's figure out who 'A' is," I said. "Maybe he'll talk to us."

"What are you thinking?"

"That he's a cop. He ran a plate for Eli, so he has to be either someone official or some kind of hacker. Either way, he's a resource."

"I hope he is a cop," Tom said. "It would be good to visit him and get the local police perspective."

Handling the old address book carefully, I flipped through it page by page until I came to an entry under "R": Ruhl, Sgt. Abraham, St. John Police Department. The listing included a phone number and e-mail address.

"Here's our boy," I said. "I'd bet the 'A' is for Abraham."

I was just about to dial his number when the phone rang in my hand.

"Callie Webber," I said.

"Use a landline," a man's voice said.

Then he disconnected the call.

"What was that?" Tom asked, noting my perplexed expression as I hung up the phone.

"I don't know," I said. "Somebody said, 'Use a land line,' and then they hung up on me."

We looked at each other.

"Windward Investigations," we both said at once.

Going as fast as the speed limit would allow, Tom drove us toward town, both of us looking for a pay phone along the way. I was so accustomed to using my cell phone that I sometimes forgot it wasn't all that secure. A person with the right equipment could easily intercept my conversations.

"There's one," Tom said, slowing to turn into a small parking lot. It looked like a body shop/mechanic's garage, and there was a phone booth to the side of the lot, near the road.

Fingers shaking eagerly, I dialed the number for Windward Investigations. Chris answered the phone.

"This is Callie Webber," I said. "I'm at a pay phone."

"You're in St. John now?"

"Yes."

"Take the next ferry to Red Hook," she said. "I'll meet you there."

Twenty

The sun had set by the time we walked off the ferry into the small St. Thomas town of Red Hook. The area looked a bit questionable, with a string of bars along the waterfront and a vagrant sleeping on a nearby bench. We weren't quite sure where to go now that we were here, so we simply followed the crowd down the ramp and toward the parking lot.

There was a queue of taxis waiting for passengers, with a lot of good-natured shouting between cabbies. We turned down several offers for a ride until one fellow greeted me by name.

"Callie Webber?" he said under his breath. "You can come with me."

Tom and I glanced at each other and then followed, wondering if we were making a mistake.

The man held open the door of his cab for me and then seemed surprised to see Tom getting in behind me.

"Wait a minute, who are you?" he said, putting a hand to Tom's chest.

"Tom Bennett," he replied calmly. "Where she goes, I go."

"It's okay," I added from inside the cab. "He works with me."

The man hesitated for a moment and then let Tom climb inside.

Switching off his meter, he pulled out of the parking lot and drove for about two miles without saying a word. Finally, he came to a sign for a small neighborhood park, put on his blinker, and turned in.

The place was deserted. He drove to the far end, passing a small playground and a few built-in barbecue grills, and came to a stop at the edge of a beach.

"Chris said to wait over at the picnic table," he told us, pointing.

We looked out to see a rickety picnic table under a tree. With the area deserted and the sun now below the horizon, it didn't appear to be the safest place to be dropped off.

"She will be right along," he added.

Tom and I hesitated and then did as the man instructed, getting out of the car and walking over to the table as he drove away. We didn't sit but instead stood there on the sand, looking around anxiously. We had closed up Eli's spy stash back at the house, but I was wondering now if he'd had any weapons in there, and, if he had, if we should have brought something here for our own protection. I wouldn't use a gun, but a billy club seemed like a good idea right about now.

Just to be on the safe side, I picked up a big stick for one hand and a pinecone-looking thing for the other. While I was scoping out the place for possible exit routes, another car turned into the park and drove to where we had been dropped off. Once it was parked, the door opened, and a man got out.

He was pretty scary looking, bald with a goatee, heavily tattooed, and at least 250 pounds of pure muscle. We watched as he walked to the passenger side, opened the back door, and took out a wheelchair. Then he opened the front door and lifted a woman from her seat into the chair. She was a big woman, but he seemed to handle her with ease.

He shut the car doors, wheeled her over to where we were waiting, and then walked back to the car and stood facing us, arms folded across his chest.

"Callie Webber?" the woman said in a deep voice. "Chris Fisher."

I introduced Tom and we all shook hands. Then Tom and I both sat so that we would be down at her level.

Chris Fisher was a hefty woman, quite muscular, with a square jaw and long blonde hair. She flipped the hair back from her face, and in the dim light I could see that her eyes were bruised and swollen.

"So Eli Gold got shot, huh?" she said, shaking her head. "Tough break. He was a nice guy."

"He's still alive," I said. "But just barely."

"Yeah, I know. After I hung up with you, I called his wife in Florida to verify things. She said you're on the case."

"What can you tell us?" I asked.

"Not a lot," she said. "If I were you, I'd pack up my bags and go home."

I was having a little trouble reading the situation. I wasn't sure if she was threatening us or warning us.

"Why do you say that?" Tom asked gently, obviously giving the woman the benefit of the doubt.

"I don't know what Eli was getting into here, but it is some nasty can of worms. If I could do things over, I would've turned down his business the minute he walked through my door."

"Why don't you tell us about that?" I said.

She wheeled her chair back a bit, rested her elbows on the arms, and brought her fingertips together at her mouth. She seemed torn between leveling with us and calling her man over to get her out of there.

"About a month ago," she said finally, "Eli came into my office. He asked me what it would cost for me to evaluate someone's home security system and give him a full report. Not the kind of work I usually like, but the electric bill was due. Life in paradise doesn't come cheap, you know."

"You took the case," Tom said.

"Don't think I didn't check him out first," she said, pointing a finger at us. "I wasn't about to hand some thief a blueprint for breaking and entering. But from what I could see, he was a legitimate PI working a case. I didn't know what that case was about, but he seemed earnest. It wasn't any big deal for me to make a few calls. I know all the security companies around here because we refer people out."

"You called your contacts."

"Yeah," she said, rubbing the space between her eyes. "A girl-friend of mine works for Island Protection Systems. IPS. She looked up the house address for me on her computer, and it turns out it was one of theirs. She printed out the work order and faxed me a copy. I wrote things up on a report of my own and gave that to Eli. End of story. An easy couple hundred dollars."

Things were quiet for a moment. There was so much more here she wasn't saying.

"Did you tell Eli where he might be able to buy a few handy tools?" I asked. "Like, surveillance stuff?"

She hesitated and then shrugged.

"I told him about a guy in San Juan I've used from time to time. I don't know what Eli was buying, but this fellow has a nice selection."

Tom and I shared a glance. A nice selection indeed.

"So what did you think of the security report your friend faxed you?" Tom asked. "That was a pretty significant list of security protections for one house."

"Tell me about it," she replied. "IPS does a lot of business in the islands, mostly corporate security. But I haven't ever seen a house that protected."

"What do you think that's about?"

She laughed, a loud, sharp bark.

"It's *about* none of our business," she said. "None of our business. Whatever's going on there."

I cleared my throat, leaning forward.

"When Eli left the island, he seemed to feel he was in some danger," I said. "In his notes, it sounds like you warned him they might be onto him."

She nodded, her features grave.

"My friend at IPS, the one who faxed me the work order? She got fired."

"Because she sent you details about the security of that house?"

"Yeah. Somehow, someone found out what she'd done. Her boss said if she'd tell them who had been inquiring about the house, she wouldn't lose her job. She gave them my name and they fired her anyway."

"Wow."

Chris exhaled loudly.

"Soon as she called and told me, I contacted Eli and said I was sorry but that my little investigation for him hadn't gone unnoticed. He didn't sound surprised. He just said don't worry about it; he would try to get at it from some other angle. I thought that was the end of it."

"What happened?" Tom asked.

"Last Thursday, some men came to see me. One of them brought along a baseball bat."

Tom and I gasped.

"They wanted to know who hired me to run that report. I wouldn't tell them, so they busted in my kneecaps."

I felt a surge of nausea.

"Then what happened?"

"When they started in on my face, I told them what they wanted to know. I gave it up—Eli's name, phone, address. The whole thing. I felt really bad, but I thought they were gonna kill me. I would've called and warned him they were coming, but I was in and out of consciousness for two days myself. I just got out of the hospital yesterday."

"What did the police do?"

She shook her head.

"Not much. They showed me some mug shots, but I didn't recognize anyone." She gestured toward the man by the car. "My brother got his hands on some company photos from IPS, but they weren't in there either. We hired a sketch artist at our own expense, but that's about all we've got. Two drawings of some thugs nobody recognizes."

"Did you bring them with you tonight?" Tom asked.

She waved to her brother and said, "Get the pictures."

He opened the car door, reached inside, and brought out two photocopies of the drawings. He handed them to Chris, who gave them to Tom.

"The only reason I came here tonight," she said, "is to give you these drawings and ask you to keep your eyes open. If you spot these two characters in the course of your investigation, I want to know about it. Names, addresses, anything you can give me. Nobody messes me up like this and gets away with it."

Tom studied their faces and then handed the pictures to me. They were both Caucasian, looked to be in their mid-fifties, and ugly.

"So what will the cops do now?" I asked.

She shrugged.

"Probably nothing. I've run into trouble like this before. They know I'm a PI. Comes with the territory."

I sat back, my heart pounding.

"No it doesn't, Chris," I said. "I'm a PI, and I've never, ever been injured like this."

She looked at me, an ugly grin on her face.

"You're a *corporate* investigator," she said scornfully. "Things can get a lot nastier down here in the trenches."

Tom put his hands on his knees and exhaled slowly. I knew he was agitated, and some of it had to do with concern for my safety.

"So how can you help us?" he asked finally.

She shook her head and then looked up at her brother. He bent over her chair and disengaged the brakes.

"I can't help you," she said. "And I don't want to hear from you again unless you can tell me who did this to me. I just...I thought it would be fair to come here and warn you. Whoever these people are, they're not playing games."

Twenty-One

Tom and I were silent on the ride back to St. John. After all of the events of the day, we were exhausted and confused and just a little bit terrified. I kept seeing Chris' face, the mottled blue and purple around her swollen eyes.

Jodi was still up when we arrived home, sitting out on the deck with a group of four friends—two women and two men—playing cards and drinking what looked like margaritas.

"Join us!" she cried, sounding just a little bit drunk. She scooted her chair to one side and grinned at Tom and me.

We declined, saying it had been a long day and we were exhausted.

"Well, at least meet my guests," she said, slurring her words just a bit. "Callie, Tom, this is my friend Sandy, the archeologist I was telling you about."

The woman politely stood and shook our hands. Attractive in an athletic, no nonsense sort of way, she didn't seem as if she had been drinking.

"That's Sandy's little sister, Fawn," Jodi added, "and this is Zach, and that's Larry."

Fawn gave us a little wave, and I realized that she was young, maybe 16. Zach, on the other hand, looked to be in his early thirties, and Larry was older still—in his late thirties or early forties. The two men made an interesting contrast. Zach was tall and model-handsome, while Larry was short and a little bit dumpy. Though he had a crooked nose and thinning hair, there was something familiar and engaging about his smile.

"Nice to meet you," Larry said, standing also to shake our hands.

"Yes, very nice," Zach added, sounding not at all as though he meant it.

They sat.

"Does everyone work with SPICE?" I asked.

"Zach volunteers there," Sandy said, gesturing toward the good-looking fellow. "Larry's been involved lately as an insurance appraiser, and Fawn's just here for a visit."

"My parents went to Greece for a month," Fawn said, not looking happy about it. "They dumped me here on the way."

"That's not true," Sandy corrected, putting a hand on her sister's arm. "I asked if you could come. I knew you'd like the dig."

"Whatever."

"Fawn's the designated driver tonight," Jodi said.

"I'm seventeen," she said, holding up a bottle of coke and rolling her eyes. "That makes me the designated driver every night."

"You sure you won't join us?" Larry asked us, and I had to wonder if he wasn't hoping to add a few people to the mix who were a little closer to him in age.

"No, thanks," I said. "We're heading to bed. It was nice to meet you, though."

"Goodnight," said Sandy.

"Goodnight," echoed Larry.

"Don't do anything I wouldn't do!" cried Jodi, and then she and Fawn burst into giggles.

Tom walked me to my bedroom, stepped inside, and closed the door behind him. I knew I needed nothing more right now than for him to hold me. That he did, in the darkness of the bedroom, gripping me fiercely, pressing his hands tightly into my back. I held onto him as well, my face buried against his chest.

"If anything ever happened to you…" he whispered.

"Shhh," I said. "I'm not going anywhere."

We held each other for a time and then reluctantly we parted.

"In the morning we'll visit the police station," I said, "and see what we can learn there. Tonight, let's just try and get some sleep."

He ran his hands through my hair, kissing me on the forehead.

"I wish I could stay in here with you," he whispered. "I just want to hold you all night."

I knew what he was saying. He wasn't asking if he could, just stating what he wished. Truth be told, I wanted the same thing.

I kissed him goodnight, his lips warm and soft and gentle on mine.

"I love you," I said. Then, because I loved him, I showed him the door.

Because he loved me, he took it.

I got ready for bed and then pulled out my little travel Bible before climbing under the covers. I needed to find something that would comfort my soul. After skimming around and flipping pages, I finally settled on Isaiah 41:10: "Do not fear, for I am with you; do not be dismayed, for I am your God. I will strengthen you and help you; I will uphold you with my righteous right hand."

I repeated the verse to myself until I had committed it to memory. Then I put the Bible on the nightstand and turned off the light. Finally, I drifted off to sleep, my mind filled with the comforting thought of God's righteous right hand.

The next morning, I didn't stir until almost 9:30. By the time I was up and showered, it was 10:15. I used the last of the shampoo in the bottle to wash my hair and then tossed it in the trash. I would either need to get to the store to buy some more, or borrow some from Jodi. I also needed to do laundry soon. A trip to St. John hadn't exactly been in the plans when Tom and I left North Carolina.

Once I was dressed, I came out to find Jodi at the kitchen table, sipping coffee and looking hungover.

"Hey," she said softly, squinting my way. "What's up?"

"Nothing much," I said. "But I feel like I was run over by a truck."

I thought of Chris Fisher and her battered face, and I realized I shouldn't even use an expression like that. If anyone felt as though they'd been hit by a truck, it was her.

There weren't any eggs in the fridge, so I made a light breakfast of juice and toast and then joined Jodi at the table, listening as she talked about how good it was to be back in the islands, especially to be able to spend time with her old friend Sandy.

"We had a good, long talk about the charity yesterday, before the margaritas came out. She gave me the names and phone numbers of all of the board members, and she promised to round up the paperwork I asked for—the salary info, meeting minutes, stuff on fundraisers, and audit reports for the last three years."

"Jodi, it really sounds like you did your homework."

"It was fun. She said it might take a few days to get everything together. In the meantime, she arranged for me to help out on the dig site. They've turned up all kinds of artifacts. Larry thinks it's going to end up being a very significant dig."

"He's not an archeologist, right?"

"No, he does something with insurance. I think he catalogs the artifacts or something."

"Cool. How about Zach?"

"Believe it or not," she said dreamily, "when he's not volunteering at the site, he works as a masseuse at some of the big resorts on the island. Can you imagine, ordering a massage and *he* walks in the door? I would just *die*."

"Hmm…" I said, not daring to comment.

"Yesterday, he got down with me in the pit and showed me how to brush the dirt off this little zemi. Gosh, I don't know how the other women who work there can stand it. I didn't hear a word he said."

"What's a zemi?" I asked.

"Some kind of Taino idol, I think. They've already found hundreds of them. This one was cool. It was carved with the face of a crocodile, about the size of my fist."

We finished the dishes and I wiped off the table while she recounted some of the more interesting finds the team had already uncovered. Apparently, there was a long process that only started with unearthing the artifacts. Then they had to be extensively mapped and photographed, sorted, cleaned, weighed, counted, logged, analyzed, radiocarbon-dated and finally put into climate-controlled storage.

I only half listened as she recounted the process, my mind already working toward our upcoming visit to the police station. After a difficult night, I was eager to get moving on this investigation. The conversation with Chris Fisher had left me rattled and apprehensive. The sooner Tom and I could get down to the truth of the matter, the better.

"While you're waiting for Sandy to get you the paperwork," I said, forcing myself to focus on Jodi, "there are also a few other things you can do."

I dried my hands, and then I found paper and a pencil and wrote down some websites she could visit to check out the nonprofit.

"These are mostly watchdog groups like the Better Business Bureau and Guidestar. See what pops up for SPICE. You might be pleasantly surprised, or you might find some red flags."

"Thanks, Callie," she said, taking the list from me.

"Just remember one rule of thumb," I said, putting the cap on the pen. "Don't make up your mind one way or the other until all the facts are in. You're not trying to prove if it's good or it's bad based on some preconceived notion you have. You're just trying to find all of the information out there so then you can make a wise and informed decision."

"So I guess I should put the bearer bonds away for now?"

I looked at her.

"Tell me you're kidding," I said. "Did you really bring three hundred thousand dollars' worth of bearer bonds down here?"

She shrugged.

"I thought I might be giving them away to SPICE."

I tried not to groan.

"Well, until it's time," I said, thinking of Eli's spy closet, "would you like for me to put them in a safe place for you?"

"Sure," she replied, and then she stunned me by simply pulling them from her purse and handing them over.

I waited until she had left, and then I opened the hidden closet and put the envelope on the top shelf, out of sight. It wasn't a perfect hiding place—a safety deposit box at a local bank would've been better—but it would have to do for now.

Twenty-Two

Sergeant Abraham Ruhl wasn't too hard to find. We called ahead to the police station and were told he had just left for Francis Bay. Some tourists were trapped there, feeling threatened by a trio of feral donkeys, and Sgt. Ruhl had gone along to save the day.

We followed the map to the bay and then stopped the car beside the road in beach parking that was empty except for a police car and two other vehicles. We weren't quite sure what "feral donkeys" would do, so we left the car unlocked and made our way up the path toward the beach in a cautious manner.

The sound of braying came from up ahead, and Tom and I moved closer together as we walked. We could also hear a man shouting over the sound of the donkeys. As we stepped through the brush, we could see the gorgeous beach and the water and the scene that was unfolding down the way. There seemed to be two couples there, all in bathing suits, standing beside their towels and kind of huddled together. A dark-skinned man in a crisp police uniform was tossing sticks and rocks toward a small donkey that seemed to be stuck in a bush.

"Can we help?" Tom asked as we drew closer, making a wide arc around the other two donkeys.

"Ah, the baby is separated from the mama!" he cried, tossing another rock. "He can get himself free from dat bush if he just want it bad enough."

The little donkey did seem to be growing more agitated. As the two large donkeys made even more of a ruckus, and the policeman threw rocks at the little guy's rump, he started kicking and jumping until, finally, he burst free of the vines that had ensnared him. Once he made it clear to the sand, he shook himself off, flicked his tail, and then the three donkeys turned and simply walked away.

The two couples thanked the officer, all looking greatly relieved. The sergeant waved away their thanks before turning to head back to his car.

"The donkeys won't bother you if you don't bother them," he said. "It's their island too."

We tailed along behind him back to the parking area. When we were out of earshot of the people on the beach, Tom called to him.

"Sergeant Ruhl."

"Yeah, mon?" he asked, not seeming surprised that we knew his name.

"We need to talk to you. The dispatcher said you would be here."

He glanced back at us and kept walking.

"What is it?" he asked.

"We're friends of Eli Gold," I said.

That stopped him straight away.

"Eli!" he said, turning to face us with a wide grin. "Well, why didn't you say so? How is the old coot? Are they back in town?"

Tom and I glanced at each other.

"No," I said. "Eli's been hurt, actually. He was shot by a sniper. He's in a coma. In Florida."

The man stepped closer.

"Shot?" he asked. "Will he live?"

"It happened Friday night," I said, "and he's still hanging on. According to the doctors, every day he makes it through increases his chances of surviving."

"What happened?"

The three of us walked to the shade near the rental car and leaned against the hood, talking. Tom and I explained the entire incident. The sergeant took it all in while chewing on a toothpick he had produced from his pocket.

"So now we've taken over the investigation that he had been doing," I said, "because it seems like the sniper shot was a direct result of that."

He nodded thoughtfully.

"So what has any of this to do with me?" he asked. "I'm glad to know about Eli, but how can I help?"

"We're not quite sure," Tom admitted. "Your initials are in his case notes. He came to you to run a license plate back in December. It's relevant to the case somehow, and we're wondering if there's anything you can tell us."

He shook his head, flicking the toothpick into the brush and standing as if to go.

"I'm sorry," he said. "We don't run plates for civilians. It must've been somebody else."

He walked to his car and opened the door.

"Please," I said. "We're not here to make trouble. It doesn't matter if you ran plates or not. We just want to know about Earl and Dianne Streep. We want to know what you know."

"Sorry," he said abruptly. "Can't help you."

"Don't worry, Callie," Tom said quickly. "We can just go down to the police station and ask around until we find out who else has the initial 'A' and is a friend of Eli's. I'm sure we'll find the man who ran that plate."

That seemed to give the policeman pause. If he had already done something he wasn't supposed to do, giving us the cold shoulder now would only make things worse for him.

"Did you say Callie?" he asked, pulling down his dark glasses to look at me.

"Yes," I said, walking toward him to hold out my hand. "I'm sorry, we didn't introduce ourselves. I'm Callie Webber. And this is my associate, Tom Bennett."

He pulled his glasses off and shook my hand, finally looking me in the eye.

"Callie Webber," he said. "I know who you are. Eli has talked of you many a time."

"He has?"

"You are the protégé. He say you are almost a better detective than he is."

I smiled.

"That's not true," I replied. "But I'll be sure to thank him for the compliment."

"But now, who are you?" he asked, gesturing toward Tom.

"Tom's my boss," I replied. "He's helping me with the investigation."

The officer looked at Tom skeptically for a moment.

"I don't know you. I won't talk to you."

"I understand," Tom said, holding up both hands and stepping back.

"You, on the other hand," the officer said, turning to me, "at least I know who Callie Webber is. Tell me something to prove it's really you."

"I have ID," I offered, reaching into my bag.

"Anybody can get ID. Tell me something about Eli that only Callie Webber would know."

I thought for a moment, my mind racing.

"He puts mustard on French fries instead of ketchup," I said finally.

Both men laughed.

"Something a little more personal," the officer said. "From his past, maybe. Do you know the real story of how he lost the tip of his toe?"

I nodded, wondering if *he* knew the real story.

"Eli tells people it was frostbite," I said. "While hiking in the Alps."

"Yes, he does."

"The real truth is that when he was eight years old, he accidentally slammed his toe in the icebox."

Tom chuckled, the story new to him.

The sergeant reached out and shook my hand a second time.

"If you'll excuse us, Mr. Bennett," he said, "this lady and I have some talking to do."

"By all means."

"We'll be back in a bit."

The cop pointed toward the police car, and I climbed in.

"For starters, you can call me Abraham," the officer said, starting the engine.

"Should Tom follow in our car?" I asked.

"Nah," he said, "we're just going for a little ride."

With a wave, we drove away, leaving Tom standing there on the beach.

Twenty-Three

"What we have here is a very unusual situation," Abraham said. "A lot has happened since Eli showed up at my door on New Year's Eve and traded a bottle of champagne for a name and an address. Because you are a detective and a friend of my friend, I will tell you some of it."

"You can trust me," I said, glancing back toward Tom, who gave me a small wave. I hoped he would be okay until we got back. Knowing he was a big boy and could take care of himself, I decided to put him out of my mind and concentrate on the situation at hand.

We reached Northshore Road and Abraham turned right, driving toward town.

"Do you know anything about art theft?" he asked, steering around a wide curve that went steeply uphill. "Antiquities and such?"

Art theft? That certainly wasn't what I had expected to hear.

"Not really," I said. "I've read a few articles, seen some TV shows…"

"Well, I didn't know much about it either until I got a call a couple weeks ago from Interpol."

"Interpol?"

"The international organization of police. They have an art crimes division and it seems our little island has come to their attention. I don't need to go into detail, but basically they believe there is a small group of people in St. John who are facilitating the sale of stolen art and antiquities. The group is well run and tightly knit, and so far Interpol has been unable to crack it."

"You mean someone here on the island is acting as a fence for stolen art?"

"A fence. Exactly. They've got a pretty good system set up too."

He put on his blinker and slowed, turning into the massive gates of an expensive-looking resort hotel called the Sugar Manse.

"St. John is a beautiful place, and many of our guests are very wealthy. A lot of the wealthiest ones stay in resorts like this one."

He turned down the winding, perfectly manicured streets of the resort complex, past tasteful bungalow-like structures. I wasn't sure what we were doing there, but I doubted we were on our way to visit Interpol agents. These rooms had to rent for at least five or six hundred dollars a night each, something no mere police organization could likely afford—even a big, influential one.

"Rich people, they love to buy and sell art. Sometimes the art is legitimate, sometimes it's not. Sometimes the buyer don't even care, as long as the piece continues to appreciate in value—or it fits nicely in their 'collection.'"

He slowed to make a turn that led us behind some buildings to what looked like a service area. There was a long, low building there, with a trio of women in waitress uniforms sitting out on the curb, smoking.

"This is the dormitory," he said, gesturing toward the building as we drove slowly past. "Some of the workers, they do triple shifts and live here. We think at least one, maybe more, are connected to the art ring. They work here as maids or waiters or whatever, and they are the contact to the buyer."

"Clever," I said as we pulled away, thinking that a server in a resort situation would have plenty of private access to a wealthy guest, if necessary.

"There are three parties to every transaction, of course. The seller, the middleman, and the buyer. Right now, Interpol is most concerned with the middleman. The fence."

"What does this have to do with Eli and his situation?" I asked. "Is Dianne Streep the fence?"

"That is what Interpol suspects. Now, understand that Mrs. Streep is a legitimate dealer of art, artifacts, and antiquities. But she has been caught before trying to sell stolen pieces at auction. That can happen to anyone in this business, but Interpol suspects that things aren't quite as they appear. They think her main business is dealing in the illegal art underground. They have started gathering evidence that should ultimately bring down the whole ring."

"That explains the massive security on her estate," I said, nodding. "She must be moving priceless artwork through there on a regular basis."

"Perhaps."

"Why do they suspect her?" I asked. "Other than the stolen pieces she was caught with?"

"Somebody somewhere started talking," he said. "I don't know who, but it was someone along the chain who got caught. Anyway, they have fingered Dianne Streep, saying she's the broker who moves the pieces down the line."

"Makes sense."

After driving a wide loop, we ended up back at the front gates of the resort. Abraham made a left turn onto the highway, returning toward the beach where Tom was waiting.

"When Interpol contacted me a few weeks ago to talk about Dianne Streep," he continued, "something about the whole case started nagging at me. The other day, I thought of Eli and then it all came back to me: This was the same woman he asked me to run a plate for! I don't know how he got mixed up with her, but it seems very fishy to me that the plate I ran for him back in December belonged to the same person Interpol is focusing in on now. I tried to contact him to ask about it, but he and Stella had gone back to the States. I didn't know how to reach him there."

"We have his case notes," I said. "Maybe we can tell you what you need to know."

Abraham produced another toothpick from his pocket and stuck it between two rows of snow-white teeth.

"When Eli ask me to run the plate, he say it was for an old girl-friend he spotted. I didn't see any harm in that."

"That's true, Abraham," I said. "Back in December Eli was just trying to follow up on the sighting of a woman he used to be involved with."

I didn't add that the woman was a former agent for the NSA, long thought to be dead.

"And it's just coincidence that now that same woman is the subject of an international investigation into criminal activity?" he asked.

His question sat there in the car between us. Was it also a coincidence that someone tried to shoot Eli down in cold blood? I didn't think so. I just hadn't figured out yet what the connections all were.

"So what's being done to bring her down?" I asked finally, ignoring his question. I knew he might not tell me, but it was worth a shot.

"We put a woman in over at the resort as a worker," he said after some hesitation. "A detective from St. Croix who came to help us out. Unfortunately, these islands aren't all that big when it comes down to it. Someone else working there recognized her. We had to pull her back out."

"And are they onto you now?"

"We hope not. The detective gave a hard-luck story to the gal who recognized her, saying she was working there under a different name because she was trying to get away from an abusive boyfriend back home in St. Croix. As far as we know, the gal bought it. But now we are left with no one on the inside."

"What about focusing on Dianne herself?" I asked, thinking of Eli and his closet full of bugs. "Have you done any electronic surveillance there?"

He laughed.

"We got soft taps on all their phones, but they are not stupid. So far, we've heard a bunch of nothing."

I nodded, knowing that a "soft tap" was one that was done through the phone company, rather than in equipment directly connected to the house. Interpol must have really done their homework, because obtaining a soft tap on a private citizen's telephone required a lot of legal paperwork and the full cooperation of the telephone company.

"What about transmitters?" I pressed. "In the home."

"Funny you should ask that," he said. "They were included on the warrant. But nobody here know how to do that stuff. We are waiting for Interpol to give it a high enough priority to send someone out. In the meantime we just monitor the phones and keep an eye on the house. But until something happen, there's not a lot we can do. I would like to make a raid, but Interpol say there's no way to know when the timing would be right, as far as gaining evidence goes—and then our advantage has been lost. Better to watch and wait, I guess."

"What would you say," I asked, "to hiring me to plant bugs in the house for you? I could even supply the bugs."

He gave me a long, sideways glance, nearly missing the entrance to the beach parking. The Gold Agency had done this type of work for police departments in the U.S., so I knew for a fact it wasn't outside legal bounds for them to bring in someone from the outside.

"You know how to plant bugs?" he asked.

"I'm a PI," I said. "It was part of my education."

He pulled to a stop next to the empty rental car. Looking forward, I could see Tom out on the beach, shoes off and pants rolled up, strolling at the edge of the water.

"What would it cost?" Abraham asked.

I smiled.

"I don't know," I said. "A dollar, maybe? I just want to pursue my own investigation. Looks like the best way for me to do that is to help you with yours."

He took the toothpick from his mouth and seemed to study it carefully.

"I'll have to check with legal," he said.

"And I'll need a copy of that warrant," I replied.

Reaching into my bag, I took out a business card and handed it to him.

"You can reach me at that cell phone number or at Eli's house here."

I opened the door and got out, thanking him for the information and for his time.

"I hope we can work together on this," I added. "Seems to me your investigation and my investigation have run smack dab into each other."

"So they have," he said, reading my card. "So they have."

Twenty-Four

It took less than an hour to hear back from Sergeant Ruhl. He agreed to pay me $1 and give me a copy of the warrant; I agreed to try and put bugs into the home of Dianne Streep—aka Nadine Peters—on behalf of the St. John Police Department.

Once I received the go-ahead, I explained the full situation to Tom. This was better than we could have hoped, I said, because now we could do what we needed to do legally. Together, we sat out on the deck in the sun and formulated a plan. After tossing around a number of ideas, we decided the best way to get close enough to Dianne's house with a listening station was by boat.

We needed a vessel big enough to have an enclosed cabin, but small enough to be able to handle ourselves without having to bring along a captain or crew. I called Jodi to get a recommendation on a boat rental company, and then Tom suggested we rent a 20- to 24-foot power cruiser, which sounded fine to me. I was just glad he seemed to know what he was talking about.

As for bugging the house, we both felt the simplest way to get started was with the dog bone. If it worked the way it was supposed to, I thought it would provide a quick "ear" into the place. Then we could concentrate on bugging the whole house more fully.

Our first order of business was to find out how wide of a range the bone had. We turned on the listening station, playing around with it until we could clearly hear the transmission coming through. Tom needed to drive down to the harbor anyway, so we decided that he would take the bone with him and we could measure the mileage that way. In the meantime I would stay here and go through the closet again, packing up anything I thought we might need into a big suitcase. I also started a load of laundry.

Tom drove away, the dog bone functioning almost like a one-way cell phone. I stayed back at the house with the headphones on, listening to his chatter and smiling at his jokes.

"Okay, backing out of the driveway," he said, his voice clear and strong. "Rawhide is sitting on the passenger seat next to me."

I turned down the volume just a bit.

"I'm driving down the hill, and I just set the trip odometer at zero. Taking Rawhide for a test drive."

I could hear the sound of a car passing.

"Okay, we're at one-tenth of a mile. Hope you can still hear me."

He was coming through loud and clear.

"Rawhide is taking in the scenery. He thinks he likes it a lot better out here."

He continued to chatter, pausing now and then to give me the odometer count. Much to my surprise, the sound didn't fade completely away until he was one mile and four-tenths away. So now we had our range.

I switched off the transmitter and turned my attention to the other items. I was glad for the opportunity to go through the closet again, but I found myself talking out loud to Eli as I went.

"What were you thinking?" I asked him more than once. "Where did you get this?" and "What does this do?"

Tom wasn't back by the time I was finished, so I switched my clean clothes into the dryer and then went to my bedroom to unpack everything else. Last night I hadn't had the energy to spend much time getting organized, but now I knew I needed to be ready for any contingency. Once I had everything laid out, I packed an overnight bag for myself, just in case.

I was sorting through my toiletries when I heard some commotion at the front door. I thought it was Tom returning, but instead it was Jodi with another group of friends. I recognized the two men from last night, Zach and Larry, but otherwise these were different faces. I glanced toward the kitchen, but the pantry was closed, the cabinet locked up tight. Nothing to worry about.

"Hey, Callie," Jodi said, hefting a bag of groceries onto the table. "I didn't see the rental car. I figured you were already off getting a boat."

"Tom's doing it," I said, joining them in the front hallway and wishing Jodi didn't have quite such a big mouth. It was no one's business that we were renting a boat—or anything else! Jodi introduced me around to the multiage, multiethnic group; judging by the dust on their clothes, they had all just come from the dig site.

Zach gave me a cool nod, not even bothering to remove his sunglasses.

"Hello again," Larry said more warmly. "Hope we weren't too loud last night. I think we had a little bit too much to drink."

"Well," I replied, "it's Jodi's house, not mine."

Jodi pointed several others bearing groceries toward the kitchen.

"We knocked off early today," she explained to me. "And figured we'd come here to have a barbecue."

"Oh," I said, and I knew my disconcertment shone on my face. In the midst of an attempted-murder investigation, she decides to throw a party? Unbelievable!

"It's okay, you and Tom are welcome to join us," she said quickly, misreading my expression. "Sandy and Fawn will be here soon."

"No, that's all right. We've got plans."

"Anybody up for the hot tub?" one of the girls asked. Several others agreed, and they headed off to the deck. I didn't even want to know if they had brought along bathing suits.

At Zach's request, Jodi led the way into the main living room, crossing to throw open the doors of the entertainment center.

"See?" she said triumphantly. "Told ya!"

"Sweet!"

Zach bent forward to study the shelves of videos.

"Zach's into spy movies," Larry explained to me. "Espionage, secret agents, anything like that."

"What do you have, like, every James Bond movie ever made?" Zach asked, pulling boxes from the shelves.

I smiled, knowing the James Bonds were probably Eli's. He loved all the gadgets, though if you watched them with him he spent half the time explaining why each particular item couldn't work in real life.

"Those are my stepdad's," Jodi said. "He's a private investigator, so he's all into spy stuff too."

"Really?" Zach said, still scanning the titles. "Does he have a specialty, like missing persons or something? I knew a PI once. Scary fellow."

"Oh, not Eli. He's like a big old teddy bear. I don't think he's in the business any more. He retired when he married my mom."

I gave her a significant look over Zach's shoulder. She was blabbering for the sake of flirting. What would she say next? Callie's a PI too?

"Jodi," I said, "can you help me with something in the back?"

"Sure," she said. "Be right back, guys. Make yourselves at home."

She followed me into the bedroom and I shut the door behind her.

"Was it necessary to tell them that?" I whispered sternly. " 'My stepfather's a PI'?"

"I was just making conversation."

"Well, I'd like to remind you that what we're doing here is absolutely no one's business. Do not share with them my occupation. Do not tell them we are here on an investigation. In fact, don't even tell them what happened to Eli. Don't trust *anybody*. Understand?"

"Of course."

"Fine," I said. She looked so remorseful I felt bad for having come on so strong. "I just don't want to see you spilling our business to the first cute guy who looks your way."

Her face broke into a big smile.

"He *is* cute, isn't he?

I rolled my eyes.

"I thought you were still brokenhearted over Franco."

"Franco schmanko," she said. "You only live once."

Blithely, she turned and flounced up the hall. Sometimes, it seemed as though she wasn't more than twelve years old.

Ignoring the crowd, I retrieved my clothes from the dryer, went back to my room, and neatly folded everything. Once that was finished, I killed time by cleaning out my purse and then my briefcase, nearly filling the tiny bathroom trash can with the brochures and unneeded receipts that I had accumulated over the last few days. Finally, when I had done everything I could think of to do, I got out my cell phone to call Tom and see what the status was with him.

Before I could get through to him, I heard his voice out in the living room. After a moment he found me in my room and shut the door behind himself.

"Just what we needed," he said. "A party."

"Tell me about it. How'd you make out?"

"Boat reserved and waiting at the dock," he said softly, brushing his lips against my cheek. "And here's our copy of the surveillance warrant from Sergeant Ruhl. How'd the dog bone work?"

"All the way to one point four miles," I replied, scanning the document he had handed me. "Of course, with these winding roads, I'm sure you weren't that far away as the crow flies."

"Either way, that's pretty good."

I tucked the warrant into the case of the listening station.

"Probably too good," I said.

"Too good?"

"The transmission is so strong, it'll probably be detected. We'll give it a try, but I doubt it'll last long. I'm sure they sweep for bugs."

"But if we plant this bug and they detect it, won't that alert them to our presence?"

"It might," I replied, "but don't you think that's worth the risk? We really need to hear inside that house—and the dog bone is by far the easiest way to try. If they're that protected, and they find something, they won't know who's responsible. They probably half expect it anyway."

With all of the revelers either on the deck or in front of the television, Tom and I went into the kitchen and put together some food, packing it neatly into a tote bag. Then we changed into bathing suits and boating clothes, and with a quick goodbye to the crowd, we took our things, including the suitcase full of surveillance gear, and drove down to the harbor. I asked Tom to stop at a roadside stand on the way so I could buy a hamburger, though he looked at me as though I were crazy for ordering something from a place called "Dirty Nellie's."

The boat was very nice but much bigger—and taller—than I had expected.

"All they had was a twenty-eight-footer," Tom said, grinning like a teenager. Somehow, I had the feeling he wasn't all that disappointed. He was so excited, in fact, that I didn't have the heart to tell him it might be a bit too conspicuous.

Giving it the benefit of the doubt, I stepped on board the shiny white deck, tilting my head back to look up at the area where Tom would actually sit to drive the boat.

"You have to climb up there to drive it?" I asked, pointing toward the aluminum ladder.

"Yeah. That's called the flybridge."

The deck we were standing on was about ten feet wide, with two fishing chairs bolted to the back next to the diving platform.

"Come take a look at the stateroom," Tom said, gesturing toward the door that was under the flybridge.

I took a step down then two more down again, entering a cozy room that held everything we would need in compact size.

"It's cute," I said, peeking at the combination kitchen and dining area. There was a small fridge, a two-burner stove, and even a little microwave. "I love the little kitchen."

"It's a galley," Tom corrected. "And don't say cute."

I opened a door to find a sink and toilet.

"Tiny bathroom," I said.

"It's called a head," Tom corrected.

Boating people were always so funny about getting the terms right. The dining area held a good-sized table, bolted to the floor, and was surrounded on both sides by well-padded bench seating.

"What's that called?" I asked, pointing beyond the dinette to what looked like bunk beds up under the hull.

"That's the forward cabin," he replied. "Two bunks for sleeping, with storage underneath. There's also storage under these benches, and that one folds out to make a double bed."

"Nice. It's enough to make you want to forget the investigation and just go for a little vacation."

"Don't I wish."

I sat at the table, checking the view from the windows there.

"This will be perfect for our listening station," I said. "Are you sure you know what you're doing?"

As nice as the boat was, I found myself feeling a bit apprehensive, wishing we could do this by canoe instead. Since Bryan's death, I hadn't been very comfortable around power boats.

"Of course," he said. "I'm a Louisiana boy. Don't forget, I've been driving boats since I was fifteen. We had a camp out on the Tchefuncte River."

He certainly seemed to get the hang of this craft quickly. The rental company had already given him a basic lesson, and we stuck fairly close to shore while he got a feel for it.

By the time we headed out into open water, I was confident he knew what he was doing, so I tried to let my worries melt away in the warmth of the Caribbean sun. I spent the first part of the trip down in the cabin but finally climbed the ladder to join him up on the flybridge.

"You doing okay?" I asked loudly over the sound of the wind. It whipped at our hair, the scenery surrounding us simply gorgeous.

"Absolutely," he replied, flashing me a contended smile.

I leaned into him, kissing him on the cheek and then slipping my arms around his waist.

Tom had picked up some nautical charts of the area, and soon he had me acting as navigator, watching the chart for landmarks and then noting them on shore. We passed Trunk Bay, Maho Bay, and Mary Point, rounding the end to ride along the slightly rougher waters of the Northshore. Tom said the boat rental company had warned him about going beyond the East End, where the Caribbean met the Atlantic and we would have to face strong currents, gusty winds, and rough seas. Fortunately, our destination would come up much sooner than that. Dianne's house was on a small peninsula that jutted out into the calm waters of Turtle Bay.

"I think that's Leinster Bay," I said, pointing to a beautiful, shallow cove. "We're getting close."

After we passed Brown Bay, Tom slowed the boat, and soon we reached the peninsula that we were looking for, a tiny promontory of land called Turtle Point. Looking up at the tall hill that rose from the water, I thought I could see the coral-colored roof of Dianne's house peeking from the trees at the very top. I took out the satellite photos from Eli's file and tried to reconcile the geography we were seeing firsthand with the bird's-eye view in the photos. I felt certain we had found the correct place.

We eased around the end of the point to find a protected little cove on the other side of Turtle Bay. It looked exactly as I had expected, with a small sandy beach in the curve of the peninsula and a private road that zigzagged up the hill to the compound at the top.

Not wanting to look suspicious, we didn't slow down once we were there but simply kept going. Once we were out of sight of the cove and the house, Tom turned off the engine and let us drift to a stop. I leaned over the side of the rail, and I could see the sandy bottom, about ten feet down. It had been a long time since I had been in water this clear. When the boat stopped, Tom flicked the switch for the anchor, and we could hear the gears as it rolled into place.

"The timing is good, at least," I said, checking my watch. "It'll be dark soon. Then we can make our move."

"And what is our move, exactly?" he asked.

"First things first," I said, taking the ladder down to the deck and then stepping into the galley. I found my tote and retrieved the hamburger we had bought on the way.

"We eat?" he asked, following me inside.

"Not exactly."

I put the burger on the counter and then dug through the suitcase for the dog bone with the bug inside. As Tom watched, I pulled the beef patty from the burger and proceeded to rub it all over the bone.

"You are one smart lady," he said, shaking his head.

I wondered suddenly if in his line of work he was ever required to do this sort of thing. When I thought of him working for the NSA, I had been picturing him at a computer, slaving over codebreaking programs—but for all I knew, he was some sort of field agent.

Once the bone was covered with the smell of the meat, I set it on the counter and suggested we check the nautical charts to see if there were depth descriptions for Turtle Bay.

"If it's deep enough there," I said, "we just wait for dark, sail as close as we can to the beach, and then give the bone a good throw. If it's too shallow to get the boat close enough, I guess we'll have to swim in and put it there."

We pulled out the charts and spread them on the table. All of the depths were marked as approximates, but it looked as though we could get the boat in about ten yards from the beach.

"I think I can do it," Tom said. "I'm no baseball player, but pitching a dog bone shouldn't be all that hard."

"What about boating in the darkness?" I asked. "Is that safe?"

"Not really. But we can if we have to, I guess."

We had about an hour to kill before it would be dark enough to head back, so I suggested we jump in for a swim. After gazing at the gorgeous water since we got here, there was nothing I felt like doing more.

"Last one in's a rotten egg!" Tom said, pulling off his T-shirt and diving from the bow. It took me a moment longer to strip down to my suit, but then I jumped in after him, plunging into the crystal clear water.

It was fabulous!

After all of the stress of late, to be able to lie back and simply float among some of the most gorgeous scenery in the world was priceless. Sticking close to the boat, we swam and laughed and talked and floated until the sun had dipped low on the horizon. Reluctantly, we climbed from the water and then sat on the back of the boat for a while side by side as we dripped dry.

"Can I ask you a question?" I ventured, hoping my train of thought wouldn't spoil the moment.

"Of course."

"If someone were a cryptologist for the NSA," I said, "would they go out into the field to plant bugs and collect secret messages and all of that? Would they use weapons and deal with spies and know how to do covert ops?"

Tom chuckled.

"You watch too many movies," he said.

"Well, would they?"

Tom looked around, seeming to gather his thoughts.

"I would imagine the NSA is more compartmentalized than that. If someone is good at breaking codes, I doubt they would waste their time doing anything *but* that."

"So someone else probably goes out and does all the physical stuff, and the NSA cryptographers are probably just handed the codes and the programs they need to break?"

"I would imagine it's exactly like that. Sometimes, they might know more details about the codes they are breaking than others. But either way, code-breaking is a desk job. Nowadays, mostly it's a computer thing. Though that's not to say their work can't have implications that reach far beyond the walls of the office."

"Oh, I understand that. I just wondered…" I let my voice trail off. "You seem to have some natural talent in this area."

"In what area?"

"Detecting."

"From you, Callie, I take that as high praise indeed."

"I just wondered if you learned any of it on the job, so to speak."

My statement sat there for a long time, and the longer Tom remained silent, the worse I felt about asking. Why had I ruined such a lovely moment with yet another attempt at probing?

"Cryptographers *are* detectives," he said finally, "regardless of whom they work for."

"In what way?"

"The very qualities that make me a good cryptographer are the same qualities that make you a good detective."

"Like what?"

"Logic. Resourcefulness. Patience. Persistence. For example, you're not going to let this case go until you know everything about who Nadine is and what she was trying to tell Eli. When I've got a tough piece of code to crack, I'm not going to let it go until I have found the cipher that will break it. It's that simple."

"Or that complicated."

He smiled.

"Or that complicated," he echoed.

He talked a bit about the science of cryptology, but after a while I found myself lost in the details, focusing instead on his deep voice and the enthusiasm he held for his work. It struck me that this was the first time Tom had felt free to share with me the actual mechanics of code breaking, and suddenly I felt very glad I had looked him up online and unearthed this fact about his life. Tom Bennett, Crypto Genius, was indeed an extremely intelligent man. I just wished I could know everything there was to know about his world.

Once the sky was completely black, it was time to move. After a quick debate about who had the better arm for throwing the bone, Tom won because he had been a newspaper delivery boy for a number of years and it sounded as though he would have the best aim. Our goal was to land the bone high up on the beach, out of the reach of the tide, but not so far into the brush that the dogs wouldn't find it.

As we drove past Turtle Bay, Tom went slowly, keeping an eye on the depth finder to get as close into shore as possible.

"I think this is about as good as we're going to get," he whispered.

I took over at the wheel and he climbed down to the main deck. With a slight grunt, he heaved that bone as high and as far as he could. Though we didn't hear it hit the sand, we also didn't hear a splash. He came back up and took over at the wheel, and we agreed to hope for the best.

From there it was time to get home and get to bed. We didn't know what time the dogs got their morning run, but we thought it might be prudent to be back out on the water by sunrise, watching and listening to see if Plan A just might work.

"Wonder if Jodi's having another party tonight," Tom said as we sped back across the black waves.

"With that girl," I replied, thinking of Jodi and her friends swarming all over the house, "it's hard to guess what she's up to next."

Twenty-Five

Fortunately, there was no one back at the house after all. I had a rough night's sleep, but I was up and dressed and ready to go by 5:00 A.M. Tom didn't look very chipper either. We grabbed enough fixings for breakfast and lunch and then trudged out to the car and drove back down to the dock.

It was early yet, but there were a few folks stirring. As we walked down the wooden slats to our slip, we heard some friendly "hellos" and were met with the smell of coffee from several directions.

The sun was just coming over the horizon when we pulled clear of the harbor and started out across the water. I was feeling more confident about being in a motorboat. Perhaps it didn't bring back many memories of Bryan's accident because the setting here was completely different.

The challenge this morning was to get close enough to the beach at Turtle Bay to be able to see what was happening, but not so close that anyone there might notice us. We finally settled on a spot a little further down the coast and out a bit, dropping anchor at a depth of 22 feet.

Tom fooled around with the listening station while I assembled the telescope. There was a spot inside the forward cabin, a tiny porthole of a window, where I could put the telescope right up to the glass. I doubted anyone would be able to see me, and from that vantage point I could focus right in on the sandy beach.

It took a while to find the bone, and by the time I had it locked in my lens, I was a little bit dizzy from scanning up and down the sand. Still, I twisted the knob on the telescope to secure its place and then called Tom over. Unfortunately, the boat was drifting so badly that when he looked, the bone was no longer in view.

I went out on deck to see if I could spot the bone with my naked eye now that I knew where it was. It was no use, so I came back down into the cabin, sat on the bench beside the window, and used the binoculars.

"See it?" I said to Tom, pointing. "Right there. By that bush with the red blossoms."

I handed him the binoculars, and he peered through them until he found it.

"Perfect!" he said proudly, adding that some skills gained young can last for life—particularly throwing newspapers.

Once we had a visual confirmation of the placement of the dog bone, I turned my attention to the listening station. There was a small speaker next to the recorder, so I flipped the switch to change it from headphones to speaker.

"Wow," Tom said, "you can hear the waves."

"Yeah, we're well within range," I replied. "Now all we have to do is pray that one of the dogs finds the bone and carries it back up to the house."

"And then hope their sweepers don't detect the bug. Seems to me like a lot of long shots in a row."

"Yeah, with our luck the dumb dog'll bury the bone in the back-yard."

Eli's note had said that the dogs were brought down to the beach twice a day, once in the morning and once at night. While we waited for their morning run, I dug out the food we had taken from the house and made a simple breakfast for us in the tiny galley. We were quiet as we ate, and I kept stealing glances at the bunk beds in the forward cabin, wondering if I might grab a nap later. I felt certain Tom wouldn't mind.

Finally, we had some action around 8:30 A.M. We heard before we could see the sound of shuffling feet and barking and a man whistling. The telescope didn't give us a wide enough range to catch all of the action on the beach, so we sat at the larger window next to the dinette and used the binoculars. Meanwhile, we switched on the recorder and Tom sat ready to take notes.

There wasn't much going on at first. It wasn't exactly thrilling to watch a trio of dogs relieve themselves while a man sat on a rock and read a book. Several times, the dogs ran past the bone, which was well placed just at the edge of the sand where it met the brush. The dogs seemed excited and jumpy, two black Labs and a German shepherd.

The man stayed down there for at least 15 minutes, and in that time, the dogs managed to spray every tree in the vicinity, chase a crab into the water, dig a hole among the bushes, and even engage in a little horseplay with each other. Finally, the man closed his book, stood, and whistled for them.

They didn't all come right away. One was busy chewing at something he had found on the beach, and the other one, the shepherd, was sniffing near to the bone. Suddenly, you could hear the sniffs over the speaker, and then, like magic, I watched as he leaned over and picked it up in his mouth.

"The Eagle has landed," I whispered.

The sounds changed after that. As the dog ran to his master with the bone in his mouth, all we could hear was the sound of the canine's heavy breathing. I watched the two dogs standing at the man's feet while he whistled for the third.

"Bob!" the man yelled. "Get over here *now*."

The third dog reluctantly abandoned what he'd been chewing on and ran to the man, who scolded him. The man's attention was on that dog, fortunately, which left our friend the shepherd free to keep his newfound toy.

"Let's go," the man said in a deep island accent. "On up the hill."

They started walking back up the winding gravel road, and the foliage was so dense it was hard to keep them in sight. But we could still hear them, the breathing echoing in our speakers like an obscene phone call.

"Come on," Tom whispered. "Don't drop it yet."

Once I lost sight of them completely, I put down the binoculars and went back to the telescope, trying to see if it might allow me any glimpse of the house. But there were so many plants and bushes and trees that it was no use. The most I could make out from this angle was one corner of the roof. And our boat was drifting and turning so badly in the water that it was hard to stay focused in that direction anyway. I suggested to Tom that we relocate a bit farther away, completely out of sight of the house. He complied, deftly raising the anchor, moving the boat beyond the next cove, and then tying it up to a mooring line.

Though we couldn't see anymore, the sounds continued. The man spoke to the dogs occasionally, but it was mostly mindless chatter, hard to understand over the sound of the dog's breathing. Finally, we heard the opening of some kind of gate and then, a moment later, a few beeps that were probably the entryway to the biometric security system.

"Okay, time for breakfast," the man said, and his comment was followed by what sounded like the eager scrambling of dog feet on a tile floor. "You want chicken and rice or beef stew? I think it is a beef stew day."

There was a loud "clunk" and I had a feeling the dog had dropped the bone on the floor. He must have started gnawing on it then, because the sounds we were getting now had changed from heavy breathing to a garbled chewing.

Beyond the noise the dog was creating, we could hear different muffled sounds, and I told Tom that was the problem with electronic surveillance. You expected everything to sound like it did on a radio show—clear and distinguishable. The truth was that most sounds weren't that distinct. It took an experienced ear to know what you were listening to sometimes. Eli had trained me well, but I was by no means an expert.

Nevertheless, I thought I caught the whir of a can opener running and then the scrabble of dry food being poured into a bowl. Suddenly, the chewing stopped, and it sounded as though the dog's attention had turned to his breakfast.

"This is nerve-racking," Tom whispered. I nodded.

We had to listen to the dogs eat, which seemed to go on forever. The man must have stayed there with them, because occasionally we could hear him whistling. While we waited for something more interesting to happen, I pulled out Eli's file again and studied the satellite photos of the house and grounds.

In the pictures I could clearly make out the gravel road they had taken up from the beach. That road ended at the paved driveway, and there was a flagstone walk that led in a curve around the side of the house. I was willing to bet that the kitchen was right inside that back door, because it hadn't sounded as though the man or the dogs had gone any farther into the home than a room or two.

Suddenly, we could hear a woman's voice, calling in the distance.

"William!" she said, and Tom and I looked at each other, eyes wide. "William," she said again, her voice sounding closer.

"Yes, ma'am?"

"I'm getting an alert from the sweeper. Has anyone been here?"

"No, ma'am. I just brought the dogs down for their run and then we come back. The system was on while I was gone."

"Call Earl for me, would you? Tell him I need a manual."

"Yes, ma'am."

There was silence except for the chewing dogs, and Tom and I looked at each other.

"Busted," I said softly.

"Earl, this is William," we heard suddenly, and from the crackle, it sounded as if he was using a walkie-talkie. "Miss Dianne want a manual sweep of the house. She's getting an alert on the TSCM."

"Right. On my way," a deeper man's voice replied.

"What do we do now?" Tom asked.

"We keep listening," I said.

William spoke again.

"All right, you get along outside now. Breakfast done."

The dogs' nails clicked excitedly on the tile, and I had a brief hope that our shepherd might grab the bone and carry it right outside with him. Unfortunately, he seemed to have forgotten it. We could hear the door open and the sound of the dogs running outside. The door closed. All was silent.

"We're in trouble," Tom said, leaning back in his chair.

Suddenly, however, we heard a muffled sound, and then a loud scraping sort of noise that sounded as though the man was picking up the bone. He made some kind of grunt, and then we could hear the door opening again, a whoosh, a big thud, and some barking.

Tom and I looked at each other, eyes wide.

"Keep the toys outside, you dumb dogs!" the man called from a distance. Then the door shut and all was silent.

Tom and I looked at each other and burst out laughing—not that the situation was funny, just that we were so relieved.

"Maybe they won't find out after all," he said. "I doubt they sweep outside in the yard."

"Yeah, but in the meantime, we've lost our ear inside the home. At least now we know what we need to know. They do have sweepers. We'll have to use the smaller, less powerful bugs with the transmitter box."

"Before we even do that," Tom said, "I think we need to switch to a different boat. This one's so tall, the flybridge is acting like a sail. We need something smaller and lower to the water so we don't drift around so much."

"Let's go do that now," I said. "Then it's time to send in the big guns."

Twenty-Six

The "big guns" were actually quite tiny: Twelve little low-frequency disks that would serve as undetectable bugs. The hard part was getting them inside the house—and, once that was done, placing the corresponding transmitter box near enough to pick up their signal and then send it out to the boat.

For now, we could still hear through the dog bone, though mostly we were getting silence with the occasional bird twitter or dog bark. It seemed the bone had been tossed into the garden and forgotten.

Things were getting so stuffy inside our little cabin that we turned up the volume and moved to the back deck. We sat in the fishing chairs, enjoying the cool breeze. For almost an hour, we tossed around ideas for how to get the little bugs into Dianne's house—from having Tom knock on the door posing as a salesman to sending her some bugged flowers. Almost every idea we threw out could have worked with the average person. But for someone as careful—and protected—as Dianne, we knew anything out of the ordinary would be seen as suspect.

In the end we went back through the Windward Investigations report that Eli had had done, reviewing every element of this woman's security system, looking for weaknesses.

"It's no wonder Eli couldn't get anywhere with all of this," I said. "That place is a fortress!"

"Where there's a will, there's a way, my grandma used to say."

"Yeah," I replied, getting up to go down to the galley to fix us an early lunch. "Your grandma wasn't a security expert by any chance, was she?"

"Nah," he replied. "Though considering how well she guarded her recipe for crawfish étouffée, she should've been!"

Lunch for us was a simple ham sandwich with a side of chips and a soda. I smiled at Jodi's choices from the grocery store, realizing she was probably still young enough to be able to eat whatever she wanted and not worry about her figure. I would have to get to the store myself soon and stock up on some more healthful fare.

My mind went from making a mental grocery list to thinking about Eli's notes regarding grocery delivery. I called to Tom, and he came down and joined me.

"What if we went in through the groceries?" I asked.

"What do you mean?"

"Dianne receives a weekly grocery delivery. If we can get hold of it, we can plant bugs in some of her groceries."

"You mean like inside the packaging, where they wouldn't show?"

"Yeah."

"Won't we just end up bugging the kitchen?"

"Not necessarily. There's always soap or toilet paper or boxes of tissue, things like that. There's a wild chance that a few of the items could get moved farther into the house. We have at least twelve of the little bugs to work with, so our odds are pretty good."

"How do you zero in on the bug you want when they're all over the house?"

I thought about that and finally shook my head.

"I don't know," I said. "I'm not exactly an expert in this stuff."

"Well, I agree that the groceries are her biggest weakness," Tom said, nodding. "But we can't add anything to her list. We've got to work with what's there. Otherwise, she'll get suspicious and we'll get caught."

"All right," I said, pulling out my phone. "Let me call the grocery store and find out when they deliver."

I obtained the number for Island Foods and then called to ask if they offered grocery delivery, pretending to be a potential customer.

Apparently, they delivered between 1:00 and 5:00 P.M., Wednesdays and Saturdays, with a $50 surcharge to deliver to the East End.

Once I hung up, we sprang into action, bringing up the noisy anchor and starting the boat's engine. As we sped through the open water, we talked out our plan. It contained a lot of variables, but we thought it was worth attempting.

Tom's first inclination was to do this legally and aboveboard, showing the warrant to the owner of the grocery store and enlisting his cooperation in the planting of the bugs into the groceries. I had to remind him that we were flying blind here, with no real idea of who could and could not be trusted.

"For all we know, the grocery delivery man is their contact," I said. "We can't trust anybody."

In the end we agreed that a little espionage was in order. Sometimes you have to fight fire, I reminded him, with fire.

Back at the harbor, we didn't take time to switch out the boat but simply loaded our gear in the car and headed straight to the grocery store. Once there, Tom parked us at the far end, backing into the space so that we could see the entire place from our vantage point.

"The next question," I said, "is whether they pull the groceries they're going to deliver from the shelves or from the stockroom."

"Oh, probably from the shelves," Tom said. "It'd be too hard in the stockroom—everything's still in boxes."

"Then let's go shopping. I'll do the dirty work while you keep an eye on the progression of things."

He gave me the car keys and we headed into the store, grabbing a cart at the entrance. It was 12:30, which meant the deliveries would go out in about half an hour. Our hope was that Gerald—or whoever—would be filling those orders right now.

Tom and I split up inside, but he was back in my row in less than a minute, a huge smile on his face.

"Like candy from a baby," he whispered.

Together we pushed the cart to the aisle where a young man standing with a clipboard was pulling cans of soup and putting them in a cart. He went from there to the bread section, grabbed two loaves, and then checked something off on his list.

Tom and I split up again, and I crossed to the frozen foods, where I could watch the fellow without him realizing it. He made his way up and down a few more aisles and then made a final notation on the clipboard, removed the paper he had been writing on, and put it down in the cart. Then he rolled it over to the front corner of the store, next to the manager's station, and left it there beside two other full carts. As I watched, he got another empty cart and went back to the shelves again.

I ambled over to the three carts, each of which had a piece of paper in it, a typed list of foods with different items circled and checked off. On the paper in the middle cart was the name "Streep."

Yes!

Heart pounding, I acted as though I were looking at the batteries for sale on the wall over the carts, when in fact I was desperately scanning the items that were in Dianne's cart, trying to decide what we might be able to use for the bugs.

For the bugs.

I blinked, surpressing a laugh at the irony: In the Streeps' cart was a pack of Raid ant baits.

For bugs!

Quickly, I turned and went back toward the correct aisle, my heart literally hammering away in my chest. I caught Tom's eye, found the aisle I wanted, and grabbed two packs of Raid ant baits.

I held them at an angle that Tom could see what I was getting, and his eyes widened. He nodded, also barely containing a smile. I took a few extra boxes and then walked past him to the "Sundries" aisle and grabbed a glue stick, tweezers, and a pair of fingernail scissors. Then I went to the checkout, paid, and tried not to run as I made my way back to the car.

Time was of the essence.

The hardest part was getting the box of ant baits open without tearing anything. I took a deep breath and let it out, trying to have patience as I slid one side of the flat scissors under the cardboard flap. Once I got the box open, I pulled out the contents: eight little plastic ant baits, a sheet of instructions, and a little pad of sticky pads for affixing the traps in place.

I put the pads and the instructions back in the box and then concentrated on the ant baits. I hated the thought of touching the insecticide with my bare hands, but I had no other choice. I thought I could run my finger through the small hole on the side of a bait, pop loose the little pellet of ant poison, and replace it with a bug.

No such luck. For one thing, the holes on the sides were too small to fit my finger through.

I needed to know what the baits looked like inside, so I used the fingernail scissors to cut open a bait. I was expecting to find a little hard, round pellet of insecticide in there, but instead the disk contained a gooey substance that looked a lot like peanut butter.

I took a second bait and cut it open more carefully, peeling back the top to expose the brown goo inside. I put one of the bugs directly on the goo and then closed the plastic flap. At least it fit, but even with the glue stick, I couldn't get the trap to look as though it hadn't been tampered with.

I tried again. This time, I used the scissors to widen the hole on one of the sides. Finally, I was able to get the hole big enough so I could slip the dime-sized transmitter in from the side without having to cut the whole thing open. Using the tweezers, I slid the bug into place, glad to feel that the sticky substance inside would hold it there.

Perfect. If you didn't look too closely, you'd never notice that one hole was slightly bigger than the rest.

Sweating in the hot car, I repeated the process until I had inserted a bug in eight disks. Then I put the whole pack into the box, carefully rubbed the glue stick across the end, and sealed it back. If someone knew what they were looking for, they could probably tell the thing had been tampered with. But to the eye of someone who had no idea that something was going on, it seemed harmless enough.

I called Tom on his cell phone.

"Done," I said when he answered. "What's the status?"

"I'll come out," he replied.

He met me at the car, informing me that it looked as though there would be six deliveries total. All of the groceries had been rung up and bagged and brought into the back of the store. Tom had been about to alert me to that fact when Gerald came back inside and started loading the frozen and refrigerated items into a special ice chest. That's what he was doing now.

"I would imagine once he's finished loading the frozen foods, he'll head out."

"I guess we'll have to wait, then," I said, "and somehow do the switch on the road."

"Guess so."

We moved the car again, this time so we could see the back of the store without being obvious. There was an old station wagon out there, just being loaded with the groceries. Before long, Gerald got in the car and started it up.

I wanted to take over at the wheel because I was trained in tailing vehicles and Tom was not. But as I hadn't yet driven on the left side of the road, we agreed that things should stay as they were.

"How about I'll backseat drive you?" I said. "Just do everything exactly as I say."

"Works for me."

I had him pull out onto the road with three other cars between the station wagon and us. Since Gerald would be making deliveries to different houses, our hope was that one of them would afford us the opportunity to switch my box of ant traps for the one in Dianne's bag.

As we followed along, I knew we had two things in our favor: There weren't very many roads on St. John, so the chances of losing him weren't high; and he would have no expectation of being followed, so our chances of being spotted were low.

Following my instructions, Tom successfully tailed the guy to his first two deliveries, though both times the houses in question were up winding, private driveways where we couldn't follow. After the second delivery, Gerald seemed to be heading over the mountains to the other end of the island, and I was afraid that Dianne's delivery might be next.

Fortunately, when we reached the highest point of the road, the station wagon slowed and put on its blinker to turn right into a parking lot.

"Park on the other side of that van," I said softly.

Tom did as I directed, and as we pulled in I watched Gerald getting out of his car with two big bags of what looked like bread loaves in each hand.

"Stall him away from the car," I said emphatically.

"I'll try."

Tom walked behind the man as he moved toward a little open-air roadside restaurant. My guess was that Gerald would hand the bread to someone inside and then immediately come back out, catching me as I was breaking into his car. Taking a deep breath, I waited until he was talking with the bartender at the counter before I walked over to the station wagon and tried the door. It was unlocked.

Heart pounding, I opened the door and leaned inside, searching desperately for the bags for "Streep." I finally found them, though the ant baits were nowhere to be seen.

I glanced up at the restaurant to see Tom and Gerald standing at the bar, Tom pointing off down the road in the other direction and Gerald telling him something.

"Come on!" I whispered to myself, starting again and working my way through the bags for Streep. I finally found the ant traps; they had been wrapped in a plastic grocery bag before being put in with the food. Of course.

As fast as I could, I replaced my box with theirs, wrapping it in the plastic and sticking it down in the paper bag. Then I got out of

the car, shut the door, and returned to my own car. I dialed Tom on
the cell phone.

"Done," I said when he answered.

"Hi, honey," he replied. "I was just getting directions to the ferry.
I'll be there soon."

He hung up on me. A minute later he sank into his seat,
slammed the door, and exhaled loudly. I saw that he was sweating,
and he looked upset.

"That was closer than you think," he said. "Tell me again why you
do this for a living?"

I took his hand and gave it a squeeze even as I watched Gerald
heading off down the road in his station wagon.

"Because I'm good at it," I said. "Also, my boss is really, really cute."

"Yeah, I'm real cute right now," he said, running a hand across
his brow. "That was nerve-racking."

"The hard part's over," I said. "You can relax."

"Over?" he asked, shaking his head. "Are you kidding? We still
have to get that transmitter in place near the house."

Twenty-Seven

I thought it might be a good idea to take a break, so I suggested we go back inside the little restaurant and get something to drink. There was no big rush because once the ant baits were delivered to Dianne's, we still had to wait until someone got around to distributing them throughout the house. There was also the matter of how we were going to get the transmitter in place. I had some ideas, but no real plan.

I stopped by the bathroom first to scrub my hands and then met Tom at our table. It was only then that I took a moment to look around and see what an incredible place this was. Perched on the crest of a mountain, it was a small open-air bar and restaurant with one of the most amazing views I had ever seen. From where we sat along the railing, you could look down over the rolling mountains of St. John, across the water, and at the many islands dotting the sea beyond.

"Kind of takes your breath away, doesn't it?"

We looked up to see the bartender at our table, doubling as a waiter.

"You're not kidding," I said. "What a view."

He gave us menus and then came back a few minutes later to take our order: iced tea for me, a cheeseburger and soda for Tom.

"Are you hungry?" I asked after the waiter walked away, still feeling full from the ham sandwich I'd had at lunch.

"I'm *something*," Tom said. "Might as well eat."

"Takes the edge off, does it?"

"An edge this big, I don't know. I'm feeling very conflicted right now, Callie. Very conflicted."

He rubbed his hands together and then put them on his knees, a nervous gesture I had seen him do before.

"What is it?"

"I just don't like to think about the fact that this is the sort of thing you do all the time. You do it for *me*. In fact, you get paid for it by *me*. I don't want that responsibility! What if you get caught? What if you get hurt?"

"Investigating charities isn't exactly this risky," I said. "I'm not this kind of PI anymore." I thought back over the past year and knew that wasn't exactly true. "Well," I amended, "only when something unusual comes up."

He sat back, tearing tiny pieces from his paper napkin. Fortunately, we had the restaurant to ourselves except for the waiter/bartender, who was now out of earshot.

"I keep thinking about last fall," Tom said, "when I asked you to look into the murder of Wendell Smythe."

I nodded, remembering the case where I went to deliver a grant to a charity, only to find the owner of that charity dead on the floor! Wendell had been an old friend of Tom's, and once the death had been deemed a homicide, Tom had asked me to do a murder investigation.

"What was I thinking?" he said now, shaking his head. "That you could do your job from behind a desk? That you could go around and ask a few simple questions and find a murderer? I put you in harm's way, Callie. It wasn't until all of this with Eli came up that I really understood that."

The waiter brought our drinks and I took a sip of mine, looking out at the view and collecting my thoughts. I had had this conversation plenty of times before, with someone who loved me and didn't like how I earned my living. Bryan had never been happy with my profession, and he didn't let it rest until the day I quit Eli's agency and went to work at the law firm.

"I could sit here and tell you all kinds of things," I said, "about how any risks I take are my choice, or that I'm always careful and you don't need to worry, blah blah blah."

"Yes?"

"But the truth is, my father is a cop. My brother is a cop. I know how it feels to watch the ones you love walk out of the door in the morning and wonder if they'll come back alive that night. Believe it or not, I know exactly what you're saying, and I understand."

"Yet..."

"Yet it doesn't change who I am. I'm *good* at this stuff, Tom. I have a real talent for it. And despite the danger, I actually enjoy it. When I went into law, I thought I could turn my back on investigating, but the truth is I didn't really feel complete, work-wise, until I found a job that combined law *and* investigating. My job for your foundation is the perfect mix of both. How can you feel guilty for the fact that, thanks to you, I am professionally fulfilled? How many people do you know who can really say they're professionally fulfilled?"

"Not many," he admitted.

"How about you?" I asked. "You love your work, don't you?"

He looked out over the vista in front of us.

"Yes," he said emphatically. "I do."

"Then you understand how it is. God wouldn't have given me these talents and desires if He didn't expect me to go out and use them."

I lowered my voice and looked Tom in the eyes.

"Besides," I whispered, "it's fun being one of the good guys. I like knowing that my job makes a difference in the world. With all you do as a philanthropist, Tom, you more than anyone should understand that concept. As for your other...occupation...well, would you do the whole cryptology thing if you didn't feel exactly the same way, if you didn't also like being the hero on a white horse? Why would any of it be worth it if you didn't?"

"I guess not."

"And that's my point. I love my job, and I love the fruits of my job. Please don't get all crazy about the danger it sometimes puts me in. This is who I am. Period."

The echo of my own voice sounded a little harsh. I reached out and touched him on the shoulder and spoke again, this time using a more gentle tone.

"I'm sorry, Tom, but I fought this battle with Bryan for years. I don't want to fight it with you too."

He nodded, his expression thoughtful.

"Okay," he said. "Okay."

His cheeseburger came then, looking so big and juicy I almost wished I had ordered one as well. I watched as he lifted the bun, added some ketchup, and put on the lettuce and tomato.

"Think about my poor mom," I mused as he took a bite. "Her husband's a police lieutenant, her son's a detective, and her daughter's a private investigator. Somehow, she sleeps at night. If she can do it, anybody can."

"I guess so."

We were silent for a moment, but there was something settled in the air between us.

"What about your own kids?" he asked suddenly, surprising me with the turn of the conversation. "What would you do if your daughter told you she wanted to be a PI?"

He took a big bite of his burger and chewed as he waited for my answer. I hesitated, thinking that somehow Tom always had a way of coming at me out of left field.

"I'd lock her in her bedroom and throw away the key," I admitted finally.

He offered me a bite of his burger, which I took. It was as good as it looked.

"We haven't ever really talked about kids, have we?" he said, changing the subject and surprising me again.

I dabbed at my mouth with my napkin.

"What do you mean?"

"Just this...Callie, do you want children?"

I looked out at the far islands, thinking there weren't words enough in all of God's universe to express how badly I wanted children. Sometimes the desire to be a mother overwhelmed me. It was at those times, especially, that I had to give it over to the Lord, praying He would bless me in that way only if it was His will for my life. That was not always an easy prayer for me, especially considering that I was already in my thirties.

"Bryan and I were trying to get pregnant when he was killed," I said softly, and from the flash of some expression in Tom's eyes, I knew I had surprised him in return. "He wanted four. I wanted three. Considering all that happened, I would've settled for one."

"And now?"

I stirred my drink, giving myself a moment to respond.

"And now I understand that sometimes God's plans are different than our plans. I'm much more resigned to accepting my blessings as they come."

"But do you *want* children?"

I leaned forward on my elbows and looked him right in the eye.

"With every fiber of my being," I said.

An intense expression came over his face.

"How is it," he asked, looking at me so deeply that it was as though he were seeing into my soul, "that you are the most independent, self-sufficient woman I have ever known, and yet I would love nothing more than to spend the rest of my life taking care of you and giving you every single one of your heart's desires?"

Our eyes locked. It was an important moment between us. I realized that maybe it wasn't too soon to say these things. We weren't teenagers, after all. Life had left us with a lot of scars but also with some wisdom.

"Tom, why haven't you ever married?" I asked. It was something I had wondered for a long time but hadn't had the nerve to ask.

"I almost did," he replied, sitting back in his seat. "She cancelled our engagement a month before the wedding. Actually, she left me a note calling things off before running away to Europe."

"But why?" I asked. "What went wrong?"

He shook his head and smiled.

"Veronica was a sweet girl, but she wasn't ready for marriage. She was right to break it off."

"But not to tell you to your face?" I asked. "That was cowardly."

"I don't hold a grudge. It wouldn't have worked. We didn't know how to communicate. And the things that kept us together were all the wrong things."

"Like what?"

"Obligation, for one. Our parents were best friends, and they had been pushing us together for years. 'Veronica and Tom, the perfect couple.' It was hard to disappoint them."

"I can imagine."

"History, for another. I mean, when you date someone for so long, you can sort of get to the point where you think, Did I waste all this time? Do I really have to start over with someone else? In a way it was just easier to get engaged than it was to think about calling it quits." He looked out at the distant horizon and then focused back on me. "Callie, you have no idea how glad I am it all played out the way it did. I wish Veronica well, but I didn't really love her enough to marry her. I haven't been emotionally involved with anyone since. Not to any great extent, anyway. Until now. Until you, Callie. The love I feel for you has surpassed any sort of emotion I have ever experienced."

With those words, he took my hand, and for a moment my heart stopped.

"I have something for you," he said, reaching into his pocket. "I was just waiting for the right time and place to give it to you."

In sudden astonishment I wondered if he was about to ask me to marry him. My eyes widened at the glimpse of a small velvet box.

"Can I get you guys anything else?"

We looked up, startled by the server. A few people had parked their cars nearby and were wandering into the restaurant.

The moment had passed. Red-faced, Tom slid the box back into his pocket.

"Just the check," he said brusquely, releasing my hand and reaching for his wallet.

Heart pounding, I tried to think through the swirl of emotions that was overtaking me. On the one hand, I wasn't ready! On the other hand, a part of me wanted this more than anything I had ever wanted in my life.

We were silent walking to the car and then for the first mile of driving. Finally, I couldn't take the silence anymore. I looked over at Tom and then back at the road.

"What are you thinking right now?" I asked.

He was quiet for a while.

"Just that three is a good number," he replied finally, trying to act nonchalant. "I think three kids would be just about perfect."

Twenty-Eight

~

We wanted to be back on a boat by sunset, but first we made a quick stop at the house to pick up some more items from Eli's closet. Jodi wasn't there, but she had left a note inviting us to join her and her friends for dinner at a place called "Morgan's Mango" if we were free around eight o'clock. As a P.S. to the note, she had written "Fun stuff if you're still out boating" with a smiley face and a little arrow pointing to an overstuffed tote bag on the table. I went through it quickly to see two beach towels, a pretty batik bathing suit cover-up, a big bottle of sunscreen, a bag of chips, and two sun visors.

I grabbed a pen and wrote back, saying thanks for the invite, but we would be tied up. In fact, I added, I didn't want her to worry if we never made it home tonight at all. I also thanked her for the boating stuff. Grabbing the tote bag by the handles, I lugged it out to the car along with everything else.

We made a quick stop in town at "Denny's Dive Shop" for some scuba equipment, and then we spent a bit more time hunting around for a store carrying mountain-climbing tools. Not surprisingly, we couldn't find anything. In the end, we went to a hardware store, and Tom improvised by buying ropes and clamps and things there.

Then we headed back to the harbor and talked to the rental agency about a different boat. The one we finally picked was much more suitable to our needs, a 25-foot Kiwi with two powerful outboard motors, a cabin under the front, and a much lower-to-the-water profile.

"We'll take it," I said.

I was feeling guilty about all of the money Tom had spent so far. I tried to help, but he insisted on paying for everything himself.

"This isn't a J.O.S.H.U.A. investigation!" I argued as we loaded everything onto the boat. "There's no reason for you to be footing all of the bills."

"No reason not to," he replied, holding out a hand to help me on board. "I owe Eli a lot more than just money."

This time there was no flybridge on the boat. Instead, the part where Tom sat to drive was near the back, and the part with the cabin below and seating above was in the front. The interior of the cabin wasn't as big nor as elaborate as the last one, but it would do. I brought our stuff down to the little kitchen area and spread everything out on the table. Tom readied the boat, started it up, and drove us out of the harbor.

While he guided us out on the water, I pulled out my cell phone to call my dad. He and I hadn't touched base since our conversation when I was in Florida, and I knew he would want to hear from me. Mainly, though, I wanted to know what the police had told him about their investigation.

"Callie, is that you?" my mom asked. "What's all that noise?"

"I'm down in the Virgin Islands," I replied loudly. "I'm not sure how good this connection is going to be."

"The Virgin Islands?" she cried. "My goodness, but you do get around a lot. Where are you staying?"

"Stella has a house down here, on St. John. I'm here with her daughter." *And Tom,* I couldn't bring myself to add.

"Oh, honey," my mom said, her familiar, soothing tones welcome in my ear, "I heard about Eli. I know you must be upset."

"Yeah, it's terrible," I said. "But we're...I'm on the case. Maybe something will break soon."

"Your father's been on the phone a lot. He said the police in Florida haven't gotten very far."

"Well, it's all kind of complicated. Is he around?"

She said he had just run down to the store but that he would be right back.

"Do you want him to call you when he comes home?" she asked.

"No, I'll try later," I said.

We started to say goodbye, but suddenly I felt compelled to tell my mother about Tom. She didn't know he and I were dating. It would be a shame to show up engaged and give her a heart attack.

"Hey, Mom?" I said. "You know my boss, Tom?"

"Yes?"

I took a deep breath and closed my eyes.

"Our relationship has changed. We're...dating now."

"Really?"

"Yes. To be honest I think I'm in love with him."

She chuckled.

"Oh, I know that, honey. I figured it out months ago."

"How?" I asked loudly, my eyes flying open.

"You're not the only detective around here," she said. "I'd put a mother's intuition against one of your techniques any old day."

I grinned, playing with a loose thread on the seat cushion.

"How do you feel about it?" I asked. "Do you think it's too soon?"

"Too soon?" she said. "Heavens no, Callie. You're not getting any younger, you know."

"Gee."

"You know what I mean. Time passes. Life goes on. Bryan would've wanted more than anything for you to be happy. For you to love again."

I nodded, tears filling my eyes.

"Thanks, Mom," I said. "I really needed to hear that."

When I found Tom back out on deck, I slipped my hands around his waist and rested my chin on his shoulder. He was the perfect height for me, tall enough that I fit against him just like a glove. With one hand on the wheel, he reached up the other one and put it on top of mine. We rode along like that for a while, until he needed both hands to steer through a larger boat's wake.

"What's up?" he asked loudly as I moved to the chair across from him.

"Nothing," I said. "I'm just thinking about how we're going to do this. Are you sure you can scuba dive?"

"I'm not certified, but I know how. I did a dive trip with some buddies one time."

We slowed a bit as we reached Turtle Point, and when we got around to the other side, we saw that several boats had put down anchor just past Turtle Bay.

"Oh, no," Tom said. "Looks like we've got company."

"It's okay," I told him, recalculating a little bit. "Actually, that's good. That's very good."

We went just past the farthest boat and then swung around closer to shore than the rest. We were out of sight of Dianne's house but close enough to get to her beach. And if for some reason she happened to grow suspicious, we now had all of these other boats to act unwittingly as decoys. I told Tom to put down the anchor, but then we realized that there were mooring buoys here instead.

As Tom eased us toward the floating white ball, I went to the bow with a boat hook and caught the line on the first try. Tom turned off the motor and then came forward to help me tie it off.

We practiced the dive while it was still light. First we swam from the boat to as close to the beach as we dared. Luckily for us, there were no coral reefs in the way, nor any hidden rocks. We saw a few stingrays in the shallows, but they didn't hurt us. Satisfied that our plan could work, we returned to the boat. Where we were moored, the water was only about eight feet deep with a sandy bottom, perfect for teaching Tom how to do a "bail out": At my count, he would close his eyes, jump into the water, swim to the bottom, locate the sunken dive equipment, strap on the weight belt, clear the respirator, put it in his mouth, strap on the tank, put on the mask, clear the mask, and come back up. He seemed to have the hang of it by about the third try.

"That's one of the things they teach you in scuba class," I said. "Funny, but it should really come in handy tonight."

Once I thought he was comfortable with the equipment, we stowed it on the diving platform and went into the cabin. We spread the satellite photos on the table and walked through the plan together. There was one hole in the security there, and we had every intention of exploiting it.

It was really quite simple: Tom was going to scale the rock face of the northeast end of Turtle Point—the only place on the entire property that apparently had no camera surveillance and no motion sensors. I'm sure it never dawned on the security company who wired the house that an experienced rock climber could scale the sheer cliff and reach the top from there, emerging a mere 20 feet or so away from the main house. I only wished I were a good enough climber so that Tom wouldn't have to be the one to do it.

The night was clear, the moon nearly full, the sea calm. The way I saw it, our risks in the water were minimal, even in the dark. The danger started on land, once we were up against three watchdogs, a security guard, alarm systems, motion sensors, and cameras.

We grew tired of going over the plans and finally put our diagrams away, confident that we both knew every aspect of what we were about to do backward and forward. I had hoped to make our move around 10 P.M., but at that point there were still too many people up and about on the boats that floated nearby. Instead, we had to kill more time. There was a pack of playing cards in the glove compartment, so we sat at the kitchen table and tried several hands of Gin Rummy, then Two-Man Spades, then Twenty-One. The problem was that Tom could not be beaten.

I thought about our time in the North Carolina mountains, when he had been so good at Scrabble that I finally stopped playing it with him at all. I wasn't a sore loser, but it simply wasn't any fun knowing I *couldn't* win. Now that I knew he was a cryptographer, however, it made sense. I realized that he probably counted cards and recognized patterns—and that whenever he looked at a pile of letters in Scrabble, he could see every possibility that existed! No wonder I couldn't win.

Outside, it was cool and not very windy, and it sounded as though our floating neighbors were still out and about. They weren't noisy, really, but they were talking and occasionally laughing. I could detect about four or five different voices, though their words were indistinguishable.

I went back down into the cabin and came out a few minutes later with one of Eli's spy tools: the telescoping microphone.

"What are you doing?" Tom whispered.

"We could use a little practice, don't you think?"

"On them? No, I don't think. There's no warrant for that, Callie. What you're doing is illegal."

"I need to practice," I said, turning on the power. The microphone was shaped sort of like a rifle, with a wire leading from the butt of the handle to a pair of headphones. I put these over my ears and aimed the mike toward the other boat. "There's no telling when we might have to whip this out and use it."

"You'd better hope nobody sees you," he said. "That thing looks like a gun."

"We're in the dark," I whispered. "And they're too far away to see, anyway."

I adjusted the volume and then listened to the people's chatter. Mostly, they were telling fish stories. I couldn't hear what everyone said because some of them were blocked from my view—and for a telescoping microphone to work, you always had to have a line of sight in order to get sound.

"This is nice," I said, pulling the headphones from my ears and examining the microphone more closely. "State of the art, for sure."

I gave the headphones to Tom and insisted he try the tool out as well. He did, turning the other direction and pointing the mike toward Turtle Point.

"Can you hear anything that way?" I asked.

"Just the wind and rustling leaves. And the waves."

I looked up toward the house, a shudder passing down my spine. The point was dark, the water black. As Tom turned and listened in the other direction, I prayed that somehow God would get us through the night safely, allowing us to do the job we had come here to do.

Pulling off the headphones, Tom handed the mike back to me.

"Sounds like they'll be turning in soon," he said softly. "I say we give it an hour or so for everyone to fall asleep, and then we make our move."

Twenty-Nine

In the end it was nearly 2:30 A.M. by the time everything was completely still and we felt comfortable in going forward. The moon was nearly full, which was both good and bad—good, because it made it easier for us to see; bad, because it made it easier for others to see us.

Still, the wind was almost nonexistent and everything was calm. If we moved quickly and made no sound, there was no reason for us to be detected.

We started by taking turns in the cabin getting dressed in our new wet suits. Wet suits hadn't been absolutely necessary, but then again there was no telling how long we might have to remain underwater, so I thought it was better to be safe than sorry. Also, I liked the black color; it would help us to keep hidden. We pulled on our hoods, and then I put a little black grease paint on each of our cheeks and the backs of our hands. The less light-reflective surfaces we had, the better.

Once we were properly attired, we moved half of the scuba gear into the dinghy. Tom climbed in next, and I handed him the transmitter, which we had put inside a small black backpack along with

Tom's climbing gear. I also handed him the oars and a bundle of rope, and then I used the back ladder on the power cruiser to ease myself quietly into the water.

It wasn't cold at all, especially with the wet suit on. I grabbed my scuba mask, which I put on my face, and then Tom gave me one end of the rope. I took a few deep breaths before swimming down under the mooring buoy, feeling for the chain. It ran all the way to the sea bottom and was locked in place by a sand screw. I pulled myself down the chain and tied the rope at the bottom.

When I surfaced, Tom was leaning over the side of the dinghy, watching for me nervously.

"Wow, you can sure hold your breath a long time," he whispered.

I put my finger to my lips even as I struggled to catch my breath.

Using the ladder on the power cruiser, I climbed halfway up and then swung one foot over into the dinghy, sliding into it until I was sitting. Water ran from my suit in rivulets, and I motioned to Tom to hold up the backpack so it didn't get wet.

Grabbing an oar, I pushed us off from the power cruiser and silently rowed us toward the beach as Tom played out the rope that was now connected to the mooring. We had to go around a small point, but since we had checked it out earlier, I knew just how close we could come in without hitting anything. When the beach was in sight, I rowed as quickly as I could across to the far end and then moved the little dinghy to the shallows.

Tom handed me the rope and the backpack and then climbed out of the dinghy and into water that just came to his waist. I handed him the backpack, and holding it high so as not to get it wet, he gave me a significant look along with a thumbs-up before turning and walking to the shore. My heart stuck in my throat. I didn't know how I was going to get through this, knowing he was putting himself in such danger. As he walked I rowed straight back a short way to where the water was probably about eight feet deep.

Once Tom was on the sand, he set the backpack safely on some rocks and then grabbed one big loose stone and carried it to the edge of the water. Looking up at me where I sat in the dinghy, he placed the stone down on the sand. That would be his marker when it was time to swim out of there.

He turned then to his climbing gear and I knew I couldn't stay and watch. I had too much to do myself.

As quietly as possible, I climbed over the side of the dinghy and into the water, and then I took a deep breath and did a surface dive to the bottom. The depth was just about perfect, so I came back up, grabbed the dinghy, which had floated a few feet away, and pulled it back, checking my position with Tom's marker on the beach.

Reaching into the dinghy, I lifted the scuba tank and tried to heft it over the side and into the water. It was too heavy for such an odd angle, so I finally had to climb back into the dinghy, kneel down, and pick up the tank with both hands. I lowered it over the side into the water and listened for a thud as it hit the bottom. I slid my mask back down over my face and then grabbed the other mask, fins, two weight belts, and the end of the rope. I climbed back into the water.

Getting to the bottom was a lot easier with the weight belts in my hand. Once I reached the sand, I found the scuba tank. I set the mask on the sand next to it, placed one of the weight belts on top of the mask to keep it from floating away, and then did the same with the other weight belt and the flippers. Finally, I tied the rope that ran from the mooring chain to the handle of the tank.

When I felt everything was ready underwater, I surfaced to find the little dinghy about ten feet away.

I swam to it, climbed in, and then turned myself around so I could row back to the power cruiser. As I went, I looked toward the beach, heart pounding, hoping Tom had been able to get everything set and secure for his climb. I couldn't see him, which was good, I hoped. Despite the bright moon, the rock face he was climbing was mostly in shadows.

Back at the power cruiser, I tied off the dinghy in its spot at the back and then slid onto the diving platform. Sitting on the edge, I pulled on my flippers, strapped a weight belt around my waist, adjusted my mask, and then pulled the heavy scuba tank onto my shoulders. Once the straps were secure, I fit the respirator in my mouth, turned around, and flipped down backward into the black water.

I hated night diving. Without a light I might as well have been blind. Though I knew there weren't likely many predators around, I had no desire to swim smack into a big sea turtle or a stingray—not to mention a barracuda or a moray eel. For most of my swim, I stayed near the surface, using the flippers to propel me quickly back around the point and then across the water in front of the beach. I was glad I had been so active lately with the canoeing and the rock climbing; my muscles felt capable and strong. My emotions, however, were another matter. It felt as though a black vise were wrapped around my heart, squeezing out everything except fear.

When I reached my destination, I sighted the marker stone on the beach and then dove straight down to find the submerged scuba equipment. I was a little off, but a careful search in a spiral motion quickly led me to the gear. Everything was still there, the rope taut between the tank and the distant mooring line.

Once I had ascertained that all was still okay underwater, I surfaced, pulled off my mask, and searched the dark landscape for the sight of Tom. I couldn't see him anywhere. He'd had time to get to the top by now, and I scanned the treeline, trying to pick up movements in the shadows.

Suddenly a distant alarm sounded. Lights flashed on, illuminating the house. Tom appeared then, in silhouette, at the top edge of the cliff.

Go! I willed him to hurry with my thoughts, my heart racing at the sight of him starting back down the cliff wall. Though the alarm wasn't all that loud down where I was, I knew that everyone in the house had sprung into action. There were flashlights and spotlights and, soon, the sound of barking dogs.

Tom disappeared into the shadows, and I could only hold my breath and pray that he would make it down in one piece. When a bright light shone out toward my direction, I submerged, allowing myself to sink to the bottom without much movement. I didn't think I had been spotted, but I waited a minute before going back up.

I peeked over the waterline again, this time to see Tom running across the sand toward the water. One of the dogs was loose on the beach and heading straight for him.

Stifling a scream, I held up one waving arm until I thought Tom might have glimpsed it. Then I let myself sink back to the bottom and waited, looping his face mask over my wrist and holding his respirator in one hand and a weight belt for him in the other.

Shrrruunk!

I didn't know what the sound was, but if I had to guess, I'd say it was a bullet. It took all the strength I had not to dart back up to the top and see what was going on. Instead, suddenly, I felt a disturbance in the water around me, and I reached out, connecting with Tom's arm.

He had made it.

First I handed him the respirator. Good for him, he remembered to blow out hard to clear the valve before sucking deeply in.

Next was the weight belt, which I strapped around his waist as he put on the mask. Feeling around on the bottom, I grabbed his fins and the other belt and handed each item to him in turn. Finally, I lifted the scuba tank and hoisted it onto his back, over the now-empty backpack.

Shrrruunk!

They weren't kidding around now. That one had come too close for comfort. I felt certain the shooter could see our bubbles.

Tom patted me twice on the shoulder, his signal to me that he was ready. I grabbed the rope in front of him and then he fell in behind, both of us pulling ourselves along by the submerged rope. No more shots were fired that I could hear, but above us the water was illuminated from time to time with what looked like a spotlight.

We had gone a good distance when we felt ourselves mired in a bed of seaweed. *At least it's just seaweed and not coral,* I thought, keeping my grip on the rope and ignoring the slimy trails of grass across my face. Tom seemed to be faltering behind me, and I moved so that I was the one in the rear. With one hand on the rope and one hand on his weight belt, I pushed and swam until we both made our way through the thick bed of slime. Another 40 feet, and then the rope ended, right at the mooring chain.

Once there, we knew we were safely under our own boat. We hugged then, and though we couldn't talk or even see each other, there was a distinct communication between us.

Tom was okay. That was all that mattered.

I untied the rope from both ends and wound it up on my arm, knowing we needed to wait underwater until we were sure no one was scoping out the boats. If the people at the house had seen Tom swimming away, they had to know he had gone to a nearby vessel. There was at least an hour of air in each of our tanks, and I planned to take advantage of that, no matter how claustrophobic it felt to sit there on the bottom of the sea in the pitch-black dark.

Tom, however, had other plans. He tapped my shoulder and then tugged my arm upward. I had no choice but to follow.

We surfaced at the back of the boat, releasing our respirators. I wanted to ask what was going on, but in the distance I could hear an outboard motor, and I knew if we were to get inside, we needed to move quickly.

"Just drop your tank," I whispered.

He did as I directed, unsnapping the tank and the weight belts and letting them fall to the bottom of the sea. Everything else we set on the diving platform, and then we climbed up the ladder, grabbed the gear, and raced into the cabin.

Without stopping to think, I seized some towels, ran back out, and dried off the platform as best as I could. If they were to come here and look for signs of activity, a dripping wet diving platform smeared with mud would be an easy giveaway. Locking the ladder up and into place, I brought my towels back into the cabin, and then we sat low on the floor with our backs against the door.

From the outside, it looked as though we were sound asleep in the cabin, all lights off.

Sure enough, we soon heard the low hum of an engine, much closer than before. We didn't dare look out of the window, but we could see the search light bounce through onto an interior wall. Holding my breath, I prayed until the light passed.

I had a feeling they were pointing the light at each of the anchored boats in turn. When I caught the sound of voices, I crawled to our "stash" and dug out the directional microphone. Flipping it on I slid the headphones into place and listened as two men argued.

"...sleeping here! What are you doing?"

I couldn't catch every word even with the mike, but it sounded as though a man had been awakened on his boat by the probing search light. I heard a different man's voice explaining that a home had been broken into nearby, and whoever had done it had swum out from the beach.

"Well, there's nobody swimming out here. It's a quiet night. Nothing's going on."

I finally heard the sound of the little outboard motor revving up, and then the boat sped away. I put down the mike, crawled to Tom, and pulled off my hood.

"I think they're gone," I whispered, my breath short, my heart still pounding.

"Good," he replied, his voice sounding weak. "Can you get my hood too?"

I pulled it off for him, seeing his pale face against the fiberglass wall of the cabin.

"Are you okay?" I asked, putting a hand to his cheek.

"Not really," he replied softly. "Callie, I'm bleeding."

Thirty

"It wasn't so bad at first," he said. "But now it's really starting to hurt."

Tom held out his hands, palms up, and I gasped.

The skin looked as though it had been shredded off, in some places almost down to the tendons. Though he could flex all of his fingers, both hands were covered in blood. I looked down at the pile of towels I had used to dry the diving platform, and I realized that what I had thought was mud was actually dark red blood. The front of Tom's wet suit was also covered with the sticky, slimy substance.

"That's why I thought we ought to get out of the water," he added. "I didn't want to, you know, draw things to us."

I shuddered, thinking of all the creatures his bleeding might have attracted. Though sharks weren't usually a concern in the Caribbean, the scent of blood could reach far and wide, bringing all sorts of predators.

Holding back tears, I told him to wait there while I found the boat's first aid kit. We didn't dare turn on any lights inside, but he needed attending to, fast.

I fumbled around in the underseat storage cabinet and finally found the kit. I crawled back to him and zipped open the case, glad to see it was a complete one. While Tom explained what had happened, I pulled out the supplies we needed, setting them on the floor beside us.

It was Tom's rapid repel down the cliff that had caused the damage. He'd had to move so quickly that he hadn't had time to make the proper loops in the rope. Without gloves, sliding that fast on standard-issue hardware-store rope had cut into his hands, imbedding shards of the twine and tearing away flesh.

I pulled a big plastic bowl from a low cabinet and had Tom hold his hands over it while I rinsed the wounds with Betadyne. He winced, sucking in air between his teeth, but he didn't cry out.

Once his hands had been cleaned, I took a chance on using a small penlight. I shined it on each hand, inspecting the damage. It wasn't pretty.

Holding the penlight with my teeth, I had Tom rest his hands on a pile of towels in my lap while I used tweezers to pull rope fibers from the wounds. He remained silent throughout. When I had taken out all the fibers I could see, I put Telfa pads against the mangled flesh and then wrapped up both hands thoroughly in gauze.

"We need to get you to an emergency room," I said.

"There's no rush," he replied. "It's not like they can give me stitches or anything. The cuts are too wide."

"True."

"And as bad as it looks, they really are just flesh wounds. I don't think any tendons are involved. We can go in the morning, let them put me on antibiotics, give me a tetanus shot, whatever. Again, there's no hurry. You need to do your job right now anyway."

"At least keep your hands above your heart," I said. "That'll slow the bleeding."

I told him to lie down right there on the floor, and then I put a pillow under his head and propped life jackets under each hand.

"Callie, go ahead and do what you need to do," he said. "You're losing valuable time tending to me."

"Are you sure you're okay?" I asked, leaning over him.

"I'm fine," he said. "Give me a kiss and get to work."

I kissed him hard on the mouth, and then I crawled to the forward cabin and brought out the listening station. I dragged it back out to the lightest part of the room, where the moonlight spilled in through the window and cast a soft glow on the carpet. Then I opened the small valise-type case, flipped on the power, started the digital recorder, and put on the headphones. If this didn't work, everything he had just been through had been for naught.

It took a while to zero in on the frequency. Tom said he had put the transmitter deep inside a thornbush quite close to the house.

"I'm sure that's when I set off the alarm," he said now as I worked. "There wasn't any brush to hide it in right there on the cliff point. I had to move within the range of their motion detectors."

At last I caught the sound I was looking for. I set the dials, adjusted the volume, and listened. Though there weren't any voices, I could detect movement. It sounded as though someone was pacing along with the clickity-clack of dog nails against a tile floor. The sound was so clear, in fact, that I felt certain someone had already distributed the ant baits throughout the house.

Leaning back against the seat, I smiled at Tom and gave him a thumbs-up. Closing my eyes, I thought of all we had gone through to reach this point—from planting the tiny transmitters in the bug traps at the grocery store to putting into place the larger transmitter that was now sending those signals out to us. If this didn't work, nothing would.

I tried to get comfortable, finally lying down next to Tom and putting my head on his pillow, flipping out the earphone so that he could hear too. The set had a speaker, but I didn't want to be making any more noise than necessary. And though it would have been better to have my laptop open for taking notes, I didn't want the light to be seen through the window. We could always play back the recording later and take notes then.

Together we heard a woman's voice, but it sounded as though she was talking to one of the dogs, making soothing sounds and trying to calm it and herself down. It was the same voice we had heard earlier, asking for her security guard to do a bug sweep.

Now, she simply cooed and whispered to the dogs, telling them how much she loved them. Finally, we heard the sound of a door and then a man's voice.

"William!" she cried. "Who was it? Did you catch them?"

"Earl's still out on the skiff," the man said in his Caribbean accent. "But so far he hasn't found anyone."

More clicking made it sound as though all three dogs were now in the house.

"Tell me again what you saw outside."

"Nothing much. Just a man running across the beach. Bob almost caught him, but the guy dove under the water and then he never came back up again."

"How can that be possible?"

"Earl was shooting, so maybe the man got hit. Or, more likely, he was able to swim away. There are about six boats anchored around on the other side of the point. Earl went looking, but they were all closed up for the night. Personally, I think there must've been some other craft tied up somewhere out a ways that we didn't see, and he got away."

"What was he doing here? What did he want?"

"I don't know," William said, his voice fading as he walked out of range. "I'll look at the security camera loop and see if we got a picture of him."

We heard a door open and close, and I assumed William had gone to the security area. There was some rustling and other indistinguishable noise, but no one spoke again until the phone rang. The woman snapped it up instantly.

"Where have you been?" she demanded. "We had a breach here!"

She was silent for a moment, and I was reminded that there was a soft tap on her telephone. I wondered if the cops were listening to the conversation live, or if they only reviewed the taped replays—as they would with the tape we were making. I double-checked the recorder; it was rolling along smoothly.

"No, I'm not alone," the woman said. "William is here. Earl is out on the skiff."

There was a pause, and I wondered who was at the other end of that call. It wasn't Earl or William, so that meant it had to be someone else, on the outside.

"Fine, then fine. See you in the morning. But come first thing!"

She slammed down the phone.

There was more pacing, some exhaling, some finger snapping. Whatever this woman was up to, Tom's appearance there setting off the security system had completely thrown her for a loop.

We heard a door and then the voice of William again.

"Okay, the cameras caught somebody, but I'm not sure how much good it'll do us."

"What do you mean?"

"He's only in the frame for a second, kind of hovering near the laundry room. I don't know what he's doing, but as soon as the alarm goes off, he leaves."

"He leaves? Where does he go?"

"Out of the frame. We don't have cameras on the cliff. My best guess is that he climbed down."

"Climbed down the cliff?" she exclaimed. "That's impossible."

"Maybe so," William said, "but I don't know how else to explain it. If you watch the loop, somebody else appears down on the beach just a minute later. So I guess there were two of them."

When the woman spoke again, it was in a whisper.

"Are you sure they're both gone? What if one is still here?"

"We're locked down, Mrs. Streep. There is no one on this property except for you and me and these dogs."

"Oh, William, I just don't think I can take this anymore. Go man the cameras. I don't want you taking your eyes off those screens for anything."

"Yes, ma'am."

I whispered to Tom in the silence that followed.

"You got down that cliff so fast, they think there were two of you."

"Yeah, but what price speed?" he replied, waving his bandaged hands.

I was just glad he was back here safe with me. I had planned the whole thing so carefully, but I hadn't considered the possibility that they might use guns! Tom was fortunate to have gotten away from there with only the injuries to his hands. A shudder passed through me as I tried not to picture all that might have happened tonight.

After mostly silence the dogs started barking about 15 minutes later, and then we could hear the woman's voice again, this time speaking to a different man. From what we gathered, this was her husband, Earl, the one who had shot at the water and then taken out the skiff and nosed around our area here.

"...full circle, several times. There's nobody out there any-where."

"What do you think happened?" she asked.

"I found a piece of rope near the cliff. I think somebody climbed up, set off the alarm, and shot back down. I'm not sure if there were one or two, but whatever craft they used to escape in was mighty silent."

"How do you know they're not still out there, lurking in the dark?"

"We're fully activated," he said. "There are no breaches right now. I might go back out at first light, check out that little group of boats again. But I don't expect to find anything."

Tom and I looked at each other and then at my watch. By my calculations, first light would be in about two hours.

"Earl, sit down," the woman said, and my ears perked up. There was something in her hushed tones that seemed significant. "Do you think it could've been Merveaux?"

"Merveaux? Why would he come here like that? Sneaking around?"

"Perhaps he doesn't want to pay this time. Perhaps he wants simply to steal instead."

"Nonsense. He has always been easy enough to deal with before."

She was quiet for a moment.

"I told him to watch for midnight," she said finally, "but maybe he is in a hurry."

"It wasn't him. Making it up that cliff? No, Merveaux is too old. Too fat."

"What about Interpol? I know they've been sniffing around."

"They're listening in on the phones, Dianne, not climbing around the mountain."

The woman started crying.

"Then it must be Rushkin," she said. "Who else could it be?"

"Shhh," the man soothed. "Don't jump to conclusions."

"I knew he was coming. It's like dominoes—Eli knocked the first one over and now they are tumbling down the line, whether he meant for it to happen or not. We have to finish this, Earl. There's no longer any option. We've got the passports, we've got the code. It's time to make our move."

"Not without the money from Merveaux. How quickly can you gather everyone?"

"I put it in on Sunday, for Friday."

"Good. We will wait and meet, and then it'll be done. We'll be gone from here by Sunday."

She sniffled a bit, and then it sounded as if Earl began to comfort her in other ways. There was a lot of rustling and movement, and I had a feeling they had gone into another room—one that also had an ant trap with a bug in it. They sounded distant for a moment, and then close again. I thought I detected the sounds of kissing. I handed the headphones to Tom.

"You keep an ear on things, would you? I've got to go back down and bring up the scuba gear. If he comes around in daylight, he just might spot the tanks under the boat."

"No," Tom said, sitting up. "I'll get them. I'm not hurt that bad."

"Don't be silly. You're still bleeding."

Dreading the dark water, I opened the cabin door and looked around at the windless night. The moon was gone, and though the stars were bright, there was something eerily still in the air.

I crept to the diving platform and silently lowered the ladder. I was just climbing down when Tom came creeping across the deck as well.

"You'll need help with the tanks," he whispered.

"Wait here, at least," I said.

Then I climbed down the ladder into the water.

For some reason, my heart was pounding. Taking a deep breath, I did a surface dive straight to the bottom. I found the weight belts first, lying heavily on the sand. I brought them all up at once, but without flippers, it wasn't easy. Tom was waiting for me when I surfaced, both bandaged hands outstretched to take the belts from me.

I hesitated and then handed them off, caught my breath again, and went back down, feeling the blackness of the water overtake me. It wouldn't be hard to get disoriented down here. Concentrating mightily, I swam down to the spot where the belts had been and felt around until I touched a tank. I grabbed for the handle and got something slick instead.

It moved.

I screamed underwater, letting go and kicking off for the surface.

Though I wouldn't let myself make any noise when I surfaced, Tom could see the terror in my face.

"What is it?" he whispered sharply.

I clung to the ladder, heart racing, breath wheezing.

"It's nothing," I whispered. "I thought I had the tank, but I think it was a turtle. It swam away from me when I grabbed it!"

Shaking, I clung to the ladder. I knew I needed to admit what was really bothering me here: Knowing Tom had been bleeding in the water, I was terrified that whatever he might have attracted was still around.

"Callie, this is crazy," he said. "Come on up. We can do this in the morning."

"The water's too clear," I whispered. "It's too risky. I'm almost done."

Without waiting for his reply, I took a deep breath and went down to the bottom. Feeling around with my feet this time, I located one of the tanks and swam it up to the surface. He took it from me, and as quickly as I could I went back down for the next one. It was harder to find, but finally my big toe slammed into the side of it. I grabbed it, crouched on the sand, and pushed off with my legs as hard as I could go.

Relief filled me as I handed the tank to Tom and was able to climb quickly up the ladder.

Once I was back on the boat, I carried the tanks into the cabin and then went back and dried the platform again. He pulled up and locked the ladder, and then we both went into the cabin and closed the door. By the time we changed his wet dressings to dry ones, I was overwhelmed with exhaustion.

"It's almost sunrise," he said gently. "Why don't you try and get some sleep?"

I looked up at him, at his handsome face, and wanted nothing more than to wrap myself in his arms forever. I gave him a deep hug, pressing my face into his chest.

"But you're hurt," I whispered. "You need rest more than I do."

"I'm still wired up," he said. "I'll listen now and take a nap later."

I was too tired to argue. I dug through the first aid kit and fished out some aspirin, handing them to him with a bottle of water. Then I pulled some clean, dry clothes from my overnight bag, intending to change in the tiny head.

"Why don't I go out so you can change in here?" he suggested thoughtfully.

He stepped out the door and I peeled off my wet suit in the darkness, relishing the feel of a cool, dry T-shirt against my skin.

When I was decent, I opened the door and he came back in. When he was settled down at the listening station on the floor, I knelt and kissed him again, and then I climbed into the bunk in the forward cabin.

"I love you," I whispered to him across the cabin.

"I love you too," he said. "More than you know."

I was asleep only moments after my head hit the pillow.

Thirty-One

~

I awoke to the sound of voices, and I quickly swung my legs over the side of the bunk, nearly bumping my head on the low ceiling. Peeking into the main cabin, Tom was nowhere to be found, though the listening station was still set up on the floor, the headphones lying next to it.

Creeping across the cabin, I looked out of the porthole on the closed door to see Tom sitting at the stern with a fishing rod in his hands. He was talking to a man in a small outboard-powered rowboat, who was looking up at Tom suspiciously.

I pulled on some shorts under my long T-shirt, and then I draped some towels to hide the listening station and slid the whole thing under the table. Smoothing my hair with my hands, I opened the door and stepped out into the bright Caribbean morning.

"Hey, honey," I said softly to Tom, yawning and stretching. Both men turned to look at me in surprise.

"Hi, babe," Tom said sexily, reaching out a hand toward me. "How'd you sleep?"

"Mmm..." I purred, walking to him and wrapping my arms about his waist. He kept one arm around me, and I realized he was wearing fishing gloves to hide the bandages. What a clever guy.

"Who's your friend?" I asked.

"I'm sorry," Tom said to the man in the boat. "I didn't get your name."

"Uh, it's Earl," the fellow said, looking quite flustered.

"Morning, Earl," I said. "You out doing some fishing too?"

Casually, I took the rod from Tom so he wouldn't have to hold it in his injured hands.

"No, I uh..."

"Earl lives up on the mountain there," Tom said. "They had a break-in last night, and he's just out asking around if anybody saw anything."

I feigned shock.

"A break-in? Where?"

I let him describe the placement of the home, just around that bend and up on the point.

"Gosh, I wish we could help you," I said. "Is crime a significant problem on St. John?"

By now, Earl looked as though he was ready for a quick getaway. We obviously wouldn't be of any use to him; we were just a couple on vacation, enjoying the early morning sunshine.

He babbled for a minute about how St. John was usually safe, very safe, and then he excused himself and said he had to go.

"Would you like to join us for breakfast?" I asked. "I think we've got some eggs and bacon in there."

Tom poked me sharply on the back, out of sight from Earl.

"No, no thanks. I need to be getting back home."

"Good luck finding your thief," I called after him.

When he had puttered away, Tom sat on the bench, exhaling. As soon as I was certain the man was far away, I reeled in the hook and sat next to him.

"That was a close one," he said softly. "And you are so smooth it scares me."

I draped an arm over his warm shoulder.

"How are your hands?" I asked. "Those gloves were a stroke of genius."

"I had to think fast. I heard him over the transmitter, saying he was going down to take a look around the boats again. Luckily, this rental came with some fishing tackle. I was out here calmly fishing off the stern by the time he showed up. "

I put away the rod and reel, asking if the man had noticed that Tom had no bait on his hook.

"I kept it low in the water so he wouldn't see! That would be just what I needed—to catch a fish and have to reel it in with these hands."

We went into the cabin, which was already being warmed by the sun. I opened all of the windows to get a cross breeze going, and then I helped him take off the gloves.

His bandages were dark red, and I knew we needed to change the dressing and take another look. He seemed to be in even worse pain this morning. Looking at the deep, gaping wounds, I didn't blame him.

This time I put some antibiotic ointment on the pads first and then wrapped things a little bit tighter to help stop the bleeding. He needed to get to a hospital, and I was starting to wonder how we could manage to monitor the listening station and seek treatment for him at the same time. In the end, I realized, we might need Jodi's help after all.

"I think I'll lie down for a while," he said, brushing his lips against my cheek. "Thanks for the nursing care."

"What about getting you to an emergency room?"

"Later," he said tiredly. "We'll figure that out later."

He crawled into the same bunk I had occupied, pausing only to flip on the small fan that was mounted up under the bow. I was afraid it might be getting pretty hot up under there, but after staying awake all night, perhaps he was tired enough to sleep despite the heat.

Now that it was fully daylight and the interior of the cabin couldn't be seen by someone outside looking in, I was able to bring the listening station up onto the table. Next to that, I opened my laptop and booted it up.

After taking a moment to freshen up, I made myself a quick breakfast of dry toast and a banana. There wasn't much more than that to choose from.

Finally, I settled down at the table with my meal and a big glass of ice water. I put on the headphones, played with the volume, and then brought up the database for the case on my computer. Typing quickly, I updated all of my facts.

I saw that Tom had made some notes during the time I had been sleeping—roughly scrawled notations of activity and times: 5:25 A.M.—snoring; 6:10—bathroom; 6:30—wake-up conversation; 6:47—Earl leaves. Though his notes were barely legible, I appreciated the fact he had made the effort despite his injured hands.

I loaded in that info and then went back and plugged in other facts I hadn't taken the time to input in the last few days. I was just finishing when I heard some activity through the headphones. From what I could tell, Earl was back from his early morning snooping, and Dianne was making him some breakfast.

Quickly, I opened a Word file. I would have to transcribe the tape anyway, so I decided to type as they were talking.

To the sounds of something sizzling on their stove, I listened as Earl explained to her the fruitlessness of his efforts.

"Whoever came here is long gone," Earl said. I typed:

> E—Whoever came here is long gone.

The sizzle died down, and then the clink of plates and scrape of chairs told me they were at the table. As they spoke, I typed some more:

> D—I'll start packing today. I suppose we take with us only what we can fit on an igma.

I strained to understand what she had said. An *igma?* What was that? Before I could think about it further, I heard the sound of a distant car door slam. The dogs started barking. Dianne yelled at the dogs, who sounded as though they were leaping at the door.

D—Alice! Eve! Shut up!

I heard some rustling then the sound of a door opening.

D—It's about time you got here! Where have you been? Don't you even care that we had a breach?

"You sweep?" a man asked, his voice barely above a whisper. My heart froze in my throat as I typed:

MAN—You sweep?

D—No, the system didn't show anything.

E—He's right, Dianne. We shoulda done a manual anyway, first thing.

There were no words spoken after that. I could hear plenty of sounds but no voices. I knew they were keeping quiet as they got out the tools that would detect if there were any bugs in their home. We were truly busted this time. Our tiny transmitters were weak, but they weren't *that* weak.

I had done bug sweeps before, and I knew that it could take them hours to clear the whole house. But I could imagine the scene taking place inside. Once they found the first bug, they would figure out that the rest of the ant traps also contained bugs. It wouldn't take long before we were out of business.

After a little while I heard beeping and then rustling and then a sharp intake of breath. One bug had been discovered, I felt sure. So much for having an ear inside the house. Within 30 minutes it sounded as if all eight had been located. I wasn't sure how they were going to dispose of them, but from a sudden glump followed by white noise, my guess was that they had submersed them all in water.

And that was that.

I switched the sound to the speaker and turned it low, just in case. For now, I would rewind the tape and transpose everything we had been able to get the night before. I would also make a copy of the tape for us to keep before giving the original to the cops.

Typing out all of the conversation from the night before didn't make things any clearer for me. Even when I was finished and was able to reread it word-for-word, there were certain phrases and sentences I didn't understand.

I printed out a copy of the transcript and reviewed it one last time, focusing on the main conversation between Dianne and Earl:

D—Earl, sit down. Do you think it could've been Merveaux?

E—Merveaux? Why would he come here like that? Sneaking around?

D—Perhaps he doesn't want to pay this time. Perhaps he wants simply to steal instead.

E—Nonsense. He has always been easy enough to deal with before.

D—I told him to watch for midnight, but maybe he's in a hurry.

E—It wasn't him. Making it up that cliff? No, he is too old. Too fat.

D—What about Interpol? I know they've been sniffing around.

E—They're listening in on the phones, Dianne, not climbing around the mountain.

[S—woman crying]

D—Then it must be Rushkin. Who else could it be?

E—Shhh. Don't jump to conclusions.

D—I knew he was coming. It's like dominoes—Eli knocked the first one over and now they are tumbling down the line, whether he meant for it to happen or not. We have to finish this, Earl. There's no longer any option. We've got the passports, we've got the code. It's time to make our move.

E—Not without the money from Merveaux. How quickly can you gather everyone?

D—I put it in on Sunday, for Friday.

E—Good. We will wait and meet, and then it'll be done. We'll be gone from here by Sunday.

In a way, I decided as I sat back in my seat and gazed out of the window at the gorgeous Caribbean blue water, it might have been a blessing that Tom had been spotted last night. At least it stirred things up a bit, leading them into conversations they might not otherwise have had.

Now the police would have a lead on a name, Merveaux, and the fact that Dianne shared some connection with Eli had been confirmed. But who was Rushkin? Was that the person Dianne had warned Eli about? Most importantly, what did she mean now when she said "we have to finish this"?

Finish *what*? Finish taking Eli's life?

I reread the lines one more time, trying to open my mind beyond immediate assumptions. I kept going back to her statement: "It's like dominoes—Eli knocked the first one over and now they are tumbling down the line, whether he meant for it to happen or not."

I tried to think of what Eli had done here that could have started things tumbling down like dominoes. He had recognized a woman who was supposed to be dead. He had asked questions. He had taken photographs.

I stood up, my heart pounding.

Nadine Peters had been "killed" back in the '60s. The NSA must have faked her death and then set her up elsewhere, almost like witness protection. Nadine Peters had been secretly resurrected as Dianne Streep. New name, slightly new face, new identity.

But Nadine was a traitor to the country, selling secrets to the Russians! What had she done to deserve protection from the NSA?

I stood and began pacing, feeling pieces of the puzzle popping into place.

Protection. For being a witness.

When Nadine was caught, she must have turned against the very people who were buying her secrets. She must have given up the names of those who had infiltrated the NSA and were paying good money in exchange for cold, hard facts. She must have been a traitor to all of the other traitors—a triple agent! In exchange, the NSA gave her a new start and no prosecution for her own crimes.

I realized suddenly that the security in place in Nadine's current home probably had as much to do with her art business as it had to do with the threat on her life as an informant against the Russians for the NSA.

Breathless, I exited the stuffy cabin and walked out onto the deck, the bright sun beaming in my face.

That was it! I just knew it. Nadine had been hiding away all of these years in a new place under an assumed name, working as an art dealer. When Eli spotted her and started asking questions, he put her very life in danger, for no doubt the people she had ratted out all those years ago were surely not the forgiving kind—especially if her testimony had landed them in prison or, worse, had some of their compatriots killed. Now she was afraid for her life, afraid this Rushkin person or one of his agents was on his way here to kill her. For all we knew, he already was here.

I sat on the diving platform and dangled my feet into the clear water.

Certainly, the woman was involved in things she shouldn't have been. Old habits died hard, and it looked as though Nadine had found a way to work both sides of the system again, this time selling legitimate art for decent money—and illegal art for even better pay. It probably wasn't even hard for her to act like a part of the legal establishment, all the while conducting her other, secret business. After all, she'd had plenty of practice.

But I had a hunch that the hand that pulled the trigger on Eli wasn't hers, nor did it have anything to do with her current, illegal dealings. If I had to make a guess, I would say it was this Rushkin, the very person that Nadine had gone to Florida to warn Eli about. I closed my eyes, thankful that Tom had put round-the-clock security on Eli. I still didn't understand why he would be a target, but at least he was safe now.

I felt a whoosh under my feet and looked down to see a huge, gorgeous stingray swimming past. It was the color of the sand, graceful and wide.

I thought of what I knew about stingrays. They were harmless, mostly, content to camouflage themselves against the sea floor and dart quickly away when disturbed.

The only time they were a danger and would sting was when they felt trapped. That's why, for a swimmer, stepping on a stingray was a big mistake. The pressure of the swimmer's foot would trap the ray against the sand, and then the creature's only recourse was to flip up its tail and sting the one who had trapped it.

Dianne was feeling trapped now.

The question was, who would she sting in order to get free?

Thirty-Two

Tom awoke about an hour later, so overheated from being up in the forward cabin that he wanted to go for a quick swim.

"I won't put my hands in," he said. "I just need to cool off."

It sounded like a good idea to me, because the people we'd had under surveillance had now likely turned the tables and were watching us. I thought two people kicking around in the water and having fun made us look fairly innocent. To that end I dug around in the storage compartment and found a few floats.

"Put on your gloves," I said, helping to pull them on each finger. "You don't want the bandages to show."

It only took me a few minutes to bring him up to date on all that had happened.

"That's too bad," he said, wincing at the pain. "At least we got some good stuff on tape before they figured it out."

"I made a transcript," I said. "Soon as you dry off, you can take a look."

With my help, he used one of the floats to lower himself down into the water.

"Ahhh!" he said, leaning his head back to get as much of his body in the water as possible. "That's enough to make a person feel almost human again."

Unable to resist, I changed into my bathing suit and joined him, the cool water a wonderful relief from the hot sun. While Tom rested his arms on the float and kicked around that way, I put on my face mask and did a little underwater swimming. There were all sorts of fish down there, small but colorful, and it almost felt as though I were splashing around in an aquarium. Someday Tom and I would have to come back here when we weren't working an investigation and just take in the beauty of the place.

After a short 15-minute swim, we climbed back aboard the boat—no easy feat for poor Tom, whose hands were hurting pretty badly. We needed to relocate ourselves, but the timing was tricky. On the one hand, we didn't want to race out of there right away at the risk of looking suspicious. On the other hand, we didn't need to hang around any longer now that our bugs had been detected and disarmed. In the end we decided to give it another 15 minutes and then pull up anchor and leave.

In the meantime we sat in the cabin together and Tom read through the transcript. I told him my theory about Nadine being in witness protection, and he said the thought had already crossed his mind.

"I don't believe there was an official 'witness protection program' back in the early sixties," he said, "but I'm sure there were ways that they did that sort of thing even then. A new identity, a little money to get started, and then they probably just expunged her record and let her be."

"You think the whole shoot-out was staged?"

"Almost. We know for a fact that Eli shot her in the leg. But if the NSA staged Nadine's death, then the shot she got from Eli was probably the only real bullet she took that day. Otherwise, I'd bet it was blanks and blood packets. No doubt she wore a bulletproof vest too, just in case."

"What about the autopsy photos?"

"They could've been faked easily enough."

"I wish we could talk to Eli and hear his version of what really happened."

"We'll have to call Stella and see how he's doing. You should call your dad too, and find out where the cops in Cocoa Beach stand on things."

"Soon as we get to a landline," I said. "I don't want to risk using a cell phone."

"Good thinking."

At his request I brought him a bottle of water and more aspirin and then sat across from him and leaned forward, my elbows on my knees.

"The question here," I said, looking him in the eyes, "is if you can take this information to the NSA and find out who it was she betrayed in return for her freedom. If you can learn that, we'll probably have the identity of the person who shot Eli."

"Yeah," he said. "I was thinking that."

"Do you have the kind of connections that would afford you that information?" I asked. In the past Tom's connections had nearly moved mountains.

He looked away.

"I think I can find out what we need to know," he said finally. "But I have to do it in person. The more info I can bring along about Nadine, the better."

I took the transcript from him and scanned through it.

"She's planning something big," I said. "Soon."

"I know."

I read out loud from the transcript.

"'We have to finish this...We've got the passports, we've got the code. It's time to make our move.'"

"I think she's running scared," he said. "She knows Eli spotted her and started asking questions, possibly alerting the wrong people to the fact she's still alive. I think she wants to disappear again, this time for good."

"My guess is that she's making an art sale to this Merveaux guy—a sale lucrative enough to risk sticking around for a few more days. Then they're out of here."

"What do you think she means when she says *'I already put it in on Sunday, for Friday'*?"

"I have no idea."

"What about here, *'I told him to watch for midnight.'* Maybe that's when they plan to make their move. At midnight Friday? Midnight Sunday?"

Wanting to pace, I stood and washed the few dishes that were in the little sink instead.

"*'I told him to watch for midnight,'*" I repeated. "Midnight. What is it about that word that sounds familiar?"

We were silent for a moment.

"Her code," Tom said finally.

We both looked at each other, our eyes wide.

"Her code!" I repeated back to him. "I'll get the file."

I dashed over to my bags and pulled out the file Eli had put together about Nadine. In the documents he had obtained through the Freedom of Information Act, there was a mention of Nadine having sent coded messages that included the word "midnight."

"Here it is," I said, flipping through the papers and then reading the classified ad Nadine had placed in the *Washington Post* several decades ago. "'Midnight blue couch for sale. Call 721-0800. Ask for Piper Firve.'"

"The word 'midnight' is what's called a flag," Tom explained. "Her cohorts could scan the classifieds every Sunday, looking for ads that started with the word 'midnight.' If they found one, they just decoded that same format of phone number and name, and then they had the details they needed for a face-to-face meeting."

I grabbed the transcript from last night and read it again.

"She says, *'I told him to watch for midnight.'* Meaning, 'I told him to watch for an ad to appear in the paper that started with the word 'midnight'?"

"Yes," Tom replied. "Exactly. That would explain *'I already put it in on Sunday, for Friday.'* She put the ad in last Sunday's paper, arranging a meeting with this Merveaux guy for Friday. Tomorrow. She put it in Sunday, for Friday."

We looked at each other.

"If we can find that ad," I said, "we can find that meeting."

"Let's go," he replied.

We had a lot to do, I realized, as he reeled in the anchor and I secured the dinghy. Once we were underway, I went into the cabin, where it was quieter, to call Jodi. I dialed the house and there was no answer, so I tried her cell phone and she picked up right away. She was working at the dig site.

"We missed you at the restaurant last night," she said. "If you want to go out with us tonight, we'll be at the Full Moon Buffet at Miss Lucy's."

"The Full Moon Buffet?"

"Yeah. They only do it when the moon is full. Real Caribbean food and a band and dancing and everything. It's so fun."

"I wish we had time. Listen, I need to know where to find two things," I said to her. "A good doctor and a good newsstand."

"A doctor?" she asked. "Are you sick?"

"Tom cut his hand," I replied. "We just don't want it to get infected."

She said there were probably doctors on St. John, but the only doctor in the islands she had ever used was over in St. Thomas.

"I got food poisoning once," she said. "He was really nice."

"Isn't there a doctor on this island?"

She told me to hold on, and I could hear her asking someone else.

"Sandy says there's a clinic right in Cruz Bay," she said after a moment. "It might take a few hours to work him in, but they'll see him eventually."

"How about a newsstand?"

She had no answer for that one except, again, to go to St. Thomas.

"That's the only problem with St. John," she said. "Sometimes it's hard to find the things you need. I suppose you could try some of the resorts here. They have gift shops, and I bet they sell newspapers. The campgrounds too."

She listed a few of the places she could think of off the top of her head, describing their locations.

"You won't have much to choose from at any of them, though," she said. "Besides a few local papers, there's maybe the *New York Times* or the *Miami Herald.*"

I thanked her for her help and then I pulled out one of the charts of the island and found each of the places she had mentioned. Showing the chart to Tom, he said we were nearing the campground at Maho Bay.

"We'll pull in there and run to the gift shop," he said.

While he turned in toward the bay, I called Abraham at the St. John Police Department. The woman who answered the phone said it was his day off, so I dug out the card he had given me and tried the cell phone number he had scribbled on the back.

"Hallo?" Abraham said in his Caribbean accent.

"Hi, Abraham. It's Callie Webber."

"Callie! How are you today?"

"I'm on a cell phone," I said, hoping he was savvy enough to understand that that meant I couldn't really talk, "but I have something for you. Could you be free in about an hour?"

"For you, you bet," he replied, giving me instructions to a small cove near Cruz Bay. I told him we could be there at 1:30.

Once we had hung up, I told Tom the plan and then went into the cabin to make a copy of the surveillance tape. I used Tom's digital voice recorder, the only thing we had handy. It was just a small device that hung on his key chain, but the storage capacity was sufficient even if the sound quality wasn't great. I was able to record the pertinent parts from the surveillance tape onto the device, listening back to make sure everything had recorded correctly. I was just finishing as I felt the boat slow down.

I tucked the digital recorder away and then stepped out of the cabin to see us pulling into a beautiful cove, filled from one end to the other with boats of all shapes and sizes.

"Looks like a popular place," Tom said, easing the boat to a stop in the shallow water.

"I can wade in," I told him, digging in my wallet for a few dollars. "No biggy."

"Grab us something to eat while you're there, would you? I'm starving."

"Sure. There are some chips in Jodi's tote bag, if you want."

I gave him a peck on the cheek, unhooked the ladder, and quickly climbed down. The water was cold but felt good, and I easily made my way to the beach, which was clustered with noisy children.

"Excuse me, can you tell me where I might find the gift shop?" I asked a woman on a nearby towel.

"Take those steps," she said, pointing. "Aaaaallll the way to the top."

I did as she said, quickly understanding what she meant. The Maho Bay Campground was perched on the side of a huge hill, and from what I could tell the climb to the top was going to be the equivalent of about five or six flights of stairs.

As I ran up, I took in the sight of this amazing place, a heavily wooded series of screened-in cabins, all strung together by wooden steps that zigzagged up the hill. There seemed to be a lot of families here, and I had to dodge clusters of kids running down the stairs every few minutes.

I was slightly winded by the time I arrived at the top, and I caught my breath as I followed the wooden arrows to the gift shop. My heart quickened as I stepped inside to see a pile of newspapers near the front of the store.

I took what they had—the Sunday edition of the *Virgin Islands Daily News* and several smaller free papers. We weren't sure what newspaper Dianne was using to plant her coded message, but I thought I ought to cover all of the bases. While I was there, I also looked for food, but there weren't many healthful choices. I finally grabbed a pack of peanuts, some ripe bananas, and two bottles of Gatorade. I asked the man behind the counter if they had any other newspapers, and he said they got the *New York Times* on Sundays, but it was usually sold out by Wednesday.

Going doing the hill was easier than coming up, though I kept my hand on the rail to keep from getting dizzy as I went. Once I reached the beach, I held the bag over my head and made my way to the boat. Tom took it from me as I climbed aboard.

"I was looking at the chart," he said, starting up the engine. "Caneel Bay Resort isn't too far from here."

"Go for it," I said, drying off with a towel and then pulling on Jodi's batik cover-up over my suit. It fit fine, though it was a bit more colorful than I would have picked for myself.

Tom pulled out of the bay and, true to his word, we reached the resort in just a short while. This time he was allowed to pull right up to the dock to drop me off. I left him there and ran inside to find the gift shop.

There was a definite difference in the clientele here, as everything was quiet and tasteful and simply screamed "old money." The newspaper selection was different as well. I grabbed the Sunday *New York Times*, the *Wall Street Journal*, and the *St. John Times*. I was disappointed not to find the *Washington Post*, which was the paper Nadine had used to send messages back in the '60s, but the clerk said that I wasn't likely to find it anywhere on the island, that most people were happy with just the local papers and the ones from New York. On my way back to the boat, I had to concentrate on the job at hand and not waste any time lingering on the gracious and stately grounds.

Back on the boat, I took the entire stack and stashed them in the underseat storage. Then I took one of the bananas and a handful of peanuts and sat down to eat.

We pulled into the cove where we were to meet Abraham about five minutes late. We looked for a dock but didn't see one. Instead, a man waved to us from the water. To my surprise, I realized it was Abraham, out swimming.

Tom stopped the boat and I grabbed the mooring line like an expert. Abraham called something to a group of kids on the beach, and then he waded out to meet us.

"Greetings, friends!" he cried as I lowered the ladder for him. "How are you on this sunny day?"

He came aboard and shook my hand, but Tom simply gave him a smile and a wave. I handed Abraham a towel, which he took from me gratefully.

"We're great," I said. "Are we interrupting you from your family?"

"That's okay. It's my day off. We're just limin'."

"Limin'?"

"Relaxing. Hanging around." He cupped his hands around his mouth and yelled, "Samuel, don't put sand in your sister's hair!"

"Are those your kids?" I asked, smiling at the sight of three small children who were playing at the waterline.

"Yes, and that is my beautiful wife," he said proudly, pointing at a great big woman in a blue flowered wrap. She was perched on a stool in the shade, braiding the hair of a teenager who sat on a lower chair in front of her. "She charge three dollars a braid if you want to get your hair done."

"That's okay," I replied. "Thanks anyway."

"So what you got for me?"

"A surveillance tape," I said, leading him into the cabin. "A good one."

"Really?"

I glanced at Tom, but he was busy with the navigation charts. I knew he was respecting Abraham's preference to deal only with me.

"This is probably all we'll be able to do," I said to Abraham as we stepped inside. "But then again, this might be all you need."

We sat at the table and I pressed "Play."

"*William!*" Dianne's voice said on the recording. "*Who was it? Did you catch them?*"

"*Earl's still out on the skiff,*" the man replied. "*But so far he hasn't found anyone.*"

Abraham listened intently as I let the tape roll, playing everything including Dianne and Earl's conversation about Merveaux and Rushkin. I didn't press the stop button until the voice of Earl said, "*We'll be gone from here by Sunday.*"

"There's a little more from the next morning," I said. "But nothing as important as that."

"Wow," Abraham said, leaning back against the seat. "This changes everything."

"It does," I agreed.

"Interpol better get on the stick. I think they are about to lose their primary suspect."

I fast-forwarded the tape, looking for the conversation Earl and Dianne had had over breakfast.

"Abraham, what's an 'igma'?" I asked as I fooled with the buttons.

"A what?"

"An igma," I said. "You'll see."

The counter showed my mark, so I switched the button to "Play."

"*I'll start packing today,*" Dianne's voice said. "*I suppose we take with us only what we can fit on an igma.*"

I shut off the tape and looked at Abraham's surprised face.

He burst out laughing.

"What's so funny?" I asked.

Abraham laughed so hard that even Tom came to the doorway to see what was going on. Finally the sergeant got himself under control, wiping the tears of laughter from his eyes.

"I'm sorry," he said. "I don't mean to laugh."

"What is it?" I asked.

"It's not an *igma*," he said, laughing again. "It's *Enigma.* Her boat. They will take with them only what they can fit on *Enigma.*"

Thirty-Three

Poor Abraham's family day at the beach was cut short. After a quick phone call to the station and then a brief conversation with his wife, he came back on our boat and asked us to give him a lift into Cruz Bay. He wasn't sure if the department had the necessary equipment to play a reel-to-reel tape, so as we drew near the dock, I told him to take the listening station as well.

"As far as we know," I said, thinking of the dog bone, "there's still one bug left there, outside, but I don't think you'll pick anything up from it."

"I should ask you if this surveillance ended up helping with your investigation too," Abraham said as he tossed the bumper over the side.

"More than you could imagine," I replied. "I'll keep you posted if we turn up anything else."

"You do that," he said, climbing out of the boat. There was a uniformed officer waiting at the other end of the dock, waiting to drive him home for a change of clothes and then straight to the station.

"Thanks again," he called to us as he hurried away. I felt a surge of satisfaction that Tom and I had done a good job with our assignment for him—even if we were only paid one dollar.

We backed away from the dock and then kept our speed down as we worked our way along the shore to the harbor, where we could dock the boat while Tom went to the doctor's office.

He thought it would be easier to walk than drive, so I kissed him goodbye then watched as he headed off toward town with his hands gingerly in his pockets. I would stay put on the boat and go through the newspapers, and maybe by the time he was back I would have discovered the when and where of the next day's clandestine meeting.

I wasn't sure how far and wide Dianne's coded message had to travel, but I had a feeling her new media for that was probably not the *Washington Post,* as it had been in the '60s, but was instead now either the *Miami Herald* or—more likely—the *New York Times.* That was the only newspaper offered for sale in all the shops I had gone to, and my conversation with the sales clerk told me that it was probably the easiest paper to find throughout the islands.

I flipped to the classifieds, which were extensive. My best bet was merchandise because that's how the messages had been coded before. I scanned down listings for dinette sets and purebred puppies, looking for the word "midnight."

My eyes skipped over it at first.

Suddenly, I blinked and scanned back up.

There it was!

> Midnight Cowboy DVD for sale. Call 417-0800. Ask for
> Thae Barthos.

Heart pounding, I crossed out the third letter in each word. The meeting would be tomorrow at 8:00 A.M. at a place called "The Baths."

The Baths.

Something about that sounded familiar. I grabbed the Virgin Islands guidebooks I had collected and flipped through them until I found a photo of a man and a woman floating in a giant stone cave.

The caption of the photo said, "Visit the Baths of Virgin Gorda, a Once-in-a-Lifetime Experience."

According to the map, Virgin Gorda was in the British Virgin Islands, which weren't too far away. The Baths seemed to be some sort of natural landmark there. Heart pounding, I decided to put everything away and call Tom. The sooner he was finished at the doctor's office, the sooner we could pursue this lead—though whether we should take the info to the NSA or go straight to Abraham, I wasn't sure. I also needed to call my father, to see what he had learned from the police in Cocoa Beach, and Stella, to see how Eli was faring.

I put everything away inside the cabin, locked up, and pulled on socks and sneakers, not knowing how far I might have to walk to find a public phone that wasn't too public.

The woman in the little boat rental office pointed me toward the other end of the dock, so I set off in search of a phone, admiring some of the beautiful boats on my way. This harbor was huge, and the slips grew progressively bigger as I went. Near the end were the biggest boats—gorgeous, expensive yachts.

The phone was next to a set of unmanned gas pumps, and it was in an actual booth with a seat. I sat inside but left the door open for the breeze. Using a phone card, I first called Stella's house in Florida, but, as I expected, there was no answer. I left a message, telling her the investigation was progressing and Eli was still in our prayers.

I tried the hospital next and asked for the ICU nurses' station. They couldn't give me any information over the phone except to say that his condition was listed as "stable." That was definitely an improvement over "critical," and I wondered if he was starting to show signs of consciousness. I had made Stella promise to call me if Eli came out of the coma, so I felt certain that he hadn't.

My dad was the next call, and I was able to reach him easily for a change. He said he had spoken to Stella just last night, and Eli was still intubated but his vital signs were strong. If he remained stable for the next 24 hours, they would be moving him out of ICU and into a regular room with special nursing care. He was starting to show some mild reflex responses, which meant he might be coming out of the coma.

"I've talked to the OIC a few times," my dad said, referring to the officer in charge, "but we don't really seem to be getting anywhere."

"Did they send you the ballistics?" I asked.

"Yeah. I got the whole crime report. Single shot from about half a block away, motel room, third floor. A Bushmaster semiautomatic."

"They know the make and model?"

"Yeah. The gun was recovered right there in the room. No prints, of course."

"A rifle with that kind of range?" I asked. "That had to cost close to two thousand dollars. They just left it there?"

"Sitting on the bed, plain as day. Police traced it to a gun shop in Miami, but the store there shows no record of the sale."

"Stolen, in other words?"

"Yep. I talked to the manager of the gun shop myself. That particular rifle was a demo they had used at a gun show two days before the shooting. So it hadn't been missing for long."

"How about the ID on the person renting the hotel room?"

My dad snorted.

"Paid in cash. Checked in under the name 'A. Nonimous.'"

"Some kind of joker."

"You got it."

The phone booth was becoming hot, so I stood and tried to step outside, but the metal cord wouldn't quite let me reach.

"Who do the police there suspect?" I asked.

"They seem to be focusing on one of Stella's children, but they won't say which one. I think it's that older boy. I talked to him on the phone yesterday, and it sounds like he's moved in and taken over. Couldn't be more solicitous—and couldn't sound more phony."

From the corner of my eye, I saw a group of people walking in my direction. I stepped back into the booth and closed my eyes, trying to concentrate.

"It's not one of Stella's kids," I said. "The cops there don't have all the facts. They don't understand that this case encompasses everything from the NSA to Interpol. It's not a simple situation."

My dad let out a low whistle.

"Please tell me you're being careful," he said.

I glanced toward the trio of boaters, surprised to see Jodi among them. She was climbing aboard a nearby boat, and with her was Fawn and Zach. I stood and tried to give them a wave, but they didn't see me.

"I need to go, Dad," I said. "Thanks for looking into things. I'll keep you posted."

"Posted?" he cried. "You haven't told me anything!"

"I know," I said. "But it's complicated, and there's still so much we don't understand."

"Okay, honey. Listen, your mom told me about you and your boss."

My breath caught. What a time to bring that up! I sat back down on the little bench and watched Jodi and her friends prepare their vessel for departure.

"How do you feel about that?" I asked.

"Well, Callie, if you think you're ready, then I say go for it. Just don't jump in too quickly."

"Too quickly? I've known Tom for several years, Dad."

"You've known him that long as a boss. Maybe a little less than that as a friend. How long have you known him as...as a love interest?"

I hesitated.

"Not very long," I admitted.

"Well, there you go. I don't care how well you know someone as a friend, once romance enters the picture, you practically have to start back at square one. You've got a lot to learn about each other. I just want to see you take your time."

"Okay, Dad," I replied, grateful for my father and my mother and how very much they cared for me.

By the time we hung up the phone, the boat holding Jodi was just pulling away from the dock. I raised my hand to give them a wave and then put it back down just as fast when I saw the name painted on the stern of their boat.

Enigma.

Thirty-Four

I ran.

By the time I reached our boat, the *Enigma* was just pulling out of the marina and into open water. I had a decision to make. I could try and follow, or I could stand there and watch them go. At least they hadn't spotted me.

Quickly, I ran to the cockpit of our boat, put the key in the ignition, and started the engine. I was about to put the boat into reverse when I realized I hadn't even untied it yet!

Hands shaking, I dashed forward and untied the ropes and brought in the bumpers, and then I came back to the cockpit, put my hand on the throttle, and gently tried to ease it backward.

Nothing happened. The throttle was stuck straight up. I tried pushing it more forcefully, and then I realized there was a button on the side I needed to press with my thumb first. Once I did that, the throttle popped back too easily and I jerked hard out of the slip.

Fortunately there was no one behind me, and I turned the wheel to keep from backing straight up. Suddenly, I had a memory of Bryan in the days before he died, trying to teach me to drive our little motorboat.

If you can drive a car, you can drive a boat, he had said to me then.

"All right, Bryan," I said out loud to him now. "I'm trusting you on this one."

Of course, I hadn't ever been instructed on a craft so huge—nor on a sea so wide! I eased the throttle forward and chugged down the row, getting a feel for the steering. I decided I would take this as far as the open water, and then if I didn't feel comfortable with it, I could just turn back around.

When I reached the exit, I scanned the horizon for sight of the *Enigma.* There were plenty of boats out there, but there hadn't been anything particularly notable about the craft I had glimpsed in the short time I had seen it—other than the name. Was it possible it was just coincidence, that there was more than one boat here called *Enigma?* Somehow, I didn't think so. Heart pounding, I inched forward there in the water, trying to figure out which way to turn. Finally, I pulled out my cell phone and dialed Jodi's number.

"Hello?" she yelled.

"Jodi?"

"Hold on!"

The noise on her end diminished as I guessed she went inside. Things were still fairly loud at my end, however, and I had to strain to hear her.

"This is Jodi," she said in a more normal voice. "Who is this?"

"It's Callie."

"Callie! Hey. What's up?"

"Nothing much," I replied. "Just thought I'd check in. Whatcha doing?"

If it seemed odd for me to call Jodi simply to chat, she didn't seem to notice.

"Not much. Fawn and I are going over to St. Thomas," she said. "We have some errands to run."

"Oh. Are you on the ferry?"

I wanted very much for her not to lie to me.

"No, Zach is taking us in his boat."

"His boat?"

"Well, the boat he captains for. It's really gorgeous."

I swallowed hard. *Zach was the captain of the boat that belonged to Dianne?*

"I thought you said Zach was a masseuse."

"He is. He's sort of a 'jack of all trades, master of one.' At least that's his joke."

I tried to think of a way to end the conversation quickly. Jodi was going to St. Thomas with Zach on the boat that belonged to Dianne Streep. How all of that fit into the puzzle, I hadn't a clue.

"Okay, well I've got to run," I said. "Just thought I'd say hi."

"Don't forget Miss Lucy's tonight, if you want. We're all going to meet there around eight."

Suddenly, that didn't sound like such a bad idea. Considering what I had learned, it seemed imperative that we get to know Zach just a little bit better.

"We'll try to make it," I told her, asking for directions, and then we said our goodbyes.

I pushed the throttle all the way forward and checked my compass and my watch. I would go exactly ten minutes toward St. Thomas. If I hadn't caught up with them by then, I would turn around and come back.

Though the engines were loud, I needed to call Tom. I couldn't even imagine what might happen if he came back to the slip and saw that the boat and I were both gone.

When I reached him, he said he was sitting in the waiting room and he had a feeling he might be there for a long time. He was in a lot of pain, he told me, otherwise he would give up and leave.

"You stay there as long as it takes. You really don't want it to get infected."

"What's all that noise?"

"I had to take the boat out for a bit. Long story. I'll tell you later."

"Okay, Callie," he replied. "I guess you know what you're doing."

I stifled a laugh at the absurdity of it, because no, I didn't know what I was doing at all! Still, I was willing to give it a try.

Steering with one hand, I reached into the glove compartment to dig out the little binoculars we had put there. Holding them over my eyes, I tried to focus on a boat that was speeding across the waves up ahead. It seemed smaller than the *Enigma,* and when I spotted a black family on board, I realized that it wasn't it. Adjusting my direction a bit to the left, I pressed onward, eager to get close enough to take a look at the next boat.

That one was it, I just had a feeling. As I peered through the binoculars, I could see the two women stretched out on the deck in their bikinis. Zach was at the wheel, his body muscular and tan in khaki shorts.

I cut back on my speed, glad that they weren't going all that fast. That made it easier for me to follow them. I found a speed that kept me just far enough back so they wouldn't be able to recognize me. I would simply go wherever they went, knowing that with each passing mile I was becoming more and more invested in the entire outing.

It was past 3:00 by the time we finally reached St. Thomas. I had no idea what I would do once I got there. It was hard enough trying to follow them without being seen, but it was ten times harder doing it while driving a craft I didn't really know how to drive. When they turned off and started aiming for a private yacht club, I kept going even as I made note of the location.

I kept going, praying that a public marina would turn up soon. I passed another yacht club, and then right beyond that was "Mike's Marina." I thought I'd give it a try.

Slowing way down, I called out to a man standing on a dock.

"You got any transient slips?"

"One through ten!" he shouted, pointing to the right.

I inched along, going so slow that it sounded as though the motor might stall any minute. When I reached the slips, I was horrified to find they were all full except one. That meant I would have to dock the boat with the utmost care, squeezing between a narrow dock and a big, beautiful sailboat called the *Sammy Bean.*

Hands shaking, I tried to remember everything I had seen Tom do. Aiming into the slip, I pulled the throttle up and then slammed into reverse. I did it a little soon, however, leaving me dead in the water just out of reach of the slip.

I tried again, easing the throttle forward ever-so-slowly and then pulling it up to neutral. I missed the sailboat, but the bow slid into the dock with a definite bump. Had I been landing a plane, the FAA would have grounded me.

Fortunately, there didn't seem to be anyone around to notice or comment. I manned the ropes by myself, quickly tossing out the bumpers. Locking the cabin, I simply grabbed a tote bag and stuffed into it the binoculars, my wallet, my cell phone, and the keys to the boat.

Glad that I was still wearing my socks and sneakers, I set off to the office and put the requisite $50 charge on a credit card. With a bit of surprise, I realized that was practically the first charge I had had to make during this entire investigation.

Once I was done there, I took off running, aiming out of the marina and onto a main road. Trying to make like a jogger, I sped in the direction of the yacht club and then faltered when I got there. Was it their final destination, or had they simply "parked" their big boat and walked into town?

I caught a cab at the nearest intersection, glad that it was just a car and not a van like the cab we had taken from the airport. I told the driver to take me to the Golden Sails Yacht Club. He turned around and looked at me.

"It's right dere!" he said.

"I know," I told him, "I just want you to circle through. I'm trying to find someone."

"Whatever you say, missy."

He did as I asked, but there was a security guard at the main gate.

"That's all right," I said as the cabbie rolled down his window to speak to the guard. "We can turn around right here and head into town."

"Sorry, mon, just turning around," the cabbie said to the guard. He let us through but stood there and watched as we turned and came back out.

"Where to now?"

I asked him which way someone would go from there to get into town.

"Up dis way," he said, pointing to the left.

"Okay, go that way, then," I told him. "But go slowly."

On the main road, the driver started to pull over and pick up another passenger. I whipped a five-dollar bill out of my wallet and held it out to him.

"I prefer to ride alone," I said. "Five bucks for every passenger you don't pick up."

"Okay, works for me," the driver said, taking the money and grinning a toothless grin in the mirror.

After a few turns, we found ourselves deep in the heart of Charlotte Amalie. The town was beautiful and crowded. According to my cabdriver, it was a big cruise day, with three monster-sized ships currently in port.

"Most of these folks be gone by five o'clock," he said. "Dey just here for the day."

As we drove along one of the main drags, I studied the crowd for the sight of the elusive trio. Then I spotted them: Zach and Jodi and Fawn, standing in the doorway of a record store, arguing with the vendor about a CD. I quickly looked the other way to hide my face.

"Turn left at the next intersection," I instructed the driver, and as he did I pulled out the appropriate fare plus $20 for four more skipped passengers. "You can pull over here and let me out."

He seemed pleased with the amount I handed him.

"I'll be around town all day if you want me to come back and get you," he said in a lilting accent. "Anytime, anyplace, you just name it."

I started to brush him off and then thought better of it.

"How about right here in half an hour?" I asked. "If I'm not back, don't wait, and here's another five for your trouble."

"You got it, missy."

He pulled away as I ducked into the nearest gift shop. I was still wearing Jodi's ridiculously bright bathing suit cover-up. Most of the things in the store were fairly vivid as well, but I found a long white T-shirt and threw it onto the counter with a rope-and-shell belt. As a final afterthought, I added a nice straw hat.

The sales clerk was chatty, but I mostly ignored her as I kept looking out of the store at the sidewalk. Any minute now I expected the trio I was following to come walking by, and I needed to be ready to go. Once I had paid for my purchases, I changed right there, stripping off the cover-up, pulling on the T-shirt over my bathing suit, and then belting it and adding the straw hat. I put the cover-up in the bag, thanked the surprised women, and walked out the door.

Heart pounding, I slipped on my sunglasses, walked to the corner, and stopped at a postcard rack. Pretending to study the row of pictures, I was really intent on looking at the record store across the street. I was just thinking I had lost them entirely when I recognized Fawn near the doorway, reading the back of a CD.

Ducking into the corner store, I let out a deep breath and stood where I could see through the window to where they were.

"Can I help you, ma'am?" a man asked, but I told him no thanks, that I was just looking.

I feigned interest in some St. Thomas hot plates, all the while waiting to see the three of them emerge from the record store. Finally they did, walking along and talking as if they really were just running errands.

My face turned red as I thought about it. Had I risked my life, risked the boat, just to follow Jodi and her friends around as they went shopping? If this was all it turned out to be, I swore I would turn in my PI license first thing Monday morning.

Oh, Eli, I thought to myself. *What I don't do out of love for you!*

When the three of them were well past me, I set out on foot, grateful that Zach was tall enough so that I could let them get far ahead and still keep an eye on them. They were an easy tail as they went leisurely from store to store. At the end of one street, they turned, however, and at that point things became a little tougher. That street wasn't very crowded, and if I made any mistakes, I knew I would be spotted.

I hung back, watching. They went all the way to the end of that block, and then suddenly they split up. With a wave, Zach kept going forward and the two girls turned right.

I let him walk on, wondering if he would even remember me if he accidentally saw me. He hadn't been very friendly the night we met, and from what I recalled, they had all been pretty far into the margaritas. Taking the chance he wouldn't know who I was, I set off after him, leaving about a block between us.

Up ahead, I saw him stop and then go into a bar. Wondering if I should be pleased or disappointed, I hesitated at the cross street, knowing Jodi and Fawn might still be close enough to spot me if they happened to turn and look back.

I glanced to the right, and sure enough they were only about halfway up the block, standing at what looked like the door of a private home. I watched as Jodi rapped on the door.

I stepped back, looking for a place to duck if they came this way. There was a jewelry store three doors down, and I knew I could go in there if necessary. As I waited to see what would happen with the two of them, the street sign happened to catch my eye.

Ketch Alley.

Heart racing, I had to wonder if the door they were knocking on was 3344 Ketch Alley—the very same address Dianne had gone to when Eli was tailing her!

I chanced another peek. Jodi and Fawn were gone.

I took a few steps up the road, checking out the numbers on the doors. Sure enough, it was the three thousand block of Ketch Alley. I had no doubt it was the same address.

I wasn't sure what to think or do next. A part of me was literally sick to my stomach, terrified Jodi wasn't at all the person I had thought her to be. I was usually such a good judge of character, but this time I had blown it. The police back in Cocoa Beach suspected "one of Stella's children" of Eli's shooting.

Could Jodi be the one?

There were actions I could take. I walked back down the hill toward the main street and then hiked quickly to the corner where the cabbie was supposed to meet me. Sure enough, he was there, and when he spotted me in the crowd he gave me a big smile and a wave.

"Over here, missy!"

I got into the back of the cab and had him bring me to Mike's Marina. Once there, I asked him to wait, and then I ran onboard and dug into the suitcase full of Eli's equipment. One item was an official-looking—but completely fake—FBI badge. I changed into slacks and a shirt, tucked the badge in my pocket, then removed from Eli's file one of the current photos of Dianne. I didn't think about the laws I might be breaking by impersonating a federal agent. I didn't want to know.

Back outside, I had the cabdriver take me back to Ketch Alley going the other direction so we could pass the bar where Zach was. As we drove slowly past, I spotted him still there, now flanked on either side by Jodi and Fawn.

"Turn here," I said, wondering if I dared do this so soon. I knew I should wait until they were completely gone from the area before I followed this lead, but I didn't have the heart to wait. I felt sick inside.

I paid the cabbie a big bonus yet again, and this time I resisted his offer to meet me somewhere later for another ride.

"Thank you, though," I said. "You've been very helpful."

Once he had driven away, I straightened my shirt, stepped up to the door at 3344 Ketch Alley, and knocked. I had no idea who might greet me on the other side, but I knew it was a necessary step.

After a moment, I heard some noise inside, and then the door swung open.

"Can I help you?" a man asked.

He looked to be in his twenties, with frizzy blond hair and a few days' growth of beard. I didn't recognize him.

"Hey," I said with a smile, trying to appear relaxed. "I'm looking for Jodi. Is she still here?"

He didn't respond at first but merely looked at me, eyes squinting. "Yeah, right," he said finally. "What are you—a cop? Get a warrant or get out of my face."

He started to shut the door. Thinking fast, I blocked it with my foot and then reached into my pocket and pulled out my fake badge.

"FBI," I said in a much stronger voice, flashing the badge. "I need to ask you a few questions."

Thirty-Five

He hesitated for a moment, a bemused expression on his face.

"Sure," he said finally, stepping back and holding out one arm. "Come on in."

Already, I was kicking myself for the stupid FBI ruse. It could have been so much simpler than that. All I had needed to do was tell the truth: I was a private investigator and I wanted to know what the two young women had been doing here, not to mention what his association was with Dianne Streep. I was just so flustered by the Jodi connection that I hadn't been thinking clearly.

He motioned down a narrow hall, so I went first, emerging into a living room that looked more like the local copy store than someone's home. A large desk dominated the place, with a row of printers and copiers along the wall, and mountains of paper and boxes in every available space. He pointed to any empty metal folding chair, so I sat. He went around the desk and took his office chair.

"What can I do for you?" he asked.

My mind raced.

"I need some information," I told him, "about the two young women who were just in here. Can you tell me what business they had with you?"

He stared at me for a moment and then began rummaging through a desk drawer. He pulled something out and tossed it toward me. It landed in my lap.

I picked up the item to see a vinyl case. When I opened it, I recognized it as a duplicate of the FBI badge I had flashed at the door.

Click.

I looked up to see him pointing a gun straight at me.

"Don't try to kid a kidder," he said. "I got a whole box of those things in the back. Who are you and what do you really want?"

I swallowed hard, wishing I had told someone where I was going and what I would be doing here.

"Sorry," I said evenly, staring at the barrel of the gun. "You're right, I'm not FBI. My name is Callie Webber, and I'm a private investigator. I'm here investigating the shooting of a man named Eli Gold."

"Don't know him."

"He came here on a case of his own several months ago," I said. "He followed a woman to your door. Today, I was tracking someone related to the case, and they also came to your door. Somehow, that tells me you might be able to assist me with my investigation."

"Why should I?"

I blinked, meeting his eyes. They were cold and hard and empty, and I had no doubt he was perfectly capable of pulling the trigger.

"I don't know," I said. "Maybe because you're the kind of guy who likes to help people out."

He seemed to consider his options. A few moments later, he relaxed his wrist so that the gun pointed up toward the ceiling.

"Prove it," he said, "and I might help you."

"Prove what?"

"That you're a legitimate investigator."

I dug out a business card and slid it across the desk.

"My license numbers are on the back," I said. "You can call any one of those licensing bureaus and check me out."

Much to my surprise, he did just that. As I sat and listened, he called directory assistance for the states of Maryland, Virginia, and North Carolina—the first three states in my list of licenses. He got the numbers of the appropriate licensing bureaus and then called and had mine verified.

"All right. Ask me what you wanna know," he said as he hung up the phone after the last call. "Then I'll tell you what the answers will cost you."

"Fair enough. What were those two girls doing here?"

He chewed on his upper lip.

"Fifty bucks. And this is completely off the record."

I reached into my wallet and counted out two twenties and a ten. I set the bills on his desk and he used his free hand to pick them up and fold them into his shirt pocket.

"Getting ID for the younger one," he said. "She's twenty-one, you know, but she left her license at home in the States, so they needed me to print her a new one to use while she's here on vacation."

I nodded.

"Is that your business?" I asked. "Printing fake IDs for underage kids so they can get into bars?"

"My business is my business," he said sharply. "Are we done here?"

"Not quite. I need to reach into my bag."

"Go ahead," he said.

I moved slowly, not wanting him to think I might be pulling out a gun myself. My fingers touched the photo of Dianne, and I pulled it out and handed it to him.

"What was your business with her?" I asked.

He studied the picture and then looked at me.

"Five hundred dollars," he said. "I'll have to refresh my memory."

I considered my options and then looked in my wallet.

"All I have is two-eighty," I said, counting it out. "And I need ten of that to get back to St. John."

He twirled the gun on one hand then pointed it at me again.

"Give me your wallet," he said.

I handed it over and he looked inside, counting the bills. He removed all but a ten and then tossed it back at me.

"Passports," he said. "She came here last spring and bought some passports."

"Under what name?" I asked.

He stared at me before turning to his computer screen. After a few moments of typing, one of the printers beside him whirred to life. When the paper shot out, he grabbed it, looked at it, and then handed it over to me.

It held the images of three passports—one with Dianne's photo, one of Earl, and one of Larry.

Larry?

I was so stunned I had to force myself to look again. But, yes, it was the very same Larry who had come over to the house with Jodi a couple times, the one who worked as an insurance adjuster at the archeological dig site.

On the passports, however, they were listed as Beth, Truman, and Peter Magee, and their address was a town in Montana.

"The real Magees died in a boating accident here a few years ago," he said. "When that lady came asking for passports for her, her husband, and her grown son, it seemed like a good fit. I think the son could pass for thirty-nine, don't you?"

"Maybe," I whispered, studying Larry's face in the photo. He had that same familiar smile he'd worn the night we met. Was he really their *son?* My head felt as though it were spinning.

I folded the paper and tucked it in my bag, hoping this man would now let me leave.

"Thank you very much," I said, scooting to the front of my seat. "You've been a big help."

He twisted his wrist so that the gun was pointed again at me.

"Two hundred seventy for the info, not the paper," he said. "I need it back."

Nodding, I pulled it from my bag. He took it from me, dropped it into his metal trash can, and then lit a match and flung it in on top. I felt sure he expected some dramatic sort of flame to shoot up, but instead the match just sat there, very slowly catching the paper on fire.

"How do I know you won't go to the nearest police station and tell them all about my little side business?" he asked as we watched it burn.

Our eyes met.

"I posed as a federal agent to get in your door," I replied sheepishly. "I guess that makes us about even."

He smiled and then he surprised me by putting the gun back in the drawer and sliding it shut. We both stood. He walked me to the door, opened it for me, and then he reached out and shook my hand.

"Nice doing business with you," he said. "Do me a favor and don't come back."

Thirty-Six

I jogged all the way to the marina, and it was nearly six by the time I arrived at the boat. Afraid that I didn't have enough gas to get back to St. John, I knew I would have to pull up and buy some. In my mind, I could just see the resulting explosion when I crashed the boat into the gas pump.

I wasn't sure where the gas cap even was, exactly, so before I went to the pumps and made an idiot out of myself, I dug out the owner's manual and turned to the chapter on "Gasoline." Much to my surprise, I realized the boat had two tanks. From the indicated gauge, I saw that the first tank was, indeed, almost empty, but the second tank was completely full. I flipped the switch that would allow the boat to pull from the second tank, and then I put away the book and started up the engine.

As I steered out of the slip, I said a silent prayer for safety. I was able to make it from the marina without incident, and I followed my compass and my sense of direction to go back the way I had come. It wasn't quite as easy as I thought it would be, and I felt an odd sense of relief when I spotted the *Enigma* up ahead. It was going faster than it had before, and I settled myself in far behind it, hoping to follow it all the way home.

At the speed we were going, the ride took about half an hour. When the *Enigma* neared the marina, I was a bit hesitant, because I certainly didn't want to be spotted here at the end after managing to hide from them all afternoon. Instead, I pulled to a stop well before the entrance and just idled there for a while. I didn't know how long it would take for them to get off of their boat and go away, but I allotted ten minutes before I proceeded as slowly as I could into the marina myself. At least the *Enigma* docked at the opposite end from where we did. Perhaps even if they were still there, our paths would not come close to crossing.

I found the right slip and slowed further. Hoping I would be a bit better at the maneuvering this time around, I held my breath and concentrated on popping into neutral at just the right moment. The boat glided into place without a hitch, thank goodness.

I set the bumpers and tied the ropes just as they had been before. Then I gathered my things, locked the cabin, and hurried to the clinic. According to the receptionist, Tom was with the doctor but would be out soon. I sat in the now-empty waiting room and caught my breath, flipping through a new issue of *Guidepost* magazine. I was just reading an interesting article when Tom finally emerged, his hands neatly covered with flesh-colored bandages. I helped out by writing the check for his treatment and taking the two prescriptions the nurse was handing over.

From there, we went to the nearest pharmacy and had the prescriptions filled—one for pain, and one for antibiotics. Tom said they had also given him a tetanus shot at the office.

"Are you okay?" I asked once we finally left the drug store, bag in hand.

"Barely," he grunted. "I think I'd like to go home and have one of those pain pills and take a nap."

"You're hurting pretty badly, aren't you?" I asked.

He nodded, and I slipped an arm around him, wishing I could bear the pain for him.

The sun was setting by the time we reached Stella's house. I was glad to see that Jodi's car wasn't there. I didn't think I could deal with her at the moment.

Tom took a pain pill as soon as we walked in the door, and when I went into his room to check on him 20 minutes later, he looked to be sound asleep, sprawled across the covers.

I stood watching him for a minute. There was something about the sight of him there, so helpless, so vulnerable, that I found endearing. He had climbed onto the bed with his shoes still on, so I tiptoed over and tried to pull them off. The second shoe stuck a bit, which seemed to make him stir.

"Callie," he whispered, his eyes only half open.

"Hey," I said, leaning over to kiss him on the forehead. "Your pills working?"

"Oh, yeah. Pain's all gone now."

The smile on his face told me he was somewhere off in la la land.

"Good. You get some sleep."

"I'll tell you a secret," he whispered. "You gotta come closer."

I leaned down to hear him whisper.

"There's blood on my hands," he said.

I looked at the bandages, which were clean and dry.

"You're okay, Tom. Go to sleep now."

"No, you don't understand," he said, trying to sit up. "There's blood on my hands. There always will be."

I pushed his shoulders back, and then I leaned forward and kissed him again.

"Shhh," I said, until he closed his eyes. He fell back to sleep almost immediately. "Just a little nap. That's all you need."

I tiptoed from the room, hoping he would stay down for at least an hour. Back out at the car, I dialed Sergeant Ruhl. I told him I was on the cell and couldn't talk, but that we needed to meet.

As he was on his way to pick up his wife from church choir practice, he asked if I would mind meeting him there. He described his car and where it would be parked.

I left a note for Tom that said simply, "Had to run out. Call me on the cell if you wake up." Then I drove to Abraham's church, following the simple directions he had dictated to me. Sure enough, by the time I got there, his car was parked out in front of the church. As I found a spot for myself and then walked to his vehicle, I could hear the rousing music coming from inside.

"Hi," I said, slipping into the passenger seat. "They sound really good."

"It warms the heart," he agreed. "And my beautiful wife, she sings like an angel."

I settled into the seat, looking out in front at the dark street.

"Where are your children?" I asked.

"Home with my wife's mother. We got about ten minutes before the choir finishes here. What's up?"

I took a deep breath, wondering even where to begin.

"I am completely confused," I said. "I learned some things today that have totally thrown me for a loop."

"Go on."

"Do you know Stella's daughter, Jodi?"

"Ah, yes. Jodi. Nice girl. She's been coming here to the island since she was just a baby."

"As far as you know, has she been implicated in this whole art ring?"

He looked at me sideways.

"Jodi? No, not that I know of. Why?"

I exhaled slowly.

"Ever since we got here, she's been hanging around with a particular group of friends. There's Sandy, an archeologist working on a local dig, Sandy's younger sister, Fawn, and these two guys, Larry and Zach. Today I saw Zach driving the *Enigma,* and then I learned that Larry is Dianne's son. I'm sorry, but it just seems too coincidental the way everything connects."

From his pocket, Abraham produced his signature toothpick, not looking the least bit surprised.

"Maybe I can tell you a bit more," he said. "It might help."

Grateful to have a connection on the inside, I sat back and waited for what he might say.

"We know all about the two men, though I don't think the women are involved. According to Interpol, Zach is just a grunt, a drifter who happened upon a good gig. He drives their boat and lends some muscle sometimes. Otherwise he's just along for the ride."

"What about the fact that he's a masseuse? Don't you think that makes him the obvious candidate as the go-between at the fancy resorts?"

Abraham was silent for a moment.

"I wasn't aware that was his job," he said. "Yes, I would imagine that changes everything. He might be the elusive contact we've been looking for."

"What about Larry?

Abraham shook his head, his lips pursed.

"Larry Streep works in insurance—primarily in insuring works of art, antiquities, and artifacts. Interpol thinks he is the main source for his mother's illegitimate art business."

"You mean it's a family affair—he insures 'em, she steals 'em?"

"Not exactly. Larry has only a slightly higher percentage of payouts than your average insurance salesman in that particular field. My theory is that he doesn't insure everything he sees. Often, I believe, when he is called to give an estimate on insuring a piece of art, he will price it high so the buyer will go with some other company. The piece ends up stolen, but since Larry has no official connection with it, no one suspects that he was the 'eye' who zeroed in on it in the first place."

"Amazing."

"On this island, we have a word for one who betrays a trust: a mingo. Larry Streep is a mingo."

"Sure seems like it."

"A few weeks ago," Abraham continued, "he started spending almost all of his time down at the archeological dig. I keep a fairly close watch on him, and it's been bothering me. I have started to suspect that the collection may have some artifacts of significant value."

"So what do you think he's doing there?"

"Keeping a close eye on what's coming out of the ground, for one thing. Trying to get access to the collection as a whole, for another. From what I understand, SPICE's collection is massive and in many ways priceless."

"Is it kept here on the island?"

"No, I don't know where the collection is being stored. That seems to be very privileged information. Even Interpol isn't sure."

I shifted in my seat, wondering if it was located on Virgin Gorda, near the Baths, the place where Dianne would be having her clandestine meeting in the morning.

"Is the collection in danger of being stolen?" I asked.

"Perhaps the most valuable parts of it, at least. Especially now that we have heard the tape."

"You played the tape for Interpol?"

"We transcribed it and faxed it over. They had no trouble identifying the person named Merveaux. He is Yves Merveaux, and he lives in Martinique. He is a multimillionaire, a collector of many fine things. Several times before, it has been suspected that he received stolen goods, but nothing has ever been proven."

"Dianne and her husband are meeting with Merveaux in the morning, in Virgin Gorda."

Abraham looked at me, his eyes wide.

"How do you know that?"

As best as I could, I told about how Nadine used to put easily decoded messages in the Sunday paper to arrange secret meetings. I explained that Tom and I had gone around today hunting down newspapers and that we had found one of her secret messages in Sunday's *New York Times* for a meeting at 8:00 Friday morning at the Baths.

Abraham slammed his hand down on the steering wheel, surprising me.

"That is out of my jurisdiction," he said. "I have to stand and watch the *Enigma* sail away from here, and I can't do a thing about it."

"Tom and I could try and follow. We have an amazing long-range mike. Maybe we could listen to some of the conversation."

He shook his head.

"There is no warrant for that. We can put electronic surveillance in the home only. Going over to the BVI cancels everything."

"Surely Interpol has jurisdiction there."

"Jurisdiction, yes, but there's no way they can get someone here that fast."

I thought about Tom and his NSA connections.

"Maybe there can be some cooperation between agencies," I said. "I know a person who might be able to help, if you can give me the number of your Interpol connection."

He hesitated and then finally nodded, pulling a pen from his pocket and scribbling the information on the back of an old envelope.

"I just don't want this happening on my watch," he said. "I've worked too hard to see things fall apart now."

Thirty-Seven

The house was silent when I got home. Flipping lights on as I went, I worked my way down to Tom's bedroom, knocked lightly, and stepped inside. He was there on the bed in the same position I had left him in, breathing the deep, even breaths of a sound sleeper. I had a feeling he wouldn't wake until morning.

It was just as well. He'd been through a lot in the last few days, and I needed him to be sharp and clear tomorrow.

Closing his door, I walked down to my bedroom at the other end of the house and went through my clothes, trying to find something appropriate to wear to Miss Lucy's Full Moon Buffet. I could go without Tom because my intention was merely to get to know Jodi and her "gang" a little better.

I was about to climb into the shower when I glimpsed the empty shampoo bottle in the trash can. That reminded me that I was all out, so I wrapped a big towel around myself and went down the hall to Jodi's bathroom, where I retrieved a bottle of expensive salon-type shampoo.

It wasn't until I was back under the showerhead and lathering up my hair that it struck me.

Why was my empty shampoo bottle at the *top* of the trash can?

Pulse surging, I pushed aside the shower curtain and looked out at the small white wastebasket. It was filled with the papers and receipts I had dumped there when cleaning out my purse and brief-case two days before. But I had thrown out my empty shampoo the day before that. It should be at the bottom of the pile, not the top.

Chills running down my spine, I finished my shower as quickly as I could, dried off, and dressed in the nearest thing I could find.

Someone had been here. Someone had searched my room.

Heart pounding, I set out on a methodical, room-by-room inspection to see if I could detect any other signs of the house having been disturbed. It wasn't easy because I hadn't spent all that much time here. But I felt as though there were some things just a bit "off": pictures that didn't hang quite straight, drawers that weren't quite closed.

In the kitchen, I opened the pantry and then accessed Eli's hidden closet. I had already taken almost everything from it for our own purposes, but it didn't look as though the few things left there had been disturbed. Terrified of what I might find, I ran my hand along the top shelf; I breathed a sigh of relief to find Jodi's bearer bonds still there. I slid the closet shut, closed the pantry, and then returned to my room.

I wasn't concerned about anything that might have been recovered from my own trash. I always kept a "to be shredded" manila enve-lope locked in my briefcase for sensitive trash. The things I had tossed out here were harmless—brochures from North Carolina, info on the Climb for KFK. But I still didn't know what to make of this, other than to wonder if it had been done during Jodi's impromptu barbecue. If not then, perhaps Zach had taken Jodi off to St. Thomas today on purpose so that Larry would be free to come here and rifle through the house alone. In my conversation with Jodi earlier, I had asked about doctors, which may have indicated to them that Tom and I would be spending a few hours in the doctor's waiting room. Chances were the coast seemed clear, so while everyone was away, somebody let themselves in and started digging.

But what were they looking for? This hadn't been the same crazed, frantic search that had been done in Stella's condo in Florida. Did that mean it had been done by a different person this time, or that it was the same person using a different method, not wanting to tip their hand that they had been here? I just wasn't sure, though at the very least I thought I should take some finger-prints. Maybe Abraham could run them for me.

For now, however, I needed to get over to that restaurant. This would be my only opportunity to sit and chat with Larry and Zach, knowing what I knew. The biggest question on my mind was, what did the two of them know about me in return? If Jodi was in cahoots with them, then they knew everything. If she wasn't, then hopefully they still assumed that Tom and I were simply here on vacation, friends of Jodi's who were simply enjoying her hospitality.

I quickly put on some makeup and did my hair, and then I changed into a lightweight tan cotton dress, belting it with the rope-and-shell belt I had bought this afternoon. I slipped sandals on my feet, and then I stepped back and checked my reflection in the mirror. I looked like an innocent vacationer, ready for a nice night out.

Before I left, I took another peek at Tom. To my surprise, he was awake and just sitting up in bed.

"Hi," I said softly. "How are you feeling?"

He ran a bandaged hand over his face.

"Like I've been to the moon and back," he replied. "I've never taken pain pills before, but my hands hurt so badly. You know, if you work for the NSA and you have to have surgery with anesthesia, they send an agent into the operating room with you."

"They do?"

"Yeah. People say some mighty dumb things when they're out of their head. I hope I wasn't…too stupid."

"No, not at all."

He sat all the way up, leaning back against the headboard.

"You look pretty," he said. "Where've you been?"

"It's where I'm going," I said. "The Full Moon Buffet with Jodi and the gang. I figured I would just go without you. You have a phone call you need to make, but otherwise, you should probably spend the evening convalescing."

"Convalescing? What am I, an old man? We've got work to do."

I glanced at my watch. I was already running late.

"Then let's move fast," I said. "I'm not sure how long they'll be there."

I gave Tom a quick recap of the things I had learned—the meeting for tomorrow morning, the fact that Zach was the captain of the *Enigma,* the shocker that Larry was Dianne and Earl's son. For the sake of time, I didn't tell him exactly how I had learned all of this.

"One more bit of news," I said, "somebody has searched the house in the last two days. Did you have anything sensitive here that shouldn't have been seen?"

He let out a low whistle.

"Anything like that I carry with me at all times."

"Good."

"Things don't look tossed in here," he added, "at least not like the condo in Cocoa Beach."

"No, it was a more subtle job than that," I replied. "This time, they didn't want to be detected. But I know it when I see it."

"I bet you do."

I pulled from my purse the contact info that Abraham had given me and handed it to Tom.

"We need to go to that meeting tomorrow," I said, "and do some more electronic surveillance with the directional microphone if we can. Abraham said his warrant doesn't apply in the British Virgin Islands, so it's not a move we could make legally. Interpol could do it, but they can't get someone here by then. That leaves you, Tom. I told Abraham I knew someone in a government agency who might be able to help out."

"Meaning me."

"Meaning you. Here's the person you would contact at Interpol to work it out."

He looked at the name and number and nodded.

"Can't hurt to try," he said. "I'll see what I can do."

Because he had to use a landline for the call, we decided to split up for the time being. I would go ahead to the restaurant. He would grab a quick shower and then find a pay phone to work out the details. If there was still time, he'd meet me later at the restaurant.

I copied Jodi's directions for him, gave him a quick kiss, and said goodbye. As I drove away from the house, I prayed for his protection and mine.

On the way to the restaurant, I called Abraham once again. I hated bothering him so much at home, but time was of the essence and I didn't think this could wait.

His wife answered, sounding none too pleased when I asked for her husband. Abraham came on the line, but when I apologized, he insisted I had nothing to be sorry for.

"This is the nature of my business," he said.

"I have a quick question," I told him, "but I'm on my cell, if you know what I mean."

"Gotcha."

"The two men we spoke of earlier," I said, meaning Larry and Zach. "You told me you've been keeping an eye on things with them?"

"Yes. Somewhat."

"Could there have been a gap in time—say, two or three days, maybe—where one of them wasn't around to keep an eye on?"

Abraham was silent for a long moment.

"You are speaking of last week?" he asked finally. "Like near the end of the week?"

Fortunately, he understood what I was implying—that either Larry or Zach could have gone to the States and shot Eli.

"Yes."

"I'm not sure," he said thoughtfully. "It's possible. Yes, it's very possible. You might check with U.S. Customs, if you know what I mean."

As we concluded our call, I felt a surge of hope. If they had flown to Miami, there would be a record—and the dates would coincide with the stolen sniper rifle and the attempt taken on Eli's life.

I kept driving, and when I reached the town of Coral Bay, I had to slow way down—first for a donkey that was in the road and then for a group of people coming out of a roadside bar. After I passed all of that, I picked up some speed, enjoying the way my vehicle hugged the road as I took the ups and downs and twists and turns of St. John.

I could hear the music coming from the restaurant before I could even see the place. I put on my left blinker and then turned into a parking lot filled to overflowing with cars. I went up and down several rows before finding a spot I could squeeze in at the very end.

Walking toward the restaurant, I could see that it was a rambling building not far from the water. Most of the people were spread out at tables across the lawn, and at one end of the patio a band was playing next to a wide slate dance floor.

I stood under a big tree at the entrance, taking in the sight of all of these folks dining and laughing under the stars and the full, bright moon. I didn't see Jodi and her group, however, so I went ahead and paid and followed the delicious aroma of the food into the restaurant.

There was a long, slow-moving line for the buffet, and I spotted the people I was looking for near the front. I took my place at the back and observed them and how they interacted.

This time, the three women—Jodi, Sandy, and Fawn—clustered together chatting animatedly. Behind them were the two men—Zach and Larry—and though they weren't saying much, they didn't seem to be having a very good time. Their expressions, at least, were rather dour. They were probably preoccupied with the meeting taking place in the morning. Judging by the fact that Dianne had bought a passport for Larry, I could only assume that when they fled, he would flee as well. I didn't know what Zach might have in mind.

As I watched, Larry turned and spoke to the woman behind him, and I wondered if perhaps she was his date. At least she was closer to his age than the kids he'd been hanging out with all week. Actually, when she turned my way, I realized she was even older than him, by at least ten years. Looking harsh and weathered with sunstreaked hair and a too-deep tan, I had a feeling she'd been around the block a few times.

Jodi finally spotted me as she came past, her plate loaded with food. She looked stunning, if overdone, with elaborate makeup, an intricate "island" hairstyle and a top and skirt set that left her stomach quite bare. A large diamond sparkled from her navel.

"Hey!" she cried, looking genuinely glad to see me. "What are you doing back here? You shoulda come up with us."

"I didn't want to butt in line."

"Well, when you have your food, come on outside. We're like the far corner that way." She paused for a moment. "Where's Tom?"

"He's coming. He had to make a phone call."

"Okay. See you outside."

She left, with the rest of her friends soon to follow.

Once they were all gone, I concentrated on the food I was waiting in line for, surprised to realize I didn't recognize a single dish on the buffet. Fortunately, the woman in front of me asked one of the servers what everything was, and I listened as he pointed out items like "fungi" and "wahoo."

Outside, I located the group, glad to see they had saved two chairs for me and Tom. The tanned woman was, indeed, Larry's date, and he introduced her as Sunshine.

"Sunshine?" I asked.

"It's that or Freebird," she replied. "Which do you like better?"

"Excuse me?"

"I'm choosing a new name for the new me. Which do you like better—Sunshine or Freebird?"

I bit my lip to keep from smiling.

"Uh, depends on your last name, I guess. Which one goes better?"

"Don't have a last name," she replied. "From now on, I'm just a one-name gal."

"Oh. Okay. Well then, either one is good."

I concentrated on the food, some of which was wonderful and some of which was just plain strange. All of the tastes were unusual, very different, very Caribbean.

The live music was especially enjoyable, and after a while I realized there was a theme to the songs they were playing: "Blue Moon," "Bad Moon Rising," "Moon River." That's when I remembered that it was the Full Moon Buffet. I looked up in the sky to see the bright, shining orb that lit the water like a beacon.

This was such a magical place, I thought. Despite the investigation, despite the problems, despite the questions, I felt myself relaxing under the fun, calming influence of evening. There was something about the warm air and the lapping waves and the twinkling stars that made so many other things seem unimportant. I realized with a pang that I missed Tom and I wanted him there. When he showed up much later and took his place in the empty chair, I felt complete again.

"How are you?" I asked, looking down at his full plate next to my empty one.

"Fine," he replied, leaning over so that only I could hear. "Not the easiest thing in the world to take a shower and wash your hair without getting your hands wet."

"Oh, no, I hadn't thought about that!" I said, reaching out to pat his arm. Poor guy. He still hadn't even told me how his visit had gone with the doctor.

"What happened to your hands?" Jodi exclaimed, pointing at Tom.

"The boat overheated," he replied. "Burned 'em on the exhaust manifold."

"Callie, I thought you said his hand was *cut*."

Everyone turned and looked at the two of us, waiting for an answer.

"The burns ended up being worse than the cut," Tom said smoothly.

"That's got to be awful," Sunshine said. "Does it hurt?"

"A little," Tom replied. "Actually, I was just looking for a way to get Callie to feed me my dinner. Hon, would you cut my meat please?"

That earned a laugh.

"Hey, buddy," Larry said, "why stop there? I think that's a good reason for her to wait on you hand and foot."

"Oh, thanks, Larry," I said. "I don't think that will be necessary. Tom's a self-sufficient guy."

Crisis averted, I seized the opportunity to change the subject by formally introducing Tom to Larry's date, Sunshine. As I had expected, she went through the same spiel with him that she had with me.

"So why are you a 'new me'?" Tom asked, awkwardly spearing a conch fritter with a fork. "Have you had some big change in your life?"

She nodded, taking a long swig of beer.

"My divorce finally went through," she said. "So I ran away from home. Got no ties there now. Might as well start over somewhere fresh."

"Do you work here on the island?"

"Not yet. I just got in a few days ago. Just me and my backpack and the shoes on my feet."

"How do you know Larry?"

"We met last night, at the Shipwreck."

"The Shipwreck?"

"A bar in Coral Bay. He's been real friendly. Ain't that right, honey?"

She put an arm around him, and he leaned toward her for a kiss. Startled and just a bit disgusted, I turned away. The longer I talked to her, the more I realized she was old enough to be his mother!

Conversation flowed as the night went on, but the more we talked, the more I decided I wasn't picking up all that much new information. Larry was absorbed with his date, Zach was as stoic and silent as ever, Jodi and Fawn were giggling and infantile, and Sandy, the archaeologist, sat at the far end of the table, looking just a little detached from the whole group. At one point everyone went to dance but her, and I seized the opportunity to move closer and ask how things were going. Tom, in the meantime, had gone back inside to see if he could get seconds. A tad more culinarily adventurous than I, he was really enjoying the food.

"I'm sorry," Sandy said. "I've been a bit rude tonight."

"Rude?" I replied. "How so?"

"I'm angry at Jodi," she said. "It hasn't exactly put me in a party mood."

"What's going on?"

She exhaled loudly, and I noticed that her hands were clenched into fists.

"Jodi took Fawn into St. Thomas today and bought her a fake ID."

I tried to look surprised.

"Why?"

"They said Fawn doesn't want it so she can drink, she just wants to be able to go where everyone else goes, to the bars or whatever."

"That bothers you."

"Of course it bothers me! I didn't want my sister here so she could party. I wanted her here to share the dig, to hang out with me. Why does she need to get into bars?"

I nodded, agreeing on all counts.

"I'm sorry," Sandy said, "because I know Jodi's your friend and all, but it's time for her to grow up. Do you realize she just turned twenty-five and has more in common with my seventeen-year-old sister than she does with me?"

We both turned to watch them on the dance floor. Jodi was dancing with Zach, sliding her half-naked body against him seductively. For the first time all week, he actually seemed interested in return. Fawn danced by herself nearby, but I had no doubt she was watching the two of them and taking mental notes for future use.

"Maybe I could have a talk with her," I offered.

"And say what?" Sandy asked. "Act your age? I've been telling her that for years."

The song ended, but when our group returned to the table, they didn't sit down.

"You guys ready?" Jodi asked, picking up her purse and wrap from her chair.

"Ready for what?" Sandy asked.

"We thought we'd head into town. See what's happening."

"I don't think so," Sandy replied. "Come on, Fawn. We've got an early morning."

Fawn started to object, but a sharp look from Sandy cut her right off.

"Sorry, Jodi," Fawn said. "Looks like I gotta go."

The two sisters gathered their things and left.

"Okay, then," Jodi said. "That just leaves the six of us."

"Count us out," said Tom, returning with a plate of dessert. "We're not really into the bar thing, and we're enjoying the music here."

Jodi looked up at Zach.

"Zach?" she asked beguilingly, and after a slight hesitation, he looked at Larry and nodded. They said goodbye to us, and then, like a flock of birds, Zach, Jodi, Larry, and Sunshine turned simultaneously and moved toward the parking lot. Tom and I watched the two couples go, not even having to wonder how the rest of their night would play out.

Thirty-Eight

Once they were gone, there really was no reason to stick around. Still, Tom and I were both reluctant to leave. He had been swept into the same peaceful easiness I was feeling. We decided to linger just a bit longer and take in the music and the starlight.

"Are we set for the morning?" I asked, dreading his answer. If he hadn't somehow obtained permission for us to listen in on Dianne's conversation with Merveaux at the Baths, then we would either have to give up or do it illegally. I didn't like either choice.

"I think you'll be a bit surprised at the turn things have taken," he said. "By tomorrow morning there should be a few more people on hand."

"What do you mean?"

"Let's take a walk."

We stood and went down to the water's edge, away from anyone who might be able to hear us. The moon was so bright that the sand under our feet practically glowed. I took off my shoes and hooked one finger through the straps.

"Here's the thing," he said. "The matter has been turned over to the FBI office in Miami. Right now they're in communication with Interpol and the Legat."

"The Legat?"

"The legal attaché for Great Britain. Because the meeting will supposedly take place in the British Virgin Islands, we can't do anything there without the express permission of the British legal attaché."

"Do you foresee any problems in that area?"

"Not really. Interpol can be very persuasive, and that transcript is pretty damning evidence. I think she'll authorize whatever needs to be done."

"So what will happen in the morning?"

"We convene at four. We'll know more then."

"Four o'clock in the morning?" I asked, glancing at my watch.

"Things are moving quickly. From here on in, you, Abraham, and I are merely observers. We're still needed on the team, but now the FBI is leading the way."

Feeling somehow enormously comforted, I didn't resist when Tom asked me if I would like to dance before leaving. I started to walk toward the dance floor, but he pulled me back, slipping his arms around my waist.

"Right here," he said softly. "We can dance right here."

With his hands bandaged, I could feel his two fists gently pressing against my back, pulling me close to him. I tossed my shoes to the side, wrapped my arms around him and rested my head on his shoulder, closing my eyes and losing myself in the warmth and strength of his body.

As we danced, I realized our time here on the island was likely drawing to a close. Everything would come to a head in the morning, Dianne and her art-theft ring would be taken down, and then Tom and I would have our answers—and justice—for Eli.

"Callie," Tom said when the song ended, pulling back a bit so that he could see my face. "I have something for you."

The expression in his eyes was almost sad, and I realized he must've been thinking the same thing I had, that soon we would be going our separate ways. Now, here in the moonlight, dancing on the sand under the stars, he seemed to want to hold on to me as much as I wanted to hold on to him.

I watched as he reached into his pocket, clumsily extracting a black velvet box—the same box I had glimpsed before, the day he almost gave it to me at the restaurant. Unable to get it open, he finally smiled and just held it out to me. Holding my breath, I took it from him and opened the box, surprised to find inside not an engagement ring, as I had expected, but a simple gold chain.

"It's lovely," I said, though I knew there was a tinge of disappointment and confusion in my voice. "Thank you."

"Put it on," he instructed, and so I did, handing him back the box as I slipped the chain around my neck and hooked the clasp.

"Do you want to know what it's for?" he asked.

I looked at him and nodded, my eyes wide.

"Eventually," he said softly, reaching out to take my hand, "I hope, anyway, there will come a point when you're ready to make this finger open and available for something else."

I looked down, realizing he was holding onto the ring finger of my left hand. Tears filled my eyes as I understood that he was talking about my gold band, the ring Bryan had put on my finger the day of our wedding.

"I would never presume to ask that you remove Bryan from your life," he continued. "But if you should see fit one day to remove his ring from your finger, then maybe you can wear it on this chain around your neck. And then there will be a empty place—an open place—for the ring I want to give you."

I was stunned. Stunned and touched and so overcome with emotion that all I could do was wrap my arms around him. How difficult it must be for him, I realized, to be the *second* great love of my life. I didn't know what I was thinking—what I was feeling—other than the overwhelming knowledge that what Tom had just done was utterly right. There were things I needed to work through before that ring could come off, but somehow the necklace would make it easier for me—for it would free my hands to reach out toward the future while still holding the ring in a place close to my heart.

Another song started, and Tom and I moved naturally into a dance. As we swayed to the music, I listened to the words...

The moon winked bright
Like a coin fresh tossed
In a blue pool too spacious to miss.
I wished and then
Threw my caution to the wind
And paid a quarter for a kiss

"Do you know this song?" I asked. "It's perfect for right now. The moon, the blue water…"

"Sounds like a good idea, actually," he replied, grinning. He paused our dance to reach into his pocket. This time, he pulled out a few coins, clumsily spreading them on his bandaged palm until he found a quarter. He tucked the rest away, and then handed the quarter to me.

"A quarter for a kiss?" he asked softly.

I obliged, knowing that with that kiss we were sealing a promise, a hope for our future together.

When the kiss was finished, we held on to each other and resumed our dance. And though across the dark lawn someone else sang the words, Tom joined along, singing softly into my ear:

How could I best convey the feeling
After all that time of longing from afar?
How could I say my heart was reeling
Without revealing
I'd let it come this far?
Your lips met mine
And I knew that coin divine
was an investment in our future bliss;
Let the Rockefellers try
To find something they could buy
That would equal the value of this—
For we found our love
Like a dividend from above,
With a quarter for a kiss

Thirty-Nine

"Coffee?"

I looked up at the bleary eyes of the FBI agent who held out a fresh pot toward my empty cup.

"Please," I said, holding it up for a refill. After only two hours' sleep, I needed all the help I could get.

Tom wasn't looking much better, though at least, he said, his hands weren't in much pain. We had changed the dressings before coming, and I had been encouraged at the sight of them. The injuries were still deep, but the skin around them didn't look quite as red and raw as before. According to him, the worst pain he was having now was from the site of the tetanus shot they had given him in his arm.

We had convened in Virgin Gorda, in the fellowship hall of a Moravian Church, which was being used as the local FBI command post. There were about ten agents there, led by a burly, no-nonsense man who introduced himself as Agent Holt, plus Tom, Abraham, and me. Our little trio hung back and watched the men and one woman at work. They were planning out a careful operation of surveillance—with possible seizure—of the art-theft ring and the *Enigma*.

I was quite impressed with the group of agents, and I appreciated the way they kept us in the loop, even though we had been asked to remain in the command center until the operation was completed.

That was fine with me. I didn't need to be in on this action—though I did want to know what was going on. To that end they had already set up a row of monitors and recorders. The two agents manning the machines here would be privy to everything that happened—and, by extension, so would we.

Before we knew it, everyone was rolling into place. I hadn't really had time to see what the Baths were, exactly, but Abraham explained it to me as we watched the monitors from the hidden cameras of the agents who were getting into place.

"The Baths are really something," Abraham told me. "But probably not what you think."

I had been picturing some sort of natural hot springs, with bubbling, mineral-filled waters, so I was surprised to hear him explain that the name was simply a shortening of the word "batholith," which had something to do with great masses of igneous rock. The Baths were an oddity of nature, a place where granite rocks—some the size of houses—had been strewn haphazardly along a beach, as if spewed up by some powerful volcano hundreds of years before. From what I could tell on the small monitors, the rocks leaned against each other at odd and amazing angles to form an intricate series of hidden pools, caves, and grottos. Beautiful.

Unfortunately, the FBI agents said, a meeting "at the Baths" could have numerous actual locations. Dianne may have meant somewhere down and among the rocks; or the area known as the "Top of the Baths," where there was a restaurant, some shops, and a pool; or the ferry dock at Virgin Gorda where one would go to reach the natural landmark. Consequently, they had put agents at all of these locations, disguised as tourists, cabdrivers, waiters, and boaters—most armed with video links and a microphones.

Everyone seemed to have a different opinion about where the meeting would take place. They were hoping to have a satellite visual of the *Enigma* and simply follow it over from St. John, but so far the connection was a bit problematic. The FBI didn't want to risk following the boat by sea, and I didn't blame them. The only reason Zach hadn't noticed me following him yesterday was because he hadn't been expecting to be followed. Today, these people would be much more alert and would certainly notice a tail.

At about ten minutes before eight, an agent spotted the *Enigma* just pulling into a slip at the marina. When the big boat was tied up, Dianne and two men disembarked and caught a taxi to the place known as the Top of the Baths. Once there, she and the two men went down a rocky trail toward the sea.

Watching the agents track all of this by shifting the surveillance from person to person and back again was like watching a finely choreographed dance—or a brilliant football play. Each agent seemed to know his place on the team, and together their efforts were nearly seamless.

At the bottom of the trail, there was a bit of concern when Dianne and the men disappeared among the giant boulders. But about that time a sharp-eyed agent spotted Yves Merveaux on the deck of a sailboat nearby. He and his bodyguard were moored out in the water about 50 yards from the beach at the Baths.

As we watched one of the monitors, Merveaux and his man put down an inflatable dinghy with a little outboard motor, climbed aboard, and started it up. They puttered in toward shore, veering off into the midst of the giant rocks.

"Point of convergence, people," the agent at the monitor said. "Craig, looks like this'll be yours for the taking."

Apparently one of the agents in a boat, a simple craft that seemed to be floating harmlessly offshore, had the best vantage point.

"She's there!" Craig whispered sharply. "She's there on the rocks, waiting for him."

There was a good sound connection, and we all listened as the little dinghy pulled up to the sand and Merveaux and his man climbed out. Then, as we watched the screen, we saw Dianne emerge from the rocks. I realized that except for Eli's photos, it was the first time I had really seen her. For such a secretive and elusive creature, the thing that struck me the most was how *normal* she looked. Sporting a black malliot and a floral skirt, she looked like a tourist taking in the early morning sunshine. The big sunglasses and matching scarf over her hair lent her a sort of "Jackie O"-type appearance.

"How are you, Dianne?" Merveaux asked in a French accent as the two stood there on the beach and shook hands.

"I'm fine," Dianne replied. "*Ça va?*"

"*Ça va bien,*" Merveaux answered. "My gout is giving me problems. Otherwise, I can't complain."

Dianne made a gesture with her hand. Suddenly, one of the men who had come with her came out from behind a rock, walked over to Merveaux, and began running a bug sweeper up and down his body. Once that was finished, he ran it on the bodyguard, who cooperated by standing there on the beach with his arms outstretched.

I bent closer to the monitor to look at the man with the bug sweeper, expecting to see Earl. Instead, this fellow was older and heavier. When the second man appeared from between the rocks, I grabbed Tom's arm.

"It's them!" I said. "The men who beat up Chris Fisher!"

"Who?" the agent asked, zooming a bit closer on their faces.

"A private investigator in St. Thomas was roughed up by two men," I explained. "Those goons look a lot like the artist sketches that were done."

"Send those images to Quantico," Agent Holt said to the technician. "They can run them through FRS."

"FRS?" I whispered.

"Face Recognition Software," he replied. "If those two guys are in the database, they"ll be able to ID them."

When the bug sweeps were complete, Dianne paused and looked out at the water, shielding her eyes to scan the boats on the horizon. She looked straight at the camera without really seeing it and then moved on.

"Everyone hold positions," the agent at the monitors said. "They are hyperalert. Repeat. Hold positions. Craig, you've got sound and picture coming in clear."

"I'm right at a thousand feet," he responded softly. "If they go for a stroll, I'll lose the sound."

For the moment everyone stayed exactly where they were. Then Dianne motioned for Merveaux to follow her, and we all held our breath as they started walking. They didn't go far, however; they simply walked to the nearest boulder and sat. Once they had done that, the other three men separated on the beach, keeping watch, stiff and conspicuous.

"You have what I want?" Merveaux asked.

"I have the location and the code," Dianne replied. "You can pick and choose as you desire."

"But I have to go in and get it myself?"

"That's correct."

Merveaux nodded, looking around for a long moment.

"That is not worth three," he said. "Too much risk. I will give you one."

"*One?*" she cried angrily. "I will give you the code for one. You want the location, that's two more."

"That's ridiculous. I can get the location from someone at SPICE."

"How can you do that?" she asked with a wry smile. "When they aren't even aware that their collection has been relocated—the best parts of it, anyway?"

"What are you saying?"

"That there's a half-empty climate controlled storage facility in San Juan. Someone's going to be very surprised come Monday morning."

"You are fearless, Dianne."

"That's why I'm rich, Yves."

"All right, I cannot resist. Three million. Give me the drop."

She spoke as she adjusted her sunglasses, breaking the sound.

"The first will be at th...ist," she said.

"What was that?" the agent at the monitor asked.

"I think she said 'At the Christ,'" the agent on the mike replied.

"What time?" Merveaux asked.

"Soon as you can make it happen," Dianne replied. "Once the first transfer has been made, the code will be there. No transfer and, well, that was your chance. I can't wait till next week."

Merveaux laughed, dabbing his forehead with a handkerchief.

"Do not kid yourself, Dianne. You are not ab…to walk away from this any more….th…I am."

She shielded her eyes and looked out at the water again.

"After you have the code," she said, "make the second transfer. If it goes through, the drop will be at F twel…" once again, her arm crossed her mouth and her voice faded. "…ake's Pond."

"You sure nobody else will be there?"

"No, the site's quiet today. You know where it is?"

"Of course. I just have to find F twelve. I assume it's marked."

"Yes. You shouldn't have any problems there, except maybe with hikers. But don't worry. They all move along eventually. You can just pause and reflect."

They both chuckled.

"Very well, then. It is nice to talk with you, Dianne, but this sun is about to burn a hole right through my head. I sh…worn a hat."

They both stood.

"It was good to see you again, Yves," she said. "I wish you…I wish you all the best in life."

"*Au revoir* for now," he said, stepping into the boat.

"Yes, *au revoir*," she replied.

Merveaux and his bodyguard climbed into the dinghy and puttered away. Dianne stood on the beach watching him for a moment before turning around and going back the way she had come.

Forty

"We just witnessed a three-million-dollar transaction," Agent Holt said, coming back into the room as the men at the monitors tracked Dianne and her two goons back to the *Enigma*. "And it looks like it's all going down today."

From what I already knew about the situation—combined with what I could understand of the conversation—my guess was that Yves Merveaux had just agreed to pay Dianne Streep two million dollars for the location of artifacts that had been stolen from SPICE. He would then give her a million more for the security code that protected those artifacts, allowing him to go in and steal whatever he wanted of them without being caught. Merveaux would be paying the money to Dianne via wire transfers, and she would be leaving him the information at two different drop points.

"The question is," said Tom as we talked about it, "where are those drop points? From their conversation, I'm just not clear."

"The bigger question," Abraham added, "is when can we move in and make some arrests?"

Agent Holt heard Abraham's comment.

"With the tape we have, we could make an arrest right now for conspiracy to sell," he said. "But we would do better to wait until the money changes hands and the goods are received. Then we can get him on possession and her for trafficking."

Of course, if we couldn't figure out the drop points, then it might be a little more difficult. At least the satellite connection was now working; both the *Enigma* and the *Cezanne*, Merveaux's boat, were being tracked as they sped away from Virgin Gorda.

"Roll the tape again," the agent said, and soon we were listening to a replay of the brief conversation on the beach.

It definitely sounded as though she said "at the Christ" for the first drop.

The *Christ?*

I was thinking they meant something in a church, but then Abraham's face broke into a big grin.

"The Christ!" he cried. "There used to be a statue of Christ on Peace Hill. It blew down in a hurricane, but everyone knows where it used to stand. There is still an old windmill there. I bet that is the place!"

"Let's go, then," Holt said.

Once again Tom, Abraham, and I were relegated to the background as the FBI did their thing. One by one the agents returned from their posts and everything was packed up quickly to shift the base of operations over to St. John. Abraham had already cleared the way legally with his warrants. Now he would work with the FBI to bring this matter to a close—hopefully today.

Meanwhile, Tom was pacing over to the side, puzzling out the second drop site.

"F twelve," he said to me as he paced. "Why does that sound so familiar?"

"I don't know," I said. "Is it an address? A beach? A boat?"

Suddenly, he stopped pacing.

"Play it again," he said, walking to the recorder.

"We have to pack up," the agent said, just about to pull the plug.

Tom reached into his pocket and pulled out his digital voice recorder.

"Just one more time," he said, holding it out and turning it on.

The agent obliged and Tom was able to record the snippet of tape.

"Are you finished now?" the agent asked impatiently.

"Sorry," Tom replied. "Go ahead with what you were doing."

He and I went back to the corner, staying out of everyone's way and listening to the exchange several times.

"After you have the code, make the second transfer. If it goes through, the drop will be at F twel...ake's Pond."

"You sure nobody else will be there?"

"No, the site's quiet today. You know where it is?"

"Of course. I just have to find F twelve. I assume it's marked."

"The site's quiet today," Tom repeated. "She means s-i-t-e. Site. Like," his eyes widened, "an archeological site!"

"A dig site!" I echoed.

"That's why it sounds familiar. F twelve is an archeological location. What is 'ake's Pond'?"

"Drake's Pond is my guess," Abraham said excitedly, crossing toward us. "There is a dig at a place called Drake's Pond, out on the south side of the island. It's a bit of a hike but quite a thing to see once you get there."

"Is that the dig Jodi's friend Sandy has been leading?"

"No, this is a different dig. An older one. I think they are almost finished with this one."

"Good work, folks," Holt said. "Now we've got both drop locations."

Everyone was ready to go, so we headed to Virgin Gorda's public marina. The place was certainly busier now than it had been when we had arrived before dawn. A group of tourists was pouring from a ferry, most of them in bathing suits and cover-ups, carrying tote bags and ice chests. As we sped toward St. John across the deep blue water, I couldn't help but think that though I would have loved being the one to race in and find the final evidence, things were out of my hands now. When we reached St. John, we quickly cleared through customs and then went with those who were setting up the base of operations in a small public works facility that Abraham had managed to commandeer, a nondescript building he said was often used for a multitude of purposes, including police training and community education. Tom and I watched with great interest as agents were dispatched all over the island—some to observe Dianne's house, some to keep an eye on the *Enigma,* and some to watch the drop points. Though we didn't have audio or video surveillance of the area yet, the agents were wired for sound, so they could describe what was happening as it happened.

Things began moving quickly.

Merveaux's boat docked at the Sugar Manse resort. He walked up the dock and into the main building, where he stayed for quite a while. Eventually, he and his bodyguard emerged out of the front side of the building and took a cab straight to the parking lot at Peace Hill. The cab remained with Merveaux seated inside while the bodyguard hiked the uphill trail toward the "Christ." We all waited breathlessly, and about ten minutes later the bodyguard came back and got in the cab.

"On the move, on the move," the agent at the monitor said as the cab pulled away. Once it was out of sight, an agent came out of hiding and ran up the hill toward the Christ. Meanwhile, Merveaux's cab returned to the Sugar Manse.

"What's he doing back at the hotel?" an agent's voice said.

Everyone was silent, so I ventured a guess.

"He needs to make the next transfer," I said. "He wants a secure place to do some banking."

They agreed, talking about moving in for an arrest at that point, but they were determined to hold out as long as possible.

"Any sign of what the bodyguard found at the Christ?" Holt asked into his microphone.

"There's something here," the agent replied. "Inside an old windmill. I don't know what it means, exactly."

"What is it?" the commander asked.

"It's just a bunch of numbers scraped into the wall. But I can tell it was freshly done."

Tom stepped forward. "Numbers," he whispered. "It's encrypted."

I looked at him and then back at Agent Holt.

"What are the numbers?" he asked. "Can you read them off to us?"

"Uh, let's see."

Tom grabbed a pen and paper and wrote them down as the man read: 32 29 24 33 12 11 41 31 14 13 34 22 26 21 20 14 34 42.

"Thanks," Tom said.

He carried the paper across the room and sat at a table, going to work.

"Maybe we should call cryptography in Maryland," the agent working the equipment said to Holt. "See what they can do with it."

"Are you kidding me?" Holt replied, lowering his voice. "We've got the king of cryptography in the room with us here. That's Tom Bennett."

The guy looked at Tom and then back at his boss, his eyes widening.

"*The* Tom Bennett? What's he doing here?"

The man shrugged.

"I don't know. Guess we got lucky."

Guess we got lucky indeed, I thought.

"We have movement on the East End," a woman's voice said over the wire. "A truck is just pulling out of Streep's driveway."

"What kind of truck?"

"A small cargo truck. All white with a few dings in the bumper. Can't read the plate. They turned west on East End Road."

Nerves were taut. There was so much at stake here—but the FBI walked a fine line between keeping tabs and showing their hand.

"Hold back," Holt advised. "This is a small island without a lot of roads. We won't lose them."

And they didn't. The truck passed various surveillance points along the way, eventually ending up at the *Enigma*'s boat slip.

Holt leaned forward, speaking into the microphone.

"All right, who's got a visual on the boat?"

"I do, sir," one voice said. "This is Craig. I'm about eight slips down the way. Looks like they're taking stuff out of the truck and loading it onto the boat. I got two men, the same two who were with her on the beach. I don't see the woman."

"This is Reese, sir," another voice said. "I'm almost there, walking from the other direction."

"Good. Craig, Reese, listen up. I need to know what they're bringing aboard."

"So far, it's mostly clothes, some boxes. A computer."

Holt seemed ready to snap. It was like fishing—he didn't want to set the hook until it was fully in the creature's mouth.

Craig continued to give us an oral report of the items that were being loaded onto the boat until the technical guy with us finally got the monitor up and running. Suddenly, the black-and-white screen flashed to life, showing the scene from the hidden camera mounted on his boat. We all watched the unloading of the truck, an endless series of trips back and forth between the boat and the vehicle. After a moment, a second monitor popped on, revealing a landscape so odd, it looked like the moon. I stared at the screen for a while and then figured it must be Drake's Pond, the second drop site. There was a body of water there, but it was ringed in some odd foamy-looking substance.

"What's wrong with that pond?" I asked.

"It's a salt pond," Holt replied. "Sea water gets trapped there, and the sun burns off the water, leaving the salt.

"Sir, we've got movement at the Sugar Manse," an agent said suddenly. "Merveaux and his guy are back in the cab. They have turned east on Northshore Road."

"They're going to the second drop location," Holt said. "Are we in place?"

Two voices answered in the affirmative.

"I've got visual and audio," the technician said.

I took a deep breath, feeling as though I might explode. This was too tense for me. I paced the room, pausing occasionally to peek over Tom's shoulder at the paper he was working on. It was covered with notations, letters, numbers, and scribbles. I realized that if Tom could decrypt the location where Dianne had hidden the artifacts, then the FBI would get the biggest, best bust of all because they could arrive at the place ahead of Merveaux and arrest him the moment he seized the stolen property.

In the midst of all of the confusion, my cell phone rang. I stepped outside and answered, expecting to hear Jodi. Instead, a voice as special and familiar as any I'd ever heard raced across the miles to me, in a sound so sweet my eyes instantly filled with tears.

"Snap out of it?" the voice on the phone said. "Did you really tell me to 'snap out of it'?"

It was Eli! He was awake!

Forty-One

I called him back on a landline from a small office elsewhere in the building. Sitting at someone's desk in a stiff vinyl office chair, I closed my eyes and let tears flow down my cheeks. *Thank You, Jesus.*

We talked at first about him, about how he had slowly started to regain consciousness last night. By morning, he said, he was talking some, but Stella made him wait to call me until she felt he was completely coherent.

"Eli, you scared me to death," I cried. "Do you understand that you may never, ever die?"

"I'll try to live forever, sugar," he said, "but I can't make any promises."

"At least not this time. Not now."

"No, not now," he agreed. "My heart's pumping strong—I know that because there's this little blonde nurse who gives me my sponge bath, and—ow!"

I could hear Stella in the background.

"A joke," Eli said. "It was a joke. I only have eyes for you, Stel."

Over the line, I thought I could detect the sound of a kiss.

"Sorry to break up the love fest," I said, "but you got us in quite a mess down here. I've got some big questions for you."

"Yeah, I want to know what's going on. Is Nadine safe? Is she okay?"

"That's the first thing you want to know?" I asked. "You get shot by a sniper, make it out of a coma, and the first thing you want to know is how Nadine is doing?"

"Callie, tell me she's still alive."

"She's still alive," I said. "But she doesn't need protecting from anybody, Eli. She's a criminal. She's about to go to jail."

"All right," he replied. "Just make sure they understand she can't go in under Nadine Peters. She probably can't go in under Dianne Streep, either. It's time to change her identity again."

"Eli, who is she hiding from?"

He coughed a bit and then sipped some water before speaking again, his voice a little less vibrant than before.

"A man named Victor Rushkin," he rasped. "He was her supervisor at the NSA—and the mastermind behind a vast network of Russian spies. He recruited her directly, and when they were cuaght, she turned state's evidence. Her testimony incriminated people at all levels. *All* levels. She got protected—he got forty years at Leavenworth. Now she's certain there's a new contract on her head straight from him."

"But why are you sympathetic to her?" I asked. "Eli, she betrayed you. She betrayed our country. You *shot* her, for goodness' sake."

"Callie," he said, his voice sounding weaker. "Don't you understand? A couple months ago, when I took photos of her on that ferry and then later brought them in to the NSA, I opened a great big can of worms. Only a handful of people knew she was alive. I started asking questions and somehow those photos made it to the wrong person. This may have happened decades ago, but these people she turned on have not forgotten, nor forgiven. Nadine told me that ever since I started snooping around and she realized she had been made, her death warrant was as good as signed. She said every time she starts her car, she braces herself for an explosion. Every time she walks through a crowd, she expects to be stabbed or shot."

"When did she tell you that? When did she talk to you?"

"The day I was shot she came here, to Cocoa Beach. I was down at the beach. You know that park where they have the wooden walkways and the little covered picnic tables? That's where I always rest after my walk. I was sitting there, catching my breath, when a woman came walking up. It was Nadine."

He went on to describe their meeting there. She had come, she said, because she wanted him to stop what he was doing—stop investigating her, stop asking questions about her. Yes, she was alive, but now she would have to disappear again, this time for good, thanks to him.

"If she dies, it's my fault. If Rushkin kills her, then I might as well have been the one to pull the trigger. By trying to get some simple information for myself, I may have signed her death warrant."

I shook my head.

"It's not your fault, Eli," I said. "You couldn't have known. We reap what we sow. She's an art thief now, you know. I just saw her make a three-million-dollar sale of stolen artifacts."

That seemed to quiet him for a moment.

"She's a legitimate art dealer," he said defensively.

"She's also an illegitimate one," I replied.

He sat with that, the silence crackling between us.

"I don't know why I should be surprised," he said finally. "She never did like following the rules."

Eli gave the phone to Stella and we talked a few minutes more. She was elated at his recovery, confused by the things he had told her, and probably even a bit concerned about the state of their marriage. Eli had kept Nadine a secret from all of us—including Stella. I urged her to forgive him but also to insist on complete honesty from now on. He may have had the right to keep the story of his first love to himself, but as a married man, he hadn't had the right to conduct the investigation he had conducted without keeping his wife informed.

"Thank you, Callie," Stella said. "I was kind of feeling that way, but then I thought maybe I was just being hard on him."

"Can I be hard on you?" I asked.

"Uh, of course."

"Your life is too full, Stella," I said. "I know you enjoy being active, but your husband should be your first priority, not your tenth or eleventh or twentieth. Do you understand what I'm saying?"

"Yes, I do," she said, bursting into tears. "And I already realized that on my own, the day he got shot."

I soothed her a bit and then asked to speak to him one more time.

"Eli, I know you're tired," I said, "but you've got to answer one more question for me."

"Okay, sweetheart. I'll try."

"Who shot you?"

"I don't know, Callie," he replied. "Your guess is as good as mine."

Forty-Two

When I went back to the control room, the place was in a frenzy. Tom had found the key to the code! Everyone stood waiting breathlessly as he went down the line of numbers, working the final mathematical steps and then converting the numbers to letters, unlocking the secret. I stepped closer to him to see the answer: S T T S E C U R E S T O R A G E 4 2.

A cheer went up from the agents, and even the restrained Agent Holt had a big grin on his face.

"That's out by the airport," Abraham said. "On St. Thomas."

"Ladies and gentlemen," Holt said into his microphone, "I would like for team one to head to St. Thomas. We are going to STT Secure Storage, unit forty-two."

Amidst the cheering, I told Tom I had been talking to Eli and that he was awake.

We embraced, and a surge of emotions swelled in my heart. Relief. Elation. Confusion. Fear.

This day wasn't over yet.

From Abraham, I caught up on all that had happened while I was in the other room on the phone. Using face recognition software, FBI headquarters had gotten a match on the two goons. Apparently, they were a pair of two-bit thugs with a long list of petty crimes but few incarcerations. Dianne Streep was known to employ them from time to time, and much to our surprise, it turned out that they were the ones who had been caught in the act of art theft by Interpol and had subsequently become informants. It was their tips that led the investigation to the Streeps and St. John in the first place. As a former turncoat herself, Dianne must've somehow figured out that they were double-crossing her, and that made them expendable.

The two goons had finished loading the truck items into the *Enigma,* and now one of them was waiting there with the boat while the other one was driving back toward Dianne's house. Merveaux was currently sitting in a taxi on the south side of the island; his bodyguard was still in the process of hiking from the taxi down to the Drake's Pond area. Using the archaeological grid to locate F12, the FBI agents had found the code there already, a weird row of letters written on a rock. At first look the agents thought the letters were hieroglyphics, but when they asked Tom to look at the screen he had simply chuckled and told them that it was a mix of letters and numbers that had been written upside down and backwards. The rock protruded out over the pond, and the code was meant to be read in the reflection on the water. I remembered Dianne and Merveaux's conversation, where they said he could "pause and reflect" there. They had been making a joke.

"Actually, that is not an original idea," Abraham said. "Some of the most interesting petroglyphs on this island are reflected in pools of water. Archeologists think it may have been done for the same sort of reason—to hide a messages by making them upside down and backward."

I listened to Holt communicating with his agents, and I thought he was acting prudently in all regards. They would keep the satellite focused on Merveaux, but otherwise they were going to lie in wait at the storage facility and catch him red-handed there with the stolen goods, thereby ensuring the greatest number of possible criminal charges for him.

As for Dianne, they were ready to arrest her now, but they wanted to wait until Merveaux was off the island so as not to tip their hand. In the meantime, they were trying to ascertain the where-abouts of Earl, Larry, and Zach—all of whom had been conspicu-ously absent so far.

Thus we waited, watching on the monitor as the beefy, sweating bodyguard emerged at the bottom of the trail, walked over to the dig site, and began checking the tags on the posts.

"What's he doing?" I asked.

"Looking for F twelve," Abraham answered. "The dig site has been divided into a grid. See the wires that stretch between the posts? That is how they catalog the items they uncover. He will find row F going down then row twelve coming across, and where the two meet is where the code will be found."

"Amazing."

Sure enough, the man found the code and seemed to know already that he was supposed to write down what he saw in the water, not on the rock. Once he had done that, he rolled up his shirt sleeves a bit higher and started back up the trail.

"Don't you have to unencrypt it?" I whispered to Tom.

"No," he replied, "that's the numeric security code Merveaux will use to unlock the storage unit."

I couldn't take the tension of waiting, so I offered to go and pick up some lunch for everyone. That was met with an enthusiastic yes, so Abraham gave me directions to the nearest restaurant, and Tom and I set off down the street on foot.

As we walked along in the fresh air and sunshine, I was filled with the overwhelming urge to be out in a canoe, paddling into the water, sailing across the shimmering waves.

"You know what I want more than anything on earth right now?" I asked as we went.

"For this waiting to be over?"

"More than that."

"To hear how much I love you?"

I giggled. "More than that."

"To get your hair braided by Mrs. Ruhl?"

"How did you know?" I asked, laughing.

"No, really, what do you want, Callie? Your wish is always my command."

I reached out for his hand but then remembered it was bandaged. I held his wrist instead.

"I want to be on a canoe," I said. "Right now. I want a paddle in my hands and Sal in the bow and miles of empty water stretching out in front of me."

"You want to go home?" Tom asked.

"Not really," I replied. "I love my river there, but that's not what I mean. I just want a canoe. I feel like paddling. Why did I ever have to have a hobby that was so utterly not portable?"

Tom slipped his arm around my shoulders.

"I tell you what," he said. "When all of this is over, I will take you somewhere and get you a canoe. With all of the water sports they have going on around here, I wouldn't doubt we could find one somewhere. How about I'll sit there with an umbrella while you paddle me around?"

"Why, sir, it would be my pleasure to take you for a ride."

We found the restaurant easily and placed an order to go for a variety of food, including salad, garlic chicken, and something called "johnnycakes." It took a while, but eventually the food was bagged and ready. As usual, Tom picked up the tab. We argued about it, until I remembered that all I had in my wallet was ten dollars anyway.

When we arrived back at the command center, it was obvious something was going on. We set down the bags of food and looked at Abraham questioningly.

"What's happening?" I asked.

"It's Dianne," he replied. "Looks like she's on the move."

Forty-Three

We all ate as we watched what was happening on the monitor. Abraham said Dianne and her goon had come out of the house and were now in the white truck. The farther they drove, the more obvious it became that they were heading to the *Enigma*. If that were true, then we all felt fairly certain she was about to make her getaway from the island. Calculating the risk, Holt decided he would rather be safe than sorry; the agents would wait as long as they could to stop her, but if Merveaux was still on the island by the time Dianne started to leave, they would have no choice but to move in and make the arrest.

We watched two satellite feeds—one of the cab carrying Merveaux to the Sugar Manse, the other of the truck bringing Dianne to the *Enigma*. We wanted Merveaux to move quickly and Dianne to move slowly. It was trying to watch it all unfold, to say the least.

"Parker, any chance you can cause a little traffic jam on the road that leads to the marina?"

"I'll try, sir," a voice said. "The street is pretty narrow here. I can jack up the back and make it look like I'm changing a tire."

"Good. Maybe that'll hold things up a bit."

In the meantime the technician was working on getting a third satellite shot, this one of the Streeps' estate. Once Dianne was arrested at the boat, agents would also be moving in on the house; but with Larry, Earl, and Zach still unaccounted for, they wanted to go in with as much knowledge as they could.

Finally, Merveaux reached the resort, and we all breathed a sigh of relief when he and his bodyguard emerged out of the other side of the building without much delay. Dianne, meanwhile, was less than a mile from the marina.

"Come on, come on," Holt whispered as we all watched, spell-bound. There were now three agents ready to apprehend Dianne—Craig on the boat, Reese on foot, and the one named Parker with the car. The remaining agents were well on their way to St. Thomas, setting up the welcome party for Merveaux at the Secure Storage facility.

The truck reached the small cluster of cars that were feeding around Parker and his flat-tire diversion. When the truck finally made it around, Merveaux was just climbing onto his boat at the Sugar Manse.

"It's almost time," Holt said.

A few minutes later, Parker announced he was back behind the wheel and heading into the marina.

The *Cezanne* pulled away from the dock at the Sugar Manse. Moving slowly, it made its way past rows of other boats and yachts and then slowly picked up speed out in the open water.

On the camera feed from Craig's boat, we could see Dianne and the second goon getting out of the truck and walking toward the *Enigma*. Her movements were tight, her posture tense. Despite the floral skirt and scarf, she now looked less like a tourist at the beach and more like a fugitive on the run.

"Gentlemen, make your arrest," Holt said.

Reese was the first to move, jumping up from behind a barrel on the dock, holding out his gun, and yelling at them to "Freeze!"

We could hear Parker's car screech to a stop, and then he also yelled for them to "Freeze! FBI!"

Dianne stopped moving and held both hands up in the air. The goon, however, surprised everyone by turning, grabbing her, and then making a dive for the boat. They landed face down on the deck, with her struggling to get back up as he sprawled out as flat as he could get. The boat roared to life and sped away from the slip, the ropes snapping just before they ripped the cleats right out of the wood.

Gunfire ensued, but the boat kept going. Both agents jumped aboard Craig's boat, and they shot out of their slip in hot pursuit.

Stunned, we all watched the scene play out in front of us through the satellite feed, helpless to do anything. As Holt cursed a blue streak there in the command center, the FBI agents at the scene fired off some shots at the *Enigma*. The FBI's boat was smaller but faster, and the distance between them quickly narrowed.

Then the *Enigma* exploded.

With a piercing *kaboom,* the large boat burst into flames. We could hear our agents yelling and we watched as they managed to veer quickly to the side, avoiding the inferno there on the water.

Dianne and her two goons were dead, the boat totally destroyed before our eyes. Despite everything, I couldn't help but feel a surge of pity for the woman who had made so many wrong choices in her life.

I looked at the monitor of Merveaux, praying his boat was far enough away so that he wouldn't see the fire and smoke on the horizon. In shock we listened as the agents at the scene all yelled at once. They hadn't been shooting when it blew, they said. The didn't know why it had exploded. With lurch in the pit of my stomach, I had a feeling I knew.

Rushkin had located his target.

Instantly, Holt was on the phone with the Coast Guard. Sirens blared in the distance.

"Sir," the technician said, interrupting. "We have satellite on the house."

We looked at the third screen, at the bird's-eye view of Dianne's estate. I had stared at the satellite photos so many times that the image was completely familiar to me.

Except for an odd black blotch that was now on the tennis court.

"Look at that!" I said, running to the screen and pointing. "What is that?"

The technician zoomed in tightly.

"It's a helicopter!" Tom cried.

As we watched, two people ran from the house to the helicopter. It looked as though they were carrying something large and square, which they put into the helicopter's side door. The camera zoomed in further.

"The house, the house!" Holt yelled into his mike. "Get to the house!"

As he directed his agents how to reach it by boat, Abraham dispatched the police. Meanwhile, the two men ran from the helicopter back toward the house. Just before going inside, they paused and looked up at the sky.

"That's Earl and Larry," Tom said, leaning forward.

Abraham put his hand over the phone.

"I have a man in Coral Bay," he said. "He'll be there in one minute."

Sure enough, though we had no sound feed, after about a minute we could see a police car racing up the driveway. The two men were just coming back out of the house when the car screeched to a stop and the cop jumped out. Unarmed, the men saw what was happening and ran back inside.

Ten seconds later, the house exploded.

This time, we didn't hear a thing. We simply watched in silence as the structure blew into a million pieces.

Flames shot toward the heavens and debris fell down to the ground like rain.

Forty-Four

The rest of the afternoon was a blur.

Between the Coast Guard, the FBI, and the local police, the command center became a frenzied hub of activity. Outside, reporters and curious onlookers swarmed around like a throng. At the center of things, Tom and I were forced to recount our stories from the beginning, numerous times. Across the room agents ran the video and satellite loops over and over, deconstructing all that had happened. After a while I found myself numbed to the horrible sequence of events in the images that filled the screen.

Somehow, the thought that Dianne and her family had been the target of an outside force seemed to come as a great relief to Holt and his men. The explosion at the house only served to confirm that the explosion on the boat had not been caused by them. They were at a loss, however, as to how Rushkin or his agents had managed to pull it off. No evidence had been found yet of a detonation device at either location.

It helped matters enormously, of course, that the arrest of Merveaux at the storage facility in St. Thomas went off without a hitch. He and his bodyguard had been caught without a single shot fired, just as they were opening the door to take possession of a large storage room packed wall-to-wall with priceless artifacts.

The fire was eventually put out at Dianne's estate, though the entire home had been demolished. FBI agents didn't find any remains, but I had a feeling fragments of the two men who had let greed be their demise would show up in time. There were plenty of remains at the *Enigma,* however, and all of the blood made for a grisly frenzy of underwater activity until the Coast Guard was able to salvage what was left.

Back at the estate, the helicopter had been searched and was found to contain a masterpiece that had been missing for many years, a Goya that had once disappeared from a Paris museum. The agents could only speculate as to what other valuable pieces might have been destroyed in the explosion. Abraham was the most devastated about that, because it was now obvious that if Interpol had let him raid the home when he had wanted to, he could have saved the art, arrested the people, and possibly stopped the senseless death of all who had been killed.

In the recapping of the events of the day for the hundredth time, I finally came to realize that the only person missing from this scenario was Zach. Unless he had been inside the house where we couldn't see him, he obviously hadn't been killed in either explosion.

Was he the one who planted the deadly explosives? Had he been hired by Rushkin to kill Dianne? As I thought about that, an uneasiness settled in around my heart. We hadn't seen Jodi since she left Miss Lucy's with him the night before. Though there was a good chance she was now merely off working at the dig site or shopping in St. Thomas, oblivious to all of this, there was also a chance she was somewhere else, either in danger—or in cahoots with him. I tried to reach her on the phone, but she didn't answer her cell or at the house. Abraham said we wouldn't be able to file a missing person's report until she had been missing for 24 hours.

Tom and I were finally released late in the afternoon. The first thing we did was call Chris Fisher, the PI in St. Thomas, and let her know that the men who beat her up had died in the explosion. She surprised me by responding with a sharp laugh.

"So what you're saying is they're fish bait now?" she asked.

"Uh, basically, yes."

"Well, thank you for calling and telling me, Callie," she said emphatically, sounding greatly relieved. "Now I can rest easy. Hey, you live by the sword, you die by the sword, that's what I always say."

After I hung up the phone, we got in the car and drove to Stella's house, hoping to find Jodi there in person or, at the very least, some evidence of where she might have gone. It didn't look to me as if she had come home at all the night before. Her room seemed the same to me as it was when I slipped into her bathroom to borrow her shampoo.

We were finally able to reach Sandy on the phone, but she said neither Larry, Zach, nor Jodi had shown up at the dig site that day. Fawn was even a bit annoyed, she said, because Jodi had promised to take her to dinner tonight at the fancy restaurant Asolare.

I was a bit surprised that Sandy hadn't heard anything about what had happened.

"A lot's been going on today," I said. "You don't know about any of it?"

"We were using some new equipment at the site that was very RF sensitive," she said. "We had to keep all cell phones and radios turned off."

As simply as I could, I explained the events that had taken place. Sandy sounded stunned at the news of Larry's death and Zach's disappearance, but when I told her about the theft of artifacts from SPICE, her shock turned to anger.

I assured her that the artifacts were safe and sound, but she was furious, telling me it must have been her fault they were stolen in the first place.

"Larry tricked me," she cried. "He said he needed access to the artifacts because he had made a mistake on some insurance tags and he needed to correct them. I didn't want him to get in trouble with his company, so I told him where they were stored, and I loaned him the key. I even gave him the security code so he wouldn't set off the alarm. Callie, he was my friend—it never dawned on me he was going over there to steal!"

"He and his mother tricked a lot of people over the years," I said. "Don't feel bad—you were up against some real pros."

Later, as I thought about it, that's what was preventing the whole puzzle from fitting together neatly in my mind. As Tom and I drove across the island toward the remains of the Streeps' estate on the East End, we talked it through together. The part that was bothering me, I said, was that Dianne was such a pro, and yet she had made some fundamental mistakes today that had ended up costing her her life.

"The problem with Dianne," Tom said, "was that she possessed the one quality an NSA agent should never have."

"What's that?"

"The need for recognition, for external validation. The life of an NSA cryptologist is one of quiet, anonymous service. Conversely, here you have a woman who seems to want the world in on her secrets. She names her dogs Alice, Bob, and Eve after well-known encryption terms. She calls her boat the *Enigma*, for goodness' sake, after one of the single greatest cryptographic accomplishments of all time. Why would you leave yourself open for questions by plastering the name of the thing on the side of your boat? Callie, that would be like you going around with a boat named 'Charity Sleuth' or something."

I giggled. "'Charity Sleuth'?"

"You know what I mean. Something that practically advertises your area of expertise when your very job depends on the fact that people *not* know what you do for a living. It's nuts."

"I see what you mean."

As we drove I thought about what Tom had said, and I realized that one of the things I loved most about him was his complete humility, his very anonymity. It dawned on me that not only was his full-time job one where he received no acclaim, his foundation took that a step further, doing good for countless others without accepting a shred of recognition for himself.

"You're going to have to call Eli and tell him," Tom said, interrupting my thoughts. "He needs to know Dianne is dead."

"I'll do it in a little while. Right now I just want to get to the site of the explosion and have a look around."

Though we were exhausted, Tom and I both felt the need to connect in person with the site of today's destruction. When we reached the familiar driveway out on Turtle Point, we turned onto it and headed up the long and winding road to the mountaintop estate. Concerned for Tom's injured hands, I had offered to drive, but he insisted that he was fine. Now he steered up the difficult drive with his fingertips, making it even scarier than it needed to be!

This place had been the focus of our entire investigation, and somehow going there in person felt incredibly surreal. As we parked the car and got out, the pungent smell of burning wood filled our nostrils. Though the fire was out, some smoke still wafted from the smoldering remains.

There were a few agents still there working the scene. Police tape had been strung up around most of it, but they let us walk the perimeter. As we did, we admired the beauty and tranquility of the place, high above the Caribbean sea, the lush greenery a marked contrast to the scattered rubble.

Tom and I walked down to the tennis court and stood at the tape line, looking in at the helicopter. The agents had removed the seats and stripped out most of the interior, probably hoping to find a secret storage compartment with more art in it or something. I asked Tom where he thought they had been intending to fly. He said that they probably had some prearranged rendezvous point on another island.

"This machine could probably go two or three hundred miles before it would run out of gas. That would give them a lot of islands to choose from, all the way from the Dominican Republic to Guadeloupe. I would imagine Dianne was planning to meet them somewhere out there on her boat."

I tried to picture it—the two men aloft in this helicopter, Dianne and her goons on the *Enigma*—and then one thought struck me. What about the dogs?

"Tom, where were the three dogs in all of this?" I asked.

"I'm sure they blew up with the house."

I shook my head.

"No, that doesn't add up. If the dogs were here while Larry and Earl were trying to make their escape, that would mean they were planning on taking them on the helicopter with them. Wouldn't the dogs have traveled better aboard the *Enigma* than on this little helicopter?"

He thought about it.

"Yeah, I suppose so. With that big painting in the backseat, the dogs wouldn't have fit in there at all."

"So why didn't Dianne have the dogs with her when she went to the dock? That would have been more logical. And you know she wasn't going to just leave them behind somewhere."

We puzzled over the dog issue while strolling the rest of the way around the tennis court. Just a ways beyond it was a bank of shrubs, and then about 20 feet past that was the cliff where Tom had climbed up to position the transmitter box the night his hands were injured. We walked to the edge there now, looking down at the treacherous rocks that led all the way to the beach.

"My hands hurt just looking at it," I said, picturing him sliding down the gnarled rope. A piece of that rope still remained, caught in the crook of a rock, blowing back and forth gently in the breeze.

"It was actually very exciting," Tom admitted. "At least the part coming up. I never had delusions of being a field agent, but I have to say that that was some wild adrenaline kick as I was doing it!"

He showed me where he had climbed over the top, and then he reenacted the steps he had taken to put the box in place.

"I thought I could just put it here near the edge, but then I realized it wouldn't be close enough to the house. I figured they had motion sensors there, so I went this way. I whacked my foot against this thing and almost dropped the box. In the end I put it over there."

I looked down at the thing he had tripped on, which was an odd sort of vent pipe that shot up from the ground about a foot high. Tucked discreetly behind a small bush, it was no wonder he hadn't seen it in the dark.

We were able to get closer to the house on this side, though the sight of it gave me a shudder. Thinking of the people who were buried somewhere among the burning pile of wood and materials made my skin crawl. We were positioned outside of where the laundry room must have been because a washing machine was still there, mostly intact, with light bulbs and laundry detergent spilled out nearby.

"What's that?" I asked, pointing to a box of clear plastic tubular-looking things all over the ground.

"UV Sleeves," Tom said, tilting his head to read the side of the box. "We use those sometimes with computers. They keep the ultraviolet rays from coming out of fluorescent lights. I think museums use them too, to protect the art and artifacts."

We walked all the way around the back of the house, pausing to speak to two of the agents before going to the car. Our visit hadn't accomplished anything, really, but there was a certain sad satisfaction at finally having access to a place we had previously been able to view only from afar.

Still worried about Jodi, I tried the round of phone numbers again, all to no avail. Tom and I decided to go into town and visit some of her favorite haunts, to see if anyone had spotted her either last night or today. I called Sandy to get a list of places we should check, and she said that she and Fawn had already been thinking of doing the same thing.

"Good. Let's divide and conquer," I said, not exactly eager to go barhopping. Sandy suggested that Tom and I start with Coral Bay, including a place called Skinny Legs, and another known as Shipwreck Landing. She and Fawn would go into Cruz Bay and check the places there.

We didn't have to work very hard at it. At the Shipwreck, a pleasant outdoor bar and restaurant overlooking the bay, the waitress knew Jodi well, and she said Jodi had been in last night around midnight with Zach and Larry and another woman who was new around town. I realized when they left Miss Lucy's, they must have come straight here.

"They stayed about half an hour," the waitress told us, glancing back toward the bar, "but Larry's date got so drunk they finally left."

"She seemed pretty far gone when they left Miss Lucy's," I told her.

"Well, by the time they left here, she was so sloshed they practically had to carry her out."

"Any idea where they went next?"

"Not a clue. Though I doubt they hit any other bars. The woman was too far gone for that."

I thanked her profusely for her help, and then I went back into the car and asked Tom to drive to the command center in town. An idea was bubbling just under the surface for me, and I wanted to see a replay of some of the video from today. On the way I dialed Sandy and told her that Jodi had been at the Shipwreck Landing around midnight, stayed for about half an hour, and then left.

"You should keep asking around," I said. "But I don't think anyone else will have seen her."

Fortunately, the lights were still on when we arrived at the command center. Tom and I parked and went inside to find the technician and one other agent there, the one they called Craig. They said that the case agent, Holt, had gone over to St. Thomas to follow up on the action there.

Much to my surprise, the technician stood and reintroduced himself to me and then to Tom, insisting that we call him by his nickname, Rig, so named because "if I got a coupla wires, I can rig anything."

He looked reverentially at Tom.

"Hey, listen, man," Rig added, "I'm sorry if I was short with you this morning. If I had known who you were and all…"

"No problem," Tom replied, obviously embarrassed.

"I'm, like, a huge fan of your work. Bennett's Theorem is so elegant, so intricately calculated and yet so simplistic in its algebraic design. It has saved me hours of work, I just can't tell you."

"Oh, well, thank you," Tom said modestly.

I was quiet for a moment, caught up in the realization that Tom actually had a theorem named after him. Other than keeping a perfectly balanced checkbook, mathematics and I didn't really get along. As this FBI agent nearly gushed in Tom's presence, I was reminded of my boyfriend's stature in certain circles. I was very glad this agent was a fan, in particular, since that might make him more willing to help us out.

"Rig, we need to see some of the video from today, if we can," I said, collecting my thoughts. "Really, starting from the beginning."

"No problem," he said, popping a CD into a drive. "I just finished putting everything on disk in chronological order."

He sat at a computer and brought it up onto the screen while Tom and I grabbed some chairs and positioned ourselves on either side of him. I had him play the available images of Dianne at Virgin Gorda, from when she got off the ferry until she met Merveaux on the beach.

"There," I said finally. "Stop there."

He pressed a key and the image froze, showing Dianne standing there on the beach, scanning the horizon. She was looking almost directly into the camera that the FBI had had hidden on the boat.

"Right there," I said. "It seems like she's looking around to make sure they aren't being observed. But what if, instead, she's really looking around to make sure that they *are* being observed?"

"You've lost me," Tom said.

"Think about it. Hit play. Watch what she does next."

On the screen in front of us, Dianne and Merveaux walked to a rock and sat, facing the water.

"For a women who knows all about security protection, she isn't being very savvy. She knows she's in the sight line of at least one boat. She knows she is sitting still instead of moving around. I think she knew we were there. More than that, I think she wanted us there."

"You're saying we were set up?" Rig asked.

"Play the conversation," I told him.

We listened to the audio between Dianne and Merveaux— crystal clear except when she told him the drop points.

"*The first will be at th…ist,*" she said, and then later, "*the drop will be at F twel…ake's Pond.*"

"Watch what she does when she says those things," I told them. "Play it again."

Rig did as I asked. Sure enough, both times, as Dianne named the drop points, she reached up and blocked her mouth with her hand—once by fixing her sunglasses, the second time by smoothing the scarf over her hair. The FBI mikes were good, but they weren't perfect. Dianne must've known she could block the sound by blocking her face.

Tom stood and began pacing.

"Callie's right," he said suddenly. "If this woman were all that smart, she would've held their meeting walking around between all of those rocks. We could've caught snippets of what they said, maybe, but for us to catch the entire conversation, we needed her to be on the beach and to be stationary. And that's what she gave us."

Rig turned around in his chair and looked from Tom to me.

"So what are you insinuating?" he asked. "That she had a death wish? That she wanted to be caught or killed?"

I shook my head slowly.

"Fast-forward to the scene at the boat, where your people move in to make the arrest. This is after she went home and came back out again."

He did as I asked. Once we had video of her emerging from the truck and walking toward the *Enigma,* I had him put it on slow motion. I leaned forward and studied the screen.

"Now look at her," I said. "At the way she stands. At the way she walks. Do you see it?"

The men were silent until Tom sucked in his breath and whispered, "You're right."

"What is it?" Rig asked.

"Keep watching," I told him. "You'll see."

In slow motion the agent appeared from behind the barrel, holding out his gun. Dianne started to surrender, but the goon practically tackled her and threw her on the boat. Once there, as it began speeding away, he stayed flat while she struggled to get up.

"There!" I said. "Freeze."

Rig hit the button. On the screen in front of us was the image of a woman, taken from behind, trying to stand. Her skirt was askew, her legs bare.

There was no scar on her thigh.

"The woman killed in the boat explosion today," I said, "was not Dianne Streep."

"So who was she?" Craig asked as we stared at the image on the screen.

"I think her name was Sunshine," I replied sadly. "Or Freebird. I don't know if she had made up her mind by then or not."

"Oh, man," Tom whispered. "How it all falls into place, huh?"

Vividly, I could picture Larry at Miss Lucy's the night before, romancing a woman who was old enough to be his mother. How excited he must have been when he first found her in the bar. The fact that she had no friends here yet and no real connections back home had made her the perfect choice.

No doubt, he had carried out his mission well—first by getting the woman drunk and then probably by dragging her to his mother's home. There, they must have played with the perfect "look"—floral scarf, big sunglasses—that would turn her into Dianne's double. And whether the woman had gone to the *Enigma* willingly or by force, I felt certain she didn't know she was walking into her death. Dianne's goons must have also been unaware that they were expendable.

My biggest question was whether Jodi had in some way been a participant in this masquerade or if she had also been held somewhere against her will. I felt sick at the thought that she might have been inside the house when it blew up.

"Now show us the satellite feed from the house," I said to Rig.

We watched the distant shot of the entire estate, then the zoom on the men at the helicopter, then the tighter zoom as they ran toward the house.

"Freeze it there," I said, and he did, catching the scene just as the two men looked up at the sky.

"Can you make the image larger, get us a better view?"

Rig tried, typing instructions, enhancing the contrast, enlarging the picture.

"That's about as good as it's gonna get," he said finally.

Tom and I leaned close. It sure looked like Larry and Earl to me.

"Those aren't doubles," I said certainly. "Do you really think Dianne killed her husband and son?"

Tom leaned back in his seat, nervously tapping his foot.

"No," he said, shaking his head. "No. Do you know what they're doing there?"

"What?" Rig and I both asked.

"They're looking right at us," he said. "They're giving us a good, clear picture of their faces. They know we've got them on satellite, and they want to make sure we know it's them."

"But why?"

"Hit play," Tom instructed, and we watched as the two men went inside the house. "Now watch."

The two men ran back into the house. The counter ticked up an excruciating ten seconds. Then the house blew up.

My head snapped back, jarred as if it were just happening again. I didn't understand what we were seeing—but I knew it wasn't real.

Somehow, those two men did not die in that explosion.

Forty-Five

We raced across the island in two cars, Tom and I leading the way with Craig following behind. Rig had needed to stay behind and keep an eye on the command center, and as we left, he was attempting to contact Agent Holt to tell him our theory about Dianne and Sunshine.

We didn't have much of a theory yet about the other two—except that somehow they had escaped that fiery blast. They must have had a preplanned escape route, a quick way into the front door and back out some other exit. Because the satellite had been zoomed in on the men, we didn't have a shot of the entire building. My guess was that they ran in the front door, ran out a back door, and somehow escaped from the top of the mountain unnoticed because of the distraction of the fire. They had either repelled down the rock wall, or they somehow snuck around the perimeter of the property until they were able to run down the private road to the beach. They'd probably had a boat waiting for them there—and then they had sailed away unseen.

I was determined to find proof they had left the building alive—and maybe find out if Jodi was still alive somewhere in the process.

A St. John cop was stationed at the base of the driveway when we arrived there, lights flashing but siren off. He checked our ID and radioed it into Rig at the command center. Once we had the okay, he let us through. It had grown quite dark by this time, but Tom was a good driver, even with his bandaged hands, and he handled the myriad twists and turns of the driveway with ease.

As we neared the top, we saw that two agents were there, still processing the scene, and they had mounted three big work lights from a generator. Craig had been in contact with them on the drive over, and they came and met our cars when we pulled to a stop behind their van, ready to examine this new possibility. The night air was chilly, and I pulled on my sweater before getting out of the car.

While the men concentrated on the back side of the property, looking for evidence or footprints or other oddities, I decided to focus on how Earl and Larry could have gone all the way down to the beach without being seen. I started in the place where I thought they might have run from and then tracked it myself, pretending that I was trying to get away from my burning house in broad daylight as it was descended upon by law enforcement officers.

I didn't see any signs that they had been there, but I kept my eyes open as I went, trying to put myself in their shoes. How had they done it? I felt certain they had given the tennis court a wide berth, so I did the same, coming dangerously close to the rock wall before realizing it. I stepped quickly back in surprise and—whack!

"Ow!"

Just like Tom, I had crashed into the metal pipe that protruded from the ground. Unlike him, however, I fell all the way down, and I stayed there for a minute clutching my toe. Ouch! I wouldn't be surprised if it were broken.

"Callie? Are you okay?"

Tom had heard me yelp and came running. Now he knelt next to me in the grass, ready to be my knight in shining armor.

"Would you believe it, I hit the same stupid pipe you did? Gosh, it hurts."

"Take your shoe off. Let's have a look."

I did as he instructed, not surprised to see that the toe was swollen. It wasn't, however, dislocated or cut, so I pulled my sock and shoe back on and then sat there for a moment, feeling it throb.

"Shall I kiss it and make it better?" he asked softly.

I put one hand to my mouth.

"No, but ow! Ow! My lip!" I whispered. "It hurts, it hurts."

"Let me see what I can do," he whispered back.

We were well in the shadows, hidden by the greenery that surrounded the tennis court. And though a million and one things were vying for our attention, somehow it didn't seem wrong to take a moment and simply reconnect.

Tom kissed me lightly at first, and then more deeply before we slipped into an embrace, just sitting there on the grass in the dark, rocking back and forth, holding on to one another. I was overwhelmed with emotion as I thought of all the times I had done investigations by myself with no one around to help me with the bumps and the bruises. This investigation, conversely, had been done as a team. If Tom never investigated another case with me again, I would always be grateful for the time we had shared on this one.

The sky grew suddenly a bit darker, and then we heard one of the agents, from across the lawn.

"Hey, Craig, why'd you turn off the—"

His voice stopped with a grunt and then a thud.

Eyes wide, I looked at Tom, who also seemed to sense that something wasn't right. We didn't speak but instead slowly and silently pressed ourselves down into the grass, side by side. My heart pounded in my throat.

What was going on?

We listened to a sudden, familiar sound, trying to place it. Then I realized we were hearing duct tape being pulled from a roll. We couldn't see anything from where we were, but eventually the noise stopped. Another work light went out.

Carefully, I raised up on my elbows and inched forward, both to reach some better cover and to see if I could see anything. I got to the thicker brush and then waved at Tom to do the same, which he did.

Silently, he motioned that he was going to crawl along to the far end and see what he could see. I nodded at him even as my mind screamed at him not to move. As he went I ran my hands along the ground searching for some sort of weapon. The best I could find was a small rock to hold in my fist.

After an excruciating few minutes, Tom crawled back to me. He put two hands over my ear and whispered as quietly as was humanly possible.

"The agent's unconscious," he said. "There's duct tape around his hands and feet—and over his eyes and his mouth."

My own eyes widened in horror.

"There's someone here," he added. "Doing something over in the rubble."

Together we inched our way along the shrubbery until we could see. We had to look through the branches of a bush, but at least there was one work light still on, behind the person, illuminating him as he worked. I couldn't tell what he was doing, but it made a fair amount of noise.

I grabbed Tom by the sleeve, pointing to his white shirt and the way it shone in the moonlight. Silently, he pulled it off, revealing a navy blue T-shirt underneath.

He looked at me questioningly, but I shook my head, not knowing what we should do next. I thought about taking the chance of making a call on my cell phone, but then I realized I had left it in the car. I cupped my hands around Tom's ear and whispered, "Just stay put for now."

We huddled there in the darkness, side by side, for at least ten minutes. Finally, I chanced sitting up a bit for a better viewpoint, and I realized what we were seeing: It was Zach, clearing away rubble to get to something underneath. With a final clink and then a groan, he seemed to be opening a door from the ground. As it creaked open, voices came spilling out.

They were hushed but angry, and Tom and I watched in amazement as Larry, Earl, and then Dianne came walking up out of the very earth. We couldn't understand every word of their angry whispers, but we heard enough to know that Zach had waited a bit too long to come and release them from wherever they had been trapped. They were coughing a lot, and I could tell they were having difficulty breathing.

"You knew there would only be five or six hours of air in there because of the power-off dampers," Dianne cried. "We could've asphyxiated!"

"This place has been crawling with federal agents!" Zach snapped back, walking suddenly in our direction. "What was I supposed to do?"

He kicked at the agent on the ground, who must have still been unconscious because he didn't react.

"Oh, no," Dianne said, seeing the agent for the first time.

"Hey, at least I got you a new boat like you said. It's fast and powerful, with plenty of room for the stuff. You'll be happy with it."

"You came here on it?" Dianne asked.

"Yeah. It's tied up at the beach."

They all stood around and looked down at the agent on the ground.

"If they wake up and hear our voices, they'll know we're still alive," Larry said. "We've got to kill them."

"No!" Dianne cried.

I wasn't sure if that was her conscience speaking or if she just knew that murdering FBI agents would be a very stupid move.

"Why don't we just lock 'em up in the back of their van," Earl said. "Maybe when they wake up, they'll think it was done by some looters."

They all seemed to agree, and so together they worked to put all three taped-up agents into the back of the FBI's van. When they were finished, Zach walked back toward us, through the gate and onto the tennis court.

"I thought you said I'd be able to take the helicopter from here," he said, furious at the state of the machine that had been dismantled on the pavement. As he walked closer to it to inspect it, I held my breath. We were a mere 10 or 15 feet away, hidden only by the shadows and some shrubbery.

"Let's go people," Earl whispered sharply. "We've got to get all the paintings down to the boat."

"I'm not helping you," Zach said. "I have to put this bird back together again."

He went to work on the driver's seat first, putting it into place and then cursing and muttering as he searched for the bolts that would hold it there. At least he seemed to know what he was doing, but my biggest fear was that he would drop a tool and it would roll in our direction.

Behind him Larry, Earl, and Dianne seemed to start an almost assembly line procedure across the wide lawn. We couldn't see everything that was happening, but it looked as though Dianne was bringing rectangular, handled cases up from the basement where they had been and Earl was taking them from her at the top of the stairs and running them out to Larry. Larry waited until he was completely loaded before starting down the private road to the beach. Zach had come here to get them by boat, and that was how they would leave.

Larry was winded when he came back up, and he walked out to the tennis court to speak to Zach.

"Jodi's tied up on the boat!" Larry whispered sharply. "Why haven't you killed her yet?"

"She's got something I need first. Then I'll do it."

"You should've killed her when you were supposed to," Larry snapped. "She's nothing but a liability."

"Just bring her with you the next time you come up. We'll throw her in that back car."

"Then what?"

"Then when we're done here, I'll get the keys off of one those agents and take her home."

"Home? Are you crazy?"

Zach spun around angrily.

"Look, Larry, we still haven't found those bearer bonds. I'll get rid of her as soon as she hands them over."

"I already searched the house," Larry said. "I told you, they're not there!"

"Don't worry," Zach replied, "I have ways of getting it out of her. When I'm finished with her, I'll know *exactly* where she hid them. I'll kill her as soon as the bonds are in my hands."

The men laughed.

"No," Dianne whispered sharply, her hands on her hips. "There's already been too much killing, too much death. First my two men, then that Sunshine woman—"

"Don't forget the old guy in Florida," Zach added.

Dianne gasped.

"What old guy? Who?"

"Eli Gold," Larry replied. "That private investigator."

"You *killed* him?" she asked, sounding as if she could hardly catch her breath. "When?"

"Last Friday," Larry said. "Zach lifted a Bushmaster semiautomatic from a gun store so we could make a long-distance shot."

Listening to them, I realized they didn't know Eli had survived their attempt at murder. Dianne's hands flew to her chest, and I thought she might faint. She staggered and Larry stepped forward to support her.

"Come on, Mom, get over it. You said he was digging around where he shouldn't have been, that his digging might tip off Rushkin. It seemed to quickest way to solve the problem."

"No," Dianne cried. "I brought you to Florida with me so you could search his house for any notes or photos of me that he might have. We never spoke of killing!"

"So what's the big deal?" Larry asked. "He was a nobody."

"You don't understand," Dianne sobbed, shaking her said from side to side. "He wasn't a 'nobody.'"

"What do you mean?"

"Oh, Larry," Dianne said, putting a hand to her son's cheek. "Eli was your father."

Forty-Six

Eli had a son.

Larry was Dianne and Eli's son.

Tom pulled at my sleeve and, reluctantly, I followed, crawling backward from the brush and toward the side of the cliff.

"Eli has a son!" I whispered.

"I know. Focus, Callie. We've got to move *now*."

I nodded, trying to pay attention as Tom said that the only way one of us could leave without being seen was to go straight down the rock wall.

"I'm going to climb down and swim around the point and go for help," Tom whispered. "You've got to promise me, Callie, that you'll stay where they won't see you. You're dead if they spot you."

"Tom, there's no way you can make it down this wall with those hands."

"Sure I can," he said, hoisting himself over the side. "Now go. Get over there. *Now*."

My mind still in a fog, I ran to the bank of trees. Squeezing between them, I felt fairly certain I wouldn't be spotted. I couldn't see much of what was going on with the gang on the tennis court, but at least I could watch Tom as he worked his way, spiderlike, down the wall.

He seemed to do okay at first. Then, about ten feet down, he faltered, losing his grip. My heart in my throat, I watched as he found another hold then, suddenly, started slipping from that one as well.

Quickly, without taking the time to think, I ran to the rock wall and started down myself. I knew if I focused on all I had learned, on all he had taught me about rock climbing, that I could do this. My injured toe was throbbing, but otherwise, at least, the rocks were good and rough with plenty of crags and crevices. When I reached Tom, he was frozen, using his elbows to form a brace against a rock.

"It's the blood," he whispered frantically. "I can't stop slipping."

Looking at him, I realized his hands were now bleeding profusely. The bandages were soaked.

"Can you go back up?" I asked, clutching the wall, trying to ignore the fact that this was the first time I had ever climbed without a harness and a safety rope.

"No, I don't think so. We'll have to keep going down."

"We can do this," I said, trying to sound confident while lying through my teeth. "Let's just overlap a bit. Here."

I inched sideways and then reached across his left arm to grab a hold in front of his face.

"Now dry your right hand on your shirt and go for a lower grip," I directed.

He did as I said, then together we took it down a step. He dried his left hand and put it in a lower spot, then I crossed over it again with mine. When I felt his hand start to slip, I pressed myself against the rocks, pinning his arm to the wall.

"Again," he said, and in tandem we went down another step.

It was working.

"*Mai pen rai,* baby," I whispered.

Without thinking how hard it was, without thinking how frightened I was, without thinking how far we had to go, we made our way down the side of the wall until we were close enough to jump the rest of the way down to the sand.

Once there, we simply embraced, holding on to one another tightly. It had taken so long to get down that I was terrified Jodi was gone by now, already being driven down the road to her imminent torture and death.

Tom and I crouched down behind the biggest rock, daring to look around the corner at the private beach at the bottom of the estate.

The boat was still there! Hopefully, that meant Jodi was still alive.

It was a big craft, but low to the water with a sleek profile. I had no doubt that once they had it loaded, they would fly out of there at top speed, never to be seen again.

"I'll have to do the swimming," I whispered, gesturing toward Tom's hands. "You know you can't go in the water bleeding like that. You'll draw sharks for sure."

He nodded reluctantly.

"I'll wait until the boat leaves," he said, "then I can run back up the trail and free the FBI agents."

"Just make sure you don't run into Zach up there," I said. "Look to see if that car is gone before you go out in the open."

My sweater was covered with Tom's blood, so I stripped it off and handed it to him. I didn't dare hug him at the risk of getting more blood on me, so I simply leaned over and kissed him hard on the forehead.

Then I gritted my teeth and slipped into the sea, swimming in the opposite direction from the beach, swimming around Turtle Point.

Except for the chilliness of the water, it wasn't bad at first. The hardest part was the darkness, the not knowing what was under me or around me. I stayed fairly close to shore, finding a rhythm that let me keep up a steady pace without wearing myself out too soon. As I rounded the point, however, I felt a stronger current tugging at me, and it was a struggle after that. I kicked off my shoes and then my pants, as the weight of them was dragging me down. In the distance, I could see the public beach, and that was what I aimed for. Making a direct line across the water, I pretended that it was daytime and that I was just out for a nice midday swim. My pretense didn't last all that long, but finally, just when I thought I couldn't swim another stroke, I paused to catch my breath and my feet touched the sand.

I walked the rest of the way out, praying I wouldn't step on a stingray or a sea urchin. When the water was to my waist, I stopped and gasped. In front of me, just below the surface, swam an octopus. Remembering that they liked to come out at night, I watched it go by in the moonlight, feeling awed and terrified all at the same time.

Still trying to catch my breath, I made it up the beach and to the road. I could see the flashing lights of the police car at the end of Dianne's driveway. With my eyes on those lights, I started running along the side of the road, ignoring the pain of my bare feet against the rough pavement. Finally, as I drew near to the police car, I ducked down a bit among the brush, not knowing what I might find there. I could hear an odd scuffling in the dark, and as I squinted up the driveway, I realized that Zach and Jodi were walking down! He had a tight grip around her neck, and in his free hand he held a gun. There was duct tape over her mouth and around both wrists, pinning her arms behind her back.

I wanted to warn the cop who was sitting inside the police car that they were coming, but I didn't know how to do that without giving my own presence away. Finally, I took a chance and tossed a pebble at the car. Though it made a loud "ping," he didn't stir.

I tried again, and on the second toss, he finally got out to see what was going on, though he didn't look up the driveway. Instead, he came around the side of the car, looked my way and gasped, spotting me in the bushes. He reached for his gun. I put a finger to my lips and pointed up the driveway with my other hand. But before the cop even had a chance to respond or figure out what was going on, Zach called out for him to "Freeze!"

The cop jerked his head up, but he was thinking quickly. Before he put his hands in the air, he let his gun drop to the road, and then he gave it a slight kick in my direction.

"That's right, nice and slow," Zach said, stepping closer and aiming his gun directly at the cop's head. As far as I could tell, Zach hadn't spotted me. "Now walk over here."

The cop did as he was told, stepping around to the driver's side, which placed the car between me and them.

"What do you want?" the cop demanded.

"I want you to shut up," Zach said. "Where are the keys?"

"The keys?"

"To the vehicle."

As the cop hesitated, I looked down at the gun that had landed on the grass in front of me. A shiver ran down my neck, down my spine. I hated guns. Though Eli had taught me to shoot when I was a teenager, I had never been all that comfortable with them. When my brother Michael almost died from a gunshot wound, I decided that I would never have anything to do with guns again.

Sometimes you have no choice, doll, I could almost hear Eli telling me. As I quickly sized up the situation, I understood that this might be one of those times. Silently, I picked up the gun, knowing I would use it if I had to to keep Zach from shooting the cop. The problem was that I really wasn't a very good shot, and Zach was holding Jodi so closely to him that I wouldn't dare try even if I was.

"The keys are in the ignition," the cop said finally.

"Thanks," Zach replied. "Oh, and bye-bye."

Zach lowered the gun to point it directly at the cop's chest. Before he could pull the trigger, however, I raised my gun, closed my eyes, and fired into the air.

The element of surprise worked. The gunshot still ringing, Zach spun toward me. As he did, the cop tackled him, knocking him and Jodi to the ground. Zach still had a gun, though, so I stood and ran around to the other side of the car, pulling Jodi free from the scuffle and then desperately trying to figure out how I could help. Zach and the cop were rolling on the ground, the gun clutched between them. I managed to kick at Zach's head, but then they flipped over and kept struggling. Jodi was whimpering so loudly that I took a moment to untape her hands. She ripped the tape from her own mouth and then started screaming.

"Kill him! Kill him!" she yelled, but there was just no way I could shoot Zach without hitting the cop.

Finally, much to my amazement, Jodi grabbed the gun from my hand, ran to the struggling men, pointed, and pulled the trigger.

Boom!

I held my breath until the cop pulled himself out from under the lifeless body of Zach.

"Yes!" Jodi cried gratefully, her body wracked with tremors. She dropped the gun to the ground and covered her face with her hands.

Suddenly, we were bathed in light as a car came speeding down the driveway. The cop picked up his gun and pointed it toward the car, but I yelled at him to wait. He didn't shoot, and after the car screeched to a stop, Tom jumped out, hands held high and eyes wide as he sized up the situation.

"It's okay," I said to the cop. "He's one of us."

The cop let his arm drop to his side, and then he bent down to pull Zach's gun from his dead hand. The officer was all business then, putting the guns away and using his radio to call for help.

"Get an ambulance too," Tom told him. "There are three FBI agents up there, alive but in need of medical attention."

I stepped forward, wanting to go to Tom but knowing Jodi needed me more. As I put my arms around her, she buried her head against my shoulder, sobbing violently.

"I think she should sit down," the cop said after he finished with the radio. "I have a blanket here."

She let him lead her to the backseat of his car, where he tucked a blanket around her and told her that a doctor would be coming soon. The way she was trembling, I think he was afraid that she was about to go into shock. I knew Tom could use some medical help as well, since his bandages were in shreds and his arms were stained with dried blood.

Tom turned his attention to me, taking off his shirt so that I could tie it around my waist. In all of the commotion, I had forgotten that I had kicked my pants off into the sea! I asked him to bring my tote bag from the car instead, as I knew it contained a pair of shorts.

Once I was decent, Tom put his arms around me and pulled me close. I pressed my face against the warm skin of his chest and held on tightly, knowing that I would never, ever let him go again.

Forty-Seven

In the end, we learned that it was a matter of car keys that had saved the day. Determined to retrieve the $300,000 in bearer bonds, Zach had searched in vain the pockets of the three unconscious FBI agents, trying to find the keys for the Explorer. Unbeknownst to him, however, that was *our* car, and the keys were in Tom's pocket. Since it was blocking the other vehicles, Zach realized his only option was to walk down the driveway, shoot the cop, and take the police car. Because they were on foot, I had time to reach the scene first and react the way I did. The only part that still had me stunned was Jodi's hubris in taking a shot at Zach while he and the cop were struggling on the ground. My secret guess was that she was so frightened, and she wanted Zach dead so badly, that she was willing to risk the cop's life in order to take that shot.

Tom explained what he had been doing since I left him there at the cliff to swim around the point. He had waited there on the rocks for a good while, but once the boat carrying Dianne, Earl, and Larry sailed away, Tom was able to use the road from the beach to climb back up to the house. Once he got there, he saw no sign of Zach or Jodi, so he took the Explorer down the long driveway, intending first to search for me and then to go save Jodi. Of course, when he made the final turn and saw us there at the end of the drive, he realized that we were okay.

Though the Streeps had seemed to make a clean getaway, it was Abraham's quick thinking that finally brought them down. Apparently, it had struck Abraham that there was one person who had been conspicuously absent all day: William, the young man who cared for Dianne's beloved dogs. Going on the theory that William's job for today might have been to keep the dogs safe and far away from all of the action, Abraham led the FBI to the waterfront park near the neighborhood where William lived. Sure enough, the agents were able to get there just in time to arrest Dianne, Larry, and Earl, who had stopped to pick up the dogs before heading out into the open sea.

Inside their boat agents found more than 20 stolen works of art, among them a Matisse and a Picasso, some of which had been missing for years. When the agents had a good look at the basement under Dianne's house, they realized it was much more than merely a basement. It was an art storage room, with fully insulated walls and a complete underground HVAC system with humidity and temperature regulators. I found it ironic that the stovepipe vent that Tom and I had both tripped on in the yard was the air intake pipe for the whole system.

Tom and I spent half of the night back at the command center, recounting the series of events and giving our full statements to the police and the FBI. Tom's hands had been tended to at the scene, but I could tell he was in enormous pain, and I was glad when they finally told us we were free to go. As we were leaving, we said our final goodbyes to Abraham, who filled us in on Jodi's status. She had been sedated at the clinic and released to Sandy, who had brought her back to the house and was spending the night there at her bedside.

Exhausted, Tom and I went home as well. On the way, we decided that we wouldn't try to fly back to the States until Monday, which would give us the weekend to rest and recuperate. At the house, I helped Tom take his medicine and get into bed. I stayed there with him until his breaths were deep and even, and then I returned to my own room, dreaming of the future when I would be able to spend the whole night in his bed, in his arms—as his wife.

By the time I got up, Tom was gone. He had left a note on the counter saying he was out running some errands but would be back by noon. I found Jodi in the hot tub out on the deck, and I quickly changed into my bathing suit so I could join her there. I lowered myself into the hot water and then looked out at the incredible view, amazed that we had been here for nearly a week but I hadn't had the time to try the hot tub until now.

Jodi seemed to have rallied, though there were dark circles under her eyes. She spoke openly about her own trauma, how Larry had tricked her and Sunshine into going to his mother's house two nights before. Once there, the women were tied up, prisoners of Zach and the Streeps. My worst fear was that Jodi had been hurt or even raped, but she said no, Zach had merely kept her tied up and hidden, waiting for the opportunity to seize the bearer bonds.

"I'm such an idiot," Jodi said now, leaning back against the tub and closing her eyes.

"Not everyone is a good judge of character," I replied diplomatically.

"Oh, it's not just that," she said. "I'm talking about the money. First I was stupid enough to bring the bonds down here, and then I didn't even have the presence of mind not to talk about them! I confided in Zach because I wanted to impress him. Little did I know, those bonds ended up almost getting me killed."

I stretched out in the warm water, feeling the aches seep from my bones.

"So what will you do with the bonds now?" I asked. "Have you made a decision about your donation?"

"I gave the bonds over to Sandy this morning," she said. "I probably didn't investigate SPICE as thoroughly as you would have, Callie, but I know it's a good group, working for a good cause. In any event, I'm going to stick around down here for a while longer."

"You are?"

"Yeah. Sandy offered me a job as their fundraiser. I think between my donation and whatever else I can drum up for them, we might be able to make some definite plans to build a facility. The sooner we can get everything out of storage and into a permanent museum, the better."

I could see that the excitement in her eyes had returned, and I knew she had made the right decision, on all accounts.

"What about the pieces that were stolen?" I asked.

"As far as I know, once the FBI releases them, they'll be returned to the climate-controlled storage facility in San Juan. Though we may amp up the security a bit."

I sat up, stretching in the sunshine. The warmth was lulling me to sleep, and I thought it might be time for me to get out.

"Hey, wait a minute," I said as I climbed from the hot tub. "How did you give the bonds to Sandy? I hid them for you."

Jodi laughed.

"I figured you probably put them in the secret closet," she replied. "Sure enough, they were in there, on the top shelf."

"You know about that?"

"It's my house, Callie," she said. "Of course I know about it. Gosh, when I was a kid, that closet was my best place for hide-and-seek."

I stood there on the deck, wrapped in a towel, looking out over the mountains to the sea beyond. It was easy to picture Jodi as a kid, running around this house, playing games with her babysitter. She had been through a lot in the last two days, but she was safe now. I wondered if all the trauma she had been through might've helped her to grow up just a little bit.

"Can I ask you a question?" I said, pulling a chair over so that I could sit and drip dry.

"Sure," she replied, spinning around in the hot tub so that she was leaning forward, her chin resting on the side.

I was quiet for a moment, trying to think how to phrase it. I didn't want to offend her, but I knew I couldn't leave here not having had this conversation.

"When you were in such danger," I said finally, "I know you must've realized you might be killed."

"Of course," she said softly.

"If you *had* been killed," I said frankly, leaning forward, my eyes meeting hers, "do you know where your soul would be right now?"

She held my gaze and then finally groaned and rolled her eyes.

"And there it is," she said. "The big attempt at conversion. You Christians can't leave well enough alone, can you?"

I smiled.

"Not really," I said. "I just can't help thinking that while you're busy making all these plans for your life, God has a better idea. He wants you to give yourself over to Him, Jodi."

"Is that what you've done?"

I waited a beat, and then I nodded. "God loves you, you know. Unconditionally. Permanently."

"God took my father away when I was thirteen. I wouldn't call that love."

I heard a car pull into the driveway, and I knew that Tom must be back.

"We live in a fallen world," I said, focusing on Jodi. "It's full of heartache. But instead of blaming God for all that's wrong, you might try thanking Him for what's right. You're young and healthy and beautiful. You have a wonderful mother, a stepfather who's a really great guy. Enough money to live your life without having to worry. A cause that's important to you. Friends who care about you."

"Friends who want to convert me."

I laughed.

"I won't shove things down your throat," I said. "I promise. But would you do me one favor?"

She eyed me suspiciously.

"What?" she asked.

"If I left you my Bible," I said, "would you read it? Just read it. That's all I ask."

"You won't keep preaching at me?"

"I promise. I'm always available if you want to talk, but I won't mention any of this again unless you bring it up."

She considered my request, and then she shrugged.

"Well, you did save my life last night," she said finally. "I guess that's the least I can do."

Tom found us then, stepping out onto the deck with a mysterious smile on his face. He told me to grab a cover-up and sandals and come with him, no questions allowed. I took a moment to retrieve my Bible for Jodi, and then I did as he requested.

We got in the car, and he drove us out the Northshore Road to a place called Cinnamon Bay. We parked the car and walked down to the sand, and then I saw why we had come: There on the beach was a shiny yellow canoe just waiting for us.

True to his word, Tom sat comfortably in the bow and let me paddle him around. Once we got out into the water, he whipped out a dainty little umbrella, which he opened and held over his shoulder. I was laughing so hard, I nearly capsized the boat.

"Hey, a promise is a promise," he said.

Once I finally convinced him to put the umbrella away, I started paddling in earnest. My arms were sore from the night before, though, so I kept the pace easy, the strokes even. I was in heaven.

After that, we didn't even talk.

And though nothing was said, I knew our minds were in the same place, our hearts were feeling the same mix of emotions. As the sun set over the clear turquoise water, I held the paddle across my lap and simply let the scene imprint on my mind, like a photograph.

I thought of Thursday night at Miss Lucy's moonlight party, when Tom and I danced to the song "A Quarter for a Kiss." The beauty of this island was due in great part to the charitable contribution of a Rockefeller, a donation that, truly, was priceless. I smiled now as I thought of the lyrics to that song:

> *Let the Rockefellers try*
> *To find something they could buy*
> *That could equal the value of this—*

For we found our love
Like a dividend from above,
With a quarter for a kiss

I understood that what Tom and I shared was worth more than a million St. Johns, more than any amount of money. We loved the Lord, and we loved each other.

And nothing could equal the value of that.

Forty-Eight

⁓

"Anybody home?" I asked, peeking in the doorway. I couldn't see the bed from there, so I stepped further into the hospital room, past the bathroom, and looked around the corner.

"Callie!" Eli cried.

I burst all the way into the room, raced to the side of his bed, and slipped my arms around him. He looked pale and weak but still a whole lot better than the last time I had seen him!

There was a chair nearby, so I dragged it over to the bedside and sat, taking his hand in mind.

"When did you get in?" he asked.

"Just now," I replied, smiling. "We came straight from the airport."

"Where's Tom?"

"He's parking the car," I said. "I think he wanted to give us a little time alone."

Eli nodded, squeezing my hand and then just holding it. We had spoken at length on the phone the night before, so he already knew all of the details of what had happened. Now wasn't a time for catching up. It was a time for speaking from the heart.

"Callie, if I had known what you would have to go through," he began, his eyes filling with tears, "I never would've asked you to come here and help me in the first place."

I studied his face for a moment, the kind, familiar eyes, the slightly-crooked nose that looked so much like Larry's I was shocked now that I hadn't caught the resemblance right off the bat.

"Sure you would've," I said. "That's what you trained me for."

He thought about that, and then he smiled through his tears.

"I guess so," he admitted.

I reached around for the box of tissues on the bedside table and handed him one, which he took gratefully. As soon as he wiped away his tears, however, fresh ones formed in his eyes.

"So Stella tells me you and Tom are an item," he said.

"Yes," I replied, grinning.

"That's good. You've forgiven him. I knew you would."

"Forgiven him?"

Eli grabbed for more tissues, suddenly looking flustered.

"Of course. Forgiven him...for taking his sweet time about things. The man doesn't exactly move at warp speed."

"Eli—"

"Think about it, Callie. How long have you known him? A couple years? And it's taken until now to say 'I love you'?"

I studied my friend's old, familiar face, wondering what he really meant, and why he was acting so strange. He reached out and took my hand, and I remembered how horrible it had been in intensive care, when I had held his lifeless hand in mine and he hadn't squeezed back.

"He's good to you?" Eli asked gently.

I hesitated, wondering how I could even begin to describe how good Tom was to me. I looked out of the window on the other side of Eli's bed, at the beautiful Banana River flowing gently in the distance.

"Yes," I said finally. "Tom is an amazing person, Eli. I'm very much in love."

"And you thought it couldn't happen twice in one lifetime."

I nodded, taking a tissue for myself.

"I was wrong," I whispered, smiling through my own tears.

We talked for a while until the conversation came around to Larry. I knew Eli wanted to ask me about him, so I brought it up myself, asking him how it felt to find out after all these years that he had a son.

"It's tragic, if you wanna know the truth. I just keep thinking that if I had been there, if I had helped raise him, then maybe...I don't know. I can't change the past. It never crossed my mind that she was pregnant. That was the sixties, you know, back when free love was all the rage and no one thought much about the consequences. I wasn't a Christian then, and Nadine was willing. Things were very passionate between us."

"What does Stella think about all of this?"

"Stella's a rock," he said. "She's my sanity in the midst of all this craziness."

"Have you apologized for keeping so much from her?"

He nodded.

"With a promise to be honest about everything from now on."

I squeezed Eli's hand again, very glad to hear it.

"Why didn't you ever tell me about Nadine?" I asked.

He shifted a bit, smoothing the IV that was taped to the back of his hand.

"I don't know," he said. "I never told anybody. That was a closed chapter in my life."

"But you loved her," I said.

"Oh, yes," he replied. "And then I found out the truth, that she sold secrets to the Russians, and it shattered my heart into a million tiny pieces. It was easier just to pretend it had never happened."

"You shot her."

"I was trying to save her life," he said. "All these guns were pointed at her, and she kept running. I thought if I could just get her in the leg, that would stop her and no one else would have to shoot." His voice caught and he cleared his throat. "As soon as I pulled the trigger, though, everyone else opened fire. I didn't know it was all staged. All these years, I blamed myself for her death.

When I saw her alive, it made me question everything I thought I knew to be true."

A nurse bustled into the room at that point, a gorgeous, buxom blonde who had come to hang a new IV bag.

"This is Melissa," Eli said, introducing us. "She's a great nurse, but I can't let her take my blood pressure."

"Why not?"

"Because just having her in here raises it by ten!"

We laughed.

After she replaced the IV bag, Melissa had to check Eli's dressing. She asked if I would wait for a moment out in the hall.

"She just wants to get me alone," Eli teased as I complied, and I felt a flash of pity for the beautiful young nurse. She must hear the same jokes at the bedsides of old men all day long.

I came out in the hall and went looking for Tom. I didn't see him, but I did spot a door with a small stained glass window on it and a sign that said "Chapel." Taking a deep breath, I stepped inside and was relieved to find it empty.

The chapel was tiny, with a few rows of pews and a small cross mounted on the wall up front. I sat in the middle row, bowed my head, and prayed. I just wanted to give a quick word of thanks that Eli had survived, but I found that other matters were weighing on my heart as well. I prayed for Eli's continued recovery, for strength for Stella, for my relationship with Tom, for the healing of his hands. Finally, I prayed for Jodi, that somehow God would reach her through His Word, in a way that my words never could.

When my prayer was over, I sat there a bit longer, feeling just a little like a hypocrite. I had told Jodi to turn her life over to God's will, all the while knowing that there was one area in my life that I hadn't fully surrendered.

I stared down at my hands, at my wedding ring. If God really did have a wonderful plan for me, I thought, then why was I resisting the blessings He wanted to send my way? If I really trusted Him, then why couldn't I let go of the past?

My heart surged in my chest, knowing it really was quite simple. The pew in front of me had a kneeler, which I pulled down, and then I knelt, clasped my hands, and squeezed my eyes tightly shut.

"Give me the strength to look forward, not back," I whispered out loud. "Give me the courage to do this."

I opened my eyes, and then I reached down and slowly slid the gold band off my finger. It wasn't hard to undo the chain around my neck, put the ring on it, and hook it back again.

"Thank You, Lord."

It was done. I had expected to feel a number of emotions along with that action, but instead as I looked down at my hand with the white stripe where the ring used to be, I felt nothing but peace.

Complete and utter peace.

I flipped up the bench and stood, my heart racing. I needed to find Tom. I stepped out of the chapel and went down the hall, finally spotting him out in a courtyard, just sitting on a bench. He was waiting there, I knew, to give me time alone with Eli. I felt a surge of love for him so great it nearly took my breath away.

Swinging the door open, I stepped outside. He looked up at the sound and then smiled when he realized it was me. He stood, and I moved toward him. Without speaking, I held up my hand to show him the empty finger. It took a moment for him to understand, but when he did, he inhaled deeply, and then swept me into his arms.

"Are you sure?" he said, and I could feel his heart beating against my chest.

"I'm sure," I replied. "There is nothing on earth that can keep me from loving you."

Finally, we pulled apart. We needed to get back to Eli, but I told Tom to go ahead, that I wanted a moment alone. He complied, and once he was gone, I sat down on the bench where he had been sitting just moments before.

I closed my eyes and tried to picture my late husband Bryan, something that was growing a little harder to do all the time. Usually, I focused so much on his tragic death that I forgot to celebrate his life. He had been a good man, and we should have shared many long and happy years together. But he was gone now, and I was not. It was time for me to start living again.

"Goodbye, Bryan," I said, clutching the ring that hung near my heart.

Then I let it go.

The hospital was cool and quiet as I walked quickly to join Tom in Eli's room. I got there and stepped inside, but because of the little hallway alongside the bathroom, they didn't see me. I realized that the two men were in the middle of a discussion.

"I want to marry her, Eli!" Tom exclaimed, and I froze, knowing I had walked in at just the wrong moment. Suppressing a huge smile, I let the door quietly shut behind me.

"So ask her and be done with it," Eli said. "It's that simple."

"It's not that simple," Tom replied. "She has to know. I have to tell her."

My heart skipped. I had to know what? He had to tell me what?

"You said it yourself, you *can't*," Eli said. "The NSA has tied your hands."

The smile on my face faded. There was more going on here than a simple discussion about life and love.

"But if I don't tell her, Eli, the secret will always be there between us. Even now, every time she looks at me with those trusting eyes, it just tears me apart. James may be the one behind bars, but all of our lives irrevocably were changed that day. Callie has the right to know the truth."

My breath caught in my throat.

James?

That day?

Heart pounding, I could only think of one thing Tom could be talking about: the day my husband was killed.

Killed by a man named James.

Mindy Starns Clark's plays and musicals have been featured in schools and churches across the United States. Originally from Hammond, Louisiana, Mindy now lives with her husband and two daughters near Valley Forge, Pennsylvania.

Mindy's fast-paced and suspenseful inspirational writing—with a hint of romance and a strong heroine—are sure to make this exciting mystery series one that will delight readers everywhere.

Coming next is the fifth book in the series, *The Buck Stops Here*. Look for this new addition to the Million Dollar Mysteries soon at a local Christian bookstore near you.

To hear Tom and Callie's song, "A Quarter for a Kiss," written especially for this book by recording artist (and brother of the author) David Starns, visit Mindy's website at www.mindystarnsclark.com.

Harvest House Publishers
For the Best in Inspirational Fiction

Linda Chaikin
Desert Rose
Desert Star

A Day to Remember Series
Monday's Child
Wednesday's Child
Friday's Child

Mindy Starns Clark

The Million Dollar Mysteries Series
A Penny for Your Thoughts
Don't Take Any Wooden Nickels
Dime a Dozen
A Quarter for a Kiss

Roxanne Henke

Coming Home to Brewster Series
After Anne
Finding Ruth
Becoming Olivia

Sally John

The Other Way Home Series
A Journey by Chance
After All These Years
Just to See You Smile
The Winding Road Home

In a Heartbeat Series
In a Heartbeat

Craig Parshall

Chambers of Justice Series
The Resurrection File
Custody of the State
The Accused
Missing Witness

Debra White Smith
Second Chances
The Awakening
A Shelter in the Storm
To Rome with Love
For Your Heart Only
This Time Around
Let's Begin Again

The Austen Series
First Impressions

Lori Wick

The Yellow Rose Trilogy
Every Little Thing About You
A Texas Sky
City Girl

Contemporary Fiction Series
Bamboo & Lace
Beyond the Picket Fence
Pretense
The Princess
Sophie's Heart

The English Garden Series
The Proposal
The Rescue
The Visitor
The Pursuit